FANCY

GAP

Fancy Gap

a novel by

Zak Jones

HAMISH HAMILTON
an imprint of Penguin Canada, a division of Penguin Random House Canada Limited

Canada • USA • UK • Ireland • Australia • New Zealand • India • South Africa • China

First published 2026

Hamish Hamilton, an imprint of Penguin Canada
A division of Penguin Random House Canada
320 Front Street West, Suite 1400
Toronto, Ontario, M5V 3B6, Canada
penguinrandomhouse.ca

The authorized representative in the EU for product safety and compliance is Penguin Random House Ireland, Morrison Chambers, 32 Nassau Street, Dublin D02 YH68, Ireland, https://eu-contact.penguin.ie

LIBRARY AND ARCHIVES CANADA CATALOGUING IN PUBLICATION

Title: Fancy gap : a novel / Zak Jones.
Names: Jones, Zak, author.
Identifiers: Canadiana (print) 20240383125 | Canadiana (ebook) 20240383141 |
ISBN 9780735249844 (hardcover) | ISBN 9780735249851 (EPUB)
Subjects: LCGFT: Novels.
Classification: LCC PS8619.O543 F36 2025 | DDC C813/.6—dc23

Cover and book design by Kelly Hill
Typeset by Terra Page
Interior image: (texture) © vejaa / Adobe Stock
Cover images: (mountains) © Christian Gideon / Stocksy;
(smoke) © Terry Schmidbauer / Getty

Printed in Canada

10 9 8 7 6 5 4 3 2 1

Penguin
Random House
HAMISH HAMILTON CANADA

For Jake

But they that escape of them shall escape,
and shall be on the mountains like doves of the valleys,
all of them mourning,
every one for his iniquity.

EZEKIEL 7:16
KING JAMES BIBLE

PROLOGUE

LOOK AT US NOW. Look at what man has done to himself. Look at what we gone and become. There's a notion I want to dispel out there, where everyone's just born good and dies saved. Some say, I suppose, that the Lord's Word is something like that. But they haven't quite seen what I've seen. All these miracles I have seen. All this despicability. Good people gone bad. Awful things happen just about every day far as I can tell. Evil exists in the world, you know. The Lord giveth, but . . . I've known heaven to be just about as far away as you could imagine. Takes a long time for some of them miracles to arrive.

That's not to say I don't believe a little bit of space between the firmament and the up above is a good thing. We need some space between good and evil, lightness and the dark. A little space at least. Need to carve it out ourselves sometimes. And I was always quite suspicious of a doctrine so Unitarian that it held everyone up as saved from the get. I think you ought to work to be saved. Either that or someone ought to come along and save you. But that simply isn't what everybody wants. I am happy to think of the Gates of Heaven as wide open. I preach it so. But that don't mean everyone's liable to step inside. The devil is gonna weigh us down so we don't want to take that step. Knee-deep in the mud of sin and it's raining outside. What I don't understand is the inclination we have to wallow in it. I been trying to crawl out of the muck and mire of evil my whole life. I've seen innocence and I've seen the rot. And it doesn't take a saint to come out and say the truth, the truth being that some people just can't be helped. But perhaps it takes a saint to go on pretending.

I have two grandsons. When they were just boys and before they were old enough for school, I often spent my days thinking deeply about these kinds of truths of the world as I watched them playing with each other. I'd get caught up in whatever little Shakespearean tragedy they were acting out, and I would cry, too.

Their mama came outside one time and caught me wiping tears out of my eyes. I had to tell her I wasn't senile, I wasn't crazy, no ma'am; I was just stricken watching her beautiful boys. Was it in them yet? Was it weighing them down?

When they were a little older and had learned to talk, I once watched the two of them come from the field where the sun was setting. I knew they were hungry because they walked toward the house with their heads held up, looking, like dinner was in the distance in front of them. Like proud hound dogs after a hunt.

I was at the house for the summer, helping Janey out with the boys. And, as often as she could, she made us all dinner. I knew it exhausted her, all this worrying and fussing, driving from home to her waitress job and sometimes out to school in Winston where she was trying to finish her degree. She was so thin and quiet then. Whittled down. I was almost nervous she'd disappear.

They'd come home as the sun set, good boys, but by the time they reached the porch the wind chimes were humming in those last heavy breezes, my head buzzing like the summer bugs calling forth the evening, and their eyes came up shining at me with that youth and peace. Sunshine from the inside out as the sun sets and hums good night. And I smiled at them, already patient and steady, ignoring the ticking down to my medication time, the nighttime, and the ugly dreams.

I said, "Dalton, what in God's name do you have all over your pants?" and the boy looked down at the red mud on the front of his jeans and asked about supper. I told them both to sit still and to keep each other busy until their mama came out and called for them. It was all I could do.

I went inside and asked Jane about the food and she hurried me back out. Well, I had told those boys not to touch the Easter lilies on the bank. I'd told them that when I was a little girl I had watched my cat rolling around in a bed of them outside my Granny's house. Back then she had a dirt floor, and the cat was always dirty and itchy. Nasty old thing. I guess I'd thought it was trying to wash itself in their dew.

I told them I'd pulled that cat, Missy was her name, right out of the flower bed to save her from getting in trouble. I said, "Missy, you know you ain't supposed to be digging up them plants," and shooed her away. I remember she was wet and covered in pollen. She licked herself dry and died later that night. And that was when I was just a little girl. And I buried that cat myself.

"Boys!" I shouted then through the screen door. "You, Dalton. Do not go messing around in them Easter lilies!"

And I had told them a thousand times. The lilies lined the bank, thick and beautiful. But, you know, that day, I was thinking about my medicine. The sun tea and peace on the porch. Time ticking by. These boys, well, I let them wander into that flower patch like I didn't have a care in the world about it.

I went in and helped Jane pour the collards from the heavy pan into a nice china bowl. She was sweating. She said, "Mama, I need you out of this kitchen," and I said, "Okay, Janey Bird, okay then," and took my pill early and in secret, dry with no water. I swallowed it as best I could but came out through the screen door almost choking.

I had heard Messiah's nervous yelling and hollering. "I don't want to, Dalton. I don't want to eat another!"

And Dalton was handing a picked-off Easter lily to his brother to eat. Not the first, either. I stood on the porch there, quiet. And I just watched Messiah chew. Worst thing I ever done in my life and I didn't do anything at all. We all got a little sin in us.

Then Jane came out and started screaming. I can see her now, running down the bank. Her blue jeans streaked with water, having wiped her hands on her behind. My daughter. Her sons. Innocent boys. And yet again, there was sin in the world.

Part I

Grace

GRACE WAS HUMMING a hymn as she looked down at the young man kneeling at her feet. The old tile of the little bathroom had been messily wallpapered over, its pattern depicting covered bridges, wavy now and peeling, as though they were being torn up out of the ground. The ink had become blue and blurred like old tattoos on sun-aged skin. Grace broke the hum intermittently to whisper "Rejoice, yes, rejoice" in an off-time meter.

She was standing in a baby-blue plastic basin full of clear, oily liquid. The young man was rubbing her feet. His hands were red and soft, the quicks of his nails white hot, almost blue. Grace watched through half-closed eyes as the young man took a handful of the liquid up to his mouth and sipped it and coughed. He went back to rubbing her feet, his hands looking not quite his own.

"That's enough, son. Go on and dry me then take this to the kitchen and dump it out and rinse it, won't you." He nodded, gently lifted one of her wrinkled feet out of the moonshine footbath, and towelled it off, sniffing hard to keep his nose from running, the disturbance from the splash having brought the alcohol up to his nose and eyes.

When he'd dried and set each foot down carefully on the plush towel laid before him, he rose and carried the basin down the hallway to the kitchen. He took a few mouthfuls more from the bath and then poured out the rest and washed the basin.

He returned to the bathroom, where Grace was standing by the claw-footed tub. She said, "All right now. Have a seat."

"Are you gonna wash my feet now, Grace?" He perched on the toilet seat.

"No, Tyler, but I am going to ask you to try out those alms you got. If they're any good I'll let you sleep here tonight, and if they're any good I might have some myself. I am feeling less feverish now. Warmed up. If you'd like you can sleep with me. We have a consequential day before us tomorrow, and I will need you well rested." She had a curious excitement in her voice that made Tyler's forehead wrinkle in thought.

"Usually, I think—I mean I seen it before—the pastor washes the worshipper's feet. Don't he, Grace?"

"Tyler," she said, reaching out and pushing back his greasy hair, "that happens during worship and with water, son. I had a fever and wanted you to help me cure it so I can preach tomorrow. Don't think too hard, boy. Just do as I say."

"Hey, Grace, what in the hell is this stuff anyway?"

Tyler took the razor blade and scraped it along the hand mirror on his lap. He scraped once, twice, three times with a sense of practice, but tapping agitatedly, his hands shaking. He sniffed and sniffed as though he'd been crying.

"Your job, son, is to tell *me* what exactly *in the hell* it is. If I remember correctly, it was you who brought this into my house. I am asking you to test it. You're testing not only that little bit of blessing there but also my patience. Now I don't want you to blaspheme, and I don't want you to be ignorant. We got a big crowd tomorrow morning, and we should have all this out on communion plates for the parishioners. You've been cussing and spitting and snotting everywhere. I am thinking it was you who laid me up with this sickness, and I am repenting now for allowing you to be disgusting in my home."

"I dunno, Grace. It looks sharp like there's glass in it. It tastes bad." He sniffed up the rest anyway. Then he licked the pane, wiped it off with the sleeve of his baggy fatigue jacket, and held it out to the old woman. She didn't accept it.

"Is it going to work as alms, son? If I get a whole half of this valley crying and blubbering as nasty as you, well I think I'd just as soon pass out shine tomorrow."

"Aw, Grace, you dumped half the shine down the sink," he said between sniffs and hard blinks of his eyes. He was talking almost out of the back of his nose he was so congested. "I thought this was the same as last time but it ain't. It's making me ill, I think."

She watched the young man as he struggled to find a place to set down the pane, still sniffing. "Where'd you get it, son?"

"Same man as last time. Same man Clyde sent me to. The one with the prescriptions."

"You think that's a prescription?"

"No, I don't think so. Not at all." He coughed. "Maybe it's a mix of something. It works but it hurts."

"We'll see if it kills you or not. I don't want anyone sleeping off a drunk in the orchard after service but I'd rather that than a dead flock of worshippers. Now go on and clean yourself up. And clean that thing up too." She gestured at the pane of glass, an ornamental mirror missing its handle.

"Yes ma'am."

Tyler stood up from the toilet and placed the mirror pane on the tank. He looked around for a towel, then wiped his hands on his pants. Then he stagger-stepped forward and, overcompensating, plopped back down on the toilet seat. Grace stepped toward him, lifted the hem of her nightgown, and offered it to him. The young man took the hem and breathed in deeply through his nose as he wiped his face. She touched his hair as if to bless him. He pulled his face away and let the fabric fall. He coughed.

"Stop that," she said. "No one's feeling sorry for you, Tyler." Then in a calm voice she added, "Just tell me what it's like."

"I don't know, Grace. I feel like I can't see."

He got up and wandered in front of the bathroom mirror and steadied himself on the sink.

She blew the rest of the powder off the glass and held the handleless mirror pane up behind him. He looked at his duplicated reflection, staring now across an infinite expanse of shrinking dimension as if there were something in there far off for him to find. A thousand of him, ever shrinking. But in the angle she chose, only one image of Grace. He held his breath as though he were about to plunge into water.

"Tyler, there are mirrors and there are mirrors, and between all that is neither forever until eternity nor once and for all. You see, son? Look here. We go on forever. There's a little God everywhere. The whole of you is stretched out into this mystery. It might be that fools like you need a little something extra to help you see it. Now you just think about that." Then, sweetly, "I thank you for bringing this to me. You ain't too bright but I need you." He hung his head. "And you and everybody else around here: first you need Jesus, but to get to him I believe that you need me."

Tyler sought the hem of her nightgown, but it was out of reach. She had ghosted away from behind him. There was blood and yellow snot running from his nose.

"Wake up, then," she called from the hallway, "and come with me. Let's prepare the offering just in case."

The young man did as he was told, following Grace out of the bathroom and toward the darkened living room of her large and austere mountain home. Crosses lined the walls of the hallway. Some plastic and new, some wooden and carved out rough and by hand. They loomed around him now, tick-tocking back and forth as he knocked them with his outstretched hands, almost sightless now with tears in his swollen eyes, feeling along the wall as he walked. But none fell.

"Grace, I need to say that I don't think I'm high, like, I don't think I'm buzzin' at all. No ma'am I don't feel good, and I don't think this stuff is gonna do the trick tomorrow."

Grace sat down quietly. She looked out the window and down into the valley, the gap in the mountains. Lights from the farms, some small-time, some big business, peppered the gap like rippling moonwake in the mountain's undulating shoals. The future creeping in. *All the medicine in the world can't hypnotize us to forgo the sins of tomorrow,* she thought as she looked at the starry yellow halogen lights shining through the mountain's mist and smoke.

Tyler was sitting on a divan on the other side of the room, bent over now, the dim light from the kitchen buzzing behind him. From where Grace sat in the dark he looked haloed by that same intrusive light, shining around him as he shrank into a pathetic ball. He was handsome, once, she remembered, and thought that if it weren't for his tendencies and ignorance he might have made for something useful, something longer lasting and dependable, like a Collie is to a farmer. She knew already that the fleeting light of his spirit was louring, and that her chemical conduit to God, as she thought of it, the alms, the drug, was undoing him.

"Tyler," she said. "Do you remember when we met?"

"Yes ma'am," he said into his folded arms, his head bent over to his knees.

"I've got it in my mind that you said you were on a mission. Do you remember? You said you were gonna do better. You were going to work yourself better through Christ. Am I correct in my memory?"

"Yes . . . ma'am," he said, heaving.

"So, you will remember what we spoke about? Your path to salvation?"

Tyler was silent now, staring at his hands between nose wipes.

"You will remember what you told me. You will remember you said 'Shepherd, I am at your whim. Shepherd, I am at your mercy. Sweet Grace,' you said, 'my journey has begun. I am yours to lead. I am at your mercy,' and on and on. Tyler, do you remember this?"

Tyler remained silent save for a sporadic sniff between short, harried breaths. Grace let the question linger for longer than she liked. She waited, agitated, and watched him. Unsatisfied with what she saw, she went from calm to angry. She shot up straight as though she'd been hit by lightning and swarmed across the room to the light switch and hit it.

Tyler sat up, shocked by the brightness of the room. He squeezed his eyes shut.

"Do you remember, boy?" she shouted.

He was shaking violently now and spitting weakly onto and between the knees of his blue jeans. She grabbed him by the collar and straightened him up.

"I am disappointed, Tyler. What did you see in the mirror just now? Did you or did you not see forever? There's a thousand of us in each moment, son. And in this moment, this very one, I'm afraid you're going to disappear. I mean all of you, boy. Every greasy strand of hair and every yellow tooth of you is about to vanish off this earth if you can't stand up and act right!" She hadn't yet decided if he should die.

"Son, don't forget what you were set here in this world to do. You were set here to help us to Jesus." She was blowing her heavy breaths in his face. She hit him on the cheeks and pinched them, sinking her fingernails into his skin.

"I don't wanna, Grace," he said, and slid off the white-upholstered divan and onto his knees. The windows had become mirrors. The spangled diorama of the valley had disappeared in the electric light, and all was stark around them. Grace moved behind him and tried heaving him up from his armpits; she pulled at his face to get him to look at their reflection in the window. Tyler began to spit up blood on himself, coughing some onto the wood floor.

"Stand up!" she shouted. "Stand up, son, and meet God!"

Tyler raised himself, shaking, to his feet, and stood looking into the translucent, mirrored windows. Grace shuffled away from him to shut off the light, clearing her throat to calm down. She hit the switch and Tyler's reflection disappeared. They were gone, and all before them was darkness through glass and the mountains lit by the moon, heaving up toward them like so many dark waves. They stared out for a second in silence. Tyler let out a grunt, a garbled cough, then collapsed to the floor.

"Amen," Grace said. She walked slowly away from the constellated gap in the mountains, shining and winking through her windows. She turned and walked back down her hallway adorned by crosses ancient and new. Tyler's blood was sticky on the bottoms of her bare feet. It was Sunday now, and she intended to rest. She closed her bedroom door behind her.

Dalton

THE AIR ON THE DRIVE through the gates of Fort Drum was polluted by trash and deterioration. It was a beautiful strip of road, but from inside the van Dalton could smell the dump half a mile away. The stench of decay from the orderly piles and containers drifted through the swaying trees lining the promenading avenue that stretched beyond the main gate. The road into the fenced-off Army base split the county's garbage facility in half. On each side sat a different kind of trash, civilian and military, the atmosphere a confluence of the two worlds. It struck him as unsurprising, somehow, this revelation as to how close he'd lived to piles and piles of it, neat and orderly as it was. It still smelled like shit.

He sat between two men, riding bitch they called it, on the bench seat. All but Dalton were unbuckled and laughing like college kids drunk on a joyride rather than Military Police performing the solemn task of removing a soldier from duty. The squad assigned to chaperone Dalton through his exit from the Army had been ordered to take him directly to the bus station, but they weren't even taking him beyond the dump.

They'd pulled through the security gate and driven just a quarter mile down the long stretch of road that led away from the post when they slowed down. There was heat and the smell of garbage in the sun. One of the MPs said "Here you go, princess" as he dragged Dalton's bag off the back seat. The sliding door of the duty van closed with a slam before he could respond. Muffled laughter. Vague shapes of staring faces from behind the tinted glass.

The van's self-locking door clicked and it did an embarrassing five-point turn before it squealed off back toward post. Dalton watched, imagining the tires exploding, sending the van off the road and into the dump, catching fire. They didn't. The gates of Fort Drum opened and the van disappeared. The road was so pristine that no dust clouded the van's wake. Immaculately clean and smelling like shit.

After the initial humiliations of out-processing were over with—the stripping of his rank, the bogus formalities of the court-martial tribunal, the name-calling, the ridicule—Dalton had decided to take the Army for what it was worth. After some fast talk and a couple white lies at the Class II Returns depot he'd managed to walk away with a few unworn deployment uniforms, new with tags, and an extra sleeping bag, after saying he'd lost his. Someone else must have "lost" the other gear he had on him: an ACOG rifle sight, some training grenades with their explosive charges removed. Then there was the Kevlar tactical vest in his duffle bag, six fully loaded .556 rifle magazines, and the expired morphine vials from his aid station. He'd tried to take as many things as he could, hiding or lying about anything he didn't absolutely need to return. He figured he could sell these to an Army Navy store, use them somehow. As the saying goes, there's only one thief in the Army, and everyone else is just trying to get their shit back.

Dalton had in fact stolen the tactical vest from a stoned private's barracks room after some late-night drinking. It still had the private's Velcro name patch on it, Dalton remembered. He stripped off his own shirt and threw it to the side of the road, then dug into his duffle bag to find its replacement. The stolen nametag was covered in mud. Dalton spit on his thumb and used it to scratch off some of the dirt around the lettering. VASQUEZ.

In his bank account he had leftover leave pay, which, combined with the status the uniform held in the civilian world, he figured could get him home—wherever he needed or wanted to go. He could hop from small-town hotel to small-town hotel, hitching rides with a gracious smile and a story about a lost wallet. He could feign trauma from a deployment he'd never endured. He could hear himself saying, "Listen, man, I'm just back from Iraq. I'm just trying to get home. Could you do me a favour?"

With the barren, stinking garbage depot on either side of him Dalton began walking toward the main county road. He breathed in the heavy, repulsive air.

He was still young, he thought, all things considered. Still in his early twenties—a young man. He'd tried to cram a semblance of normal life into the three years of his enlistment, dressing up as a civilian on his weekend passes and holiday leave. But he was never himself enough to feel like he could go home. He'd visited Syracuse, Buffalo, New York City, Montreal. Anywhere he might find women to talk to or college kids to drink with or near, anywhere far enough away from an Army base where a baseball hat could cover up his dumb haircut, where he could sit next to people without them asking him about the war he didn't know or understand, the suffering he was supposed to have experienced.

Now he was being pushed out toward that world, but still without any merit, without anything to show for all the bullshit. All the drill sergeants screaming, the dead friendships, the promotions, the demotions. Birthed again into a civilian life left doubly behind. He squinted, not unlike a newborn in the wobbly sunlight, his eyes unsteady after the weeks-long confinement in his barracks, in the always-on protective din of the halogen bulbs that hummed and hovered over him while he was on suicide watch. No story to tell worth telling, he was a man in a stolen uniform with a stolen name. At last, and at least, he was a bona fide civilian again, untethered.

Other Than Honorable. Dalton didn't know exactly what those words contained. They might have told him in one of the various proceedings they'd forced him to undergo; he didn't remember much of what had been said. He did know it meant that his service had offered the Army more detriment than advantage, more shame than pride. He hadn't seen combat or anything near it; he hadn't really served at all as far as he was concerned. Instead he'd hurt his back unpacking a redeploying unit's equipment. The pain meant trouble sleeping and Dalton had begun frequenting the Class VI liquor store to buy little spark plugs of Rémy to drink during the day so he'd be tired at night. When he wasn't manning his own aid station, pocketing muscle relaxers and painkillers, he haunted his brigade's main troop clinic with complaints of pain, persistent cough, and malaise, asking for Ambien and promethazine. What was clear to Dalton now was that he'd lost sight of the easy goals—making sergeant, paying bills, going to Airborne school, community college, whatever—and that he'd lost sight of the just plain accomplishable. In lieu of what, he couldn't say.

He'd also earned a few citations for showing up to formation drunk or unshaven, and for skipping out of duty altogether—an AWOL trip to New York City with Romerin that resulted in some attention after their motel room in Queens caught fire. He'd gone down twice, then, for fucking around with his only friend. And it wasn't Dalton who dropped the cigarette on the couch; it was the girl they'd brought back to the room. But when the pimps and druggies, the attendees of a middle-aged, middle-classed bachelorette party, the maids, the salesmen, and he and his disrobed comrade met outside in the motel parking lot after the fire alarm, the young woman was gone—with only a receipt for the motel with Dalton's signature left to account.

His commanding officers had given him more chances than any other soldier he knew. But after a year of accumulating demotions, he started receiving new kinds of accolades. He'd been awarded a DUI citation, and multiple "warnings" from friendly MPs and uniform-horny civilian police, for speeding down I-81 in a borrowed car. He'd been picked up and all but booked for fighting with civilians at a bar off-post called Crazy Legs. And finally, Dalton had got himself the "hot piss" badge—awarded to those who can't resist a couple puffs of Spice or Bath Salts or actual weed before having to piss in a cup. He'd played Russian roulette with the drug tests, always wondering if the four quarts of water and countless trips to the Battalion HQ urinal had flushed out all the bullshit drugs and gas station boner pills he'd ingested or if some was still kicking around in there. And then his luck ran out. His last rank before the bottom of the pecking order, Private First Class, was finally stripped away.

Someone, in recent days, had cut out a new label for his barracks room door that replaced his rank, formerly Corporal, then, after his demotions, Private, with "Mister." "Mr. Fuquay." No, not a soldier, not at all. And after this latest Chapter 15 for *inappropriate fraternizing,* Dalton had been half-asked, half-ordered to pack his things and prepare to out-process from the Army without ceremony.

He thought now that if maybe he'd been more committed to the idea of himself as a real person, as somebody in the world, well, then, he might have avoided all that. Could have killed himself—blown his head off with a Walmart hunting rifle as a sergeant across the hall in his barracks building had—at least that would've gotten him a posthumous Honorable discharge. Even that modicum of decency was disallowed. All options erased.

When the men asked how that soldier had managed to stick a rifle barrel in his mouth, they were told that the sergeant had bought a "kid-sized" rifle just for the occasion.

Dalton could have killed himself driving drunk through the glass-panelled building of a Pizza Hut as another man in his platoon had—and out of a different kind of disappointment than that which they now had in him, the Army would have covered that up with an Honorable as well. Draped casket. But not for Dalton. Not for what he did. Fraternizing with another man in the showers. His best friend.

There was an official court martial, but the verdict had already come down. He was moved to the entertainment room in the barracks, a glass room on the main floor with a pool table and a foosball table, all pushed to the side to make room for his cot. Those soldiers who pulled Charge of Quarters duty threw used pouches of dipping tobacco at the glass pane by his head as he sat on his cot under the buzzing fluorescent light that had to stay on. Suicide watch. Not without ceremony, then: there was this. A ceremony of humiliation.

As he stood in the road a cab crawled out through the gates of the base. Dalton figured it must have just dropped someone off and had been lucky enough to load back up on the return trip to Watertown, the nearest city. The only place Dalton had been where they hung up banners welcoming back the troops or supporting the troops, offering discounts to the troops or special cash advance rates for the troops. Everything for the troops. A real American town with real fading nylon flags.

The old blue minivan pulled up and slowed down. The driver coughed behind its yellowing, aftermarket-tinted windows. As the door slid open Dalton waited for a dip can or a half-empty beer to be thrown at him from the passing window, but the cab crept alongside him, screeching its brakes. A young, tan soldier with a fresh high-and-tight haircut leaned his head out, smiling.

"Hey, private! What are you doing standing around out here for?" The soldier spoke with the veiled accent of someone trying to lose his roots—Puerto Rican, maybe. The Army's assimilation machine going to work on him. Everyone has to fight to keep a little of themselves and fight at the same time to lose it.

Dalton was relieved the soldier mistook him for a freshly arriving private instead of an excommunicated corporal. He didn't recognize any of the civilian-clothed boys in the cab. Another, in an open-mouthed Arkansas accent, asked him, "Where you headed, man? We're goin' to Walmart. Get in if you're goin' that way." He spit tobacco juice into a can of Monster Energy drink. Wiped his mouth. The young men shuffled around and tried to make room.

Dalton got in up front with the driver who smelled of body odour. He shrugged his shoulders a few times to settle into the time-deflated seat and situated himself so as to discourage conversation from the back seat. But the boys were busy shushing each other with the side jabs and wrist-grabbing of new camaraderie and inside jokes. They drove past the Dunkin' Donuts, the dozens of no-money-down auto sales lots, the military-discount tattoo parlours, and the money wiring and lending services that lined the roads leading to and from post. All had signs saying MILITARY OWNED! or MILITARY FRIENDLY! This whole Potemkin village of "support" for the troops was set up for these types of boys, fresh from Basic Training with enlistment bonus money in so many pockets that had never seen any.

Their squad leaders, without fail, had already told them to avoid these friendly scam businesses that line every Army post, but in short glances in the rearview, Dalton watched the young men as they took mental note of each sign calling out to them. "Look at that Hemi Charger right there," said the Arkansas boy. "I'ma get me one of them." A minute later he shouted out, "Tractor Supply Company! They got Justin Boots there! I'm gonna get me some!"

This small world of strip malls and rub and tugs was all theirs now. Dalton looked again. They had their faces almost pasted to the window. Eyes darting. One of them wore a shirt somehow alluding to *The Dukes of Hazzard*. STARS 'N' BARS 'N' MUSCLE CARS it said. The Confederate flag was indeed printed on each car adorning the shitty T-shirt. The other soldier Dalton could see, the boy with the shy Puerto Rican accent, had on a severely wrinkled dress shirt. Something from Express for Men maybe, pulled right out of the duffle bag.

"Hey! Which one of you stinks up there?" asked the soldier with the fresh-buzzed hair. There were chuckles, mostly from the cab driver. A fleeting sense of relief came over Dalton. He was glad they didn't ask to pull over into the auto lot, for their sake. Their hushed laughter continued. More rib-jabbing. A dumb happiness was filling the air now, leaving no room for Dalton's broodings to breathe. A desire to jump from the moving van replaced his relief. He gripped the armrests and tried to avoid glancing any more into the rear and side-view mirrors. He felt jealous, inadequate.

"Damn, Private, where are you coming from. They ain't got showers at Basic anymore?" said the Arkansas boy.

"I think it's just the dump," Dalton said, and the cab went quiet. They had long passed the dump. He didn't want to offend the driver by rolling the window down or drawing any more attention to the smell. He thought about how he'd outranked them only a few weeks before and how he could've just told them to shut up. He counted the blurry mile-markers as they drove, trying to keep his mind off the fuzzy square on his chest where his rank used to sit. He absently fingered it all the way to the Walmart, the store's prominent sign looming above its acreage, its excessive parking lot that stretched into the street and beyond, scooping up the passing cars almost magnetically.

As they pulled in, the boy with the Puerto Rican accent chirped up. "Hey, man. What's this, Vasquez?" He reached up to snap his fingers again and again next to Dalton's face. "Despierta, muchacho!" he said. "Vas a entrar con nosotros?"

Dalton thought about grabbing the boy's arm and biting it. The boy laughed. "You don't speak Spanish, do you? Okay, you need sheets or anything? You don't really need to buy that stuff. People in the barracks have extra."

Dalton said he would be fine. "Not going to Walmart," he added.

"Where are you going, then?"

"Just into town." Dalton gently waved two fingers into the rear-view as the boys filed out of the cab one by one. Just as they'd exit a troop transit truck. Just as they'd leap from a plane.

The boys passed Dalton some money through the window to cover their share, which he gave to the cab driver. On the sidewalk just outside the store they stood in a straight line, a gradation of skin tones with varying heights and styles of clothing—the redneck shirt, some nuevo-Italian club getups, a preppy boy—all mismatched ethnicities and accents and old lives.

They turned in step and walked toward the superstore doors. Almost marching, Dalton thought, forward and organized but at different strides, consciously trying to walk normally. They waved to the greeter, fighting a reflex to salute, it seemed, as they filed in.

The cab driver and Dalton studied each other for a second. The driver was lumpy in a way particular to the ultra-sedentary: his gut overlapped his seat belt and divided his torso from his remarkably skinny legs sticking out of stained khaki shorts. The cabbie fought with the shifter and got the van into gear, his eyes still on Dalton.

"Where you headed?"

"Bus station."

The van slunk out of the parking lot and onto the rural freeway that meandered into Watertown.

"Going on leave?"

Dalton shook his head in a noncommittal *Yes/No* to each of the cabbie's questions. They stopped at a red light behind a truck lifted up on a stilt-like suspension kit. One of its decals spelled out CONTROVERSY in Old English font. The others had to do with the Second Amendment and hating liberals, along with variations on the Punisher logo, the familiar MY OTHER RIDE IS YOUR SISTER and IF YOU CAN READ THIS YOUR MOM IS BUSY WITH THE ZIPPER, and, of course, a 4-31st Infantry Battalion sticker. Another American hero.

"You got a girl where you're headed?" The cab driver exhaled long and slow. Dalton didn't answer. "I remember when I used to get home on leave, it's like the women line up, don't they? They know you've got a job. They know you're doing something with your life. Make sure you wear a rubber, kid."

The thought of having women line up for him anywhere didn't arouse Dalton. It made him feel stupid. What would they be lining up for? He adjusted his pants and looked over at the man's legs. He felt a sense of slow, delayed surprise that the cabbie had ever been at all sexual, let alone in the military.

He had the radio set to a conservative AM wave talk show: *"President Obama may be the greatest example of affirmative action in recent memory,"* the host explained. *"This is YOUR country. This is what has become of it. A nightmare for Americans. Do you see yourself here anymore? Blood—blood—the Founding Fathers of this nation shed their blood; so what? So we can just give it up?"* Dalton felt hot and started pulling at his seat belt. He wanted to get out.

"Hey," the driver said as the beeping seat belt notification sounded. "Hey, kid. Stop. Put your seat belt back on. What in the . . . Je-*sus*. You tugging at your crotch? What do they got you boys on? Get home first, son. You can jack off wherever you like but not in my goddamn cab."

Dalton reattached his seat belt and pressed his forehead against the window, watching the fog of his breath appear and disappear, its predictability calming him as Watertown slid past. The driver rolled the window down for him, knowing now that Dalton needed it, and the glass screeched along the skin of his hot forehead. The van stopped.

"Hey!" the cab driver said, as if he hadn't said it many times already. "This is it. Station right here. Ten dollars."

Dalton paid him and got out. The ranch-style, slant-roofed bus station seemed out of place. He thought about pausing before he entered, like in the movies, where the character breathes out the past and inhales the future. But he just walked straight in, feeling nothing but the cabbie's stare behind him.

Dalton's eyes adjusted to the droning fluorescent lights and the grey concrete walls that seemed to grow duller and shrink closer around him, expanding somehow but getting tighter. The sense of the place's emptiness hung thick in the air like the cigarette smoke of ghosts still waiting for their bus. Nothing moved but the intermittent shadows from slow-passing semi trucks interrupting the rays of sunshine that poured through the windows. Dalton walked back out into the gunmetal daylight.

There was a phone booth on the corner, an old one; the panes that weren't missing were Plexiglas scratched to opacity. After a fight with the stiff hinges of the folding door he dropped his duffle bag outside and climbed over it into the booth. The smell of piss and cigarette ash made him fight with the door once more, tripping over his bag on the way out. He shifted it to keep the folding door open and felt grateful for the missing panes. Then, having checked the slot for quarters and finding none, he picked up the sticky receiver and called his mother collect.

"I don't understand," Dalton's mother said over the phone. "I don't understand how it could have possibly turned out this way if you 'didn't do anything.'"

She paused, waiting for a rebuttal that didn't come.

"It's not a witch hunt, Dalton, it's the military. They don't do anything without a good reason. What happened?" She paused again. "Sweetie?"

"They didn't give me a chance, Mama." He knew he was lying and furrowed his brow to help him sound serious. "They just hate me," he went on, forcing a laugh at the end. Like he didn't care. "They just fucking hate me, Mama. I guess that's just it." He fingered the rankled Velcro fuzz on his chest.

"Well, you know, blessed are the poor in spirit, honey."

He felt the need to tell her about when the sergeant caught him fumbling with the orange cap of an old prescription bottle as he tried to pour some private's piss into the test receptacle; that they'd taken away his phone. And that other incident in the shower, the last straw. But he couldn't.

Instead he said, "I was in a room with a bunch of dope smokers." And "I lost my phone on a training exercise." Then he coughed out "It's not my fault" and smacked his hand on the Plexiglas.

"Dalton, slow down and just tell me what happened."

"I was in a fight, too. Some other things. Misunderstandings. It ain't right for me, Mama, I just can't hack it anymore. I have to come home."

He couldn't lie fast enough to keep up with her barrage of calm questions. But they weren't whole lies. Not really. It was just that when he started saying something that resembled the truth he could almost watch it careen into bullshit, pushed along by currents of shame. It was a bad habit. His mother's responses grew curt and monosyllabic as his answers grew increasingly long and broken.

"Have you hurt somebody?"

"No, Mama. I'm just not cut out for this kind of thing."

"Dalton, it can't be a *kind of thing*. You were doing so well, you said. You're not coming home because of *me*, are you?"

"No, Mama. I mean—"

"I'm just joking, honey, I know."

"No, you don't know, it's— I don't mind coming home to you. I mean, that's half of it. You're sick, you know? And no, they just won't have me. It's complicated, I guess. It's not my fault, but it's complicated. They hate me. I'll have to tell you about it."

"Well, looks like you're going to have to start applying for colleges or— Or *something*, Dalton."

"I know, Mama, I will. I'll take care of you if you want. I mean if I can."

"I know some professors here—you know I'm in school, don't you, son? I mean, do you keep up with me at all?" She paused for insult. Dalton stayed silent.

"Well, you can help me around the house. Maybe you can drop in and take a class with me. Maybe you'll like it. You know the church—"

"It's not about—" He paused. "I think I need a break."

"Okay then. Just like it always was, honey. Dalton, I don't— I'm just worried that I— Well, you get on home then and we'll talk more." She sounded tired. "And don't call me collect, sweetie. I simply don't have the money."

He pulled the phone away from his ear and tipped himself toward the open door of the booth to breathe. He sighed deeply. Time passed.

"Well, you know, I'm here all alone," she continued. "And your brother's gone for the summer. I sent him away to camp, did I tell you? It won't bother me at all to have some company."

"All right, Mama."

"Now, if that's all you want to tell me, I've got something to tell you. It's not good news. Are you ready?"

"I don't really want to talk anymore."

"Well, don't you want to know what it's like *here*? Aren't you concerned at all for your poor old mama? Your brother?" She forced a laugh. "He's away, and I've been feeling—"

"Listen, I can't do this, Mama. I gotta go." The receiver felt heavy in his hands. There was a pause on the line, static from far away. "I love you," he said, but the dial tone was already in his ear.

Jane

"GOD*DAMN* THAT BOY!"

Jane clicked her phone shut and tossed it onto the passenger's seat and jammed her brake pedal just in time to miss the rust-red tractor that appeared in front of her. The city traffic had subsided, so after the tractor driver had waved her by she had only to rest two fingers on the top of the wheel to steer down the long arcing turns of the one-lane Piedmont roads. She was leading a pack of cars, but her nerves were still rattled and she did not want to go any faster. She couldn't afford another speeding ticket, and used the caution of her bank account to mediate between her mind and the gas pedal.

Dalton's news left her discomposed. He was coming home, she thought, and that must be a good thing. She was missing the butterflies in her stomach that she supposed any other mother would have. He'd phoned her in a desperate way a dozen times since he left for the Army. She'd since realized that each time he'd smelled the faintest whiff of deployment he would call her up and revel in her hearing of the news, in her sobs and protestations. He might as well have been talking about his departure from the Earth as she knew it. This was different. He wasn't going anywhere. And this time she hadn't reacted, almost not at all. The actor, the giver within her, was giving up. The danger of it all used to—as far as he knew—overwhelm her to the point of despair; she understood that this had made Dalton feel real and needed.

So why was she showing him this side of her now? This cold, tired side? Was it in earnest? She'd known he'd come back. It was a spiritual certainty of hers. And so the overreaction must have been a favour to him. A mirage. She knew that and he knew that. But she always managed to weep for her son. Like a handshake. It was the last need for him, to feel loved. It was maybe all she could do now. All she could give, the performance.

Of course she wished Dalton would come home a caring son, that he'd stay on to look after her. But that would mean everything about their world would have to be different. Different boy. She damned her son and wished for a different one. And that revelation sank inside her, sat just above her hip bone as though she'd swallowed a stone. Jane opened her mind to the myriad alternatives that galloped in like horses back to a barn in a lightning storm, mixing what *had been* with what *could have been* with the way things were. She wished he could have gone to a university nearby, Appalachian State maybe. Something normal and good. Maybe if almost everything had been different. The boy was just always in trouble.

His teachers had always called him bright. *A very bright boy*. He was always just one step away from that bright future but managed to evade it. It hurt her to see herself in him. The self-sabotage, the meandering. The way he could find ways to make things harder on them, on her. The way he didn't see the same.

Jane closed her eyes briefly, and when she opened them a man in a pickup truck with a flaming Confederate flag decal on the hood was passing her in the oncoming lane. He glared at her, gearing up to shout through his passenger window, but froze, eyes resting on her head, bald and scarfless. After a beat he gave a two-fingered wave, lifting them up slightly off the steering wheel, and guzzled on past, less aggresively now. He waved his tanned arm out the window when he turned off, just a minute down the road.

She wanted Dalton here in the car now. Where he couldn't leave till she told him all that she wanted, all that she'd lost on him, and all that he had to do to make it right. Now that time was ticking down.

Jane had spent the morning at Winston-Salem State University. She'd had nothing but school on her mind before Dalton called.

But now she was racing home to no one, to drink while she studied. She settled back into that plan and sighed again, knowing she'd wake up harried the next morning, distressed by the clicking away of lost time as she always was, and would have to rush, again, to make it to church.

The church, the congregation, had made all this business for her, made all this stress, but it was in the name of the community and in the name of their own Christian duty that they sought to help her. Money for college, money to help supplement her dwindling Medicare. Church camp for Messiah at no cost.

As unassuming and inconsequential as she felt and tried to seem, she was known to each member of the congregation, for better or for worse. She knew she was their totem, their spiritual linchpin and shared welfare story. She knew that to some of the women in particular—the insufferable church ladies, as she privately referred to them—she wasn't so much their friend as their living ticket to heaven, the borne fruit and blinding symbol of their Christian charity.

Her predicaments were known and known widely: her outcast of a mother, disappeared up the mountain but still in and out of people's mouths; Clyde gone four years now and her all alone. Some, she knew, wondered if her mother hadn't taken Clyde with her. They all knew more than she did, all the church ladies and alcoholics, all the sheriff's people, all the PTA women from Messy's school. They knew of course the softness of Messiah and his quietness, and the school so hard on him since Dalton's adventures with guns and fights and girls and that boy Tyler. It was as if Messy had some leaking injury that wouldn't heal. It wasn't to save her, no, but to use her, somehow, right on time. Every favour from the church had Jim Hickok's fingers all over it. Inside it.

And she paid for it. Was paid for it. The church, the bureaucratic embodiment of their collective goodwill, reached out to her and took her in like an adoptee after her oldest boy had gone and done the community and the country a favour by enlisting. Jim Hickok must have felt that. Must have felt responsible, she thought. But Dalton's enlistment had impressed everyone else, assuaging some of their worries about her failures. Plus, the tying up and shipping off of Dalton as a loose and wild variable had alleviated some of the pressure to perform her expected pieties. Like she had somehow bettered herself by ridding her family of her son, that reminder of a mistake that, under the congregational leadership of Jim Hickok, they all shared but was hers to bear. "What a terrible thing to think," she said to herself. But it was true.

She primed herself to numb the pain of knowing that her son now faced another stalk in one of life's crop of unextinguishable regrets. She saw her own crop, now miles of flames set to burn finally out. The thought destabilized her. That vastness of fires before her, burning now to diamonds. Acres and acres of diamonds. She blinked the tears from her eyes to reduce the glare.

The unforeseen early return of her child came with no guarantee of anything except the church ladies' eyes and subtle judgment. Nothing Dalton could say or do would exorcise that pressure. The blaring possibility that she had failed through him and by him and to him reawakened in her, and with this fear she wondered if the scholarship cheque would still come if he returned and worked to help her. What would she say of their finances? If he came home acting like she hoped he'd act, he might hurt by helping. Help to hurt. He might make things harder just by being around.

He almost surely would. *That boy can't work,* she thought. *Can't work out.*

Messiah

MESSIAH WAS FULL OF LUNCH. He was sitting in a manicured pasture about a hundred yards from the chapel, the muffled sounds of other children playing flooding his ears like music from another room. He was inside—deep in his inner world, with fluffy walls around him that filtered and caught anything uncomfortable, not removing anything but stalling whatever forces of focus—*Focus, Messiah, focus!*—came his way until the levee inevitably broke and let the world come flooding in.

"I don't want anyone botherin' me," he'd said. He'd said it a thousand times. And here he was, unbothered. No need to focus. Between his cargo-shorted pale legs was a patch of white-tinged clover growing cautiously close to the ground as though to avoid the Saturday mower that had just run over this field. Survivors by being small. The smell of cut grass stuffed up Messiah's nose. He pushed his fingers into the ground and leaned forward.

He had a memory he was sorting through. He was sitting on the ground just like this. Dalton was on top of the tin roof of their house, waiting for their mama to get home. He remembered Dalton shouting at him, "Just sit there, Messy. Sit there and get Mama to look up at me when she pulls in!" Messiah was sitting there just like this, twisting clover between his fingers. Looking up at the black-clad image of his brother pacing on the roof. And when Mama pulled up Dalton jumped before Messy could say anything to her. She didn't even see him up there but only saw him there on the ground, his leg sideways. Just like this, he remembered.

"Messy!" a kid shouted from behind him. The noonday sun was hot on the top of his head, and he could feel his scalp starting to burn where his hair was parted. The camp counsellors had encouraged the boys to wear ballcaps, but Messiah had no hat. He did not turn his head to look at the boy who called to him, instead murmuring "What?" under his breath, assuring himself that he was doing what he'd so often been told: to always respond when people spoke to him so they'd know he was listening. It was *very important* that he remind everyone he was there. That he was listening.

He could hear the boy running up, dragging his feet in the sloping run of an exhausted child. He approached out of breath and wheezed, "Messy, they're calling us to go in. You gotta come now. You gotta come in with the rest of us."

"I know," Messiah muttered.

"Well then, come!"

"I don't know if I wanna do any more school."

"It ain't school, Messy. It's prayer group. Come *on*."

Messiah pulled his fingers from the damp ground and blew the shards of grass off their tips. He looked down one more time to see if there was a worm or a four-leaf clover there for him to find. Something to justify his staying. He turned his head and looked beyond the boy to the group of children being herded inside by the camp counsellors. He looked for a soldier in the parking lot. He looked for a small bald woman with a head scarf.

The boy started tugging on Messiah's shirt, pulling the collar around his neck. It felt like a string around him. Tightening.

"Come *on*," the boy pleaded again. "Messy. Come *on*!"

When Messiah heard the heavier footsteps of a counsellor approaching he began pulling up clumps of grass, digging, now, to see if he could get at anything at all, anything to keep him there just for another moment. The counsellor reached his hands under Messiah's armpits to lift him up. His big body hung limp against the effort.

"Messy. Come on, buddy," the counsellor said. "Come on, buddy. Time to go inside."

"No!" Messiah wet himself as the counsellor pulled him toward the chapel.

Grace

THE NEXT MORNING Grace undressed Tyler where he lay on the living room floor, unmoved from the night before. The sun spilled through the large windows, beams finding their way to light her gently shaking hands, pulling the blue of her veins to the surface of her skin and casting a golden glow on the dead boy's face. It was still frowning in pain.

Tyler had evacuated overnight. She bathed him with Dawn detergent and rough washcloths. She cleaned up all that had come out of him. She bundled up his soiled clothing and folded them neatly and tucked them under her arm. She left his body lying naked there in the sun.

The air was still and already humid as Grace went with the clothes and washcloths to the nickel tub out behind her barn. She filled the tub from the rusted rain barrel suspended above. She ran the garments along her washboard, working diligently. Birds began to sing, and Grace took note of each: the thrush and towhee, *drink you tea, drink you tea*. The wash revealed a new, effervescent green to the camouflage. A pattern emerged that looked oddly foreign and insufficient once the local grime had been cleaned away. Tyler had pinned many pins and sewn numerous patches onto the old Army jacket. She washed clean a white eagle that looked like a rank from the Second World War. She held up the right shoulder bearing a convoluted flag—lightning bolts, skulls, a torch, a snake—something she hadn't seen before. On the other shoulder were the stars and bars of the Confederacy, and on the chest the white cross of the Klan. She tsked to herself and laid the jacket out on the wooden bench to dry in the steaming morning. "Idiot boy."

She'd found Tyler at what she thought was the end of his militia fascination. After a stint in jail and the ensuing absence of his father, Tyler looked to her to be ripe for reform. She thought his zealotry might translate directly to her mission to help the world find Jesus. She needed strength and she needed an outsider. And she knew Tyler.

He was the son of a quietly famous lost causer in Mount Airy, Harold Flowers, a mechanic with long stringy hair and hands stained forever black. The town knew him as the man in camouflage who walked with a limp, having been injured by friendly fire in a shootout with communists in Greensboro in the seventies. He was a Bircher, a casual Klansman, and only somewhat Born Again. They lived in an unnamed red-dirt cul-de-sac of trailers offshot from Route 52, closer to Pilot Mountain. Grace knew Tyler's father from his sporadic interest in old-time religion. He was just an attendee, much as she'd been then, a kind of travelling casual worshipper. Couldn't bring himself in to join a real church. Lots of the revival types were like that, needing the open air to sing and be seen in the eyes of the Lord. The father would haunt the backs of revival tents, brown-bagging liquor, trying to keep up with the crescendo of worship, slurring in mock tongues. He often had prepubescent Tyler in tow, dressed in his daddy's baggy Gulf War fatigues, his head shaved down to the bone.

The boy had gotten mixed up with her grandson, or her grandson, also an idiot, had gotten mixed up with him. He and Dalton had taken one of Tyler's daddy's guns from his bedside and brought it with them to school, passing it back and forth from one to the other throughout the day, scaring the pretty little freckled girls with it and pointing it, unloaded, at the other redneck boys, squeezing the trigger and dry-firing those indelible, empty clicks at all those children. So the story went. Dalton confessed to firing it in a field by the school, popping cans and milk jugs on which they'd written people's names and drawn penises and breasts.

When the police came for them after so many parents had complained, the two were arrested and separated. There was no confusion about who was guilty nor about who was the owner and the instigator. One slightly more idiotic than the other, she thought, and shook her head. That same night Dalton was released on the recognizance of his pastor, Jim Hickok. But Tyler had remained in jail as the stories ran again and again on the local news about a near-Columbine that had scared all the parents in the Piedmont Triad region of North Carolina. Tyler's father had, on that very same day, mysteriously disappeared. Questions abounded.

She could hear voices gathering at the edge of her winding gravel driveway, as they did every Sunday. She had the thought to send Tyler down to tell them to assemble in the orchard and to wait for her sermon, then she looked at the hanging and dripping clothes. She'd have to bury him or get Clyde to do so. She wiped her soapy hands on her nightgown, pinkening it here and there.

Dalton

DALTON HAD REALLY LOVED ROMERIN. His best friend. And then the fight. What had presented itself as a moment of anger now looked like something else. That was all. Their inseparability had turned into a talking point. Rumours started—first with the other men in his platoon, then his company, and eventually with the whole battalion. Don't ask, don't tell.

He wished he'd been able to say goodbye to Romerin, but after that day, after they were separated by laughing, panicking men, naked and bleeding, knees red from their violent tousling on the floor, Dalton couldn't lock eyes with him. Not when they sat half-dressed in their lieutenant's office, not afterward in the barracks. Not in the chow line. Then Romerin had been transferred to a different platoon.

Now, leaning against the bus station wall, the soft pressure reminded him of the shower divider, of Romerin's bearing down on him, breathing on him, grasping at him like an inverted drowning victim. He remembered the violent rattling of the shower door as Romerin battered it and shouted at him. He felt again Romerin throwing him on the floor, hitting him hard, both men naked and struggling and grunting, all parts of him heaving and sobbing in the steam. The slipping grips of wrists struggling to violently cover over the inexcusable evidence of what had spilled out from their bodies, covered with watery blood, erect and gasping.

"What in the living fuck," one soldier had said as he and another had dragged Dalton along the tile floor. Romerin screaming. The men yelling for an NCO and almost punching him with bleached towels to clean him up. "No!" Dalton had shouted as they pulled him away, whether in defiance of the implication his priapic body welcomed or in protest of his separation from Romerin he didn't know.

They had met their court martials separately. The process was a lonely one. That initial anger and longing returned. Something unfinished that couldn't finish. Dalton went through his paperwork to double-check the wording for mistakes, for clarity. But there was nowhere else to go but away, nowhere else to go but home. His discharge papers read *Inability to Adapt.* Underneath all the rest of his condemnations, those words and *Other Than Honorable* burned to the quick of him and punctuated his loneliness.

Dalton closed his eyes and squeezed them tight, opened them again. He looked through the chalky, salted plastic windows of the bus station at the sun as it hovered just above a string of stores—a massage parlour, a vape shop, a Chinese buffet, a cellphone store—and closed them, relaxing his eyes behind their lids. He was in his mind. The pink and orange shadows of the now-setting sun blanketed the memory of the barracks' shower tile still in his eyes, simply washed over it. The bismuth light grew like a nebula, eclipsing overturned mop buckets, the drain next to his cheek clogged with mucus and body hair. Dalton remembered his outstretched palm supporting their collective weight on the tile. He'd moved his hand and let Romerin drop on him. Screaming now with the laughter. He was in his mind, yes. He could feel again the tearing of his underarm skin when they dragged him to the commanders' offices.

He slowed his thoughts or just paused them on that frame. He had to get his story straight. He couldn't let the bus that would shuttle him across the country drag him as he'd been dragged out of the shower. He might be dragged forever, he thought, until he died, perhaps of disgusting dreams and dehydration shouting "No!"

You can jack off wherever you like, the cab driver had said. To where, now, was he being dragged?

He told himself to stop acting stupid, to cut it out with the dumb thoughts. He got stuck on the word. It had been forbidden at home, to protect his brother. "Dumb" and "slow": disallowed. He tried to picture his brother, sweet, solemn boy that he was. Dalton found that he hardly knew anything anymore about Messy, but he knew for certain that he wasn't dumb. He must be in middle school by now. Dalton wondered if it would make any difference to his brother how he was, exactly, now that Dalton, as Messy might have known him, was so extinguished. Maybe alive was good enough. Anger at himself for betraying his brother came down on him. Dumb, he thought, his brother wasn't dumb. What's dumb is to come home like this. *Other Than Honorable*.

Dalton tripped on his bag as he moved toward the ticket window, kicking it a little and just catching himself on the countertop. The bus station attendant had a chain-smoker's yellow hands and nose, and sunspots dotted a forehead that extended past his ears. He wore a translucent green visor like a bookie. He blinked incessantly and arrhythmically.

"Where to?" the attendant said with a smile.

Dalton shuffled more on his feet and dug through his pockets but couldn't hide that he still hadn't figured it out. He was flustered and wanted to tell the attendant anything, anywhere. He wanted to tell the attendant to go fuck himself, really, but after a glance back at the board, said "Roanoke" instead. "Winston-Salem, if it'll take me there. Mount Airy, North Carolina, if I can."

"Well," the attendant said as he checked a chart beneath a scratched sheet of plastic on the counter. "There ain't no bus direct, but you could get there. You'll have to go through Syracuse, then to New York City . . . down to Philadelphia, then to Richmond, and then you could get to Roanoke through there I figure. You got any bags?"

"Just that," Dalton said, pointing to his green duffle with a kick and a little anger in his voice, thinking the attendant wanted him to relive his stumble from moments before.

"Going home?"

Dalton nodded and blinked back at the attendant, suddenly aware of his own eyelids.

"Where's home, son?"

Dalton blinked again.

"Son, do you want to go to New York first? You could stop anywhere along the way. That's Greyhound. We've got buses to Washington, Newark, Pittsburgh . . . You don't have to go nowhere you don't want to go. Could go anywhere you *do* want to go," he said like an ad.

"No," Dalton stuttered and blinked.

"Son, are you mocking me?"

"No," Dalton said again, but softer, and blinked rapidly, hoping the attendant wouldn't notice. He couldn't help it now. He looked away.

"This is just something that happens, boy, when you get older. My eyes get watery."

"I just need to head down to North Carolina." Dalton's hands were shading his eyes now.

"Well, you can pay for your tickets all at once with transfers or go from station to station."

"I'll do that."

"Which?"

"I'll just go a little at a time. I've got a long leave ahead of me. I'll take my time."

"Thank you for your service," said the attendant. He blinked.

Jane

JANE WAS TIRED, but she pulled down her sun visor and in the little mirror watched herself redraw her eyebrows with one hand as the country turned rural and sparse. She took the exit nearest her house and pulled into the heat-cracked parking lot of a beige-painted strip mall. She fussed with her makeup a little more but decided there was just no fixing the real problem—the lack of eyebrows and the brown patches like medieval counties on a tea-stained map that were slowly growing along her face. She situated, then tied and retied her head scarf, cool and silky on her hot head. Finally she swung open the door and got out of the car slowly and with great effort, then limped into the ABC liquor store with the scornful Carolina sun in her eyes.

She was welcomed by one of Dalton's old classmates who knew her a little too intimately. He'd always known her from chance sightings around the public schools, elementary and middle, and from the news after Dalton's *incident*, but had come to know her quite well over the past couple of years through these interactions at the store.

Each week, she knew, he'd watch her struggling to get out of the old black Toyota that was always in various states of disrepair, sometimes on a doughnut wheel, sometimes with one headlight. He'd watch her through the whole ordeal: scooting one chubby leg out and lifting herself up with one arm, fingers splayed wide and white on the car's roof. The tumours in her spine that had made her legs weak had also turned her into a kind of physics expert in moving herself, relying on the steering wheel and door handles as fulcrums to push her out of the car. He never came out to offer his help or even go so far as to open the door for her. But he was polite enough to keep buying wine from, she thought, even if she despised the show she felt she had to put on for him with each visit. She armoured herself with the thought that the boy would never know what she was capable of, where she'd been in her life and *who* she'd been, and who she'd been *with* and all the rest. He didn't know anything, she told herself, and she forgave him each time the door chimed. Forgiveness. Forgiveness each and every time.

But maybe something about her slow, squinted walk into the sun compelled him to come and open the door for her this time. Jane wanted to shout "No!" She wanted to remind him that she attended university. That she'd worked her whole life. That she was a cancer survivor, a mother. She hated him for his smile when she walked in, his knowing about her, his casual air. She smiled. Did she suffer, did she limp and wheeze a little bit more for show? Or was it real?

"How're you, ma'am?" he said as the door shut itself behind him. He walked over to his usual station behind the register, pleased with himself.

"Well, Ralph, just fine, just fine."

"I got that wine you used to like, it's back in." He was leaning over the counter now as she walked past him in her little half steps, putting her delicate, ornamental shoes one in front of the other. This was a brisk pace for her, and her feet couldn't move her fast enough. She strained her neck instead to look over to her usual section.

"Which one was that? The pinot gris?" She shuffled on.

"Yes ma'am." Having lost her behind the aisle, the young man moved out from behind the counter and eyed her from above the short wall of liquor during the minute or so it took her to respond. She could hear her own laboured breathing above the hum of the air conditioning.

She came back with a bottle in each armpit, digging through her pocketbook. "Well I guess I'll just try a new one. I couldn't find any others I like."

"I've got that one, ma'am." He motioned to go and fetch the bottle.

"No, no, no. I feel like experimenting, Ralph. Live a little. Listen here," she added, feigning coarseness, "I'm more interested in that girlfriend of yours. How's she doing?"

"Going along all right," he said. "Do you ever run into her at school?"

"No, and I'm glad I don't. Bad enough being a dinosaur, worse being an old bald dinosaur. Makes me feel sometimes like I'm wasting my time. I'm getting so tired. But thank God it's Saturday! If it weren't, I might not have the—"

She paused as she stood, now with the pocketbook on the counter, looking as though she didn't know what to do next, her vision going soft and fuzzy. She felt like a little girl trying to blow a gum bubble. She glanced up at the young man and smiled, recomposed herself, remembered that she was still holding the bottles beneath her arms, and set down one then the other. He waited patiently. The look on his face made her feel pitiful.

"I might not have the energy to return," she said at last, but had lost the name of the school, the place she meant to return *to*.

"All right, Ms. Jane," he said. The boy scanned both bottles without saying anything else, and Jane watched her hands as she moved them, feeling as though they were disconnected from her: crinkled with a thousand hair-thin white wrinkles, white sun specks dotting the tops like touch-ups from mismatched paint. Her nails were a bitter colour and felt brittle; she fought against worrying too much about them as she worked to find her card. The door chime sounded but without her glasses she couldn't see who it was. One prolonged squint for no new information. She looked back down at the bulging mess of receipts and dollar bills.

"Well, hello! Hey there, Ralph!" came a voice with a practised, diaphragmatic boom.

The face of the young man brightened. "Hello, Pastor Hickok!" he said. "Goddamn," he said under his breath.

"And hello to *you*, Ms. Fuquay!" the voice said, and Jane turned.

"Why, hello to you, Pastor Hickok."

"Are we having some kind of celebration tonight, Ms. Fuquay? A nice bottle of wine with dinner? I'm expecting you at service tomorrow, I'm sure."

The condescension was not lost on her. A lecture about why she shouldn't be drinking, not after her *promises* to the addiction groups in the church basement she'd long since stopped attending, would have been less humiliating than his feigning a kind of understanding about the drinking habits of a dying woman. "Why yes, I *am* having a dinner tonight, Pastor Hickok," she said. "Dalton is coming home for a spell."

"Well, that is an occasion indeed. Yes ma'am! An American hero!" Jane thought his look turned strangely nervous, as though he'd lost his keys. "How's he doing, anyway?"

Jane searched his face for ill intent and, disappointed to find none, smiled in return. Sweat dampened the crux of her collarbones, and her forehead warmed beneath her scarf. "Yes," she said, trailing off, absentmindedly flipping through the contents of her wallet. "Yes, that's right. Something to be proud of. He seems to be just fine."

"I am happy to hear he's coming home on leave. You look happy yourself, Jane," he said to her shoulder, more warmly now. Ralph had begun to busy himself behind the counter, probably not wanting to be expected at church himself. He watched them with quick anticipatory glances that, to Jane, seemed to suggest an expectation of conflict.

Jim Hickok was a big man with a full head of white hair that seemed unnaturally thick for his age. He was tall and broad, a little over sixty, and had a stomach that told of his indulgences but didn't make him any less handsome. Jane watched him, smiling as he laughed amiably, a little lost in himself. He let the conversation deflate by putting his hands in his khaki pockets, smiling and rocking back on his heels waiting for Jane to say something nice.

"He's lucky to have such a strong-willed mother." He winked. "May I ask how you're doing?" Jane knew now that he was performing. For her or for Ralph wasn't clear.

"Well, just fine," Jane said again, performing in return. "Stronger every day."

They spent several seconds studying each other, adjusting their smiles. As the pastor wiped his hands on his khakis Jane turned to face the wall behind the cash register. "Well, good night, Pastor Hickok." She waited for him to move. He reached out a big hand and touched her shoulder with it. Not a palm-heavy, religious touch, but a thick-fingered caress that grazed across her bra strap, his rough fingers catching in the silk of the blouse she wore over her camisole.

"All right then. Enjoy your dinner party," he said and walked toward the bourbon aisle, shouting to Ralph about baseball.

Abandoning the search for her debit card, Jane counted out seven dollars in change, put that and a five down on the counter, and said goodbye to Ralph. Then she walked out into the parking lot, crumpled herself back into her car, and sighed, happy to have survived once more the great swing of her body required to plop herself straight in her seat. She hoped Jim hadn't seen.

Jane slid her hand under her scarf and then back out. Wet, as if she'd dipped it in a glass of water. She felt naked and surveilled.

She wished Jim hadn't been there and wished even more that he hadn't touched her—a pity touch, she thought, serving only to remind her of the way he'd once held her with his big hands. Of how he never would again, of how she'd never be touched by anyone like that again. She reached down through the neck of her blouse and felt the clammy skin of her chest, sliding her hand over the bridle-thick scars where her breasts had been. Dusk was setting in. A little gas to get the Corolla going again, just a tap. Just a little gas and she'd be gone.

Down the road, Jane stopped at a grocery store and repeated her groaning car exit once more. The burning lines of hanging halogen made everything in the place pop with colour. She hadn't spent too much time cooking or shopping for anything in recent weeks, and felt she was getting too old to distinguish between all the products that seemed to float by her like an inverted parade.

She asked a young woman in a green apron for help and had a harder than usual time getting the words out. She was just looking for breakfast food, she said. The girl took Jane down to the cereal aisle. Once Jane caught up—trying her best to keep pace and breathing heavily, leaning on the shopping cart, avoiding other customers as best she could—she looked around at the animated boxes and started to laugh a sad laugh, looking down at her feet.

The girl, her eyes now brimming with a new sympathy, scanned Jane's figure from beneath her sharp bangs: Jane's posture, her eyes, the loud head wrap. Jane raised her chin. "I thought it might be here. Just one aisle over. Of course. I'm sorry to take up your time."

With warmth in her voice the young woman said, "Ma'am, how about you just tell me exactly what you need, and I'll run and get it for you and meet you at the front?"

"Don't worry," Jane said. She took a beat to catch her breath. "Sweetheart, I must be having what they call a *senior moment*." She surprised herself with her own use of the word. That wasn't the problem.

"Do you mean breakfast like pancake mix?"

"Oh, I'll be fine, sweetie," Jane said. "I'm fine now."

Determined now to get what she needed, Jane made her way to the meat, to the milk, to the eggs. All cool to the touch as she tossed them in the cart. She leaned on its bar, thinking about her sons and about Jim Hickok and about the medicine in her purse. It wasn't so much that her body screamed for morphine, but there it was: the eerie feeling that the morphine was screaming out for her. A noise from behind her, a mix between a buzz and a honk, made Jane turn slowly, her feet moving three times each to make a half circle. Coming down the aisle was the young clerk in a motorized wheelchair shopping cart, waving at Jane and smiling.

"I got you this, ma'am."

And it was real redemption, Jane thought, to be so defeated and so saved.

After the whole polite hassle of transferring Jane and her groceries was over and the woman walked away, Jane keyed off the electric cart and rested in its seat. The aisle appeared to elongate before her; the ceiling seemed to shrink. She dug through her purse, found her morphine, clicked out an extended-release pill, and took it. She noted the time on her watch and pinched herself as she said aloud the number out of ten pain she was in so that she could update her doctor. She wouldn't remember anyway. In their steady insistence the long tubes of light shone like an orderly, all-encompassing spotlight above her. The music played over the intercom, buzzy and static. Jane laid her head on the handle of the cart. People walked past her. It was a race against time, now, to get out of the store and drive home safely, but everything was so still.

At the top of her gravel driveway Jane killed the Corolla's ignition and meditated in the static quiet of home: cicadas droning in the humidity, the cooling engine popping and humming as it settled into place. Sitting there in the single lamplight on her road, she opened up her mind again to memory. She looked out at her house, a kind of irradiated yellow in the night. The green front door. Clyde had painted it. It was black now, dark in the shade. The green box that divvied out energy to the other homes in the hills hissed at the foot of her driveway and she found herself calmed by its persistence and power, by the guarantee of white noise that gave her permission to meander through her thoughts with her eyes closed.

She thought about her own mother, the ghostly whiteness of her skin and her tar-thick hair and stubbornness, and how before she left she'd warned Jane about Pastor Hickok. And, of course, Jane thought about how Pastor Hickok had warned her about her mother.

But he was just the last in a long string of men who'd made their way through her life—miserable and dissatisfied men, all boyfriends and short-lived partnerships. Jane and her boys had since stopped bouncing from apartment and townhouse to apartment and townhouse and selected one of her mother's inherited properties in the foothills to settle down in. This house, sitting half-lit and tin-roofed, wet with dew in the summer, this house bloomed like a weed up out of the ground, securing the dirt beneath them to make their spot on the earth real. It was their refuge and their remembrance of aspiration. A headstone, now.

Her mother had come home from her knee surgery to rule the roost. She'd come to convalesce but stayed, Jane thought, to raise Cain. The two women had gotten along symbiotically, even if it felt a little parasitical to Jane. Times seemed best when Grace went on her medication; when she was what she called "a little resentful of age except for these little miracles," shaking her pill bottle—peaceful except for needing a cold washcloth here and there for her forehead. Times when there was still a little OxyContin in her purse and church to look forward to.

When Jane had dates or had to work late, Grace would look after the boys. She would tell them stories, read to them from the Bible, or sit them down in front of televangelical shows on the stale

Christian channels, the pastors and preachers asking for money and prayers. That was the extent and the worst of her influence on Dalton and Messiah. Stories from the Bible were preferable; both Grace and the boys were fans of the ugly parts—the more belligerent and worrisome parts, Jane thought. But when the pain kicked up and the swelling flesh around Grace's knees tightened, or when rain came, or when any noise drew her out of her focus, she would turn ornery and the mood in the house would change, sometimes for weeks. In these hurricanes the whole atmosphere of the house felt stifled and slowed. She was the eye. Angry as the devil, Jane thought, and half-sobbed, half-laughed to herself there in the car. The medicine was working now, and she wished she'd gotten new knees of her own; hers sure hurt enough to warrant it.

But Jane knew that beyond the bills and the paperwork, Grace's knee surgery took a more significant toll on her mother than any surgery ought to. An operation ought to kill you or make you better, she'd thought, but when her mother started screaming at the children, sometimes hitting them with her big Bible, Jane knew that something was happening beyond the pain from the surgery. A drama, and a pain of deep meaning for Grace, as though the sin of the boys' laughter was burning her up inside.

Like any child, Jane didn't want to believe that she might lose her mother to dementia or to drugs, to God and Jesus, or to the irrevocable calcification of old Southern orneriness, either. She knew that her boys had come to fear Grace. That she was losing her mother to something. But when Jane was diagnosed with cancer, any hope of doing something about it disappeared. And her mother disappeared shortly thereafter. Taking the whole energy of their shared life, and all the money, with her.

Messiah

MESSIAH FUQUAY WAS SITTING alone at a picnic table under the breezeway adjacent to the chapel, busying himself. The screams and shouts of the other boys came to his ears as though he was underwater.

He kept mostly to himself at camp, just as he did at school. He'd been on the receiving end of some nicknames at first—Pukeway, F-U-kway, and so on. The camp counsellors had tried "Mez," but he hadn't warmed up to that one. He was Messy like his mama and his brother called him, or the formal Messiah. But that was like a curse word around here. The head counsellor winced whenever he said Messiah's name.

He tried to curb the new nicknames by taking on an air of impartiality, a delaying tactic so that he wouldn't have to resort to saying "Don't call me that." He wanted to save any true protest for "retard," a designation he'd hoped to escape out here at Mountain Heights Youth Camp. He knew from his brother that it wasn't a true designation. Not medical, anyway. "You've got to just talk more, Messy," Dalton had told him. "When people talk to you, you gotta talk back, buddy. Just talk back like I talk back to you when you ask me questions. Try to pretend like you got something to say and then maybe you'll find you got something to say."

They eventually settled on *Messy*, however, which here felt like an ironic nod to how neat and minimal his bunk and belongings were. This satisfied Messiah. The camp had no uniforms, but Messiah had his own. Walmart-bought white Hanes T-shirts and blue jeans that rose above his ankles more and more by the day.

There were voluntary haircuts available once a week. The barber, a member of one of the churches, would drive out to the country and set up a chair for the boys to sit in while he clipped their hair with shears affixed to a thirty-foot orange extension cable that ran from the back door of the concrete cafeteria. A Marine veteran with a squiggled blue bled-out globe and eagle tattooed on his arm, he could cut hair only one way: high and tight. The haircuts were not very popular. Messy liked to watch his blond, almost white hair fall on his jeans. He liked the feeling of the barber sweeping his neck with the brush after he was through. The buzz cut felt good on his neck, like he was new. In the communal shower rooms he would stare at himself in the mirror and think about his brother in the Army, imagining himself in Dalton's uniform.

Messiah was surprised when Graham, his youth pastor, had told him at the beginning of the summer that he could come to the camp with the other boys if he wanted. It would be free, he said. He'd talked to Messy's mama.

Messiah had wanted to but hadn't even entertained the idea when the flyers advertising the camp were passed out each Sunday in the bundles of little Jesus comics and prayers and simple hymns. It wasn't the camp itself that drew him but rather learning that Graham would be there. He wanted to go wherever Graham was going to be. But like most things he figured it wasn't up to him, desire aside. He'd never been before, and thought it wasn't in the cards.

Messiah had gone so far as to throw the flyers out each week so his mom wouldn't have to see them and regret his absence from the "Christian tradition" the camp claimed to maintain. He thought of it as freeing her from a guilt that was beyond her control. Protecting himself, really, from having to listen to a recurring explanation of why he couldn't go and the lies he'd have to tell her about not wanting to anyway. Same discussions as when they went grocery shopping and he wanted Lunchables. Same sort of discussions they'd had about Dalton coming home. Not up to them.

Now Graham appeared as he typically did, late in the week in the church van with its name, SACRED HOLLOW PRIMITIVE BAPTIST, on the side. Messiah had been putting together a puzzle as the blue van drove in, kicking up dust in its wake. He got to his feet, lumbered in a husky jog toward where he knew the van would park, and met it as it came to a stop, putting his splayed hands on the driver's-side window and smiling.

"You weren't drivin' as fast as you do, as you could," Messiah said. "Graham, why you driving so slow?"

Messiah, who'd be turning fourteen soon, looked at Graham to let him know that he considered cars and he considered speed and he wanted all the mystery of it to fade away behind his posture. He stood up straight as Graham got out of the van. Messiah was taller than the other boys, almost as tall as the counsellors and administrators.

"I just got off work, buddy. At the mall."

"You bring me anything?" Messiah didn't need to pretend with Graham.

Messy had studied Graham, and he took him in carefully now. He took note of the curve of Graham's white ballcap, which was dirty. The letters LSU on it surrounded by some straight and squiggly lines. He took note of the unbuttoned top of Graham's shirt. The holes in Graham's clean jeans. Messiah thought about how his mama patched his jeans, Dalton's old jeans, and wished she hadn't.

He had often considered Dalton through Graham, and Graham through Dalton. It sometimes felt like he had to choose. He told his mama that one day, and she said "That's ridiculous, Messiah. You've got one brother." But Messiah didn't want Graham to be his brother. Not like that. He wanted Graham to be something else.

The two walked side by side across the dusty gravel circle around the camp's central building.

"Listen, buddy, I heard you've been actin' up," Graham said. They'd stopped outside the big steel doors that opened into the cafeteria where all the children would be coming together for supper soon. The moment felt like a secret.

"I don't act up," Messiah said. "I act right. I just don't feel good. I don't feel right."

In a hushed voice, Graham said, "Do you miss your mama, Messy? Lots of kids miss their mama here."

"Yeah, I guess so."

"That's all right, buddy. And we got Jesus, too, though. Right? Don't forget. You ain't missing Jesus, are you?"

"No, I ain't missing Jesus." Messiah stood up straight again.

Graham lifted one of his grocery bag–laden arms and pulled the door open. "I saw your mama the other day. She looked happy, I think. She's doing good. She came down to the lunch after the sermon. Do you ever want to go back to church on Sundays and see her? I could come get you if you do."

"Maybe." Then, at least pretending a little to know and to want and to be able to say, Messiah added, "Yes I would."

"Well, all right then, Messy. You miss your brother too? I heard he was coming home. Did you know that? We were just talking about him at church on Sunday. Hey, we even prayed for him! You can *bet* he's with Jesus."

It was like that. Graham would come and talk and then Graham was gone. And it was Graham who Messiah was missing now as he was getting ready for bed. The pleasure he took in his fresh haircut and in his reverie with the image of his brother in the bathroom was short-lived. Messiah was sitting on his bunk with a big-texted and illustrated edition of the Bible lit up by his headlamp. A counsellor came in and shouted, "Lights out!"

And Messiah thought about his friend. Graham was tall and broad and tanned. He'd made Messiah feel special in Sunday school. When he had Graham, Messiah felt as though he were on equal ground with his peers. Like he was flowing with the stream current of the world. He understood just about everything that Graham taught them and could sing the songs from the sheet as loud and as good as anyone else. So different, he thought, from the remedial classes in the trailer that he and other special students were assigned to. The stale walls of the trailers emanating heat and keeping it in. Slide shows of new words and drawings of pigs and animals. These humiliations of difference weren't lost on him, and that alone should have distinguished him from the other students in his classes, he felt. Because he at least knew just where he was and knew that it was shameful.

And maybe sleep wouldn't come. He felt he'd been blown up too much too fast with all his thinking and that he'd bust like a balloon. He often thought maybe he'd just run away. He'd just go to where Dalton was. And where was Dalton? It was hard to tell people everything he knew. Hard to pretend to find the words.

Laughter was moving like waves across the bunks in the big building where they all slept. The boys had come up with some prank, he thought. Messy lay there listening intently and warily on the off chance that he might hear his name. Waiting to hear the news of whatever trick might materialize out of the hushed, conspiratorial laughter.

But the giggling slowly faded. The various flashlights and Game Boys dimmed, and the sound of the lake plodded and splashed against the shore like a big baby playing in a puddle just outside the window. The wind rustled a branch that scraped against the tin roof like fingers and bones. The sounds of sleep replaced the laughter, and the kicking off of sheets and gentle ebb of creaking mattress springs signalled to Messiah that there was no impending danger.

He relaxed and started slipping into a dream where he was with Dalton, both of them in uniform and at church shaking hands with people he was sure he'd never met. In the dream he was very good at having very much to say, to talk back at everyone. He heard a voice shouting at them in a language he recognized but was struggling to understand. People smiled and nodded at him, their faces inflating to grotesqueness and their smiles widening into Cheshire caricatures of smiles. These smiles that hurt him—the practised encouragement of a special child to break through to the other side of the simplest of tasks: tying one's shoes, blowing one's nose, tucking in one's shirt. Not hard, just hard to do right. The drowsy and stupid smiles and nods. *Good job, Messy.* Then Dalton was gone and Messiah was on his way down the brown corridor of stairs to the Sunday school classroom in the grey basement where Graham waited. Then the stamping of feet and the slamming of doors. The very real energy of rushing authority. And Graham was there, somewhere, and Messy could hear him. Dalton's face—Graham's face now next to the bed.

"Messy—wake up, buddy."

Grace

GRACE FUQUAY HAD SPENT HER LIFE CLIMBING: up from Beulah and the lowlands. She'd climbed up and over the hardships, the men who'd beat her, Jane's daddy; she'd climbed, quite literally, out the front door of his house. She'd climbed the spurs and tight-cornered country roads on foot, ignoring offers of rides, and walked the thirty or so miles to her Granny's mountain homestead. Later she'd climbed back into Jane's life, and into her grandsons' hearts, then up the many-runged ladders of evangelical leadership, scattershot and irregulated as it was, and rested then for many years among the countless low-landed, gently curving roads that intersected and flew across tobacco fields and furniture factories, flea markets and dollar stores. And now she was at the top, alone with Clyde and her parishioners, her own Gospel. The last rung was up to God. Yes, she had climbed from the red dirt of the earth in Beulah, North Carolina, up halfway to heaven.

In Beulah, in the thirties, she was birthed onto a barn plank floor, the last of four siblings and one of only two who would live into the new millennium. Her older brother died from polio. Her father from drink and pneumonia. Her other brother, lost in the war.

They were sharecroppers and traders, before all the loss, their lives humming along without electricity. Learning of the war in church rather than from the radio. And with the conscription of her remaining brother and the passing of her own mother, she was left to her homesteading Granny, who grew all that she ate and the tobacco that she snorted. Her home then was a holler near Lover's Leap in Virginia. And when she was a little girl she'd stand at the ledge and look down on the lowlands and wonder how much higher she might possibly rise.

There was no nook or turn or hole or gap in the mountain, no backcountry state route leading from the flatlands to the peaks where she was raised that Grace wouldn't have called home. But now, Grace came to think of one road, the Blue Ridge Parkway, as a red carpet to heaven, and it led right to her front door on Buffalo Mountain, of which she owned just about every square inch.

Spread out down on the various plains and valleys between the deceivingly steep but still rolling hills and mountains lay oases of fertile ground near an acre apiece, and upon each acre to her name Grace purchased over a hundred micro crops of tobacco for which she hired workers—some legal, some not—to till, plant, sucker, top, pick, and prime. At first these workers were mostly migrants, hearing of land that needed tending and chores that needed doing, and through their networks they would inform one another about a big payday waiting for them up on the mountain. Seasonally they would come, hauling tents sometimes, sometimes bedrolls, and during the spring to late-summer seasons of field labour would haunt the edges of the cleared fields, and those fields would stay cleared.

Old shacks, some ancient and some newly erected, came to occupy most of Grace's properties. Trailers and little jungles of campfires and hanging clothes. She watched them all from her perch on the mountain. Occasionally a sheriff's deputy would traverse the seldom-travelled snake of road that led off the parkway up to Grace's network of land. Mistaking the migrant workers for squatters he'd harass and threaten them, demanding identification and evacuation or money.

This happened almost yearly, and for a time Grace, almost always in a floral nightgown, would walk out onto her porch and greet the deputy with a smile, assuring him that they were her men out there working. Harassing the workers was just his job, he would convey to her. "Have to scare them straight, make sure they aren't stealing from you, ma'am," and at her reassurance that they weren't, the deputy would mosey back down the mountain to town and conduct similar business in the Home Depot parking lots and tractor supply store parking lots, often with great success, running the workers out of town.

Then something changed. Perhaps these sheriffs and deputies had been too successful, as the workers from Mexico dwindled and stopped returning. Grace was convinced that it had nothing to do with the pay or with her treatment of them, but rather with the sinners in the shoals—the sheriffs, the county commissioners, the sugar-coaters.

They were God-fearing people, Grace thought, and she liked having the migrant workers around her, people who knew work and knew God. In the final year that her properties swelled with Spanish and the smells of nighttime cooking, she had an orchard cleared and planted near her house, happy to provide work beyond the tobacco and cornfields—clearing out tangled flora and installing order on the mountainside.

But thereafter, these people did not return. They'd been chased from the region, to where Grace did not know.

In the season that followed Grace became familiar with the smell of rotting fruit emanating from the newly minted garden, The Orchard, as she called it, the ground plush with soft muck. The sweetness drove her indoors. Day after day: no visitors. There was no map to her house, and she imagined the roads—the interconnected countryside highways and mountainside parkways, the unmended retaining walls garlanded with hanging rhododendron—shrinking up toward her heart like veins. It was a cold year, and Grace spent it staring out at her browning land and growing angry and cold.

Advertisements taken out, Baptist periodicals called, a classified square bought: FOR HIRE – MEN – CHRISTIAN – ANY TYPE – BUFFALO MOUNTAIN – LABOR – FARMHAND WORK – GOOD PAY. Underneath, in small print, she put her address. By and by some men showed up to inquire. They came in groups, shoved in the backs of pickup trucks, sometimes three or four men, sometimes seven or eight. She regretted having not put SEASONAL STAY in the title. These men were hard to communicate with, hard to bargain with. They wanted pay upfront; they wanted to head home at night. These were not the men Grace needed to know, were not sent from God as she would have liked. They were sharp, and were hungry, but could find other work. Grace wanted someone chosen, someone lost.

And she found them. In the change there came a great hunger in the neighbouring foothills. There were layoffs in the factories in Bassett, in Stanleytown, High Point, Saltville, Canton—decades-old layoffs—and the children of the old workers, impoverished, grew up fighting and aimless, not strong enough for the direction of God. But they found Grace.

These boys, now in their twenties or thirties, caught wind of the opportunity to escape for pay, to tend and to be tended, and the season after her season of loneliness, Grace was gifted her revival. The boys came asking not for food and shelter and good passage as the men before them had, but for money and legitimacy, for the shelter of work, for sustenance. The shacks doubled in number in a week. The cornfield was retilled and cleared, planted anew, and grew just fine. The tobacco blossomed and opened to the warming sun, and before long there was a functioning, a coming and going, roadside selling of corn and hushed sales of illicit tobacco and marijuana if a curious motorist asked nicely. No apples went wasted on the ground. They were picked, and pressed into cider, and a year came and went, and more worshippers returned for the next.

But there was a change again.

Grace's knees failed her one morning and she fell down her sloped overlook to the south of her house. The fall brought with it broken ribs and a fever, and pain that was hard to subdue. Her confident walking and vigilant surveying ended, her outward-looking smile turned inward, and, money and profits be damned, she lay in bed. Some of the workers offered to take her to the doctor, an idea she cursed until fever took over, and finally a doctor was sent for and prescriptions written. A live-in nurse got hired and shooed away, but not before Grace began to take religiously the medicine she needed to bear walking again. And so, straight-legged and zombified, compelled by the rush of good feeling in her bones, she would shower and once more leave the house to shout and corral her workers and hold court.

It was then that Clyde appeared, haggard and coming down off a drunk. He said he wanted to mend tensions with Jane. Thought that if he could get Grace to go back down to Jane, let her daughter help her now that she was sick, he could get things right with what he felt was his last love. Grace never did return to the shoals, to her old house with Jane. She kept Clyde instead.

He felt obliged to stay with her while she was mending, looking after the paying of her workers and wielding her chequebook like it was his own. In her hazy recuperation there was almost nothing she wouldn't approve. Clyde stayed and gained a truck, hauled in a trailer just down the road, helped erect a semi-permanent tent in the orchard and advertised visiting preachers, began to normalize things.

But it wasn't long before those workers who'd settled into Grace's part of the Blue Ridges brought their own eccentricities and problems. Whiskey was carried up weekly to nighttime revivals and Grace would preach when she could, finding strength in their communion, the old fire again back inside her, coming out in flaming sermons to the workers gathered around a bonfire on top of the mountain. But it was as though the decrepitude of the foothills began to creep up the mountain. Factories closing in Bassett, stores shuttering in Stuart. There was an accumulation, the mass amalgamation of lean-tos and junk, outdoor stoves and Dutch ovens, bedrolls and trucks, tractors and emptied-out minivans with mattresses, shacks with kerosene heaters, clotheslines, water buckets, hanging camp showers and disguised corn whiskey stills—it was as though this part of the world was heading backward in time. But religion was a constant, and any hope for money or relief was an encouragement, and more people came. The families grew. The new workers, black sheep in all their flocks before Grace's, brought dangerous attitudes that weren't foreign or new but were hayseed, far-flung, and rootless—as though these people had shrunk what they knew of the world to a hostility for anything beyond the kudzu borders of their holler.

They saw in Grace what they saw in themselves. They shared a suspicion that they'd become the refuse of modernity. They shared a belief that the towns and the computers and the people who had pushed them away had fallen into the hands of the devil, the lake of fire. And they, drug addicted and uneducated and cold and alone, they, the victims of modernity, had become lost to their old families and communities, and feeling unmissed, had found Grace.

Grace's predicament had begun years before, one Sunday morning when she had lain in bed and skipped church. In the nineties, it had gotten so that Grace's interruptions at Baptist and Pentecostal churches, reports of her breaking out into tongues and her writhing and shrieking and eye-rolling and hysteria, had come to precede her, and even travelling revival outfits coming through northwestern North Carolina would know about Grace and would ask a few men to wait outside the tent to look for her. Occasionally a curious pastor would come out to greet her, just to see, to try to ward off any chaos that followed her. One might ask her if she could play by the rules and let others worship half as fervently as he knew she would. Grace would just stare at the pastor as she snuffed some powdered tobacco from a vial at the entrance to his tent.

Laughing, one pastor said, “Grace, gracious Grace from Pilot Mountain,” and smiled with dentures so porcelain white the nubs looked almost green in the sun. “Don’t you look like a cool glass of water?”

“You dirty old man! If you thirst,” she said, “drink from me,” and laughed maniacally, coughing up back-of-throat tobacco and spitting on the ground. But the phrase suited her, and she kept it in her mind as a mantra. *If you thirst, drink from me.* It was as though she’d never be empty. She turned to the makeshift parking lot in the field where families were straightening out their clothes and shutting car doors. She waved her arms and shouted at them and said, “Do not enter here, friends! There’s a haint in here, something that your weak, carpetbagging minister here can’t muster the strength to encounter. Satan, my people, travels along here with this man, here in this tent. Do not enter!”

The ensuing pause signalled to Grace that she had their attention and, at the very least, had gotten her impromptu audience to consider her words. She saw that she had the power. She discovered her soul, she thought, her gift. There existed, she was sure of it, a whole lineage of prophets such as herself, likewise betrodden and cast aside. She found her message. And out of her mouth came more hellfire and damnation than any church was prepared to handle. The women and men, their children, stood before her and breathed out of their mouths, not knowing how seriously to take her. Then eventually filed in. This was always the case, the ambivalence of sin.

She went on a pyrrhic crusade to terrorize all such preachers, those who she found were weak in the knees and weak in their faith. There were months of forced exits, physical removals, Grace kicking and screaming in the arms of the sheriff, of returns home to her daughter, her sinning daughter. Returning to Clyde and how he looked at her. Then there would be the disapproval, the hiding of car keys to stop her from going to church, the shouting matches, the zombified children watching, listening to it all. Grace became a cup too full, until she began to boil up and over. And now on the mountain, her mountain, she regularly let her spirit run over the meagre cup of her body and onto her followers, and they did drink from her.

Jane

PERHAPS SHE'D TAKEN TOO MUCH MEDICINE. Perhaps not enough. Jane pushed open her car door, but there on the hill of the driveway gravity kept pulling it shut. She opened it again, slipped her arm through the crack between the door and the frame, and set her hand on the roof of the car, feeling the pasty dust of late-season pollen. The door closed hard on her arm but at least she wouldn't have to throw it back open. She lurched back and forth in her seat to get the pendulum of her weight going, and all at once lifted herself up. Trusting her left leg too much, she pushed through the door with her body and fell onto the gravel.

She didn't cry out but instead felt a sense of calm. She could taste dust in her mouth, and when she pushed her hands into the gravel to sit up the sharp rocks dug into her palms, sending pain as if she'd been burned up her arms and to her chest. There it was muted by the morphine, and she breathed heavily in relief, almost in ecstasy, as it slipped away.

Clouds had come up low over the trees beyond her house. The bugs around seemed to reply to the humming electricity box. The street light flickered in Morse code. The wave of cicada calls was extended and exaggerated. The shell-like leaves of the magnolia in her front yard made a shushing noise when they brushed up against one another in the wind.

Dalton was coming home. Things were going to be different. She rubbed her hands together, freeing them of the little rocks pushed into her palms. The thought made her smile. She sniffed and straightened herself up and breathed in the short silence between the call from the bugs and the response from the box. She dismissed outright the idea of crying.

Jane propped herself up on the car's runner, still wedged between it and the door, and hoisted herself up noisily and unladylike until she was on her feet, a little dizzy, her body in much pain from the effort. She thought she might need to take a little more medicine. At the thought of what the shorthand of that next pill was—*breakthrough* morphine, they called it, for *breakthrough* pain—she began to yearn for it, and had to force herself to first collect her things from the passenger seat before walking slowly and cautiously across the lawn and up the steps of her porch, navigating each one at a time, leading always with the stronger leg.

She leaned up against the porch railing and stared out into the fuzzy nighttime. The grown-over bank that ran down from the house to the road had been beautiful once. She'd gotten so tired that she couldn't bring herself to walk back and forth from the kitchen with a watering can to tend to the more fragile plants that used to flourish there. The pride of Old 52, she used to think. She remembered her sons always rummaging in the mulch and picking the flowers. If she'd had a hose she would have sprayed them with it, then. She had torn up all the Easter lilies.

When she swung open the screen door the creak of the hinges blended with the night sounds and the buzz of bugs, the cloud of Carolina noise. It pleased her. The image of her boys on the bank stuck in her mind; she could almost smell the hot grass and summer pollen. Her back was cool with sweat. She sighed and collected herself, maybe just in case he was home. Yes, just in case. She turned the key and stepped through the green front door of her old yellow house.

She went through to the kitchen, put the groceries away, and then sat on her favourite couch, a recreation mid-century modern cigar-style thing, something truly hers. Something comforting about antiques, emanating so many past lives, places, ways of living. She was grateful for her couch and grateful for Messiah's time away at summer camp. She was glad he didn't have to watch her dip again into a fresh bottle of wine. And what should she be ashamed of? She'd told Pastor Hickok there was to be a party tonight and that was all right, surely. *Some party*, she thought. She pulled the cork with the antique opener she was fond of. The anticipation of the wine stirred a latent feeling, the oncoming wave of euphoria she felt she had to keep in store. The doors to the world opening. *It will be nice to have Dalton home*. She tried on the thought again and waited to see if it was genuine, but nothing came.

Jane had left her heels on the intricate hallway floors that had been painted, years ago, by Dalton and Clyde, the kind of man who was never there, but of course now he was everywhere, having spilled himself and the memory all over the house. Any consideration of a piece of that house, touching the upholstery of the sofa or scuffling her slippers along the redone floors, would remind her of her mother, or Clyde, or of the two of them, disgustingly, according to the gossip. He who'd been so hard to pin down, the story went, was now waiting hand and foot on her mama in the mountains.

Before her diagnosis she'd been working in child protective services in Stokes County while she tried to get her degree. She'd made a career of taking children away from their parents; after a while, she had a hard time committing to any future of her own when she altered the futures of so many others. Then came the Bush tax cuts and, less bona fide than her peers, she was let go. Then the diagnosis. Then the groups. Then Jim Hickok, then

Dalton and the gun, Dalton and the Army. Clyde gone; her mother gone. And poor Messy. Her little boy.

She caressed her couch and felt at once worthy of the indulgence and afraid of the reality and precarity of the moment. When would Dalton be home?

Those little children had been taken away at her official request. Back then she would torture her psyche each night, doubting herself, wringing her shaking hands between sips of wine that grew into gulps. One bottle turned to more and then to whiskey. The faces would fade into a cloudy remembrance, and her worry and management of worry would numb her into a contentedness that let her forget even her own children for a time. The next morning she would invariably wake to panic and aspirin and cold showers and cold coffee brewed knowingly the night before, and the children's bus long gone. She would speed down the shoal roads and almost push her boys out of the car with harried kisses; her late arrivals at work were met with condemnation and more aspirin and shaky drives to the first case visit of the day with the sighing and the shaking head of an accompanying officer. This ritual comedy had consumed her in a whirpool of predictable setbacks and apologies until she was let go. The tax cuts were to blame, she told herself. What else could she do? What else could she have done? And with no more doctor visits for her aching breasts until some money had been settled, and Dalton was gone then and then Messiah, and now . . .

She picked up and perused a few prescription bottles. Shopping, almost, for which pains she'd like to numb, how she'd like to sleep, measuring that against a sad familiarity with how difficult all this would make getting out of bed in the morning. She opted instead for another glass of E&J she'd unhidden from a kitchen drawer, listening to the last of bluegrass hour on the local public radio before the news came on.

Jane shut her mind to her past and shook her head in cadence with the events of the day, murmuring along and tsk-tsking the news. She took her wine to her seat in front of the mirror of her dressing room, as she called Dalton's old room. It now served as storage, crowded with furniture and paintings, vintage Jackie O–style hats and clothes hung on every corner, a chaise lounge where her dog, Sumo, liked to sleep. A room for what she had left. Where was that dog? She set her glass down next to a tackle box she used as a jewellery box and put her earrings into it as if enacting a ceremony. They were a gift, from Clyde. She thought of his rough-hewn face, smiling as he dangled these silver hoops from his dirty fingertips. She closed the box.

If it was Clyde who refinished and lacquered and made the house real for her—the floors, the antiques, the painted walls, the refinished bathrooms—it was his absence that made all this cumulative history so tepid and stale. Nothing more to be changed, to be preserved or shaped. Unless Dalton—unless. But there were too many steps to arrive at that kind of rejuvenation of the place, the mood of it. Too many holes to fill, and Dalton, despite what he'd learned from Clyde, wasn't a big enough man to do it. He wasn't a man at all, she thought, not quite yet.

But was Clyde? Run off with no call for years. Her mother had always called him a loose recreant, pulled to the ends of the earth by magnetic waves unseen by anyone else, his motives his own. Disciplined somehow and principled, but recalcitrant and childish. His shoulders stretched wide across his hairy back, his hands like the roots of a chestnut tree. No other roots to speak of. How had she pushed him away? By losing her hair, by needing something soft? It was like asking a rolling boulder to be soft.

Jane looked hard into the mirror. The static voice from the radio made a joke, and the audience laughed. Her hair was returning—little sprouts of ghost-blond wisps that shot out too quickly and grew stringy, falling in front of her face and tickling her forehead after a week or so without vigilance—but her eyebrows were still drawn on. At first, when she started treatment, they'd been caricatures at best;

back then she'd made a habit of looking at herself in the mirror and pursing her lips to perform the stoic if worn-out mademoiselle. She did so now, but the gauntness of her face and the newly grown wisps of hair, despite her much practised and much more acceptable eyebrows, did not humour her.

She tried on a few new faces and a few new characters. She squinted to warp her expression into an ancient daguerreotype, as though she were somewhere in a boudoir in New Orleans, fanning herself. But the image looked silly, and toying with it was just part of the medicine, she thought. Just her mind sagging into something familiar.

She got up to feed Sumo, her last responsibility. After finding his bowl full of food, she realized she hadn't seen him in a couple of days. Not unusual but not comforting either. Even her dog was uncommitted and liked to roam. She went into her bathroom, which had drying pantyhose draped like Spanish moss across the rail.

She washed her face. Removers and toners and micellar waters ran into her eyes and stung her awake. There were orange streaks of mildew running down the porcelain sink and the scent of too-used towels wafting with each pat and rub. There was the sound of her breathing, an inhuman new heat inside her, this sting that had come up her chest to torment her again. Eruption. She rubbed her eyes and blindly turned the water to cold; with rigid hands she cupped the water and opened them over her head. The cool water streamed down her forehead and nose, and some fell down the notch at the base of her neck and down her back. At the shock of it, she knew the breakthrough morphine had worn off. The warmth of the brandy chilled in her and she was again numb and empty, just a sick woman in a small bathroom.

Grace

GRACE WAS SHOWERING with the door open, the water running cold over her skin, the lye soap dragging across her coarse, wispy hair, scrubbing and scrubbing as she was to get the mess off her hands, off her skin, out of her nose. Then she heard a knock.

She wrapped herself in a towel and walked to the door, opened it, and turned back around without greeting. It was Clyde. She knew him from the smell of whiskey and the exasperated huffs that followed her as she withdrew into her home.

"Shepherd," he said, "I ain't sure if this is what you wanted or not. Well, we got a lot of angry people out there. It ain't like normal religion, I told you this before. We can't hinge on this, we can't—" He stopped.

The two were standing now in Grace's living room, Tyler's white body lying between them. Grace, her hair wet and dripping, unthoroughly rinsed, was staring coldly at him across the room. Clyde looked down at the young man, naked and turned upward, his arms crossed and his eyes open, gazing blankly at the ceiling. Grace began dressing in front of him.

"I called you this morning," she said.

"You didn't say it was Tyler."

"I said we lost a son today."

"He been here longer than just today, Grace," Clyde said, breaking the measured calmness he'd been attempting. "I thought it was just somebody. You didn't say—"

"Yes, that's right. Upon us a light has dawned. He died last night."

"Well, what did he die from?" Clyde was staring, still, at the body.

"I'd say it was from natural causes, given what came so naturally to him," Grace said. "In truth, Clyde, it was whatever that poison you two acquired. It was impure. I am beginning to think you mean to turn our little revival service into something like a Jonestown."

Clyde removed his hat and ran his fingers through his black hair. He wiped the corners of his mouth with his fingers, then covered it with his arm and looked away. "Jesus Christ," he said. "Jesus Christ, Grace."

"Clyde, you know that there's but one moment a day that Satan cannot find?"

"I think he done found us here. I don't want this. I don't want anything to do with this. And," he was becoming as serious as he could be, "it wasn't us *two*, it was just him. That's his job. I got other jobs I gotta do. You got a whole group of people down there wondering what happened. Some of 'em are already asking, well, they're acting like they know something's wrong."

"Many moments, Clyde. Many moments such as these. Satan finds all but one. I just about had a moment of peace, and you come knocking on my door, smelling like a whiskey still."

She watched him try to hyperventilate. He was trying to work himself up into fear or misunderstanding, but it was all too much of a performance. So much of what they did together was a performance. However, Grace thought, the question of for whom they were performing seemed never to cross their minds. She willed the heavy breathing to stop, willed Clyde to regain his composure, and he did.

"They're waitin' on you," he said.

Grace stepped around the body and tied her grey hair back. "Follow me, Clyde," she instructed, and walked out through the front of her house to meet all those people strewn across the orchard. The summer heat pulled up the morning dew from the ground, and the world smelled ripe.

Barefoot, her cotton-white dress wet and clinging to her body, Grace strode across her gravel drive toward the voices, hushed but collectively anxious in their hum. Grace let their nervousness draw her forward. The crowd grew silent.

One man, thin and gaunt-faced, removed his trucker ballcap. "Shepherd," he said. Grace floated toward them, coming to a stop a few feet from the man who stood at the front of an amalgam of chairs. The apples swung green from their branches as the wind ceased to blow.

Grace, hesitating only ever so slightly, lifted her arms and smiled.

"We are waiting," she said, and the anticipation on the faces of the crowd did not subside but seemed to work to remain attentive and not look away. "Today I have the great honour to ask for your help. I need a helping hand. Jesus preaches a sermon suggesting you can cut out an eye if it encourages you to sin. Would you not take out an eye but offer up a hand against sin? Is this so marvellous to ask? So fantastical?"

A great pause elongated itself across the crowd in the orchard. The people fidgeted in their seats. The ritual discipline of washing on Sunday and donning their best clothes had yet to leave most of them, though most other anchors of normalcy had long since evaporated among the group. They were waiting for something from Grace. As though a deal had been shaken on and the goods yet to be delivered. And now she was asking them for something new, something else. Red ears, rough-shaved jaws, pale and raw in contrast to the men's leathered upper cheeks, stood out and burned in the sunlight.

"I am asking your help in dispatching a soul to God, my friends, my lovers, and wanderers. We have lost a soul. We have lost a dear, dear soul," she said. "And he was such, the hand and the arm of the Lord," She held out her hand and examined it in the sunlight. "Mine hand has proven cripple now, and as such I have forgiven its mis-movements and offered it up to Yahweh himself. I have taken it off." She closed her hand into a fist.

No new emotion seemed to strike the faces before her. However, many of the congregation turned to look at Clyde. In their world loss was an unfortunate if commonplace occurrence, but they seemed to have trouble gathering who it was that Grace had banished if he had yielded temptation toward so much sin. They waited for something more. They waited for the implication.

"Failure is a sin. And my hand groped for failure. I need a stronger hand. We need help, as we are all one family. I do not think that our ministry, here, in these hills, can continue without a miracle. I need each of you to put away your Godly hesitations, your distractions and temptations. There are more eyes that need putting out, as there are many, many sins that weigh heavy on us today. And onc fewer hand to help carry the load. And it is sin that cost us the life of one of our own. I need each of you to open your eyes to the communion that moves around you now like the waters of Baptismal streams. Redouble your ministry and your outreach. I am praying now for the Lord to deliver us a new worker. Someone to be with me so that I may do unto the earth, unto and for my flesh, you, my family. I need done from his body what mine cannot do. I hope he will arrive in time. I know it moves fast. I know, as you know, that the world turns around us and daily condemns us to a harder and harder existence. What do you need to get through? What do *we* need to get through? Pick up the next drowning man, the next drowning woman so overwhelmed by such tumultuous waters and bring them up into the gasping lung of the real, bring them up to the advent, the now, with us."

Her voice demanded emotion, but she was still met with almost none. The crowd was silent, still waiting, glassy-eyed, for her pronouncement of the name. They waited for her to bring the tragedy down onto them.

"Who was it?" a wide-eared man asked from the back of the orchard.

"Your son," Grace said to gasps.

"My son is here, Pastor Grace?" the man said.

"Your son. My son. Jesus's son. You, there. Your brother. You, Miss Boles, your brother, your husband. You little James," Grace gestured with an open hand to a little boy whose hands were up his shirt, holding his belly. "Your brother."

"No ma'am, my brother's over there," the boy said, pointing to a slightly older boy across the scrum of bodies. That boy had straight bangs and thick, brown-framed glasses pulled tight to his face with an elastic ribbon. He stared at Grace, uninterested.

"Yes, your brother's right there. But is that your only brother, James? All of you," she said, pointing now and waving her arms, canopying the sleeves of her dress in the sun. "Is that your only husband you hold? Your only son? Your only brother? Have you learned nothing at all? Have you not learned about the menace of the world outside this mountain, this break in the mountains? Have I failed you so?"

She paced back and forth like a professor or jail guard. The crowd shifted now, readjusting itself in unison, open-mouthed and transfixed. She turned and slowed, then pounced into an outstretched pleading posture, bent at the waist.

"Look how precious," she said, forcing a break into her voice and collapsing her shoulders. "Look how full of potential. *This* is what I need. I need life to give salvation. A pure life," she added, gesturing at the children who'd risen from their seats and blankets to stand nearer their parents. "I need the new and unbroken. We need to save this, the covenant of our young and the Lord. We have so little time to lose."

She breathed, rested her arms, and looked around solemnly.

"Tyler has left us," Grace said. "And so, good people, my friends and neighbours, I worry there will not be the usual alms to share with you this morning."

At this there was a susurrus of irritation and shock, as though through gritted teeth. The parents held their children in a way that implied Grace was asking for a sacrifice of some kind to replace this familiar if quiet presence in their communion.

"I feel my power to teach, my power to lead us, is draining from me. I feel the dissipation of belief, I feel our understanding is breaking. I fear the enemies at the gates, and I spit and flail at the devil encroaching. And yet I feel nothing from you, my cared for, my died for, my calling, my cousins, my family. WHERE are we to go if not to one another?" she roared. "The coarse machine of the world is thrashing just outside this orchard. I can hear the chainsaws. I can hear the end. And, my brothers and sisters, I weep in my soul."

With that she reached her arms behind her, lifted up her dress, and from the waistband of her underwear pulled Tyler's sweat-stained military patrol cap. Grace laid the hat on the ground before her and bowed to it ceremoniously. "I will return to my weekly preaching just as soon as I am able," she said. "And we will have a Messiah on this here mountain. I know it to be so. The Alms of the Lord will continue when the weather cools. I believe it. Destruction cometh and those that seek peace will escape to the mountains. Stay with me here and wait for my heart to mend."

She turned away, and as she walked down the path through the trees and up the driveway toward her home she could hear the swell of voices shouting and arguing with one another. She could hear someone follow her just halfway down the path. She did not turn, and soon the footsteps retreated. She heard one man's voice rise above the others.

"Right here," he said. "Ain't it clear, brothers and sisters, ain't it clear? There ain't another way to fix it?"

"Well, Michaelson, find another ministry why don't you?"

"Just try me, goddammit. Put it right here."

"Put it right where? I ain't putting my money nowhere till we turn this around."

"Clyde, what happened?" They were shouting now.

"Please, God, we will turn this around," Clyde said. "Pray with me now, pray with me that to us a new hand will be delivered, one to hold the torch, one to light the way."

"Well, I ain't puttin' any more money into that basket until there's some more alms to go around," one man muttered. "I'm trying to get *mine*."

He was shushed. They bowed their heads as Grace disappeared up the gravel drive. Clyde looked over his shoulder at her retreat, a dozen hands on his back, his arms, waiting for him to begin.

Jane

SHE WOKE UP Sunday morning with a headache, the birds informing her that it was too early. *This is not your hour, Jane*. They sung out to her to go back to sleep. Her body ached in its stillness, in its presence. She reached for her bedside table and took some pills without checking which they were. Any would do. A whole night had gone by after the rush of Saturday afternoon, and she had no new revelations to show for how hard she must have thought, given her headache. She wondered when Dalton would get home. Certainly not in time for church.

Jane clenched her sheets, nails gripping one of the two foam toppers of her mattress like forks into tough meat. She sat up and swung her legs over the bed in one laboured motion, then rested. The walk downstairs to the shower was a chore, and she needed more rest but wouldn't allow herself. At the bottom of the stairs she listened to the interstitial breath of the house: the slow creaks of the beams expanding; the muffled birds; the ticking of old fuses checking themselves for their limit; a rattling windowpane, hand-blown and warped, still not set right in its frame after a hundred years; the off-time clicks of her antique clocks; and, of course, her own breathing. To distinguish herself from the rest she breathed fully, purposefully robust and with conviction, before moving again. To shout, to have the energy to just shout. But to whom?

Before reaching the bathroom she walked into her dressing room, stopping for a rest on the chaise lounge, reclining and massaging her temples, coaxing the blood back to her brain. More windows than usual banged slightly with the wind. In her mind it was as if Dalton were slamming pots and pans in the kitchen making Eggos and eggs like he used to when he was a little boy; as if two-year-old Messiah were crawling around the linoleum of their old apartments, dirty-kneed and laughing at his brother's labour. Those mornings—French Toast Mornings, she called them, when a big breakfast wasn't expedient, and when the boys longed for syrup and sugar to accompany their cartoons. The noise of it those mornings. The noise of the empty now.

It was early enough to go back to bed and still wake up in time for church, she figured, but then the doubt set in. What if she felt worse when she woke up? Jane had gone to church a few Sundays in a row now, which should have been enough to quiet anyone from thinking she was unappreciative of all they'd done for her. The donations, the team's name in the Relay for Life, *Jane's Angels*. She had received a great amount of attention, and both hated and loved the feeling. "She's so brave," the women of the church would say, at any event or into any microphone loud enough for her to hear it.

Jane scooted herself to stand, half-grunting out loud. She walked to the mirrored desk and rifled through the antique tackle box for her favourite earrings. What if she didn't go? She'd already told Pastor Hickok to expect her, but she'd also told him to expect her son. She couldn't imagine answering another question about Dalton.

Every Sunday she would field questions about him, feigning a knowing, martyred smile for the women who would inquire and a slight air of pride for the men who would intone "God bless him." But now she wasn't sure what to say. She wouldn't wait for him. Perhaps it was best to go, alone as usual, and tell Pastor Hickok that

Dalton had been held up by *orders*. She stopped short of exploring the possibility that no one would notice or care.

She went to her bathroom and, avoiding the mirror, used a stool to climb into the tub, knowing she'd have to pick it up and place it in the tub to use again to climb out. The ritual terrified her with its potential for broken bones, for being trapped in there with no one to find her. She was resigning herself to go to church and was working at her resignation as she rinsed but a dizziness hung over her. She felt a new ache as she ran her sudsy hands over her midriff. When she pushed down on the right side of her belly the cloud of pain that worked up with every ounce more of pressure made her feel nauseated. Every new pain like this had resulted in bedrest and bills and negotiations with Medicare and work and time, but here on her abdomen cratered a soft spot that screamed like a fevered baby.

She tried convincing herself that if she *did* go to church today it would be splendid. She would make it so. A return of sorts, where she'd remind the churchgoing ladies why they called her brave, and would revel in that for the next few weeks. She breathed through her mouth and salivated after pushing gently, but still too hard, on her stomach. Yes, she would go, and then Dalton would come home to tend to everything else. She allowed herself a surge of hope and smiled as she splashed water under her armpits, feeling the swelling lymph nodes, and let her fingers trace the scars across her chest. Her hand inched down again toward her side and she pushed in and squinted at the pain and felt her leg weaken, then pushed again, breathed, closed her eyes, and vomited.

She made it. God willing—and He must have been—Jane made it to church. After finicking with her dress, her fake breasts bulging insincerely out of her bra, she finished her makeup in the rearview mirror of her car in the parking lot of Sacred Hollow Baptist Church of God. The car turned hot on the blacktop, soaking up the sun and magnifying it through her, and her mascara refused to stick.

But she felt determined. She wanted to let them know she'd always heard the embedded disdain in their praise and that today she'd reply with pride. She would revel in their feigned prayers and well-wishes and accept them as deserved, and to punctuate, she'd eventually move off to the men and talk to them without shame, without care or airs—she'd soak it up and she'd put it on display. All cards on the table today.

She looked forward to watching the children, planning to stand by them, to enter their centre of attention—something like a maypole with all the mothers' eyes on her, living and being. Not like a ghost. She would not be a ghost.

These were her preoccupations, in the parking lot, hesitating to key off the ignition, sweating in her car. Perhaps she'd drive home instead. Perhaps she'd go to a bar somewhere off the Blue Ridge Parkway and watch a football game and have a beer. Maybe there wasn't anything to show anyone, maybe she'd just wait at home for Dalton. *Enough*.

After the familiar acrobatics with the car seat and door handle, she lunged into the sun. With imperfect makeup and an eyeful of smudges, still determined to convey a holy, proud indifference to the praise or the hatred she'd encounter, Jane slammed her car door and walked across the oak-shaded blacktop. She slowly climbed the stairs, not supporting but pulling herself up by the handrail with each step, and headed into the church.

Jane stopped in the narthex. The greeter had already taken his seat, so she listened to the muffled beginning of the service from behind the tall closed doors, alone. They were singing a familiar hymn but the words didn't quite register for her, their meanings evaporating as the quotidian, dispassionate voices droned on.

After a brief quiet, with the organ player still pressing on her damper pedal, Jane opened the doors and walked in.

In the resonant pause that follows any kind of break in the service, Pastor Hickok looked up and smiled. "Why Jane!" he announced into his microphone, and everyone in the church twisted in their suits and dresses, khakis and polo shirts, to face her. The air conditioning whirred louder; a baby made a warning cry. Jane waved and went to take the closest seat, a row of people shifting down the pew to accommodate her. The pastor's smile followed her in what felt like a slow-motion spanking. She briefly curled her lips upward with a tilt of her head back to acknowledge the congregation, and sat, finally, adjusting herself snugly in the pew.

"Good morning," the pastor began, "and a beautiful Sunday morning to you, Ms. Fuquay; and to all who come into this, our house of God, and who care to share their time with us; and to God, who knows us all to be ready to love and ready to welcome each soul into this church. I will open with this: 'Rejoice and be exceeding glad, because great is your reward in heaven, for it was in the same way they persecuted the prophets who were before you.' Bear that in mind today, my friends. Bear that in mind.

"I've got a story for you. There was a woman I know, and you may know her, too. She's had her hiccups. Sometimes public ones. A lot of people think she's crazy. She's got some demons. She's got some issues that need to be taken care of, sure. And, important for us to remember, there's something she carries with her through history, and that's doubt. Hers? I don't know, but ours?

"My friends, her name is Mary Magdalene. She was a sinner like you, and you and you and you. She was someone who gave herself up for Christ and wiped away what once was for the terrible promise of what will be. Are you all prepared for what *will be*? Are you still hung up on what was?

"We've got a lot of *what was* in here, don't we? Don't we? We've got a lot of *what wases* walking through here, walking through your mind now! Walking through the door and sitting down in a pew. What *will be* today? I ask you, what *will be* today? Will today be redemption? Will today be the day you take Christ's hand in yours and walk down that Jericho Road? What does it look like? Iraq?

Mesopotamia? Jerusalem? No! Is it Old 52? Is it I-81? Is it here, the road here, right outside this church? The road of your life? Your Jericho Road is the bedroom floor where your feet touch each morning and the road of your dreams at night and everything in between. And we walk down it either alone or with Christ. Amen! Look here. Look here at our own Mary—look here in yourself, a knowing penitent. Look down into the souls of everyone you love and know that there are miles and miles ahead of you on your way to heaven. These stairs getting up to this here church, these stairs are our Jericho, these pews!

"Now, I don't want to embarrass her, but I had a feeling last night, as I was preparing this sermon, that I might not see Ms. Fuquay today. No, it is not because I think she or any other member of this congregation might not want to come, no, I know that y'all are just itching for our Sundays together. I worried that—well, after my conversation with Jane, I worried that we'd miss her this morning."

The church was quiet, and still, and the baby had begun crying a low, muffled moan. Jane looked down at her shoes and began to pull at a chunky hymn book that was snugged too tight into its wooden holster. Realizing it wouldn't be set free, she handkerchiefed the sweat from her brow and looked around at the congregation, but looking through them as one looks through an aquarium window. She put on an expression of joy and curiosity as though each pair of eyes directed at her were part of a whole, conglomerated subject that fascinated *her* rather than the other way around.

"Not because of any reason other than she might be at the airport this morning," he said. He had teased out the desire to judge from each person in the room and knew it.

After what seemed to Jane a spiteful, nasty pause, Pastor Hickok continued. "Her son Dalton is coming home to us. Not just home from the Army, but home to us in spirit. Home to Jesus, home to

God. In due time, I'm sure. We thought it might have been this morning. I'm sure he's on his way. It has been a long journey. But it's wonderful to see you, Jane."

She wished it would stop, this benediction serving only to reprimand her for her trip to the liquor store.

"In Second Corinthians, we hear that God, who comforts us in all our tribulations, asks that we may be able to comfort them who are in any trouble, by the comfort wherewith we ourselves are comforted by God!

"Yes, for as the sufferings of Christ abound in us, so, by God, our consolation also abounds.

"I asked Ms. Fuquay last we spoke about what she would like to hear about in our sermon today. I asked how I could bring the word of God closer to home for her. How could I put God in her heart? In all our hearts— And that was selfish of me, Lord, forgive me. I asked her what she wanted to hear, and she said strength! Strength, dear God! And here she is today. God bless you, Ms. Fuquay!"

"Amen," said some in the congregation, hesitantly and without the usual fervour. Others muttered; several stifled knowing laughter. Jane sensed that some of the women were working hard not to turn and look at her.

"Ladies and gentlemen! Look now at Ms. Fuquay, who despite an ongoing fight with illness has joined us here today! Look now to Ms. Fuquay, and know as well as you can know that she herself is suffering for God while we are comfortable. She herself is here as the piercing blaze we need to see our Lord, the strength, Dear God, we need to carry us home to heaven. Praise Jesus!"

Jane held back tears, staying still and without visible breath. And the people in the pews praised Jesus, uniformly and unenthusiastically, only a few now looking at Jane. Her body itched to get up and walk out but she remained stoic and smiling, scanning the room to see who was looking. The rest of the sermon proceeded, she thought, as he might have planned it before their meeting at the liquor store yesterday. His arms opened wide to the congregation and he smiled so broadly that his body seemed to swell before them. She opened her mind to thoughts of Jim beyond a deliverer of personal sermons. She remembered his breath, the gentleness of his hands.

He talked on. When the sun outside broke through the stained glass of the church a triangle beamed violet and green on her arms and warmed them. She thought of the pastor holding her wrists above her head, years ago, against the church wall in the same coloured light and she thought of the ensuing nights in his office after the stale meetings in the very basement of this church. Her coming upstairs for air when the conversations grew too dramatic or too sour or pathetic and slipping into his office for her own communion.

She thought of Jim Hickok as she'd first met him, in his office with the green desk lamp glowing on his papers, his shoulders hunched over, his shirt slightly untucked at the back, his broad collar undone and his sleeves rolled up, smelling like bourbon and toothpaste. That was how she'd come to know him. Even years later she'd yearn for him when Clyde was away in Kuwait, away on a drunk somewhere up in the mountains. And Jane would find him. Jim, there, writing in his office, just waiting for her to slip out while her mother was at home with the boys. Their secret always precarious but intact.

But after her mother disappeared and Clyde left she would circle the drain, as she thought of it. Swirling around in herself, tumbling about like the swishing wine in her mouth. And in their Wednesday night intra-AA meeting forays and afterward that was how she'd always see him, how she'd leave feeling drained from the spectacle, from the electric heat and used air, from the performance.

Here, now, on the pulpit, after turning his sermon to unity and community, his was like a voice from another room. Jane drifted downstream, away from it and from the congregation entirely, returning only when the bodies around her began standing and voices came to wake her from her quiet cell of nausea. Alone in the pews holding her stomach. Thinking of her son. Thinking of all that ought to have been but would never be.

Dalton

DALTON COULD SEE the whole front of the house. It was a looming relic of Southern heritage. The rusted tin roof had been painted black again, as it was when his Nana had inherited it, when Dalton was just little. It was spread much wider than it was deep, three windows wide on the top floor, and was painted bright white then. The house now was yellow, tea-stained by pollen and time. The shutters were flung open permanently, bolted to the summer-soft wood that overlapped itself, paint like frozen waves, shrinking up in the heat and made brittle by time. A swing—a wide, circular cut of wood that hung suspended from a tow rope taken from an industrial air field—creaked off to the right of the house, hanging from a monstrous, knotty oak tree. Further off to the right was the old tobacco packhouse, more slanted now than it had ever been, and with fewer rotting boards than he remembered protecting the piled up unsalvageables that his mother liked to collect and store there in her mausoleum for furniture and beat-up homewares. He paused on the gravel driveway and searched for a nostalgia that wouldn't come.

He looked at the cracked paint and the warbly windowpanes of the house. He remembered watching the rain fall from the inside.

He shook his head in disappointment, though at what, exactly, he didn't know. Looking out; looking in.

The door was locked, which was unusual. No car in the driveway. *I told her I was gonna come home,* he thought. *Church must be over by now*. He dropped his bag on the porch and went around to the side of the house. It was surprisingly empty of noise. There were no cicadas ringing, and Sumo wasn't patrolling; the day was getting on, and the smell of curing tobacco from one of the little farms a way off was the only thing that felt in place. He sat on an upturned wheelbarrow next to the chicken coop and waited.

Dalton started thinking about ways to break in. This scheming drifted into an intense noticing of each detail—the ramshackle bricks, stacked up and never righted, that marked the entrance to the crawlspace under the house. There was a trap door there that opened from the crawl space into what they called the mud room. He could go in that way, he figured, then saw himself covered in dirt and thought about how he'd like to look when his mother returned.

He rose and walked around, always keeping an eye on the driveway. He had a feeling that every detail of this place would become so important to him that they should already be so. He wanted to be comforted by all it encompassed, and was looking and remembering, trying to will these scenes to matter: the vegetable garden, bare now but still full of dirt, built with old railroad sleepers stacked two high so the soil was nice and deep; the magnolia tree's dinosaur leaves and strange brown pods with their bright-red seeds; the sound and variety of his mother's wind chimes, some glass, some copper; the split wicker porch chairs, upholstered with reproduction Chinese pagoda scenes on faded toile and stained with coffee, wine, and juice; and the stains themselves, faded too—all these little bits of the past kept stabbing at Dalton as he circled the house.

He focused on the mound of dried mulch on the bank in front. On that bank, and in the front yard, there used to be a flower garden, set there like a little stage of nature, like a roadside stand selling children's performances. He remembered Messiah eating plants from the garden and watching him as he chewed. They had fought; Messiah must have been only four or five, and Dalton got blamed and switched for letting Messy eat the plants, which had made him very sick. Dalton figured it was around then when things changed with his mother, who distrusted him after that.

"A place of my own," his Nana had repeatedly said. "A place for God." His mother had never wanted their house to be such a place, especially as it became less and less a place of God or for God and more a place to house antiques and junk. His mother loved these things. And she fought always to keep them, even when they had little money. His Nana was always trying to sell something out from under his mother's nose. To pay for what, he didn't know. That was before she seemed to have all the money in the world.

In the snarling, tongue-twisting, scattered arguments that Grace had with her daughter, and the insatiable lashings of switches that she doled out to her grandsons, she'd become alien to them, had worn out her welcome in her own house.

Then, in the unsettling way that miracles bequeath themselves to the unsuspecting, Grace had won the state lottery. That's what Dalton's mama had told him, anyway. This made her grow only bolder in her belief that she was the chosen one of the Appalachian piedmonts, some kind of saviour. Jane had wondered aloud more than once if perhaps one of the "friends" Grace had made at some revival or another had given her the winning ticket, but no evidence of that ever materialized. Either way, Grace took her winnings with no photo or fanfare, moved out and on, further and further northwestward over the next few years, appearing once or twice in a regional religious newspaper or revival flyer. But there were no specifics of her whereabouts or goings-on. It was as though she had finally been called to heaven where she thought she belonged. Dalton hadn't seen her since.

During this reverie, Dalton had wandered all the way around to the backyard. He headed through the trees toward the train tracks that ran behind the house, leaving his shoes on the small back porch. He thought about whether it was still his house. He had left.

Maybe it wasn't "his" anymore. Perhaps it was his mother's and only hers now. He wanted to take off his uniform and did so. In his underwear he made his way beneath the thinning canopy to where he used to have campfires, further south into the woods. The air in the shade of the trees blew cool. The moisture from the upturned dead foliage dampened his ankles as he walked. This cooled him. Everything had grown over.

Beyond the woodline lay the triangle of rotting logs where he and Messiah used to sit, cooking frogs from the creek or telling each other stories until it got dark. Dalton began to feel good, sitting shirtless in his old haunt, and he began to think about his brother, away at camp.

In North Carolina you were either gifted, regular, or you rode the short bus with children of all different ages and issues. Bad kids, slow kids, kids with bum legs, they'd all be in the same remedial class. That made Dalton angry, then, sitting down and thinking it over, and it made him hurt for his little brother. Messiah wasn't slow, just spacey. He didn't need to be in those classes. But Dalton well knew that the fire his mother had once possessed—scourge of the PTA, shouting and fighting with the more well-to-do mothers in the area; impassioned defender of her own mother at their church—all that was over, swallowed up by illness.

Dalton followed the train tracks for a while, looking for old flattened pennies or loose railway spikes, coming up out of the ground as tombstones sometimes do when it floods. He found one, kicked up the tie and held it in his hand, six inches long and heavy and rusted.

He remembered one time when he and Messiah played chicken. They hid in the brush in the ditch of the track just to rush out onto its ties as the train came around a bend, knowing it hadn't enough time to stop.

Messiah would want the train to come so badly. Even when there was no sound of its approach Dalton would catch him kneed down to the ground, feeling the rail for vibrations. Messy almost wanted to believe he could will the train to come by, touching the track as in a prayer. He'd be fifty paces behind Dalton as they walked, stopping once in a while to lay both hands on the ties. But sometimes he was right. It was coming. The excited look in Messiah's eyes. They'd stand there on opposite sides, each touching a foot to their respective rail, eyes flicking back and forth between the train and each other. The temptation of tempting fate.

That one time playing chicken they'd waited until the train was just a little less than a hundred yards away. It came faster than he ever thought it might—and anything less than that distance wasn't a game of chance but an invitation to misstep and disaster. Dalton had rolled away to the ditch and looked up, expecting his brother to have done the same. But Messiah was still there, staring down the train. Dalton had called out "Messiah! Move! You win! Go on!" but the train was so close that Messiah couldn't hear. He didn't look toward Dalton in any case.

Dalton scrambled up the bramble-lined edge of the ditch, leapt across the track and pushed his brother out of the way, knocking him down and tumbling with him down the other side. They'd fought there for a second, Dalton terrified by the realization that his brother would do that to him, would be so stupid—for what?

The train had passed them slowly, slow enough for the conductor to shout curses at them. They watched the engine go by, then car after car towing coal, nice and easy, heading north and east.

Now he thought that perhaps Messiah had been trying to eke something out of him, risking himself to pull Dalton toward him, to make Dalton save him, just to see if he would. Dalton's ears filled with the buzzing of the shallow forest, his brother everywhere except with him.

Jane

"YOU'LL BE DAMNED TO HELL!"

Jane found herself outside, alone, the tails of her head scarf swaying along with the tablecloths in the slight wind. She was turning the corner toward the entrance of the church basement when a little boy with blond hair—like Messiah's when he was young, almost white—poked his head out from the back door of the church and caught a glimpse of her before poking it right back inside.

Bathing, now, in the orange-toned, new-afternoon rays of sunlight. The alien yells of children playing—a sound so nostalgic and so abrupt that it panged her, pulling her straight out of the meditative feeling of peace she'd found in the morphine-blanketed comfort of her memory. She felt she was sweating out the medicine.

The kids were fighting as they broke through the rear door into the makeshift picnic area adjacent to the graveyard, flooding out into the daylight, some toward Jane and others toward the basement where lunch was being prepared, flowing up against the choir who pushed past the crowd on their way to change out of their gowns.

Directly after the service Jane had tried to pray or to manifest some young man to hold out a hand and help her down the front steps as she descended, feeling vulnerable as she went, leading slowly with the same strong leg each time. No such saviour availed himself and she reached the bottom alone, tired and disappointed.

Jane rarely stayed for these post-service potlucks, but after Pastor Hickok had targeted her so, she felt the congregants would want to continue his encouragement. She had a chance to extend the limelight this once, for good. She imagined people sidling up one by one and speaking to her as a woman rather than the topic of prayer. She didn't want to be alone in conversation with herself.

She entered the church's basement and found herself among people sloshing about as though they'd just crashed into a cove. It was raucous in the big beige room, but she could still hear her own breathing. The children who'd made it outside, briefly, were already behind her trying to get back in. Not wanting to pass her, they slowed their runs and patiently matched her step for step, a show of manners she both appreciated and resented.

The basement was not at all arranged in the way she'd known it. No circle of folding chairs, no lone table of addiction pamphlets, no smoked-out beer-gutted men and skinny women with tobacco-stained smiles to welcome her and insist she share her name. The people here knew her name in a different way and for a different reason. She was the unfortunate woman with the troublesome son and an illness who needed help. But here she was, alone.

She watched as the church ladies set to work. Some were still fully adorned in their church clothes, others had changed into jeans and cap-sleeve T-shirts, all of them hovering around and moving out of the way of one another as tables were dragged from back rooms and closets, polyurethane tablecloths laid and set with plates and plastic utensils, bowls and trays of food carried in by the men from their cars.

She shifted between the potluck plates and the Tupperware laid out clean and picturesque. *Gauche*, she thought, and then thought badly of herself as she hated the word and hated to have thought it.

Feeling eyes on her, she patted her finger to her lips in a cartoonish gesture to feign indecision. She didn't want to eat anything, really, but also didn't want to appear rude or hesitant to participate lest someone comment on her choice or recommend something, obliging her to "simply must try" something she couldn't stomach. She walked the length of the tables as though in a cafeteria line, loading her plate with simple things one could eat in small bites, anticipating the moment when people would approach her. Then she stepped away from the tables, waiting for them to congratulate her on the news of her son's return, to ask her about how her treatment was going, to inquire about her studies, anything—but none did.

With plate full she looked around, picked out a spot to eat.

The children, having been accounted for by their parents, had separated from them again and were chasing each other in circles, playing a loosely ruled game of tag but mostly just cussing at each other from behind dresses and khaki-panted legs. "You'll be damned to hell! You'll be damned to hell!"

She watched as the newly-frocked, now-official youth minister, a spindly, small-hipped child of God with shoulder-length hair, corralled them in his arms and shushed them until a quick quiet came. Jane sat down near the end of a line of brown metal fold-out chairs and dipped into her potato salad, trying not to smell it. The wall behind her was brick, painted white and adorned with the Sunday school children's stencilled hands in Easter colours, baby blues and light greens and pinks, each with a prayer scrawled on its palm. The hands surrounded a large, amateurish portrait of Pastor Hickok hanging directly above her. She could feel the huge montage pressing down on her shoulders, framed by it as she was.

The youth minister looked at Jane and then just above her head, giving her a stern nod. A woman Jane had never seen before came near, bent over a little and said quietly in her ear, "He's just come from preaching his own sermon at a Baptist church in Winston.

Ain't he something to admire?" and more loudly, straightening and gesturing toward the children, "Which is your little one?"

Well, how polite. She wants to make friends, Jane thought.

Smiling through a mouthful of half-chewed food, Jane said "Oh, mine are grown" and sighed, her eyes following the group of children roving around the nucleus of the young minister. He lunged on long, strong legs around the room in free association with every person and thing.

"But yes, he sure is handsome," Jane said. "His name is Graham, I think. Should I introduce you?"

The woman blushed, and shaking her head, put a large bite of food into her mouth. A moment later she stood and shuffled off.

Jane missed her boys then. Dalton would have made a good youth minister, she thought, and started to plan a conversation with Graham about the possibility. She noticed, now, the women of the church looking up from their plates and blinking their mascaraed lashes in her direction, but none made a move toward her. Feeling the heaviness in her legs and knowing she couldn't stand without the freedom of both of her arms, she let the subtle invitation pass. They soon circled around one another, talking about what, Jane couldn't say. But their backs were toward her, mostly.

Jane settled on watching the children playing and the youth minister's short-sleeved biceps herding them. To these children, to these young and unquestioning spirits, every detail of the room, every interaction, might hold Jesus or the devil, she supposed, a gruesome dichotomy that turned to punching and more shushing. As if he knew Jane was studying their rowdy idleness, the little boy with Messiah's hair looked up at her and said, "Bald lady! You're the devil!"

She dropped the last remnants of her plate on her lap. She closed her eyes and, with food still in her mouth, began breathing deep choking breaths in through her nose and coughed on her food.

She let her head sink and held her abdomen, pushing on it while trying to catch her breath. The pain radiated through her. She looked back up at the boy who still stood before her, smiling. "You! Now *you're* the devil!" he said happily, waiting for a response. She spilled her plate on herself.

"Oh honey," she coughed. "No, I'm not playing devil with you!"

The boy tagged her, pushing his little palm against her knee. At this Jane smiled, and, still coughing, motioned wildly in embarrassment for help with the spill, trying to keep smiling at the boy.

A woman nearby stepped over quickly and reached out a hand to Jane's back while she finished chewing and coughing. She steadied herself enough to smile. Without a word the woman gently shooed the boy away. Jane let his accusation lie. "I'm fine," she said, but the woman's hand circled on her back a few more times before locking eyes with her. Then she smiled at Jane, seeming satisfied to have done something, however minimal. She told the boy to run along then bent over, scooped up the clumps of potato salad from Jane's lap onto the Styrofoam plate, and walked away.

Jane got up, picked the little bit of potato salad off her blouse, and began moving around the room. She didn't want to stay if she wasn't going to receive any kind of praise for being there. She felt like a ghost as she walked, orbiting some of the tight circles of women conversing. Many of the congregation's men were outside smoking or chewing, she knew, or else puttering about the smoke and the spit, participating in that solemn masculine pastime secondhand. She had one eye on the door now, but felt sick just at the thought of the smoke smell. She decided to be patient: someone must be curious about her condition; someone must want to follow Pastor Hickok's lead. She'd ride it out and wait.

You just can't look forward and back at the same time, Jane thought. She refused to consider what her past might mean for her prognosis. She thought of power lines, canned food, roll-on deodorant, X-rays, and MRIs. Maybe this maternal yearning she was feeling wasn't going to be quenched by anyone in this church today. *When Dalton comes home,* she thought, she'd feel safer, steadier, more complete. She hoped so but couldn't count on it, and was willing herself away from counting on it. Jane watched as the women started cleaning up. The window of opportunity to feel like part of something bigger than herself was closing.

The teardown of the chairs reminded her of the AA meetings in this same basement. The same process, although not one of those here had been to any of those gatherings. It was as if they prayed to two different gods. This was a different kind of worship, she thought. She looked around at the pastel colours, the airy, embroidered dresses of the girls and women, the uniform side-parted haircuts of the boys, the blond cowlicks, the newness of their skin and faces—it's about money today, she thought, and surprised herself by feeling so political. Was she the only one so moved by the Lord to pack her sin in her purse and carry it right back to the place where she was expected to have effectively vanquished it?

But she had to come to Sunday service. She was their beneficiary. Pastor Hickok had arranged it so, had obliged her to come to these Sundays *and* to the basement meetings, even when she thought she had it under control. Perhaps when Dalton returned—perhaps he would come with her here. Perhaps he, as a hero of sorts, could help Jane get to the bottom of what these people wanted from her in return for what they'd given. Maybe his uniform would convince them. Of what, she didn't know. If he could still wear it. She didn't know if he could. Nausea rose and made her feel faint; the walls became wavy. She sat down again on a lone chair set near the exit.

Jane wanted an acknowledgment of her attendance, of her attention to the sermons, of her presence at all the useless meetings. She wanted the salvation so often talked about. Here she was, hoping for it, but she didn't want any answer that came out of

Pastor Jim Hickok's mouth. Did not want the damning done unto her by these nasty children, the rude offspring of their insincere parents. Wanted still less the spiritual debasement of the church ladies' unceasing looks and hesitancy to know her. Perhaps what she sought was simply in the church itself.

The building was nothing more than an unexceptional concrete stack, a suburban monument to order, the site of a weekly pilgrimage of privilege. *Our community*. She thought of old churches her mother would drag her to, growing up. Churches situated on plain roads, generally at a turn, with tiny parking lots and narrow driveways to really send home how narrow is the path to salvation. Those churches worked like meccas of the mountains, where all the hillbillies with any sort of property or time slid down and gathered round to talk about their woes and misfortunes with a tinge of hope, their vision of heaven guided and provided by a local loudmouth, given for free, outside of hat-passing of course, and without too much judgment coming along with it, just as long as one was *there*. But of course there was judgment. Communities have to push people out. What was the purpose of a community so insular without those outside of it?

Having sat alone for a conspicuous amount of time, she held her stomach and felt the pain radiate from her abdomen up to her armpits and out to her fingers. Jane caught herself before she gagged, rested her hand on the corner of a table. She looked about for the woman who'd rubbed her back but couldn't see her. She stood and walked, stiff legged, into the family restroom where she could sit herself down on the toilet with the help of a metal bar that ran alongside it. In the bathroom she cried dry tears that she tried to work up, just to get them out. She smelled herself to make sure she wasn't stinking people away from her.

When she emerged the pitchers of tea were empty, the cookies gone, the doors open. The cut-grass air blew in, warm and thick.

Outside, girls, members of the youth choir, stood in a circle facing one another, sang, and laughed in the sun.

Jane followed the song outside, working hard to avoid the attention of the youth minister who was directing the impromptu choir, speeding up their delivery. Satisfied by their tempo and synchronicity, he began miming the act of passing out money to all the children. Jane, the recipient of so much of the church's real money, had had enough.

She waved curt goodbyes, avoiding making eye contact with Pastor Hickok as he stood watching the children sing. She didn't want to congratulate him on being the only person to notice her nor condemn him for being the reason no one else would. She walked off slowly, her clutch under one arm, the other swinging, giving her the momentum to climb the slight hill toward the parking lot. Folks walking by made a point of waving, but none said "God bless you, Jane."

Finally she reached her car, which out of pride she'd parked far off from the handicapped spots. Now she stood beside it, waiting for the families around her to load up their vehicles and drive off before going through the ritual of getting in her own. This was a last-ditch effort to make some meaning out of the day. And as they finally did look her square in the eye,

"Well, I'm sure things will turn out just fine, Jane!"

"Okay now, Jane, you take care of yourself, and you just call if you ever need anything."

"Jane, so good to see you, must have missed you in there."

"Are you bringing anything to the potluck next week? Well, if you change your mind, you know just to call me, so we don't have doubles of anything. Rest up, now."

"All right then, Jane, well, it is good to see you. I love your scarf. Tell your son we're proud of him when you *do* see him. Okay now, yes, goodbye. God bless you."

And then she was alone in her far corner of the parking lot, the car door swung wide open.

Jane struggled with the starter, easing the gas and then cranking it, the whole time hearing "You're the devil!" and with each blink of her eyes seeing the little face of the child like the ghost that appears after staring at a light bulb. The boy's voice had been low and snide. In it she'd heard Dalton's own quiet tones.

Jane gave up on the car and rested with the door open and the sun beating down. Behind her closed eyes Dalton's face appeared. As he aged he'd grown darker and oilier in both his complexion and in his attitude toward her; now, as a man, he wouldn't in any way resemble the boy from the church's basement.

They had grown distant. At first she'd felt it was herself and her work to blame. He was just a boy, angry and petulant, and along with her illness he'd grown into something painful. She'd gotten sick in secret and had later often wondered, if Dalton had known, had properly known, if she'd told him how dire it might become, how sick she really was, if he might've warmed to her, might have stayed. To hell with the church, the school, the news, to hell with the men and with Grace, it could have been the three of them—

"Hello, Jane."

Pastor Hickok stood in the sun next to her car. He had his sleeves up and his shirt pulled out somewhat from his pants, his collar undone and his glasses low. His watch caught the sun and reflected in Jane's eyes.

"So, what did you think? I didn't get a chance to talk to you at all during the potluck."

"Well, I wanted to get a chance to talk to everybody," she said. "That youth minister. He's very good with the children."

"Oh, that young man must have done or said something strange today. I don't think I've ever heard that amount of vile language from the children before."

"I hadn't noticed."

"Well Peggy told me that she was talking to you, and one of the children said something awful mean to you, Jane, and I'm sorry about that. There isn't anything to it you know, they're just children."

"I know about children, Jim." Jane realized she'd used his name. She wanted to lecture him further but left it there, his name hanging in the air.

"This head scarf is pretty," he said, and smiled. He raised his arm up to touch it but stopped. "I am so glad you were able to make it today."

She winced. "Well, yes, thank you. I did want to be early. I just can't seem to get anywhere on schedule. I think I've got to set my clocks an hour fast at this point, but I always feel like I'm running out of time."

"Where's your *son*, Jane?" Pastor Hickok said, declaring an end to the niceties. His eyes darkened with a touch of serious concern.

"I was expecting him last night, really. But I think he might have gotten bogged down by orders, you know. It's hard to know these kinds of things, you know, what they do in the military."

"Well, how was the wine?"

"Jim. I don't care about how the wine *is*. I know you know that."

"Okay, okay! Off-limits question. It all tastes the same, I know, I know. I don't want it to be too difficult to be alone up there in that house of yours, Jane. So, really, now, how are you holding up?"

"I don't need any more money, thank you, Pastor Hickok." She tried the ignition, praying it would start, but it choked itself out. She tried again and gave it some gas, and it almost clicked but failed. "My starter's not quite right," she said and sighed out in exasperation. "Maybe I'll just move into this goddamn church."

Hickok's face brightened with purpose. "You want me to have a look?"

"No, I think I'll be quite all right, thank you."

"I can call a truck, or a mechanic, Jane. You don't need to be so hard. I can give you a lift home if you'd like. I think I would want to see Dalton."

"Oh Jim, I wouldn't like. I do not like. I don't like for you to sermonize about me, for you to ask about Dalton, and I don't like for you to come and talk to me out here and look at me. I'm— I'm melting. Will you please just let me be?"

"All right, then." He bowed his head. "I'm sorry. As you know. If that means anything. And if you ever find yourself needing some help, you know where to call me. I haven't heard from you. It doesn't have to always be money."

"No. Well, yes, I know. Thank you," she said, and closed her door.

▪

Jane drove down winding Old 52 as fast as she could. Driving as usual by memory. As the day and the years caught up swiftly behind the struggle to start her hot black car on the hot black parking lot in the hot black tobacco basin of North Carolina, she took some medicine from the trail mix of pills in her car's ashtray and knew she had failed. She held her breath for what felt like miles.

Jim had looked at her with pity—a practised look, as though he'd done it a hundred times before. It pasted over every other look he'd ever given her like a fresh coat of paint. She took more medicine, washing it down with a hot, flat can of Diet Dr Pepper from her cup holder, the lipstick stain on the rim almost gluing her lips to the tin. She hadn't liked the way he'd looked at her before but resented the way he looked at her now. Strength? What in the hell in that ad-libbed sermon had been about *her* strength? She wished Dalton had been there with her, wished she had the money and the family that would give her the key to get what all the other women were getting from the church. Whatever the fuck it was.

Turning into her drive, Jane resolved to never go back. Before keying off the ignition she was stung between the eyes with a reminder that she'd drunk both bottles of wine the night before. She breathed and waited and sweated.

Feeling her morphine break through, she put the car in reverse and headed back in the direction she'd just come from, to Winston-Salem where the wine shops would still be open on a Sunday afternoon, bars too. And along Old 52 she buzzed the yellow line, then the white. She stared past the incoming cars, past the guardrails and treelines of the turns, her eyes wide and unblinking.

She hated to think of that child seeing her for what she worried she was. She hated what the child might become and she hated those women, hated the people of the church now, hated how she wished so for them to circle around her, covering her with their bodies and hands and dirtying their nice clean clothes, and as they did they would crawl around, lifting her now, holding her with their hands, arms tangling with one another—and shout, "How brave!"

Clyde

CLYDE RETURNED TO THE HOUSE after seeing that Grace's congregants were at work reassembling the orchard as she liked it, back to its Edenic state, as though they'd never been there. The chairs were put away and the tent pulled down, wrapped up, and carried to the barn. It had been four years now he'd been working for her, and he knew that any variation from her desires turned quickly to suffering, like a wrong turn into oncoming traffic. He took a deep breath before kicking off his roper boots one at a time, balancing a dollar store Easter basket in one hand and his hat in the other, careful not to spill any money out of either. A pitiful job it was, asking these poor people for money. Tyler's job, before. But more pitiful in his absence, especially today, with nothing to exchange but blessings and prayer. And of course that's all that was ever guaranteed, but not all that was expected.

When he came into the house Grace was clean and changed. She'd sprayed herself with lilac, too much, he thought, until he got to the living room and saw Tyler's body, still arranged in its peaceful pose, but now with a clean sheet over his nakedness, damp splashes darkening the white of it. Some kind of spray or disinfectant. Lilac and bleach.

He could see Grace's shadow emanating from the kitchen. Her hands shook softly but quietly, betraying themselves only by the irregular clanking of the spoon against the glass as she stirred sugar into her sun tea. He thought how lucky he was to get to see her like this, her grey-white hair pinned up behind her head, her long neck shooting from the back of the laced collar of her nightgown. She wasn't a leader now, not the dealer or zealot, the roles she played in her performances. She wasn't the Shepherd of Buffalo Mountain, but Grace. His Grace.

"Get my cane, Clyde. I do think I'll be needing it today. I feel quite unsteady after the sermon. The sun is too hot. So hot, Clyde. It is exhausting. The whole world is burning up. Hell ascending, it is." She drank from her tea.

Clyde arranged the change in loose piles and laid the bills on the kitchen table face up and stacked in kind. None over twenty. Only one twenty, in fact, and that one was his.

"Well, what do you want to do with . . . this, this boy, Grace?" He tucked his hands in his pockets. "With Tyler?"

Grace set down her crystal glass of tea sternly and turned to face him. "Do you know who this boy is?"

"I know who he was."

"I said, do you know who he *is*, Clyde. Do you know who he is to me now?"

"No. No, I do not." He fought the urge to sigh. He'd played this game before.

"This boy lying in there, Clyde, he's got more stake in this ministry than just about anyone but God. Do you know how I come to be here, all alone?"

"Yes ma'am. But Grace, you ain't alone. I'm here. I been here. And, furthermore, I don't believe he's got any stake in anything at the moment. I want to know what you want done with him."

"I come up here to the side of this mountain because this boy here made it so I didn't have nowhere else to go. I was tossed out of every godforsaken church and prayer group this side of the Cumberland Gap on account of this here boy. Do you want to hear the story, Clyde?"

She breathed heavily but steadily. Clyde hiked up his pants and tucked in his shirt. He wiggled his toes against the hardwood. He felt as though he might have to run. "I know the story, Grace," he said sternly. "And I don't want to change it."

"I said I'm gonna need my cane."

Clyde went into the bedroom where the bed was made and grey light poured in through the drawn, sheer linen curtains. On the floor before him was the dress she'd worn to her sermon, her underwear on top. A towel beside them. Everything else about the room looked like a museum, still and regal. Preserved through time. Clyde stepped over the pile to where Grace's ornate cane—cypress, from somewhere far from here, with a woman's face carved into the handle like a pirate ship bow—leaned in the corner, facing him.

Grace was standing beside Tyler when he returned.

"Yes, this boy," she said, accepting the cane as Clyde passed it over the sheet that covered him. "Yes, he took me for quite a ride. Sit down, Clyde."

He sat, waiting to hear her new sequence of events. Every turn in the road of her life required justification anew. Clyde was well aware of this habit of hers, his own entanglement in her life having been justified and re-justified until the revisionist order of how things had happened to her and to him and why became more hassle than it was worth to argue against. He waited to hear how the body came to lie before them, priming himself to subscribe to that history no matter how far beyond his own reckoning it appeared.

Slowly she knelt down and tugged at the sheet to reveal Tyler's face. It was peaceful, if gaunt, and looked as though he might cough himself awake. She caressed it.

"This boy here was involved in some bad business, you know. He, well, there was something about him, deep within him, and I don't know if it was his daddy or if it was somethin' else, but this boy here just hated anyone who wasn't white. And look at him now. White as a ghost," she lilted.

"He's white as a ghost—and I'd like to think maybe that'd make him the happiest little bigot in the world. Well, you know what happened, don't you? This young man, he went to school with my *grandson*. Yessir! And they were the *best* of friends. Yes sir! The best. Like two peas in a pod. And when I thought I might have *just* been on the cusp of getting my little old grandson to come back with me, to come home from whatever awful, heathen sort of dog life he'd been living, smoking dope, messing around with the girls and all that, just when I saw the look in his eye that said 'Nana, I'm gonna need you soon,' just then this little sonofabitch did the damnedest thing. He gave my grandson a gun. Why? I don't know."

Clyde nodded along. This theory was already well established. That just when Grace came close enough to Dalton's trust to get him back on track, Tyler came into their lives and interrupted it. "I know that, Grace," he said. "I was there too."

"No, you were not, Clyde!" she snapped. She huffed and looked around the room and walked to the window. She must have wanted to check to see that the orchard had been cleaned up and that the congregants were clearing out of there. She did look exhausted, Clyde thought.

"No, no you were not. Where you went, I don't suppose anyone knew. Some marathon of whorin' and sinning. Off on a drunk. But Jane certainly didn't have a handle on things. I still wonder why. Why? I do not know. I do not know why, Clyde. But my grandson wasn't too bright and he decided to bring that little old handgun to school and show people. What a nightmare. What a curse."

Clyde stood then, and bowed to look her in the eyes. "Well if he was such a problem, Grace, why did you bail him out?"

He was teasing her. She looked older than she'd ever looked and he felt sorry for her. Protective, almost.

"Well, the rest of the story kind of writes itself there. My grandson had to go and leave his school. Finished the rest of the work at home, from a juvenile house arrest."

She was saying it all again like he'd never heard it.

"And I was living with Janey you know. And the boys. And where were you? Damned fool. And I'll be damned if there wasn't a reporter, one, two, ten reporters on my front porch just about every morning come to talk to me about this for a little while. And I made a mistake one day, Clyde, and I went out there to talk to them and I brought my old shotgun out there. That shotgun was a gift from my daddy." She nodded toward the gun leaning next to the kitchen door.

"That's right, Grace. I know about the gun."

"And this boy right here"—she paused to look again into Tyler's face—"this one right here went off to jail. Either jail or prison, I don't know, but I was assured that he was never ever to be heard from again, not in my house or in any others. But of course I'd met them reporters and of course, Clyde, I was on the *news*. And when a nice old lady like me gets on the news, mixed up with guns and white power kind of people, well, it gets a little hard to make biscuits for the church suppers and sell cookbooks at the flea market. Do you know anything about that, Clyde?"

He was confused by this question and didn't know whether it was his to answer. He had been there, despite how she'd recast the story, and knew all about it.

"No, ma'am!" he said, then thought for a second and added, "I don't know if it's all so simple as that, Grace."

"Well, you *should*. You should. You should. You should," she said, enunciating her words with a thumping of her cane on the floor. "You ought to because there ain't no one in this county that had to go through this but me, and it's this little shit right here. This little sonofabitch that did it to me."

"Yes ma'am."

“Then I was taking my money and moving on. My daughter hating me, sinfully, you know, resenting me. And I took my money and moved on and came up here and started preaching myself. I was travelling then. And one day we were down the mountain in Fancy Gap. We pitched a tent out in a field owned by some farmer, and he let me use it. And it was hotter than hell out there and not a fly wing of air blew around. And I’d finished my sermon and this young man right here, he come up to see me after. The trucks were all but packed up and everyone had said goodbye, and this young man right here came up to see me, yes, and he said, ‘Pastor Grace,’ which is what I was going by then, and he said, ‘Pastor Grace, I owe my life to you.’”

She was fake blubbering, now, mimicking the dead boy in front of her. “*‘Pastor Grace, Pastor Grace, Pastor Grace, I am so sorry for what I done to your boy. I know better now. I know better. I will do anything you tell me, please. Please tell me.’* And on and on. And I knew he just needed someone to sign off on his community service papers, but, Clyde, I put this boy to work!”

“Yes ma’am.” Clyde had heard this all before. “And you put me to work, too, Grace, and I do so appreciate that. I do, ma’am. But, Grace, do you remember how we came to be together up here? Do you know what *that* means to me?”

“I know, Clyde, I know. Now, what are we gonna do with this?”

Dalton

DUSK WAS SETTING IN HEAVIER. Dalton tripped over a mass of something as he crossed from the tracks to the berm, flies starting to buzz around him in the muddy grey of the cloud-heavy evening. It smelled terrible. Dead animal. Dead large animal. Dalton kicked the mass away from him, tried to dust himself off but only smeared dirt and sweat on his chest, then headed toward the house.

He put his uniform back on and sat on his mother's porch. He'd not waited long when the old Toyota came slowly up the driveway. Dalton watched as his mother wiggled in her seat, back and forth, pushing herself up and out of the car onto one leg planted and ready to hold her, and, not quite making it, fell back into her seat and rested. Dalton stayed on the porch looking out over her, not wanting to ruin the surprise of his return by running out and helping. He was almost shocked to see her moving, static as she'd been in his mind for the past year or so, somewhere between still in church and still in bed; he hadn't considered her moving around. He was ashamed.

He watched her go through the motions again, grunting and sighing as she shot both her arms out of the car and then pushed, in breast-stroke fashion, to pull herself out. In the momentum she caught herself like a slow-motion Olympian after a sprint, stumbling in short steps and slipping a little in the gravel of the driveway.

Dalton couldn't take it anymore. He left the porch but stopped just beyond it, watching her open the car's rear door and gather her things. She'd gone bald and was frail; she clutched a scarf in one hand, wrapped in her fingers between plastic grocery bags. In the other arm she cradled a large brown paper bag. The veins on her head looked blue under the white glow of the street lamp but faded back into the shine of her skin as she approached the yellow of the porchlight. It was as though she was growing older with every step toward him, becoming clearer now but somehow more unreal. She finally saw him. "Dalton . . ." She slowly set her things down on the ground then hobbled up to him without her arms open.

He hugged her tightly to his chest and felt the uneven distribution of her breasts against him. He thought about what they might've looked like under her jacket, torn and sewn. She slid away from him with a little push, sniffing, and apologized.

"You know, since I started treatment, even the dog won't come near me. I think because of how the medicine smells. I can smell it on me sometimes. Isn't that sad, Dalton?"

He was thinking she smelled like wine. Beer, maybe. Sweet. She breathed out heavy and wiped sweat from her brow and from under her eyes, gently, with splayed fingers.

He hugged her again all the same and she reciprocated this time, holding for a second then letting him go with a pat, leaving the bags on the ground and walking with little unsure steps up to the porch. He picked up the bags and followed her. She took some time getting the keys out of her purse, then jangled one of them up and down in the latch.

"Let me help you with that, Mama," he said as she jangled again. She wrenched the key out of the lock, said "Goddammit" low under her breath, inserted a different key, then swung open the door and looked in, hesitating at the jamb.

"With what?" She looked up at him, feigning confusion; the way her head was cocked made her seem shorter than he remembered, and thinner and sharper around the edges. She did smell like medicine, too, behind the wine. Bitter, the way aspirin tastes.

Inside Dalton smelled potpourri and the remnants of some collard greens she might have reheated for breakfast. Or maybe that was just how the house smelled now. They walked down the hallway, its floor painted with red and blue intersecting vines, delicately preserved beneath the polyurethane that he and Clyde had laid over the hardwood.

"Look at the floor, sweetie. It held up, didn't it? How pretty." She moved slowly into the house, flipping on lights. "Just as pretty as it ever was." The faded lilt of her old Deep South accent sounded as if it had been taken from her, as if it had been made impotent by time spent alone, a jouissance of social grace she hadn't exercised. Her voice was ancient.

Dalton dropped the bags off on the little kitchen table and walked back into the dining room. His mother passed by him, seeming eager, on her own way to the kitchen where he could hear her rustling through them, putting things away. Even her movements sounded sick, clumsy and unsure. For how long had he done her wrong? He wanted to start at his father's departure, but that wasn't his fault. He wanted, then, to begin with an apology for his performance in high school, for all that happened after, for the journalists, the expulsion and resulting bad attention everywhere they went—*but she don't care about that anymore,* he thought. She knew he was sorry for it.

She came out of the kitchen and sat down and looked at him hard, rankled as he was, grey and unshaven after two days of travel.

"I'm sorry I left, Mama."

"Oh, Dalton," she said. "We've talked about that." She started moving things around on the table, sifting through the bills and coasters absentmindedly.

"I don't hold it against you, son. I think that, at the time, you just needed a change."

"Yeah, I think I did."

"I've needed some changes myself! I don't remember if I've told you, but I'm not in a good way."

"That's all you've really told me, Mama, but I didn't know—like this. No, Mama, I'm sorry about leaving, regardless." He wanted to push out tears to show her that he was real sorry, but instead ended up squinting dryly.

She sat down next to him, crossed her legs, and sighed. He took in all the parts of her face that weren't her eyes: her wobbled jowl and turkey buzzard neck made her face look like she'd seen too much sun and was giving up holding on to itself. The makeup around her eyes didn't stick like it was supposed to. He looked at her bald head, the veins on it pulsating under a cobwebbed wisp of hair that floated above her. He tried so hard to divert his eyes but couldn't.

"Where *were* you?"

"I was right here," she said with put-on cheer.

"No, I mean today. It's Sunday, where did you go?"

"To church." She uncrossed and recrossed her legs, the opposite side. "Then to town," she said after a moment.

"What were you doing in town? In Winston?"

"I was running errands, Dalton. My pharmacist is there, and . . . What happened, baby? How did you get kicked out of the damn *military*?" After a pause she added, "You can tell me, sweetie."

"Well, here's—I don't know—here's the thing. I wasn't in too good with anyone. I ran out of chances. I did a good thing in signing on the dotted line, you know, that's the first step in making something of yourself. That's what the recruiter told me, remember? In the first place, I mean. I told you that already. Well, I don't know if I did. I guess I'm sorry that I haven't called you more."

"Right, honey, but what *happened*?"

"Well, I met a bunch of guys, a whole bunch of guys that I liked, and we got along just fine—that, well that was in basic training in South Carolina. But then you get split up. Everyone goes to different places."

"And you went to New York, yes, I know. And what, you didn't end up making friends there?"

"Yes, I did. I mean we split up before that too. South Carolina, San Antonio—remember I was there for a while doing medic training. Then New York. Fort Drum. You know all this."

He paused.

"But it wasn't like what you think of when you think of New York at all. Just in the middle of nowhere. I don't know. It was too much like here. I kept having to restart everything. I felt good for a while." Dalton caught his old exasperation creeping in and fixed his tone.

"It's just that when I got there, I didn't know anybody. I was the *only one* who wound up in Fort Drum and I had to start all over. I made one friend though. Romerin. I told you about him. He reminded me of Messy, kind of. He was all right. Then, I don't know. People were nice to him. When people were nice to him, and we were together, it was like—well, it was nice. You know?"

"He wasn't getting you into any trouble, was he?"

"I don't know." Dalton's face was splotchy now, and his leg was bouncing up and down.

"I just wanted to get a sense of this friend, son. No need to be so nervous. I am trying to learn what's going on. Are you coming and going or are you here to stay? Are you in some kind of trouble or did you call it quits? I can't get a straight answer out of you."

"Well, so, I got written up for a few things, stupid things. And, well, Romerin and I had a falling out, and we got into a big fight and people misunderstood, like, what it was about."

"And so."

"So I was already in the hot seat. That's all. And we got in a fight, and I caught the brunt of it. I didn't like the way they were talking to me, and everyone was calling me different shit, and no one would listen to me anymore. I was a corporal, you know? But no one would listen to me. Not about anything. So I just kind of quit."

"How do you mean, you *quit*?"

"I mean I quit trying. I took my uniform off one day and didn't go to formation. I didn't want to play ball with them anymore so I just stayed in my room. They were so nasty. Anytime I showed up it was like I was in more trouble. I had to do more push-ups, or get coffee, or, you know, whatever I had to do, and I didn't want to do it anymore. Clean toilets. I got treated like everybody's bitch. They started calling me *Mr. Fuquay* like I wasn't in the Army anymore. Then I really wasn't. I mean I'm really not. Not for much longer."

"And that's it? They let you go, like a normal job?"

"That's it," he said, and wiped his hands on his pants. "Yeah, that's it. How's Messiah?"

"Oh, now, I thought you would never ask."

She stood and started performing a chore, really performing, moving into the kitchen, wiping the counter, wringing out the washcloth and running more water over it, wiping again, wringing again.

"Thought maybe you'd forgot about your old brother."

"No, Mama, I hadn't forgot. Goddammit, I'm stressed out, you know. I've been worried about myself." He stood and went to the kitchen doorway. "I assume he's all right, or you would have told me. Right? He's a good boy. He's being a good boy? A good kid, right? Normal?"

"More normal than you, son."

"Well, I don't know. You sent him off to some evangelist camp. He wasn't helping you at all?"

"No need to be cruel, Dalton. And I don't need that much help."

Dalton noticed something about her change. She was shifting a bit, moving under her clothes as though they might be itching her. "You all right?"

"Yes, son, I'm a *good kid* too." She stared at him without smiling.

"Did I say something wrong?"

She eyed him for a moment, then turned away. "Just a misunderstanding about a fight, huh? Do you want coffee? Have you had dinner?"

She dug in the refrigerator and pulled out a bottle of wine, twisted the cap off and poured herself a glass.

"You want some?"

Jane walked around the kitchen, occasionally looking around at Dalton as though he might have moved what she was looking for. She didn't ask for his assistance in finding it. He saw her purse but didn't want to tell her. Only when she got to the door did he say "It's on the back of the chair, here, Mama!" She put it on the counter next to the wine, pulled out a rectangular box with seven compartments—one for each day of the week printed in pharmacy-blue lettering—and starting sifting through one compartment then another, the pills rattling around. She finally got to Sunday. With all the little plastic compartment doors swung open, she tipped the container over and spread her pills out on the counter, sorting through and examining them.

"That's a hell of a lot of medicine," Dalton said.

"Well, son, I got a hell of a lot of cancer." She pushed out a little laugh. "I wish you knew how much it's cost me, Dalton. One of many costs. I can't tell you what it's been like here."

"Well, shit, Mama, why don't you keep Messiah here? He's a good boy! He can help you. Don't you know I would— Why ain't Messiah here?"

She used her browning and brittle fingernails to scratch the crust out of her eyes. He was waiting for her to cry, but she didn't. *Maybe she can't cry,* he thought.

"So where's the dog?" he asked, but she was rubbing her eyes and face.

He tried again. "So, are you happy I'm home? I can— I'm home."

"What was the *reason* it says again, son, on your paperwork?" Jane looked as though she were about to burp for a while but didn't.

"'Failure to adapt.' That's just what they put when they can't put anything else. It's not the worst. Hey, Mama, are you okay?"

She nodded, corralled all the pills in one hand, and dropped them in a clean, short Mason jar. Then she turned and walked past Dalton toward the stairs.

He watched her go, wanting to talk more. He needed to tell her the story again, maybe add in new details to make his case a little more convincing. "Hadn't done anything," he wanted to say. "Just got in a fight with a guy who everybody liked more. Couldn't fix it." Something like that. Or maybe not, maybe just the half-truth again in case he'd glossed over some crucial aspect. But the truth of it was that the details weren't even clear to him. He half-whispered "I missed you!" toward the open door behind him.

Only after thinking he might like some wine himself did Dalton discover that she'd taken the bottle with her.

The bedroom Dalton once briefly had to himself was junk storage now, but he saw that his mother had made up a poorly upholstered couch for him with a comforter and some mothball-preserved sheets. They smelled like gingivitis smells, he thought, like flossing. Beneath them, coming up from the cushions, he could smell Sumo, the old dog, and figured this must be where he spent his days, sleeping here in his old room. The floorboards above Dalton warped and flexed beneath his mother's slow-moving weight. It sounded like two old women dancing with each other.

As he lay there, listening to his mother listen to an Al Green CD play itself over and over, he imagined all the ways he could make it better. This could be a good time, a happy time. He could start fresh, tell everyone that he'd signed only a three-year contract, was back early, was injured, whatever. What did they know? He could go to night school and work during the day. He could help his mother out with the bills. He knew she had so many; of course he could do that. He thought, *Maybe I could go up there and make her a promise. That'd make her happy*. Instead he stayed still, and promised, again and again, to himself. He would help her. He would take care of her and make sure everything would be all right. His brother. His mother. His failure—not burdens, he promised himself, but reminders of how to be, why to live.

The night around him crept—as it does—in buoyant loneliness indifferent to its occupants. Through the dusty windows came fuzzed projections of the magnolia, the one white light of the street lamp throwing shadows that wormed around the walls, made large and stark every once in a while by the headlights of a passing car. There were clusters of ladybugs on the wall. Too many of them, and they moved all in unison as if being shepherded from one spot to the next by his mother's footsteps. Her hoarse humming, off-tune and off-time. Dalton closed his eyes and took big deep breaths of the stale air, like gulping water.

His dreams were populated by the thrum of cicada screams, the noise blooming into a blacker-than-black shape behind his eyes, swarming him alone in the dark.

A wave of electric panic came to him at the tail end of his sleep, squeezing him until his eyes opened. In the blurry disillusionment of morning, as he resigned himself to his surroundings, he felt the stress of the past few weeks hit him again, all at once. He checked to make sure he hadn't wet the couch. Just sweat. He remembered his promise to himself from the night before, and looked around his old room piled with accumulations of things—things bought from yard sales still with their tags, an old clothes dryer, drying racks with clothes still on them, a dusty exercise bike. An arrangement of glass slippers caught glares of sun striking through the east window, its rays made prominent by the dust he'd unsettled and continued to unsettle by pulling on his jeans. Dalton felt circumstantial in this very personal museum his mother had curated in his absence. It's all junk, he thought, and was still wondering about its purpose as he walked down the decorated hallway floor toward the kitchen.

The time flickered on the stove, green numbers telling him that it was either quite early in the morning or quite late in the afternoon, which surprised him before he realized it was inaccurate. That was something he'd been used to before he left for the Army. The power would cut out, sometimes because of poor wiring, sometimes longer because of overdue bills. The time, he thought, wasn't important now and he wondered briefly if it ever would be again. It *was* important, however, that he find another clock, if only to verify that he hadn't slept for a whole day. He figured that this sense of lost time was more a product of his mistakes, his recent untethering from function and usefulness. That problem, the big problem of his future—compounded, of course, by his past—of his mother's future, would be his clock from then on out. He'd spend every minute wisely, and as long as he was moving toward something it wouldn't matter what time of day it was. He had to focus on something; he needed purpose. He settled on starting fresh and natural and sweet, with breakfast. He'd bring up two plates and have breakfast with his mother.

He turned on the radio and NPR played, the local news rambling on. Listening to it felt good. It felt like home. He romanticized this new path, the path of the good son. He pulled his mother's watch out of her purse, trying not to look at anything else in there. Nine-something in the morning. He used it to sync the clock on the stove, plus five or ten minutes fast to help her be on time to things, then programmed the coffee machine to match. He filled it and set it to brew. He whisked the eggs, heated the cast-iron pan, preheated the oven, cooked sausage with onion and made a roux. He measured flour with his hands and sifted it through his fingers into a mixing bowl with soda, powder, and salt, added old but good-enough buttermilk, then rolled the dough and cut out circles with the empty, tarnished tuna can that he found, reassuringly, still sitting in the utensil drawer.

She must really have been expecting me, he thought. Everything but the buttermilk was sealed, fresh and unopened before he pulled it out. These were the groceries he didn't help her with the night before. She had prepared for him, and for the first time since his arrival he began to feel welcomed. He put the biscuits in the oven and added milk to the sausage roux to make gravy, fried the eggs and then, firm onto this feeling of welcome, he set and spooned the finished meal onto plates.

Dalton picked up the tray and walked back down the hallway, past the room where he'd spent the night. His movement had stirred the air and kicked up that old-dog smell again, overwhelming the good smell of the coffee and biscuits and gravy. He climbed the stairs, lit by the dust-thickened rays of sunlight that poured through the windows.

At her door, he stopped for a second to put on a smile. He balanced the heavy tray on the corner of the banister and opened the door with his bare foot. Her bedside lamp, a faux oil lamp—a brass thing with an upturned vase painted with angels sitting atop the bulb that had followed her around all her life—was still on and, old as it was, buzzing slightly, joined by the static of the CD player. Amid the buzz Dalton called in a cheerful whisper, "Good morning, Mama!"

The covers were heaped up where she was lying. Dalton noticed the half-dozen empty pill bottles by the lamp. He hated to look at them; some were stacked on top of one another like a sleeve of cups, some knocked over, unscrewed and topless: a collection of them. He looked back at the mound beneath the blankets, still as a painting in the tight, sun-hot, dust-shimmering air.

"Mama?" He set the tray right down on the floor.

He walked up to the side of the bed and pulled the sheets back just enough to notice that his mama was still clothed. He stepped back and looked around the room as if someone might be watching how he would react. He reached toward her, touched her, and shook her to come awake. Then he dug his arms underneath her to lift her toward him, bent over at a severe angle, and started breathing into her blouse, weeping. She wasn't cold, but heavy.

Messiah

"HEY, MESS," Graham said softly. "Wake up, man. Hey, man, I've got something to tell you, could you wake up for me?"

The way Graham said "for me" confused Messiah. Graham had never asked Messiah to do him a favour. He rubbed his eyes and pulled his T-shirt down over his belly and waited for Graham to say something else.

Graham was still shaking him even though Messiah was obviously moving and awake. *Graham is here* was all he could think, so he repeated the thought to himself, reflexively and reassuringly, as he sat up and looked at him.

He *was* there, there in the long dark room, his face illuminated by the hallway light spilling through the left-open door.

"Hey Graham," Messiah said. "Why are you here so late? Are you going to prank me?"

"Mess, I've got something to tell you. I'm so sorry. Can you come with me?"

The camp's director, Mr. Albright, was sitting in a wrinkled shirt and smoking a cigarette while looking displeased. Graham waited outside, the door just ajar.

"Take a seat, there, son," the director said.

"Am I in trouble?"

"No, not at all. No, no. Shhhh, shhh. Hush, now, boy. I've got some bad news for you, Messiah. I'm afraid it's about your mother. She has passed on."

"Passed on to where?"

"Passed *away*. Your mother, I'm told, has succumbed to her illness, in bed, alone at home. The right people have been called and they're taking care of her."

Mr. Albright paused, outed his cigarette, and said, "I'm sorry, Messiah." The two sat in silence in the lingering smoke. Messiah's eyes, hurting from the foreign, powerful glare of light and irritated by the smoke, started to water.

"Go ahead and cry, boy, that's all right. Would you like to join me in prayer?"

Mr. Albright took a Bible out of his desk and pulled his lips inward into a jowly frown. "What this means for you, Messiah, as a boy at this camp, is complicated. Now, we'll pray first and then we can talk about what happens next."

"I don't want to pray," Messiah said. His thoughts were of his mother, her reading to him in the lamplight. The silk of her nightgown, her deep voice almost singing the words to his favourite books, rubbing his calves when he had growing pains. He thought of her putting on makeup with curlers in her hair. He thought of beef stroganoff for dinner and the creaking floors of their house. He thought of quilts and of the early mornings at the bus stop, his mother waiting with him until the last minute, the car idling and the exhaust floating in the blue, chilly air. He thought about Christmas, the few, immaculately wrapped presents, the mirrored ornaments, the soul records through the crackling old speakers, her "Good night, Messiah." He thought of her excitement about autumn leaves on the Blue Ridge Parkway and their drives across it, listening to *Prairie Home Companion*, of her laughing at the jokes he didn't understand.

The voice from the radio resonating calm within him and the feeling of drifting off to sleep in the blowing heat from the car's vents, heating her hair then, the Pantene shampoo warming so that it radiated throughout the car making it smell so pungently maternal and real.

Mr. Albright began to pray anyway. Messiah turned and looked behind him for Graham, but the hallway had darkened.

"My brother's in the Army," Messiah said, interrupting.

Mr. Albright finished, then said "Amen," opening his eyes and looking at Messiah. "All right, then. We can try to get someone to call him."

"I don't know the number."

"That's just fine, Messiah. We will try and get someone to call him."

"What do I do now?"

Dalton

DALTON WOULD REGRET not following her as she left him the night before. He would regret so much: the hug, their conversation, the fantasy of getting a kiss goodnight. But now he was having a flash of stoic pride, like he could pull energy and focus, somehow, from his resistance to the feeling itself, this feeling of being south of rock bottom. Flawed logic. There was a dry-mouth feeling all over him, and no denying the whirling nausea of that long slow walk to the front porch, something like pure loneliness. Like he was out of time, or in a cage getting lowered into the depth of things. Floating loneliness. Weightlessness with no other sense of freedom. Leaving the door open he hoped would attract the neighbours' attention enough for them to call the police. Someone would come and find her. He hoped they would, anyway.

But it was the walk down their ornamental hallway that kept recurring over and over in his mind now; the quiet silence of it, the grim tension, the feeling that she'd known something he didn't. The vines painted on the floor looked like veins under their polyurethane. Did she plan on this happening? *Is this what she wanted?*

He had turned off the buzzing lamp and the CD player and unplugged the alarm clock that had gone off like a bomb as he sat beside his mother, petting her.

He had combed shaking fingers through her sparse hair, clenching his other hand into a fist and biting it, not out of a real need to silence or to calm himself but in a gesture he knew to be one of grief. *This is how it looks,* he thought. *This is how it is supposed to be.* But the sting didn't cut through the unreality.

He had left the door to her room ajar and opened the windows in the hallway, the ones that still had their screen intact. He tried not to think about bugs getting in. He took the breakfast tray back downstairs, walked back along the hall, its painted red and blue vines almost glowing, growing more intricate as he went, entangling themselves then spreading and branching beneath him. In the kitchen he gulped down one of the lukewarm mugs of coffee and tossed the breakfast in the garbage pail—plates, coffee, and all. He swiped a kitchen towel across the countertops to clean them of crumbs then ran it under the sink until it got warm but thought better of it and switched the faucet off. Not the kitchen towel. She's not a thing, he thought.

He had found a couple of clean washcloths in the bathroom, wetted and wrung them, and went back upstairs, pausing at her door. With a deep breath that made him see stars he stepped back into the room.

Dalton was nervous about her not being stiff. He feared that she may still be alive somehow, that he was wasting precious time. He pressed his fingers hard into her neck and wrists looking for a pulse, but there was no use. Why was he afraid? Her jaw was agape and there was no breath. He folded up one of the damp cloths and wedged it just under her chin. He straightened her out in the bed, folded her arms across her hard chest, wiped down her forearms and bald head. He wiped the dried-white spit from the sides of her mouth. He kissed her forehead and held her hand, and the sun blared on his back from the window. He felt himself sinking. He told her he loved her, and he did.

He came to himself. Once the cold ran out of him and his face got hot he started to think he couldn't wait anymore. He slowly removed the cloth from under her chin and felt relieved when her mouth stayed closed and peaceful. Dalton went back into his old room, the junk room where he'd slept, smelled the dog and thought about Sumo. He wanted somehow to find the dog and take him with him, wherever he was going, and then thought he needed to get his brother, too. The order in which these ideas occurred to him made Dalton feel ill and deeply dissatisfied with himself. He couldn't get it right—and worse, he knew he wouldn't.

Messiah surely didn't know he was home; their mother wouldn't have called to tell him yet. Messiah was at camp, enjoying a summer in a carefree way that would almost certainly never be possible for him again. Dalton walked through the house and looked at envelopes, notepads, at papers in his mother's address book—all over—but he couldn't find a number for the camp. He didn't even know the name of the camp. There was no internet at the house.

Finally he picked up the phone to call an ambulance, or whomever they might send in these situations. With the dial tone ringing, he stared at the phone's console and hung up. He lifted it again, lightly fingering the 9 button, then hung up again. No one knew he was home.

He wandered into the room where he'd slept. Looking through a chest of drawers, he was surprised to see that it still housed some of his clothes. They'd been scrunched into the two bottom drawers and were musty and smelled like dog. He took every shirt out and considered it, opting for a church-only dress shirt, baby blue. He put it on, worked ineffectually to smooth out the wrinkles, gave up, pulled on some civilian pants from out of his duffle, packed everything else back up, and sat on the comforter that his mother had laid out for him on the couch.

That's too much shit, he thought. He unpacked his bag and looked carefully at each item. He laid aside all but one spare military uniform and one spare set of civilian clothes. The loaded magazines, the helmet, the Kevlar battle armour, a knife, the spare ammunition, and a training grenade hollowed out on the inside all went into the drawer, replacing the clothes he'd just pulled out. He smacked himself a little on the face to remember this moment, to know that when he got a call from Messiah or whomever he could come back for these things and sell them at a gun shop or gun show. An insurance package. He closed the drawer.

He wished he knew how to call Messiah. But what could he do for his brother now? Maybe it was best for him, for Dalton, that no one tell Messiah he'd come home at all.

Dalton realized he was sobbing, not having noticed when it began. He knew only by the tears falling on his shirts as he folded them up, each drop creating a small dark circle on the fabric. He didn't wipe his eyes.

His mother's purse was still on the kitchen table. He took the few dollars from it, weighed the car keys in his hand. Thought better of it, lest he get blamed. An awful thought. He picked up his duffle, walked out to the porch, and looked around. The house left him feeling charged—as though if he were to touch anything it would shock him. Maybe that was why he left the front door open as he stepped off the porch and away from the house. The real reason.

Before his head and his eyes had cleared, he found himself heading toward town.

Cars passed him along the road. He walked in the tall grass between the shoulder and the train track that ran parallel through the county. It would take an hour to get there. Dalton stopped twenty minutes in and pulled out his Army patrol cap and started making eye contact with motorists, but nobody picked him up. He curled the brim and stuck it in his back pocket. It hadn't done any good. He thought about donning his beret but figured that down here it was just as likely to get mistaken for a beatnik beret, making it more likely that he'd get run over than in anyone picking him up. He weighed the pros and cons of stepping off into the woods that ran alongside Old Highway 52 and changing back into his uniform. But then they'd surely know he'd come home. He'd save that for the next place. *The next place.* He squinted, walking with his eyes shut for a little while.

In town, cutting across familiar strip mall parking lots and gas stations, Dalton meandered between cars, and, in a habit still not shaken from his youth, looked through their windows for valuables on passenger seats, finding none. He stepped into the ABC store across the street from the bus station. He scrounged for change in his pockets and kept his shaking hands there. The store's air conditioning reignited the damp must of the old clothes clinging to him alongside the leftover images of the morning: the serene face of his mother, her skin white and paper-thin, the peculiar smell of an old house sitting in the direct sun.

He put a few spark plug bottles of whiskey on the counter and ordered Camel Lights. The young man who accepted Dalton's change was around his age, someone Dalton never would've talked to in high school, a real country boy. Dalton stared at his Auburn University hat with the fish hook through the brim. In turn the young man studied Dalton, which made his hands shake worse.

"Hey, whoa, hey there! *I know you.* You got a haircut! I heard you was in the Army."

"Four dollars? For cigarettes?" Dalton said. "Damn. And, no, I think you're wrong."

"No, no. I *know* it's you. You was in the news. You brought a little gun to school or something. West Stokes High School. I remember you from one of them YMCA dances. You used to have your hair dyed. Used to wear chains, like a, uh, like a gay punk rocker or something. Army boy, now. Look at you! Yeah, I remember you. How you doing—uh, what was your name? Sorry, what is your name?"

"Just visiting, man. I think you got the wrong guy." Dalton knew he had to get out of there—the store, the town—he had to get out of that room with his mother. It was like he was still there. The stale air.

"No, man, c'mon! You don't remember me? Ralph? You know me man, we had church together a few times. Your Granny brought you to our church. Don't you remember? I told people I knew you when you was on the news. Man, I can't believe you're the same guy. How's your mama? Jane? She comes in here. Yeah dude, I *know* it's you. I remember. Wow, look at that goddamn haircut. Army guy, huh?"

"No, not really," Dalton said. He asked how much.

"All right, well, let's call it ten bucks. But hey, I seen your mama just the other day. She comes in here a lot. She said you was coming home. Can't believe you're the same guy." Ralph was shaking his head.

"All right, well, thanks," Dalton said, leaving the money on the counter.

"You sticking around long? Tell your ma I said hello!"

Clyde

CLYDE WALKED DOWN from the house through the orchard, checking, as he went, for leftover Capri-Sun juice boxes, orange peels, Dixie cups, and the like. He found none and was satisfied. The sermon itself hadn't felt like a success. More of a spectacle, he thought. He'd have to write it all down to remember how it was and how it felt. Not so much how it was said, but whether this one did what it was supposed to do. She always wanted to talk to him about the sermons and he didn't usually have the right words.

His trailer sat a few hundred yards from Grace's main property, hauled into a clearing in the woods on some of Grace's spare acreage. It had been his parents' before they died. Up until today he'd shared it with Tyler. The two of them, regardless of their proximity, had never spoken much outside the passing on of Grace's directives and the exchange of casual insults and slurs over a Budweiser or maybe a pipeful of whatever was going around. Call it subsistence living. They never got around to talking about the past. How they came to be there together. They'd each let Grace dictate the terms of their shared history. He regretted that now.

He had running water pulled from plumbing installed in the nineties when Buffalo Mountain was gearing up to be a retirement home community, a project that was culled along with so much else just before he moved up there, sometime around 2008 or 2009. He couldn't rightly remember.

He flicked the lights on, walked into Tyler's room, then balled up his bedding that lay matted and brown, sweat-stained on the pull-out couch. He put them in a contractor bag, tied it up, set it down by the door, and began to undress. It was going on three o'clock now; time to shave again. He hung up his church clothes in the sliding-door closet, the mirror glancing at him before he slid it away behind the faux-wood panel. The tattoos and scars on his arms and chest had raised, as they did whenever he got nervous. And Grace had made him nervous.

Clyde put a pot of coffee on to boil and stepped into the shower. He washed with the Irish Spring, the last of it, rubbing the bar on his head and feeling the tug against his scalp as the soap sudsed up and disappeared. He used the remnants to spread what was left along his body, stamping their goopy shards down the drain with his big toe. He rinsed quickly and stepped out before the water had even begun to warm. At the sink he prepared his shaving bowl and set out his straight razor, a safety razor, and an electric razor, a tool for each part of his face. He'd left the beard behind for good. No disguise of any kind when he was working for Grace. She said once she didn't like to be debased in such a way by his unkempt facade. Her words. So, he shaved for her. That was to be a new him. *A second coming,* he'd laughed.

His parents hadn't owned but had run the tail end of a pig farm when he was a boy, and he'd helped them work it ever since he could walk and talk. They'd lived in the same trailer he lived in now. This was the last of them—the economy and the life they'd worked so hard at having whittled down anything they'd had to these four walls. He was bearded before they died. Stayed bearded for Jane. But he shaved now. Didn't have to hide himself anymore. Didn't need a disguise.

At seven years old he'd slipped halfway into a pot of the boiling water and lye used for sloughing off the hair from hog skin before it was processed and sent to market. He'd caught himself, but it was too late. The skin fell off his arms like a silk nightgown falls off women in the movies.

They were scarred now, as was the right half of his face, which had grazed the top of the chemical water. He used the electric razor on the uneven right side, the straight razor for the left, and the safety razor for his neck. Trying to get as close as possible to the skin under the scars. He splashed Aqua Velva on it all, neck and chest, and let it sit there, stinging him and waking him up. *Need to be sharp,* he thought.

He spit in his hands and slicked his hair back, flossed his towel between his legs, and began to dress.

Grace had told him to make a poster and to start flyering an advertisement for her sermons and the revival, a flyer that ought to bring people in from all over, beyond their little corner of the Blue Ridge. She wanted it posted everywhere he could think of, a thousand of them up before Sunday. He considered this task when he pulled on his jeans over his still-wet behind and a new T-shirt right out of the Hanes bag down over his head. It itched him.

Clyde sat down and wrote out what he figured were his instructions as best he could. Then he wrote in his journal the little things that had happened, leaving out Tyler, the stained sheet that wrapped him, Grace's body, and anything else damning to the revival. He'd always considered himself a writer. He had his stories, and he'd tell them when he could. He thought all this might one day add up to something, like a movie or a TV show or something. Just a fantasy. It just got hard, sometimes, to believe the world would ever listen.

He washed his hands again and smelled them, making sure they were truly clean. When the owners of the pig farm sold it off to a chicken conglomerate, Clyde's parents called it quits and he took on the family tradition of working oneself to death. The smell of the processing plant was still on him, he felt. All that fat and bone rising up in the warbling Carolina heat and sticking to everything in Surry County. Anytime he drove through that part of the world he could remember the early mornings, checking in, setting up his station, pulling birds apart. Sometimes they'd move down the line so fast they'd get to Clyde's station before they'd even half died, and they'd fight him. He became a kind of vegetarian. He hated the smell of chicken, even when it was packaged up sitting in the supermarket cold. Even when it was cooking.

His thoughts were getting away from him. After writing about the burn of the Aqua Velva and some memories of Jane, the chicken farm, his beard, his boiling face, his disguise—all these recurring worries—he turned his attention to the poster. Grace had said she wanted all kinds of people, but he thought that might come at a cost. He knew that her revival could never be so open. It had to be the *right kind* of person, someone who needed something. Someone who was missing something.

She'd handed him the jacket Tyler always wore, adorned with stupid gang symbols and signs and flags for local militias Tyler wasn't even part of. Clyde knew those types of men, those men in militias. Typically they were fat old ex-cops, sometimes vets, and they just loved guns and absolutely hated most everything about the future that always seemed to come too soon for their liking. Simple as that.

Grace had made him take note of the signs and patches, reproducing each one on a sheet of paper. She'd watched him, sitting there at the table a yard or so away from Tyler's body, ensuring that his little renderings were close enough to match what was there on the boy's jacket. This kind of history-making wasn't so unusual for Grace but still felt like overkill to him. They weren't there to document Tyler like some kind of religious martyr. But she insisted.

"Good enough," she'd said. "You don't have to find out what the hell any of this means, or what they are, just put them, real small, on the paper when you do the flyer. Get that flyer out now, Clyde. I want people next Sunday."

I want people, he repeated to himself, and sketched out the little signs: 3%, a snake, a jumble of letters beneath a cross. He did just as she said. And when he was done marking it up in pencil, he thought the flyer would do fine:

REVIVAL – GRACE'S CHURCH OF THE REDEEMER – EVERY SUNDAY – EAST SIDE OF BUFFALO MOUNTAIN – COME ONE COME ALL – ALL WELCOME – PATRIOTS WELCOME – MOTHERS WELCOME – OLD TIME GOSPEL – PAYING JOBS WEEKLY – REFRESHMENTS PROVIDED – SHINE AND MUSCADINE WINE – GOOD PAY WEEKLY FOR VOLUNTEERS – EVERY SUNDAY – NOON

He packed up the drawing and a stapler and went down the mountain in his pickup, ready to head into town, into town, into town, and into town, all towns feeling the same and feeling far away and too close at the same time. He'd put the flyers up, hand them out. He'd hunt a little and fish a little. He'd be back Sunday, early.

As he was driving he felt the sun on the left side of his face. He reached up to feel the smooth skin but felt the stubble sticking up already, refusing to stay cut down.

Clyde set off on the Blue Ridge Parkway, aiming for all the little towns and strip malls and diners along its route he could get to with enough gas to make it back. He still worried about cash, despite his knowing that Grace had the money to keep him driving for the rest of his life. All things with her were quietly conditional, dependent on his successes. And the goalposts were always shifting.

He'd stuck to recruiting, mostly, real missionary stuff, he thought. He saw himself not so much as her partner—or whatever he was to her—as her mentee, someone she tried to guide through the haze of unknowing, the fuzziness and unreality that seemed to be part and parcel of his life. It didn't hurt that she happened to hand him some cash once in a while.

He knew what kept him living in separate quarters from Grace, though. He knew his side of things, anyway. It was the shame they each carried with them, having left Jane down in the shoals to fend for herself. That and his tendency to go in search of those entertainments of which she did not approve. She called them *drunks*, as though he was off doing only drinking, sitting next to a still and tying one on.

Clyde had a preternatural sense for finding where that country was coming unravelled. Biker bars along the highways, trailer park dogfighting nights, unlicensed bars on the outskirts of Winston-Salem, militia musters, gun shows. And when he found these places, it would go one of two ways. He might keep his head and seek out the kind of people to whom Grace's ministry would be attractive, explaining to them how to get up the mountain and how to find the weekly service. It was real missionary work. The other way would drag Clyde down among the unredeemable damned, leaving him sleeping off some high or another in his truck, pill bottles and liquor bottle empty on the seat beside him, sometimes with blood on his hands.

He drove with the radio off, taking stock of his situation as it stood. He cautioned himself against scheming, in any way, against Grace, but was feeling vengeful about Tyler's erasure. He felt like he could lose it all too. As if Grace needed him more than ever—that feeling of being wanted and appreciated, he was sure he'd have it—but also saw him as ultimately replaceable.

He finished stapling the last of what he hoped would be the only poster he'd ever have to make onto a diner's bulletin board just outside Meadows of Dan. A thirty-mile radius was about all Grace could expect. He'd spent the past few days going from town to town and staying with old buddies from high school, one night in his truck, once in bed with a woman, refilling the necessities of his shaving kit and restocking shirts from the Dollar Generals peppered throughout the piedmont and lower mountains. Sunday was fast approaching, and he worried that if he didn't bring more people out then Grace might punish him somehow in one of the strange ways she'd found to hurt him.

He'd talked to some people, too. Some down-and-out-looking couples waiting for pizza or hot dogs at a gas station, a man struggling with a fishing worm vending machine in Rural Hall, a group with Gadsden flags outside a county courthouse who said they were protecting monuments, folks he thought looked lost. The way he was lost. The way he had been lost, anyway.

The stack of remaining flyers on his front seat bothered him, reminded him that he hadn't lived up to the thousand-flyer promise he'd made to Grace. But it was taking up too much time at this miserable pace. Driving from place to place, from all-you-can-eat buffets to gas stations to tackle-and-bait shops, for what?

He put off the other thing he had to do. Grace had asked him explicitly to run Tyler's errands. "Collect some new alms, Clyde!" she'd said as he was pulling away. Tyler had made a whole life for himself just by procuring little tastes of illicit drugs and shine for Grace's congregants, making it so they were always available when needed, providing a nice exchange for those who managed to pull themselves together to attend the revival ceremonies in her orchard every Sunday. They'd put whatever little they had into that Easter basket, sometimes the same monies Grace had just paid them for some kind of work or other. It was a cruel cycle, but only if you looked at it that way. He figured most people who came to hear Grace preach were better off than they would've been without her. Clyde knew that to be a fact, having pulled them from the squalor himself.

And he was pretty sure she didn't need the money at all. Sometimes the parishioners would talk among themselves, wondering if they ought to put more money in—maybe with a little more in the pot they'd get a little more of what Grace offered for communion. Usually some kind of OxyContin or methadone. He knew that some of Tyler's connections cooked up meth and that some of them had a corn whiskey still near the orchard. He could smell the still tenders' mashing-in some nights, the cooking malt catching the air just right and mixing with the fig-like smell of curing tobacco when it came time, autumn in the lowlands, and the wind would carry all that up the mountains and mix it with the sweet smell of the whiskey stills and it felt like old times, as far as he could imagine it. It felt right.

But that didn't assuage him at all insofar as he didn't know those folks, the ones with pills and guns, mostly. If he did, he didn't like himself when he was around them. He didn't want to go looking for them, let alone sniffing them out from the congregation, though he thought it might be easy to do. It would be too late anyway. Grace wanted alms for Sunday, and she wanted something easy and impressive—something, she'd said, to open the eyes and ears of her people to see the disappointed face of the Lord. No, it wasn't for money, and it wasn't an exchange. It was like the alms were a means to an end rather than the end itself. He felt he had to believe it. There was still something out there—God or what, he didn't know—but it spoke itself through Grace with a power that stopped him where he stood anytime she turned it on. She had saved him, that was right, but he thought of the gun in the glove compartment of his truck and questioned his role in all of it. Is this how miracles happened?

He knew about the pill mill in Mount Airy. The problem was that the cops had raided it once or twice in the early part of the millennium for filling forged prescriptions and now they had security sulking around like a zombie guard, as if the problem emanated from the outside. One of the men he'd stayed with a few days before explained to Clyde that even to get in you had to relinquish your ID, drive through the gate with cameras on you, walk through bulletproof sliding doors with cameras on you, then sit down in a waiting room with cameras on you. After that you had to go talk to a doctor. Clyde thought of ways around the cameras. His ways, if he could make them, wouldn't be quiet. He pulled out his map of the region and figured he could be in Mount Airy in an hour.

He waited in the Goodwill parking lot, keeping an eye out for anyone who might look like a pill addict. The plan was he'd take their car and drive in, pulling his hat over his face and peering down, avoiding the cameras. Then he'd wait until someone came out of the office where they issued the pills and take the lot from them right there, either in the parking lot or—

An old woman emerged from the Goodwill hobbling on a walker, making her way as Grace would if Grace had aged about fifteen years. She was bent over a little and struggling with her walker, caught now on the lip of the sidewalk. Clyde got out of his truck and walked toward her.

"Evening, ma'am." He smiled.

"Good evening young man."

"Can I help you?"

After some exaggeratedly formal haggling, Clyde was driving the woman's Buick and she was sitting next to him in the passenger seat. She'd said she had to go to the pharmacy and then head home but was, she was glad he noticed, quite tired. When he'd asked which pharmacy she named the very one, the pill mill just as he'd hoped. He said he'd take her down there and drop her off at home if she'd like. She said that would be just wonderful, tired as she was. She noted how they were sonofabitches there and laughed but promised to say he was her grandson. Her grandson often took her down there, she remarked, and no one seemed to give a damn who he was.

They pulled through the gate and Clyde passed the woman's ID over to the guard and told him she had an appointment.

"Need to see your ID too now, mister."

"Can I talk to you for a minute?"

"Sure," said the guard, and Clyde keyed off the Buick. The woman didn't protest at all.

Now Clyde was telling the guard about his grandmother's dementia, and the guard grew suspicious. "Okay then, will you let me talk to her?"

"All right," Clyde said with a shrug.

The guard approached the vehicle, and despite its not being quite dusk he shone a light into the woman's face and startled her. She reared back as if he were attacking her and said "Clyde, Clyde!" which Clyde grimaced to hear, but he ran up and said softly, "It's okay, Granny, it's okay."

The guard let them pass through, apologizing for being tough on them and wishing them a good night.

Clyde waited in the car after he pulled the woman's walker from the back seat and set her up to head into the facility. It was agonizing watching her navigate the concrete ramp zigzagging up to the building. The doors finally opened then closed behind her. And in a quarter hour she was hobbling back on out.

She fell asleep on the drive to her retirement condo. He tried to wake her to some avail. "You've got to keep driving, Granny," he urged. "Let's go, let's get you into the seat." He got her out and gently ushered her to the driver's side. She held on to the sides of the car throughout the rigmarole, shaking and wobbling. He sat her down behind the wheel, buckled her in, and told her to wait there.

She looked confused and betrayed like a baby being woken up mid-nap, and he felt like he might've been really hurting her. He went back to the car and tried to reassure her, saying, "Don't worry, ma'am, someone is going to come get you. Wait just right here, ma'am, I'll go and get some help." He walked in the building and told the concierge there was a woman outside who seemed to have fallen asleep at the wheel and that they should call someone to come get her.

Outside, he took one last look at the car and the still, grey head of the woman sitting there and thought of Grace. From one old woman to another, he thought, and walked slowly back to his truck.

Clyde thought he might not return. He thought about selling those pills and taking whatever gas that could get him and driving toward the coast. There, he thought, he'd just fish until he died or got thrown in jail. He imagined for himself a life out of a song, fishing in the ocean and drinking at one of those Uncle Joe's Crab Suckers kind of beach bars. Maybe it was the lower altitude, the flatness of the Piedmont down here in North Carolina, that made him feel free to roam, to go as he pleased and where he pleased. The magnetism that had kept pulling him back up the mountain toward Grace, to his trailer there, the sermons and the trees, the bugs and the quiet—it evaporated here in the lowlands. All that Old Tyme romance, flat-footing to fiddlers, corn whiskey, mountain girls, all of it was pressed to the back of his mind, overwhelmed by the grey monotony of modern America: KFC, Bojangles, a dozen pharmacies; a church here, Baptist, another church there, Primitive Baptist, growing big and ugly out of the long scar of asphalt that cut through the surrounding green country.

This was the very same thing Grace was fighting against. She wasn't just crazy like people thought she was. Aside from all the handling of serpents and talking in tongues, she had a vision of an America that was fading. Grace wanted to reanimate these highway towns, all connected together and tethered by overhead wires, tangled and marionetted by bogus modernity; she wanted to make them real again, to bring them back into the kingdom of heaven. The only America that'll be left after the flood, he'd heard her say a thousand times now, was in nature, up on the mountain, yes, closer to God. And then the magnetism was back.

He believed in Grace. He worked for her. She worked *through* him.

And he owed her, after all. It wasn't just Tyler she'd rescued from jail. Despite what she'd said about each of them, Clyde knew she'd paid the sheriff in Surry County to let them both go. Tyler had been in a cell just down from his, in for his exploits with his daddy's guns, and Clyde for drinking and driving a car without its title and insurance. It was on that afternoon, the three of them in the Sheriff's Department parking lot, that each told Grace they'd work for her until their debts were paid off.

He never did go back to Jane and tell her what had happened. He didn't want to become some go-between from Jane to Grace and vice versa. He wanted to put his head down and work, then to pack up and leave off for somewhere else. The problem was that he couldn't separate what was paying off his debt from what he did out of something like love for Grace. She had a hold over him. She'd often raise her voice at Tyler, hitting him and threatening him with her shotgun, but never Clyde. He was obliged to do the tasks she set out for him and was rewarded with a little money and the freedom to go and do as he pleased, more or less. In all that he did was something of Grace. He even brushed his teeth for her, he thought. Sometimes he could almost feel her hand guiding his along the steering wheel, on the grip of a handgun, running his fingers through his hair.

Dalton

HE WANTED TO GO somewhere between Fort Drum, New York, and the foothills of North Carolina. The logic of this was that, whenever the news of his mother's death caught up to him, it would look like he hadn't quite made it home yet. The logistics were complicated. He wanted to get himself a hotel under the Vasquez name and a story of a lost wallet, and to do that town by town until he settled somewhere good enough to call and inquire about his brother. To feign surprise at the news of his mother. To make it so he was still on his way home. To roll back time.

He gripped his stomach when he realized that Messiah would learn of his mother's death alone and how confused it was going to make him. He saw images of his mother, at once glad and crippled by the knowledge that Messiah wouldn't see her when he'd seen her, as he'd seen her. Peaceful.

Messiah wasn't a dumb boy, or even really *special*, as the nice teachers used to say, or *tetched*, as Dalton had overheard a lady at church put it. He was unique. He processed things in a manner that, to Dalton's mind, was suggestive of a higher intellect than most kids his age. And what *was* his age, now? Thirteen? Fourteen?

It took him quite a while to make his way back to Winston-Salem, and that was the opposite direction he needed to go. He changed into his uniform, far enough away from home now to attract the right attention with it. To cash in on those thank-yous he'd received for his bullshit service.

He decided to head back just the way he'd come, retracing his route to maintain plausible deniability of his presence in his mother's house. He hated to have seen that goddamn Ralph boy in the goddamned liquor store. It reminded him of the spark plugs of whiskey. He cracked one and drank it in anger, still standing in front of the route map.

The bus ride to Charleston was long and its views monotonous, the interstate repeating itself in the green and brown grasses of the highway waysides blurring into a line, the trees breaking only for exits and pull-offs for hidden cop cars to radar motorists. He saw vehicles of all types pulled over by highway patrolmen, their red-evil lights flashing above black Dodge Chargers, leaner than he remembered them ever being and more sinister. Orange-jacketed prison workers appeared occasionally, peppering the grassy medians in bright blazoned workwear and bright-green gloves, picking up trash and debris, sometimes weed whacking, sometimes mowing, but doing everything in slow motion, it seemed, as the bus hurtled past.

In Charleston, Dalton stopped to stare at the gold dome of West Virginia's state capitol building, buttressed by scaffolding and covered partly with a tarp, no workers or politicians either coming or going. The sun was setting.

He sat down in a newly renovated diner, too nice to be the real thing. It was empty except for the young server playing a game on her cellphone. He ordered a coffee.

A gale of loneliness, or something like it, blew straight into him. He was stretched out all around it like a balloon, was empty except for it—like he was maybe only a tornado in a box. Nothing was pinned down and it was all swirling inside. Messiah. He had left his brother behind.

"You can have as many refills as you want," the waitress told him, "but if you're not gonna eat anything you need to promise to tip me." She smiled as she said this, in a half flirt, then went back to looking down at her phone.

"Just holler if you need anything more," she offered, tapping and swiping. Dalton only knew she was talking to him because no one else was around. He stirred the coffee and looked at her. Then he looked at his coffee, then back at her.

"Have you ever lost anyone in your family?" he blurted.

"None that I was too worried about losing." She smiled again without looking up.

"I'm worried," Dalton said.

"Do you want a refill on your coffee?"

"My mama died. Just this morning."

"Aww, I'm sorry." She put her phone in her apron and glanced nervously at Dalton before stepping behind the counter.

Dalton got up and walked toward the corkboard by the door. He looked at the notices pinned there, gathered up the loose papers and advertorials and tracts on display, then returned to his seat. His mug was full but not steaming. The server had disappeared somewhere in the back. He heard her laughing with the cook.

There was an ad in a newspaper-style publication that seemed to be nothing but ads, and it seemed to call out for anyone to come work.

LOST YOUR JOB? COME WORK FOR US – FAIR PAY – ALL WELCOME – NO CREDIT CHECK – DRUG TEST REQUIRED – FREEDOM WV COAL PROCESSORS – FRIENDS OF COAL

Then, just under it:

> ¿PERDISTE TU TRABAJO? VEN A TRABAJAR PARA NOSOTROS – SUELDO JUSTO – TODOS BIENVENIDOS – SIN VERIFICACIÓN DE CRÉDITO – PRUEBA DE DROGAS REQUERIDA – FREEDOM WV COAL PROCESSORS – AMIGOS DEL CARBÓN

He tore the page out of the paper and folded it up, taking note of the address and directions there. Then he laid five dollars on the counter and left.

Dalton spent the night in the lobby of a big hotel near the capitol building, having told the concierge he was waiting for someone to come check in. He didn't have the energy to try to persuade her of his desperation. He watched the television news all night, half-waiting for a story about his mother's death to run, even here, a couple hundred miles away. Something so momentous, so quiet.

In the morning the concierges switched shifts, the nighttime one pointing at Dalton and explaining his presence to the sleepy-eyed man who replaced her.

When she was gone Dalton approached the reception desk. "It looks like my friend isn't going to come. I don't have my wallet, I lost it somewhere from Fort Drum to here, and it was in a bag with my phone. I appreciate you letting me sit here all night, but is there any chance I could use a room for an hour or two to get my things in order?"

The concierge politely declined, but showed Dalton a guest services corner with maps, attraction brochures, and a phone he could use free of charge. A gym with a free trial.

Dalton found the number for a cab company and dialled it. He unfolded the ad and laid it out in front of him as the agent on the phone explained how to get to Freedom WV Industries and Coal

Processing. She sounded like she was driving, and Dalton had the thought that she might be the only cab in town. She said she'd be there in ten or fifteen.

Dalton made his way through the front gate of the plant. It stood in front of mounds of black and grey dust that stretched back into the deep-green mountains behind it, a beachline cove pushing into a slow-flowing river that ran between all the industry, the trucks and the rusted towers and the chutes, the smokestacks and the flumes and plumes they billowed into the grey mountain air.

The plant's main building almost vibrated in its staleness and sheet-metal sweep. Dalton walked through two steel doors then past a warehouse with steel shelves lined with barrels of chemicals and discarded forklifts scattered throughout its wide expanse. He felt small. The front desk man walked him through a maze of these towering aisles of drums and boxes marked HAZARDOUS and into a drywalled stall at the corner of the building. Another man sat there, in a red trucker hat and a shirt bulging at the buttons. He was smoking intensely and purposefully, speaking sternly into the black phone receiver whose cord he'd wrapped around his giant, non-smoking arm.

"I'll call you back," he said, and set down the phone with a light ring. Dalton adjusted his uniform and smoothed his nametag.

"Habla inglés?" the man asked and frowned, determining whether this was necessary.

"Yes, yes I do," Dalton said. He pointed to his nametag. "I don't really speak Spanish, actually."

"Good. Me either. I do the payroll here. Hirin' and firin'. What can I do for you, Mister, er, what is it, what is that rank?"

"Corporal."

"What can I do for you, Corporal Vasquez?"

"I saw your ad. And I'm responding to it."

"You look like you got a job," the man said. "I mean it looks like you already gainfully employed, my friend. You don't wanna work here, brother. I ain't sure that ad is really for you."

"No sir. No, I do want to work here. It said, well, the thing is I need a job now. Almost today."

The man sat for a second and moved some things around on his desk, as though this was his first time having one of these conversations. He looked uncomfortable.

"Well, Mister, er, Corporal, we don't get a lot of applicants coming in here in uniform. We don't really got a position that gives us a tax break for hiring vets. My name is Wyatt. You can call me Wyatt. You are a vet, ain't you?"

"Soon to be," Dalton said. "My leave ends in a few days."

"And you don't got no job to come home to? You got family around here?"

"My mama died. Recently." He steadied himself.

Save money to go to Canada, he thought. *Get Messiah when you can.* Something about standing still in front of this man's desk made him feel like the past few days were catching up to him.

Wyatt explained that, if he was really interested in the job, it wasn't a very good one. A lot of men he might be working with indeed didn't "hablo anglais," as he put it, and Dalton might find the work not too demanding for a vet, no, but maybe unfulfilling. He got up from his desk and walked around and placed a hand on Dalton's back. Dalton stared at the wall behind where Wyatt had been sitting.

Wyatt got a worker to go fetch another worker to *come here, pronto*. He asked Dalton where he was staying.

"Nowhere, yet."

"Clark! Come here and take this boy to the worker housing. *Yes*, that one. Set him up with the tenant manager and get him a cot or something."

He turned back to Dalton. "Son, thank you for the service. I don't know or want to know what sorta trouble you in, but I look forward to working with you nonetheless. We'll sort out your pay. Don't worry, we'll sort it out."

After a series of doors and warehouse lights trailing overhead, Clark and Dalton stepped out into the noon air. The piles of coal dust were radiating warbling heat and scattered throughout the concrete yard. The mountains of West Virginia loomed, great waves of shadow against the hot blue sky just beyond, poised to come crashing down onto the slim industrial valley. Clark cranked on a diesel truck and told Dalton to hop in.

They drove about five miles on a road cut out of a dip in the hills, pulled into a turnoff unmarked by street signs or otherwise, then headed down a dirt road for half a mile. Finally they pulled into a three-acre red-dirt clearing populated by trailers, tucked away in the woods off the highway that led into Charleston.

Clark stepped into one of the trailers, spoke with the superintendent of the park, and came out again to where Dalton was smoking one of Clark's cigarettes.

"She said she'll get you sorted a little later. It seems she's real busy right now." Clark spit into the dust. "You're in number three."

The two walked past the first ring of trailers, some meant to get towed behind a truck, others more permanent, hoisted up on mounts of bricks or elevated by stacks of old car wheels welded together. A double-wide with a big number 3 painted on its side was situated so that you could drive right up to it, with a view of the forest behind.

Two men smoked outside. "You on the night shift tonight?" Clark asked.

"Si," one said.

"Si," said the other. "Yes."

They nodded at one another and studied Dalton, taking in his uniform. Staring at him as he pulled his duffle from the back of Clark's truck.

Clark muttered "Fuckin' Mexicans" under his breath. "No offence, I mean."

He swung open the trailer's screen door and gestured to Dalton, who nodded to the men and followed Clark in.

A bedroll lay in each of the four corners of its main area, undivided by any kind of wall or blind. The kitchen was at the far end, the bathroom and shower just beyond that. Little towers of plastic drawers stood next to each bedroll, with a duffle or gym bag beside each tiny living section but one. Clark pointed to the available roll on the floor, the only one without a cot, sheetless and tea-stained with sweat.

"This is it," he said.

Clyde

THAT EVENING HE ATE from the tenderloin of the deer he'd hit on the highway, leaning over a campfire down the road from a hunting resort and not far from a trailer park Tyler had often visited to collect alms. He figured he'd go down to the park in the morning and see what he could scrounge up for the service the next day, but for now he'd rest and camp and eat whatever good parts of the doe he could salvage from the mess he'd made of her on the road.

That would be the last of his errands till the morning, when Grace would be expecting him along with the alms, new tidings, and gossip from the parks and hollers in Vesta and Cana, Meadows of Dan. He was parked in a clearing off the side of a winding spur in the road, and from there Clyde could hear music playing in the distance, the bass rattling whatever vehicle contained the noise. He finished carving out the rest of the good meat, put all but a few pieces of salvaged tenderloin and backstrap in an old plastic Walmart bag, and dropped it in his truck bed. He tossed the rest of the carcass into the woods and returned to his fire to cook another portion.

He knew he was on private land, but if anyone told him to move on he could maybe just say he was hiding out from his old lady. Not necessarily untrue. He could say he'd wanted to get a hotel but had lost his wallet. He was always getting ready to lie if it came to it, and it always felt like it was going to come to it.

If he couldn't work up the guts to go back to Grace he'd have to find a new way to live, a new place to stay. The remaining venison was charring on a rock possibly too near the fire. He pulled at the pieces, burning his fingertips, and flipped the tattered steaks over on the hot rock. Then he sharpened the end of a sapling twig and stabbed the meat. As he sat and ate the thin slices he heard whooping and hollering back beyond the treeline, maybe two pastures over, up near the hunting lodge. A party, maybe. Then came a succession of gunshots from the same direction. Then another and another. It sounded like a dozen or more guns going off more or less at once. Automatic guns. Big, high-calibre rifles firing in unison.

If it was a funeral of some kind or a ceremony, he figured he could go and hand out some flyers there. Clyde hadn't considered postering the hunting resort since he couldn't see how anyone there would fit in with Grace's country parish, but he thought he ought to go just to see. The whirr in his head that compelled him to act stupid was humming along as he might expect.

Clyde went back to his truck, put the Ruger in his waistband and some flyers under his arm, and walked toward the voices. He moved slowly, listening for whistling in the leaves that would've told him the bullets were headed his way. No disturbance of that kind. He lost the fire behind him. When another volley of shots was let off into the night Clyde saw a tracer round shoot up into the sky. Who could have access to something like a tracer round?

He broke through about an acre of woods, some of it familiar to him after tracking the doe, but changed now in the deepening twilight. Two clearings, then woods again. The clearings were fear and vulnerability. In the daytime a place where God might go to breathe and meditate, but at night it might be like a turkey shoot. The forest was thick now and his steps were loud.

He was hunched over following a small-game path that made a tunnel through the underbrush. He could hear the voices and laughter of men in the next clearing. It might be better to crawl toward them to see what he was getting himself into but if they caught him like that they might shoot him on the spot, so he kept on as he was, cracking twigs under his feet.

"All right, mister—"

Clyde froze.

"Come on out of there, now. I got a twelve-gauge trained on your dumb ass and if you fuck with me I'm gonna blow your fool head off."

Clyde shouted, "I'm friendly! I just want to talk. Join the tailgate."

"The what?" Clyde heard a lightening in the man's tone. "Just get the fuck outta them trees and come over here."

Clyde stepped through the last few yards of bush and stood up straight with his hands in the air. A man in his forties approached him, walking heavy and breathing hard, chuckling to himself through wheezes. He was wearing full battle rattle as if he'd just come back from Iraq, but he was so out of shape and round in the middle that he looked more like an overgrown toddler playing dress-up. A lookout guard or scout.

"I been watching you for about fifty yards now, sneaking around. Thought you was a black bear. Lucky I didn't shoot your stupid ass."

"I was camping out with my truck a few hundred yards back that way," Clyde said. "I got a stack of flyers here for a church. I was hoping to see if you all would like to join us."

"What kind of church sends you out to Pulliam Resort at nine o'clock?"

"Only need a minute of your time, that's all."

The man let the shotgun hang from its sling and clapped his hands. "You armed?"

"No," Clyde lied, "just the flyers."

"All right then, go on over there and talk to them. You lucked out, son. I woulda been just fine to kill you."

Clyde stumbled out onto the manicured lawn of what looked almost like a golf course, but the only building was way up on a hill, behind a bonfire that lit up fifteen or twenty men in fatigues. The fire reached higher than a storey or more in its flames. It was something miraculous. To the east stood a line of pickup trucks parked in an orderly way.

The guard shouted over to them, "Friendly approaching! Hey! You got a visitor coming up your way!" And despite or maybe because of the warning the men dropped their cups and spun toward Clyde, fumbling their weapons and steadying them, their stances wide.

"Don't fucking shoot him!" shouted the guard. Clyde was sure, then, that he was going to be shot. He approached the men with his hands up, holding out the flyers for Grace's revival like a white flag.

"Hey, *visitor*, why didn't you show up at muster time?" said the first man he approached. "Where's your weapon? Where's your gear?"

The only man without a weapon and fatigues whistled and gestured for the others to lower their rifles. As Clyde entered the halo of the fire, the man, regal and silver in the moon and bonfire light, passed him a cup of corn liquor and welcomed him with a nod. Clyde nodded in return, took the cup and downed it, then tossed it into the fire. He thought he recognized the man but couldn't place him. When he nodded again the man patted him on the shoulder. The militia members around the fire looked briefly at their visitor then went on talking and smoking.

The tall man in civilian dress said to Clyde, "All right now. Go ahead. Where are you from and what are you here for? Did you hear about the muster and you're late, coming the backasswards wrong way through the woods, or are you some kind of lunatic?" He said all this with a smile.

"Just heard the party through the woods. I was camping off the parkway. Heard what sounded like a gun salute. Thought I'd come and tell y'all about a revival we've got going on not far from here. Up Buffalo Mountain near Meadows of Dan."

"Lemme see that." The man gestured for Clyde to hand him a flyer. "Oh, Grace! Well, no kidding and I'll be damned. You working for Pastor Grace, then?"

"Yes sir." Clyde checked his voice and posture. He didn't want to seem too eager to appease the man, but there was something about him that put Clyde in his place whether he liked it or not. The man had a voice full of gravitas and authority.

"Well, now. Me and Grace go back a long way. You might have known her daughter, Jane. She was a good friend of mine. Grace, too. We've known each other for a few long years. Happy to see she's still preaching. I'll hang on to this and think about what I can do to help her ministry. I guess you better get to handing out the rest of them flyers."

The man shooed Clyde away with his eyebrows, a full-toothed smile, and another head nod that said *Go on, git!* Like he was a dog being scurried out of a kitchen. "Don't worry," the man said as Clyde restacked the papers and looked around. "These men are good people. They won't bite. All right, then . . ." The man trailed off and turned from Clyde toward a group of musterers.

Some of the men really tried to read their flyer. Some folded it up and stuck it in their pocket. Some threw theirs into the fire.

"Hold on now," Clyde said to those who scoffed at him. "Have y'all ever even *been* to a revival?"

The men had indeed been to one or two, they reassured him. And some even claimed to have cousins who were attendees of Pastor Grace's Church of the Redeemer, as this particular flyer called it. Clyde had given it that name only a few days ago.

And so he felt this encounter to be a strange homecoming, one where he or someone just like him had come through already, evangelizing and making meek attempts at recruiting. And yet these men were already well recruited. They were organized and self-measured, confident as to where they stood in relation to God and Country. But less confident as to why they stood so, Clyde thought. None seemed to want to volunteer just what they were doing there.

He worried at first that he might have stumbled on a Klan rally. Perhaps the burning cross was sitting in ashes, smouldering now at the bottom of the roaring fire. But there were no hoods among the men. No need to disguise themselves. None of the cowardice that accompanies that particular sort of backwoods bigotry. They seemed open in their enthusiasm for their military regalia and the chance to wield big guns. His arrival had energized them, as though they were putting on a show for his benefit, performing how righteous this little ceremony was, how natural.

He approached a big, grizzled man with inset eyes and a harried expression. Like he was shocked. Like every minute he lived was just after he'd seen a ghost. The man's mouth was agape, staring at the fire.

"Howdy," Clyde said. He handed the man a flyer and watched him read it, mouthing the words as he went.

"A revival, huh. I like me some good, old-time church." He scratched his beard and tugged on it. "Friend, do you want to really see God?"

"I guess that's what we're trying to do," Clyde said. "Bring everyone a little closer to Him, you know, the Lord."

"Well, shit. Here, eat some of these."

The man held out some sticky grey mushrooms and gestured to Clyde to pop them in his mouth. Clyde did so. The whole handful. They weren't dried as he'd seen before, but slimy and wet, as though they'd just come off a cow patty. They tasted awful.

"Warsh 'em down with this here." The man gave Clyde a pull

from his flask. Moonshine. It, too, unaged and sharp. The combination didn't help. Just made Clyde's eyes water as he gulped it back to keep it all from coming up.

"Yeah, I see what you've got going on," the man said. He crumpled up the flyer and threw it into the fire as some of the others had. "Seen flyers like this before. People living out near an old-time revival that doesn't move. Seen that before. You ever hear of Elohim City?"

"I think so. Maybe? Sounds sort of familiar."

The man seemed more irritated than surprised. "Ever hear of the Oklahoma City bomber?"

"Yessir, I read the news."

"Okay well, never mind, then. You all don't seem like the kind of people we need. Nobody here gonna care about some kind of woman preacher. A big storm's a comin' and we need women who can cook and make children. Preachin's a man's job."

"Hold on a minute, now. I'm just asking if y'all would like to come up and attend our service. I think you'll see that Pastor Grace is one of a kind."

Clyde was still fighting to keep the liquor and mushrooms down, but felt his shoulders relax a little. "We're friendly as you can imagine," he continued. "And thank you for the drink. I didn't mean to get off on the wrong foot there, I just wasn't connecting any dots. I asked if you wanted to come to church, and, well, I guess I just couldn't piece the rest together."

"You already drunk then, I guess. Hope you're staying in the woods tonight, buddy, because I don't know if you're going to be able to drive after them mushrooms settle in. You said you wanna talk to God, well, you're about to meet him."

The man spit tobacco into the fire and wiped his mouth with the back of his gloved hand. "I asked because I was thinking this was maybe meant to be. Maybe it's the case that God brought you out here to talk to us. We're waiting for a bit of a sermon ourselves. I think you'd like to meet Mr. Hickok, and I think he'd like to talk to you. Probably will after he gives us a little sermon himself."

"Hickok," Clyde said. "Is he a pastor?"

"Sure is." The man made a big show of finishing his flask and smacking his tongue and sighing. "Ahhhhh, that's good," he said. "He's gonna run for office. We're thinking of starting up a kind of new township out here off the parkway, maybe near Fancy Gap, maybe somewhere near Kibler Valley. I dunno."

"Like Elohim City?" Clyde asked, but he was preoccupied now with the man in the golf shirt milling around the crowd across the way from the fire. *Hickok, Pastor Hickok. Jane's pastor,* he thought.

"Well, look at you—maybe you're not the dullest knife in the drawer after all."

Clyde looked back at the man. He smiled at Clyde condescendingly. The fire was reflecting off his wide eyes, burning inside his big pupils. He spit again into the fire. He had an upside-down American flag patch affixed to his tactical vest. America in distress. He wore another patch on his arm, this one with a cross, a sword, a shield, and a snake all bound up together. Most of the men were dressed similarly, but not uniformly. Punisher skull stickers on their guns. Crosses and swords and shields and snakes. Clyde thought he saw the snake on the patch move, slithering along the sword and tightening its body around it.

"Y'all part of a group of some kind?" Clyde asked.

"All part of the same group as you. Ain't you a Christian?"

"Yes, I am a member of this church right here in the flyer." The conversation was getting muddied. Clyde didn't know if he was missing what the man was saying or the other way round.

"Are you a cop?"

Clyde started to feel dizzy. He watched the thin smoke from the fire trail up into the sky, joining with the mist blowing off the top of the Blue Ridges. That fog itself, thin now and fast-moving, was high up from where they were in the Kibler Valley, but it seemed not too far away from the Milky Way itself. It was as though the fire they stood by was supplying all this spread-out haze of soft white that pulled across the sky.

Now Clyde scanned the men around the fire. Many were crowding around the only man other than himself not in fatigues. Hickok: broad, handsome, older. Maybe in his late fifties. Jane's Hickok, then. That Jim.

Clyde felt a tug of anger as though it was pulling at the nape of his neck, urging him to get mad. To be defensive. He craned his neck back to the sky, the Milky Way like dried semen on dark silk sheets. Jane. Her thighs. The white smoothness of her thighs on the dark bed, his hands and face running over the tight fat of them. He felt himself getting an erection, feeling bad underneath the sourness in his gut. He tugged on the front of his pants and fixed his slackened jaw, feeling the beard, three days old, growing out. His unkempt facade hiding who he'd become. Grace's Clyde. Jane's Clyde. The freckled sky was the hair on his jaw, his beard dragging itself across Jane's body. Her legs on the shiny dark sheets. The softness of them, unroughed by sun. His legs, gone now, to the earth and planted in the ground. Her legs in the thin air, borne away and mixing with the smoke, the fog.

Then a thousand images and memories buried beneath the years of disciplined effort at forgetting came crawling out of the sky before him like spiders out of an egg sac. Jane's thighs, the sheets, the preacher, his smile, the whiteness of the church steeple and the whiteness of her body, his grease-stained hands running up the flesh of them, through to the hair of her ankles up to the hair of her thatch there, where she was, where his heart was, there where she would swallow him up like the Rapture, pulling him back into where he came from, where she came from, up to her mother then up to Grace and to God. Had he been raptured? He'd been pulled into the darkness. He'd been swallowed up by it all. All long gone. The

Saturday afternoon reveries, whiskey-breathed and stiff and musky, and maybe he'd never come back down to his heart. He checked now to see if it was beating. It was beating fast. He'd known that he'd been gone then, floating through some darkness, never finding the end.

He looked back over to Hickok. The fire was dancing on his wide, clean-shaven face, orange in the firelight. Clyde was watching the man he'd shared her with, standing now in a cleared field surrounded by guns. And where was his consolation? Where was Grace? The effigies of her work, her name, falling apart now in the roaring flames before him.

He heard a voice close by as though from underwater. The man next to him had been monologuing about Elohim City and a new church and a new state. Christians and whites. None of it had registered with Clyde. He just nodded along. Tried to look at Hickok again in the blurry firelight.

"Well, you know all about that. Just like you said, know all about it," the man said, finally breaking through to Clyde. "Well. We got somethin' goin' on here, that's for sure. Started out as a regular militia muster we'd have every once in a while. It's growing though. We all know each other now, more or less. Talk on Facebook and on forums. Internet. People here from around the Blue Ridge, people from the Piedmont too, North Carolina. We try to get together about once a month to stay well-regulated. I don't wanna say too much though. You just talk to Mr. Hickok, and he'll sort you out."

"Is this still a—a hunting resort?" Clyde said, stupidly. He was trying to come back to earth. "I went skeet shooting around here a few years back."

"Yeah, it is. The tail end of one. Pulliam Resort. Twelve thousand acres. Owner's a friend of Mr. Hickok. We set this fire up just between state and private land for the meetings. But you know, all the land belongs to the people of this country, not the politicians and bureaucrats. Ain't no such thing as federal land, state land. You gotta go through here to get to the fenced-off public access point anyway. Kind of makes it like you can't get there at all without permission from the Pulliams. Anyway, it's all fenced off. I guess except the part you came in from. Squirrelly sonofabitch, ain't you?

"Cops really can't come in without breaking some of their own laws. Some of these guys are cops anyway. They told us that they can't come on in. Need to be invited. Them's the rules, you know. We ain't breakin' any laws that matter. We're just waitin' to hear what Mr. Hickok's gotta say and then I figure we will fall out for the month. You missed a helluva good muster." He trailed off again and fingered his weapon.

"Boy am I high as hell," the man said. "What about you?"

"I'm . . . I'm just gonna listen to what Hickok has to say and then I guess I'll be on my way," Clyde said.

And as though on cue, the tall, broad man in a golf shirt and khakis stood up on a overturned milk crate and cleared his throat. Some men knelt before him. Others shushed one another. Before he spoke there was only the sound of the crackling fire.

"Patriots," he said, "there are more of us coming to these humble gatherings each month. And for that I'd like to thank you. Some of you are old friends and some new. If all the world is at an impasse—which, I assure you, it is—if all the world has turned on itself, people turned on each other, on their neighbours, what is it then that pulls us toward one another so? What is it that brings us together here, under God's vast expanse of sky, by the roaring fire of the primordial knowledge and understanding, all this peace above and scorching destruction below, what is left, my friends, other than true brotherhood to bind us?

"We have said, many of us, *God and Country, God and Country, God and Country* until our eyes bleed. But what do we mean when we say Country now? Do we mean the nation? The state? What can deliver real power to that concept other than the God that undergirds it? He who gives it strength? He who gives us what we have mistakenly called progress? No, there is only God left. God and the people of the faith. What other than the people who form it, this Country of ours, can shape it? What and who other than the people who hear the beck and call of the Lord are here and strong enough to make it real?"

At this Hickok began pacing back and forth in front of the fire, and the men all around it slowly fell into a loose formation before him. More men looked down as though they were praying, but really, Clyde thought, they were thinking about the wet grass and their knees before they knelt. Some did so. They were rapt in their attention to his words, nodding and touching their hearts. Clyde resisted any kind of movement that would draw attention to himself, but still felt unable to blend in; the mass of camouflaged men seemed too aware of his presence. He may be imagining their suspicion but stood as still as possible anyway, trying to mimic their enthusiastic, masculine gestures of affirmation as the preacher spoke.

The preacher, Clyde thought, *son of a bitch*. And he was there again, with her. With her and her boys. Sunday mornings hurrying them in and out of the shower. The whiteness of the boys, too. Sick and soft like pneumonia patients. The young one light-haired and uneasy. Shy. Messiah. The older one dark-haired and brooding. Baggy clothes and chains with all kinds of evil shit on his T-shirts. Dalton. His eyes like the tops of old wells, dark and still and wet. Had he done enough for those boys in those fuzzy years?

Damn this Hickok, he thought. He'd never attended church with Jane but had accompanied her and her two boys to a few of its events. Picnics in the park, fundraiser auctions, estate sales. Maybe a funeral. He'd always been half-cut and aloof, somewhere between guarded and discontented anytime he'd been coerced into going, into acting like a husband out there with the pretty church ladies and their brown-necked children in polo shirts. He knew about Hickock and Jane. But he hadn't done anything to stop it, and all he

would have had to do was stick around. Be a man. *That's always how you deal with it,* he thought, *fuck off, go and run away*.

The fire was quieting now, and the man's voice seemed to blend with it. Hickok was smiling and looking at Clyde. Knowing in his eyes.

"We have stood up for what we believe in," Hickok was saying. "For what we have always believed. But when the nation is corrupt, and the government is soon to be discovered for what it is, divorced from the God of its founding, dissolved and absolved of its merits, then there will be nothing left but brotherhoods such as ours. Small, new nations such as ours. Proud nations of people who remember. People of real faith, of real belief in what we used to call America. What could be America still. But the time now is calling for action.

"We want to start a new church, yes? A new community. Well, something will have to be done about all this invasion, all this segregation and disintegration. We need our brothers and sisters to be under one big tent, one church, one government. One new community here in the mountains. I am working on these elements, but you all need to be my strength. You all are called, now, to be the arm and sword of the Lord."

This line wrenched up grins on the surrounding men. They began jabbing one another with elbows and jawing their chaw more enthusiastically. Like he was talking directly to them about something Clyde didn't quite understand. The arm and the sword.

Hickok continued: "And look at you, all of you, you men in the dress and stature of America's wars. You *are* in a war now, my friends. You are in a war with the future, and the future is against you. The future is now, and the future has abandoned Christ on the cross, and the heathen hordes are at the gates. And what will we do about it?"

Fight! the men yelled together.

It was raining now. A storm was gathering overhead as if fuelled by fire smoke and Blue Ridge fog, building up above them. Lightning popped quietly in the clouds. Hickok grew taller now among the

shrinking flames. His laughing mouth broadened. Clyde felt that if he could shine a light into the preacher's mouth he'd be able to see all the way through to the other end of the world. He wanted to reach into it. Down deep into the man's jaw, all the way to the beginning of the world where there was nothing but darkness. This is what Grace had spoken about. The maw of the beast. All that's given, taketh away.

He wanted to climb in there, into the man's mouth, to crawl in there and go back to the beginning of time. The opposite of the Rapture. The devil swallowing you whole. This was the force against which Grace wanted him to fight, this yearning for the belly of the beast.

"These musters are not just for drinking beer and making friends." Hickok laughed. A stage laugh. The laugh of a politician. "No, these are to train and to practise for the coming End. To build toward purpose. To build toward strength. Not just in your body, friends, not just the strength of your body. But the strength of your convictions. The strength of your morals and the strength of our principles.

"The talk about a new township here, my brothers and friends, is ongoing. I have been speaking with the Pulliam family who owns much of this land. Half the land off the parkway from Vesta to Fancy Gap, from Meadows of Dan down to Stuart, a little more than half of that is Pulliam land, and he's looking to give it a home. To give our mission its own mandate. To give us the rights we deserve and need. To let our families worship, to let our constitution thrive, and to drive forward the sword into the belly of the future and pierce it with history. With a little grace . . ." He paused, and, as though Hickok could slow time, he cut his speech there, Clyde could have sworn, wrenched his head right toward Clyde and froze the flames behind him. Hickok winked and winked, slow and torturous. Clyde was sure he heard the tin echo of Hickok's eyelids touching, could see the heat and spark of taunting provocation

burst from his face. Then everything resumed. The ex-preacher continued:

"And with a little luck, we will start the next chapter of this movement where it should have always begun: a fellowship here, in God's country. In the Blue Ridge where the mist only just barely covers the miracle of life, the reality of freedom as we know it. As we want it. I am working to found a church here to suit our needs, and we will work together to build it. The new America needs a place to worship. Amen!"

Amen!

Clyde was clenching his teeth so hard he thought they might snap. He pulled a lighter out of his pocket and wrapped his fist around it. *A sword in the belly of the beast.*

"And the rest will follow suit. The world has yet to witness how far our eyes can see from these hilltops, how fertile are these valleys. Stay now in communion. Eat something with each other and welcome any new brother you might see among you, because you are now in the foxhole together. The time for playing around is soon to come to an end. It may not be us who makes the first move; it may be the government as it stands, but we will gain a foothold in the foothills, and we will climb the mountain to glory. Amen!"

Amen!

And as Hickok stepped down from the milk crate, Clyde straightened his shoulders and lunged at him through the fire.

The next few moments were a tangling of huge snakes falling down on him, the firelight flashing through the knots of grunting figures pulling at him and dragging him through the grass and ash of the fire.

"Don't hit him! Don't you dare strike this man," Hickok was yelling somewhere out in the darkness. Clyde's face was pressed into the soft, damp T-shirt of one of the men's bellies. Armpits and chests, wet and heaving and laughing and wheezing. "Get him over here," Hickok ordered.

They pulled Clyde closer to the fire where Hickok was still standing. "Look at him!" he heard one of them say. "Here, wrap him up in this."

A sheet of some kind was pulled around Clyde's arms like a straitjacket, and the man he'd been talking to earlier pulled up Clyde's chin and showed him what he was wrapped in. A Confederate flag, wet and sopping, covered in ash and mud.

"Okay, men, hold on," Hickok said. "Let me speak to him."

Clyde was lying on his side, his arms tied up in the flag with a corner laid out before his eyes, muddied by the sooty ground. Hickok leaned down and spoke quietly.

"Well, now. I was looking forward to running into you, but I didn't want to have to break it to you like this. Quite surprised to see you here after what Grace has told me. And I must say that I never liked you much, Clyde—all I heard about you makes me sad to know. But like I said I'm happy to break some news to you myself.

"This whole thing you've got going on with Grace—that little pissant church and all the trash up there is going to get cleaned up." Hickok was almost whispering now, talking right into Clyde's ear. "We're going to take that mountain and turn it into a new world, you understand? This whole side of the Blue Ridge is about to be a real place of God. The entire country is going to shit, and we need a new nation. Do you understand me?" Then he shouted, "A new nation!"

The men around them erupted in shouts and stomps and whoops. Hickok relished it for a second, then said, "Now, we're gonna let you go. You just go on up there and get your things and leave. It would behoove you to do just that. Grace isn't gonna need you around anymore. You just leave it at that."

Part II

Dalton

FREEDOM INDUSTRIES
4-METHYLCYCLOHEXANEMETHANOL

THE BARRELS SHOUTED AT HIM. There were toxin signs and warnings, too, all of it making Dalton feel ragged and dirty and sick of swishing the partly emptied barrels with water, washing off equipment in the mixture, then pouring out the rest into the Elk River. He watched the oily, sudsy water tumble and swirl toward Charleston.

Every little bit of the shiny minerals, these gold flakes as they called them, was glittering out from the dirt and dust, distinguishing itself among the little mountains of soot just to tease him. Sinister, knowing where it had all come from, dug up from the earth and put somewhere it didn't belong. Valueless and ethereal. Picked up and carried by the wind and water. The guilt in the process, the poisonous procedure of coal power; it flowed downstream and through the air.

The other men worked around him diligently, as if they were digging a grave for a family member. They weren't tired of it, he thought, not spiritually tired. Did the guilt not get to them? All this stabbing and digging up, the drilling and sifting and washing off of

toxins; they'd spit into piles of black dust and the wet would sizzle in the sunlight like an egg just cracked, disagreeing with the air and with their work. The guilt piled up in him like those black mounds in the sorting yard. But it was as though no one else could see it. No one else felt it. Dalton watched for any hesitation among the men who laboured next to him, any understanding or knowing of what they'd done, what they were doing to the earth, to themselves, to their families.

He thought he was dying of it, was absolutely littered and filled with black. He blew his nose and the black came out. More black dust than snot. Each little fine particle was like a tiny devil getting into you and you could never exorcise it afterward. Not entirely. It was part and parcel of him now—the gold flakes and chemicals and dehydrated work and cramped muscles, the easy pay and the "Hey don't worry" that the foreman would utter—it was all amassing into a black congestion that stopped up his brain and his heart. It was rotten, and he knew that the soot and ash he was moving around that country was in him. Was blowing everywhere and pouring out into everybody else.

Dalton hadn't tried to contact Messiah in the year or so since his mama's death. He'd disappeared himself as best he could.

He worried about his brother during his long days out in the sorting yard. Messiah's image was all around him. His voice in the echo of a slammed-shut iron hitch, the finality of the truck full of waste, the cloud of fly ash and silica in its wake, in his eyes; Messiah in his eyes; Messiah in his dreams late at night, in his sleepy haze when he and his bunkmates were woken up to drive out to the river to dump waste into the stream; Messiah was in the stream, playing in the water, the gold flakes sticking to his skin, smeared with ash and burned red with runoff; each gold flake in the mound of ash was a devil's wink from hell, popping out at Dalton, reminding him that all this, all the winds and streams of ash and

memory, led back to where Messy was. The tributaries of memory. All led from him to where Messy was. Where Dalton wasn't.

He wondered sometimes why no one had come looking for him, someone to force him to face the problem. But after a year, maybe more than a year, of monotonous rotation from trailer to yard, from yard to river, from the adit of the mine to the truck, from the truck to his cot and bedroll in the trailer, from the bedroll to his dreams, from his dreams to the trailer, from the trailer to the yard—no one came looking until one morning, just after sorting began, Dalton was called back into Wyatt's office.

He walked between the grey mounds of ash and pulverized coal piled neatly around the yard, then through the same door he'd walked in a year before.

"Glad you're here, er, Corporal," the boss said. "Listen, and I want to be clear that this has nothing to do with me. You keep your head down and I appreciate that. We got all sorts of men here who gotta keep their heads down. Of course I appreciate that. The problem comes only when the problem sees fit, and today you're the problem for me."

This was rehearsed. Wyatt lit a cigarette and straightened in his chair. "I figure we need to talk. I got some bad news today." He blew out a long pull of smoke from his nose. "I guess some strange news. I'm going to tell you something that I don't need to get around and, well I don't think it will matter too much to you soon anyway. But it does concern you. I got a tip that we're about to be hounded by the sons of bitches in D.C. about our payroll and who's on it. Ah, you know." He laughed now to make it seem easy. He was sweating. "You know this happens all the time. The thing that bothers me is that just as I put the phone down about that I got another call. It was from the goddamned Army, some kind of lawyer. He wanted to know, and I am going to repeat this exactly, if I had a, wait, Dalton Fuckway working here. I said, 'No sir, I do not,' and that was that."

Dalton sat uneasily in his chair. Wyatt put his cigarette out early, stabbing it dramatically into a bottle cap upturned on his desk.

"And I got *another* call. It was the fuckin' Red Cross asking the same thing. Now, do you know why I might've gotten all these calls on the same day, Mr. Vasquez?"

Dalton stayed silent but shook his head. He looked down at his lap.

"Well neither do I. But I am beginning to suspect that all this shit is coming from the same place. I got a runaway AWOL Army guy here and now we're going to have the NLRB come and count heads and who knows what else. Do you understand why this is a problem?"

Dalton nodded.

"I cut you a break, you know. You got a job, a place to stay. You can save some money and work when you want. What you do with it and how you pay the taxes on it and all, that is your business. We just contract out. My hands are clean. Maybe I'm a little stupid for giving you a job but they always say we gotta hire veterans, support the troops. And you come in without any resumé or anything, I figure this is the best I can do."

Wyatt lit another cigarette and stood halfway up, hiking his pants. He nudged the oscillating fan next to him and it started rattling on the desk.

"I didn't like how you showed up with your uniform on. I didn't like how you didn't seem to have any concerns about where you were or what you'd be doing, but I figured hey, what the hell do I know? Maybe he's a PTSD guy or somethin'. I thought maybe you were a gambler. I don't know. But I'll tell you what, I'm starting to think that your name ain't Vasquez, and I'm startin' to think that you're a little more trouble than you're worth."

Dalton looked at the nicotine-yellow floor between his ash-covered boots.

"So, this is what we're going to do. I'm going to give you this envelope here and you're going to take it. I'm going to erase you from the payroll, regular or irregular, whatever. I want you to take this envelope here and get the hell out of Freedom, and, if I could offer my advice, right the hell out of West Virginia if I was you. How does that sound, Dalton?"

Messiah

"GIMME HERE THAT string you found—I'll make a necklace," the Perkins boy said. Only then did Messiah notice he was pulling loose string up from the fraying carpet.

"No, wait, I don't want to do that," the boy said. "Let's go for a drive down near the railroad tracks." He paused. "You hear me? Why don't you listen when I talk?"

The older boy was getting restless, the energy of his angst mixing with everything in the room. Messiah listened to the rustling of the boy's shaking legs. Old episodes of *Looney Tunes* played at low volume on the TV screen. The flat symphonics reminded him of French toast, which, in another life, he almost always got on Saturday mornings when he was little, at least when things were good. Dalton piling up more French toast on his plate while his mother slept in. Messiah being very careful not to puncture the Styrofoam plates they used to make fewer dishes. He was hungry for that now, that feeling of peace. French toast mornings—his brother.

"Hey! I'm talking to you! Is *anyone* listening to me in this house?" the boy said with an air of exasperation that seemed put on. The mimicry of adults at the end of their rope.

At just about fifteen years old, Messiah had aged into one of the oldest boys in the state-run children's home, then was bureaucratically ushered out into a "transitional family," the Perkins household, who agreed to foster him until he finished high school. "Paperwork's still in the mail," the mother had said. "Don't you go giving us any trouble and we'll see about keeping you. Could use the money, son, not the trouble." That was about all any adult had expressed to him since he'd shown up a few weeks earlier. Messiah had tried to sit still and stay out of everyone's way, like a pudgy piggy bank being told not to break open till things were set in stone. He kept mostly to himself.

But he *had* tried. He'd insisted, to anyone who would listen, from the very first day that he'd learned of his mother's passing, that he had a brother to call. He had the number for Dalton's Army unit. He had Dalton's now-inactivated cellphone number. But no one could get ahold of Dalton. Pastor Graham had tried too, asking the men in the local community college ROTC office if there was a way they could help find Dalton. It was to no avail. Graham had said the office was reluctant to share personal information, even in an emergency. "Put in a Red Cross request," everyone had said. Except that it seemed no one knew what that process was or how it would work.

But Messiah hadn't given up. He called a local recruiter, digging the number out of a local Yellow Pages in the waiting room of some doctor or social worker's office, pretending to be eighteen and feigning interest in joining up like his brother had, but also surreptitiously inquiring about Dalton, asking the recruiter if he knew him, had ever heard of him. The recruiter laughed into the phone.

"Is he dead?" Messiah had asked, and the recruiter stopped laughing and apologized. Then, in a last-ditch effort, Messiah had asked the recruiter to look him up. The recruiter said he would if he could, but the database was so big that the best he could do was get

the local police on the case. Messiah dropped the charade and started choking into the phone. He asked if the recruiter at least might pass on the news of his mother's death to his brother. He didn't remember how the rest of the conversation had gone but was given the number for the local Red Cross.

Messiah took that Red Cross number and gave it to his new caseworker, then the next new one, another caseworker, another one still. The sweet, busy, sugary women. They made a lot of promises. But Messiah was outgrowing his bunk at the boys' home, and he had to return to school. A report finally came, a judge handing down an order. Messiah was delivered the news by an unfamiliar social worker who said simply that his file, his search for guardianship, had been closed.

From the Red Cross report they learned that Dalton had been discharged; that he'd been transported in a military vehicle to a bus station near Fort Drum. The log read, *Pvt. Fuquay (Discharge: OTH) escorted to Greyhound Bus Station, 127 Arcade St., Watertown, NY,* and was dated only days before his mother had passed away. The police had told the social worker that they were still looking for Dalton, but suggested it was best that other arrangements be made for Messiah. The social worker patted Messiah on the back and told him to pack, to get ready to meet his new parents. She said, "I know that's hard to hear."

Messiah was told that this new home would be a new start, and that he'd have all his needs met. He'd be back in school and could start classes where'd he left off. But he was already behind.

The Perkins boy started talking again, and Messiah felt as if he'd woken up.

"Well, let's go on a drive up the parkway," the boy was saying. Messiah hadn't bothered to remember this boy's name among all the foster children in that crowded house, but he was sure he actually belonged to the Perkins parents. "I know a swimming hole off the Dan River—a place where a hundred little creeks and streams

meet," he said. "It's off the parkway near the Pulliam lodge. My daddy used to take me huntin' up there." He was talking very proud. A skinny, stretched-out prince of unfolded laundry piles, sticky kids, and cat piss.

Messiah's mama had dropped him off at homes like this when he was a kid. Sometime before she trusted Dalton to start looking after him. Homes where babysitters promised parents low fees along with home-cooked meals that by the end of the summer almost always turned into microwaved hot dogs or cold macaroni and cheese chased with jugs of home-mixed juice and off-brand Rice Krispie squares. He'd always been nervous without Dalton and hated these places. Now he felt like a giant among babies, overgrown and stinking through his T-shirt. Was this how far behind he was? Gym shorts sticking to the inside of his thighs.

When he heard the number of foster children in the Perkins's home Messiah had fantasized about a huge, colonial-style house with plenty to do, basketball courts nearby, maybe four-wheelers. But it was the same old stale, hot, vinyl-sided house he'd always known. The same feeling. The stomach aches and loneliness. He felt he deserved it, somehow. Not too distinct from the Bible camp or the boys' home except it felt like he was piled among more kids and more talk, more dirt and more clothes rarely washed. And he felt so alone.

The operation was run by Mrs. Perkins, a woman not taller than five feet and a half but who moved with the fatigue of a just-from-training bodybuilder. That physical exhaustion was on her like a wet jacket she couldn't take off and moved with her like chains she was condemned to drag behind her forever.

Messiah counted around fifteen children living and staying in that house. He figured six were her own and the rest were either fosters or something like long-term babysitting stays.

Her husband worked in construction. And when this fact about his new foster father was first told to Messiah he imagined the muscular

image of the jackhammer-riding worker, with big arms and a prominent chin. He was hoping Mr. Perkins would be strong and caring. Funny in an old movie kind of way. Catcalling women in city steam, hard hat tilted maybe with a toothpick in his mouth. He saw all this in black and white and was satisfied with it, the construction.

Instead, and this was immediately clear to Messiah, Mr. Perkins was worn and tired, shuffling around their home with the same exhausted movements and belly sighs of his wife, but skinny and empty like an old pop straw with cracks in it. Mr. Perkins never paid much attention to the children who haunted and crowded his house. He hunched and he drank and he occasionally shouted at them, seeming to have difficulty remembering their names. Another foster had said, slyly and not without condescension, that Mr. Perkins's job was to flip the two-sided STOP or SLOW sign for the county's roadway workers, and that was a good job because you could do it drunk.

The smell of kid spit and dust and general uncleanliness of children crawling around on an unvacuumed carpet with the cats permeated the whole of the house, sank into their clothes. The whole place smelled.

"So," the Perkins boy said. "What do you say we get out of here? I'm allowed to drive the truck, you know. I can drive that old thing anywhere I want, when I want. I'd bet you'd like to get out somewhere. You wanna go somewhere with me?"

"Yeah, I don't like it in here, really." Messiah spoke as though he had a choice in putting up with it. "TV isn't great. All these kids want to watch is old cartoons. Better at the home I was at. We had cable."

"Why don't you go on back there, then?" the boy said. "Go on back to your orphanage, then."

Messiah said, "I can't. Too old. Gotta transition. They said I couldn't stay." He was speaking very matter-of-factly.

The Perkins son had the long arms and legs of a man but the birdlike chest of a boy, an exaggerated nose, and a short forehead

that crinkled when he spoke. Messiah was careful around him for reasons unclear to himself. He saw this older boy as wielding a kind of influence that could be either very good or very bad. Messiah almost couldn't bear to look at him, because when he did he thought of Dalton.

"Okay, well, we ought to pack a bag," the boy said.

"Can I borrow one of yours?"

"Yeah, sure. Come in here." He motioned to the master bedroom, such as it was. The two stepped over the clothes at the threshold and the Perkins boy shooed away a sick-looking cat. He opened up his parents' closet.

"Here, put this in it, and this, this too. Okay. This too." The boy began rummaging through a closet that held piled fishing gear, jackets, underwear, tools, towels, and a couple of old rifles. He stopped stuffing the bag and held the rifle, looking at Messiah with wide eyes.

"You ever shoot a gun before?" Messiah shook his head no. "It ain't loaded," the boy said, and pointed the rifle at Messiah, who closed his eyes and pressed his hands to his ears. The gun clicked, and the boy started to laugh.

"You're a little pussy ain't you?" Messiah shook his head again and started looking in a set of drawers, hoping to find swim shorts. The boy cocked and clicked the rifle, still pointing it at him and saying "Bang! Bang!" under his breath in a stage whisper. Then the boy put the gun away and started rummaging again through the closet, still laughing.

"I ain't a pussy," Messiah said.

"Well, I pointed a gun at you and you covered your ears. What the hell you think that was gonna do?"

"I dunno. Don't do that to me."

"It's okay, you— I didn't mean to bug you. Maybe you ain't a pussy. I guess we'll see."

"How we gonna see?" Messiah said curtly, hoping the boy wasn't going to touch the gun again, or worse, make Messiah do something to prove him wrong.

"We'll just go on up to the swimming hole and we'll see."

"Any extra swim trunks?"

"No, we don't need those. Now c'mon and pack up your bag quick, we're not gonna get there for a while. I know how to get there and all, but just in case, we gotta go soon before he gets home."

He meant Mr. Perkins. Messiah had seen the man drunk and in an isolated rage, mad and yelling at the television or slobbering at his wife, grabbing at her or anything he thought was her—anything from a coat rack to a reclining chair. Children crying. Mr. Perkins throwing beer cans and cans of baked beans around the kitchen.

Messiah wasn't nervous about being on the receiving end of that anger but saw that the boy might be. Maybe he wasn't allowed to take the truck after all; maybe he was just bullshitting to impress him. Messiah steeled himself, knowing now the risk they were taking.

With their bags swung over their shoulders, they walked past two little boys sitting in cartoon-patterned pyjamas. "Open them windows! It smells like cat shit in here," the Perkins boy ordered. With their eyes staying glued to the television, it was as if the volume had increased in the living room.

"Go! Open them windows or I'm going to throw you out in the damned yard!" he hollered, wide-striding over to them with a huff and ripping the remote from one of the boys' hands. Acting like his daddy. He began bonking them on the head with it and they cried. The other boy began picking up toys and pieces of toys and food and throwing it all at Messiah and the Perkins boy, who was laughing now. The other fled on his hands and knees and was crying bloody murder, visibly pissing himself and shaking.

They stopped in the kitchen to load up on food. Messiah climbed on the countertop to get to the top cupboards, pushing aside ant traps

and cereal boxes to retrieve items hopefully long since forgotten. The older boy finished loading his bag up from the fridge.

"C'mon," the Perkins boy said. "Let's get outta here before they tattle."

The two boys came out proud—their backpacks filled with knockoff Capri-Suns, Jell-O cups, and an assortment of pocket knives, slingshots, matches, a pair of binoculars—and were surprised to feel unnoticed. More kids cried and shoved each other under the magnolia where Mrs. Perkins drank sun tea and smoked.

She finished her cigarette and hiked up her blouse by its shoulders to air out the sweat that made it stick to her before letting it fall back into place. "Come on, *y'all!* Quiet now!" she yelled. "Quiet now you little— Quiet, you!" She comeonyalled again and again until the children stopped wrestling, and, lulled by the summer heat, rested in the grass, picking at it and looking for bugs.

"Which ones are hers?" Messiah asked.

"None of your damned business!" the Perkins boy said. "Why? You want her to be your mama?"

"No," Messiah said. "She looks like Jabba the Hutt with them little aliens crawling all around him. You know?" He regretted saying that as soon as it came out of his mouth. He didn't want to upset the Perkins boy and found he didn't even like hearing the word mama now. It hurt him in his stomach and behind his head. It hurt him in his eyes. He looked at the sun to wash them clean with afterglare shadow and blinking.

"Oooh-ooh buddy," the boy said. "You gonna say that about my mama?" He stomped off toward the old Chevy truck parked on the other side of the house beneath a grove of trees. Once royal blue, it was now spotted like a cow with rust, buffed out and touched up and rusted back again. No licence plates.

"You ain't even got a fuckin' mama!" he said and forced a laugh. "Rather a fat mama than an old dead one. Anyway, you trying to

go swimming or get an ass-whoopin'—I don't know. But come on anyways!"

Messiah followed, eyes watering and the world so blurry.

The boy kicked the truck's tires and crawled in through its passenger side. "Looks good!" he said as he slammed the door. Now he struggled to sync the clutch and the ignition. The truck let out a crunching, choking sound. "Dammit! Goddammit! God!"

Mosquitoes buzzed in Messiah's ears. Maybe he'd made a mistake in trusting this older boy. *My brother was his age.* But that didn't make sense. Dalton was older, he was in the Army, he was long gone, he reminded himself. Dalton was a memory. Dalton had forgotten about him, but Messiah couldn't help remembering him. He was trying to find the way to say it. He took stock of the two brothers he kept in his mind: Dalton as Messiah had known him: lanky and dark, a punk band T-shirt, a book in his pocket, his hair in his eyes, and Dalton the ghost: an action-movie man in uniform, evaporating, vanished.

The truck started up. The boy yanked at the three-on-the-tree shifter, wrenching it into neutral, then crawled out and ran around the engine to pull out an old wooden chock block from under the tire. He looked past Messiah toward the house to see if anyone had noticed. When the truck started to roll Messiah got in front of it, pushing against it to keep it in place.

The boy returned. "Damn, forgot to put a brake on. They don't work too good." He climbed back into the truck and waved for Messiah to join him. "Are you snifflin'? You're gonna have to stop that 'fore we come back to this house or you'll get a switching. They don't like grown men crying around here."

"Who's they?"

"My mama," the boy said. "So, you still wanna go to the swimming hole? Or did I do all this work just because you think I got *all* the time in the world." He was performing again, and Messiah

found that, strangely, it cheered him up. The boy looked at him. "You're just standing there like an idiot."

Messiah got in. The boy said the truck was rightfully his, but that he hadn't gotten his licence quite yet. He said he'd "inheritit" it from his grandfather, but Messiah didn't believe him. It wasn't a question of how impressed he should have been, but that he couldn't care about this sort of deep-dyed lore yet. He didn't want to cut a switch to be whipped with.

Messiah's soft stomach, doubled over from slouching in the truck, was eating the middle of his shirt. He untucked it. Situated himself. It was a grey Gap shirt that his mom had gotten him at an outlet store—his mother. There was a camo-printed ballcap on the dashboard. Messiah put it on and looked at himself in the dirty side mirror and thought of his brother.

They pulled out of the yard and into the gravel driveway while the boy's head swivelled all around to make sure no one noticed the sound. Messiah was happy to leave that damp house, its creaky makeshift porch balanced by bricks and unbalanced again by time. To leave the fake plastic window shutters glued permanently open to the sides of the built-right-here oversized trailer, the relic of a fleeting prosperity; to leave before the sun-bleached siding fell away and fell further apart into dust that he breathed in and out with the after-dinner cigarettes and the breath of the other children. Messiah, yearning to drive away faster, sweated in anticipation.

The Perkins boy drove the truck out slowly onto the road. Looking back, Messiah saw that Mrs. Perkins hadn't moved.

"You ever been to the ocean?" the boy asked after an hour of mostly silent driving up the winding Blue Ridge Parkway. They were flying through Blue Ridge backroads, grinding the gears only a little bit at each turn and slowdown and staying mostly between the lines.

"The beach, man. You ever been to the fuckin' beach? I bet you'd look funny in a swimsuit anyway. I wonder if they even sell swimsuits at the surf shop that would fit you. Look at you. Bunched up like spilt oatmeal. I wear board shorts. They're long. My brother wears the same ones. So, you ever seen sand before?" He poked Messiah in the stomach.

"Which brother?" Messiah crossed his arms over himself.

"None of your damned business."

As the boy looked at Messiah he felt he was being assessed and smiled back instinctively. Then he decided it looked too premeditated and sucked his gut in a little. "Of course I seen sand."

"I mean from God, not from a sandbox. I mean God's sand. Long miles of sand. My brother got me to count the grains in my hand one day, and when I was just about done he blew them all out and said sand is just one word, *sand*, like that." He looked to Messiah for affirmation.

Messiah smiled again and didn't blink. "No use in counting all the sands one by one, I guess." He was trying to appease the boy, to keep him from swerving all over the road whenever he wanted to scare Messiah or get his attention.

Finally they pulled up to a pasture where the road spurred between two elevations. A coyote ran up the berm to the left.

"I wish I had my rifle," the Perkins boy said.

"I thought it was your daddy's."

"I can use it whenever the hell I want, makes it just as much mine as the food in the fridge or this here truck," the Perkins boy snapped. He mimed firing at the coyote's tail, disappearing now in the drying grass stalks. "We'll park the truck behind one of these here bales and make it look nice and natural so the sheriff don't investigate."

They cut across the field toward scattered hay bales and cornered around two that were close together, hiding the truck from the road. After they'd climbed out of the truck the boy rummaged

through some of the wet garbage and chains in the back till he found the chock block slick with mildew; he pulled it out from inside a crumbling tire, stuck it behind a rear wheel of the truck, and looked at Messiah. With the sun low and hanging just above the boy's cowlick, Messiah felt open and okay, like he could breathe.

The boy kept turning back and looking at Messiah as they walked westward together into the early evening sky, and once or twice Messiah thought he made to reach back and hold his hand but fought it off. It must have been only a flinch or a twitch of some kind.

"This creek ain't clean, supposedly," the boy said as he cleared the dried brush in front of him. "I know because I came home soaking wet from swimming over there, where it's shallow, and I got whooped on and yelled at—something like 'There's all kinds of chemicals in it' or 'There's cowshit in it,' you know? But I figure I'd die if it was so dirty. No, I wasn't even sick at all. You wanna swim in it or walk further to get down to the hole? Hole's clean."

Messiah motioned that he wanted to continue, flicking his wrist forward as if they were on a mission and surrounded by enemies. He kept a stern look on his face. He didn't want to swim in the shallow water where his body wouldn't be all the way under. They started along the creek, and soon came to a bend that, over time, had pulled out the silt and wet mud and moved it further down the stream, making a slight whirlpool that slopped along the banks of the bend and calmed in the centre. Around it was a ring of fine sand, unsuited to and discordant with its halo of red mud and crown of fallen, rotting branches. A bright white beach around the deep water.

"I figure we go naked and then dry off after. No, I know, but I'm telling you she's wrong about the water. Yes, *my mama,* she ain't a doctor, you know that. She ain't the brightest bulb. Okay, you take your shirt off first."

The way the boy was staring at him made him feel challenged, like it was a dare. Messiah wondered how it had become a contest.

He lifted his shirt up and his hands got under it, wet with sweat on his belly. He hesitated.

"What do you want to see so bad?" Messiah tugged his hands free. "I'm going to swim with it on."

"No, that's stupid. What's wrong with you, go on and take her off."

Messiah sighed and, turning around, wrestled himself free from the shirt. He balled it up in his hands and turned to face the boy with his eyes closed; he opened them to find the boy still looking intently at his body.

"You've got fat underneath your nipples." The boy laughed sharply. "Look at those juggers!"

Messiah clutched his shirt before him, hiding behind it as much as he could. "That's just how they are, I can't help it."

"If that's 'just the way they are,' how come mine ain't like that? See I told you you'd look weird at the beach. Well, go on and take off your drawers too."

Messiah met his eyes again, trying to figure out the end of this game. He'd been losing faith in the boy since they came off the parkway. But this was where they'd ended up. So he put his fingers in the waistband of his pants, hesitated, and then without breaking eye contact slithered the shorts down.

"Well, how else are we supposed to swim? I ain't lookin' at you. You're just funny, that's all. I'm taking off my drawers, too." The boy's voice was getting higher and faster as he spoke. They were both exposed now, standing stark against the glory of the sun as it broke through the veiny canopy of the forest edge. "Vanity's a sin, you know. Okay, get on in there and I'll cover my eyes. I ain't near you . . . stop worrying so much and just swim around."

Messiah watched his steps as he crept toward the bank of the hole. His toes were catching on turned-up roots where people had dug in their fishing poles. His feet were white and soft, unused to going without shoes. He was sensitive to the pain he felt just walking

on his own feet, and to the sight of them beyond the whiteness of his soft belly, melting down into the fine sand.

He knew the boy was still staring him down and felt examined right through. If he didn't look up would that be enough? He tried to hurry faster into the hole to cover himself. Its water was cold and viscous with loose mud. Messiah worried about catfish biting his pecker off, and was starting to ask if that could happen when he got a splash of water in his open mouth. He choked and spluttered.

Once they were both fully in the water, Messiah couldn't swim in any direction without the boy swimming toward him. It was like the boy became sweet. The boy was sweet. So Messiah let him come a little nearer. They swam, and the boy splashed Messiah, but it wasn't mean. Then Messiah let him come near again. He let him come very close. They splashed and clambered out and jumped back in and resurfaced, and the Perkins boy spit out water at Messiah and splashed him very hard.

"Well, splash me back if you don't like it. Go on. Go on. No?"

Messiah went under, holding his nose. He saw the boy's white figure squirming and kicking in the murky green water. He came up for air.

"Let's swim over there to the bend, over to the deep part. You go first. I already been here swimming my whole life! And you just been staring at your pecker this whole time!"

Messiah looked up. Behind the floating, staring boy was a line of smoke rising from near the top of the mountain in a clearing; the little scar of creek seemed to climb the mountain itself. The image comforted Messiah, to see someone having a fire. He was soaked through and getting cold.

He closed his eyes and floated on his back. He felt the water creep into the uncomfortable place in his ears but didn't let it bother him. Then as he drifted, with his big toes stuck in the mud at the bottom of the creek, he felt the boy's hand on his head, in his hair.

Messiah didn't open his eyes but tried to thrash and twist away. Yet the hand just came up under the tense knot at the back of his head, supporting it; the boy's other arm scooped Messiah up by the ankles and then slipped toward the bend behind his knees; now he was being carried in the water like a baby. Messiah opened his eyes to the Perkins boy staring at him and blinking rapidly.

"How come you don't acknowledge me?" the boy said.

"I do acknowledge you." Although he was bent up in the boy's arms, he remained stiff. He let the boy spin him around counter-clockwise in the water, slowly.

"You didn't even never introduce yourself to me."

"I'm Messiah."

"That ain't no name for no orphan. Your mama ain't a Christian, is she?" The boy said this in a soft voice, one that betrayed the nastiness of the sentiment.

"She is too a Christian."

"She's dead."

"I know that, but it don't make her less Christian." He paused. "And that don't make me less Messiah."

"Look at me!" said the boy, and Messiah did. "Look at me now! How come you don't ever say my name?"

"I don't know your name. I ain't ever heard anyone call out your name. I ain't ever heard anyone pay you any mind."

"How come you figure they pay *you* mind?"

"They don't. I thought you was an orphan too," Messiah said, lying. "I figure maybe they feel guilty or something."

Both of their eyes went wide.

"I ain't an orphan," the Perkins boy said. Then, after a moment: "And you don't know what they got to feel guilty about. I know more about you than, well. What's my name?"

"What? I don't know your name," said Messiah again, and the boy spun him faster, and the trees seemed to wheel around them.

"Well, what do you want to call me, then?" said the Perkins boy. And he smiled.

"Can I call you Dalton? That's my brother's name."

"I don't want to be your brother." Slowly, he put his nose almost to Messiah's nose and said a thin cold voice: "What's my name?"

Messiah stared into the boy's eyes but tried to look past him.

The evening sky had set in. The clouds rolling by were spread out against the sky and streaked with grey, the halos that outlined them as hard as polished silver. Messiah felt now as if he hadn't really gotten out at all. He felt in fact as if he'd sunk deeper into the cushions of that house, that everything had gotten greyer as he looked out past the boy staring at him and blinking the water from his eyes. The boy dripped face-warmed water on Messiah's nose, the boy's eyes just as grey as the spread-out clouds.

"I couldn't tell you," the boy said in a quiet voice, as though his indifference were a secret. It was, and it had become a dangerous one.

"I couldn't tell you," he said again.

Then the boy crooked his neck forward like a nearsighted old woman and put his lips in front of Messiah's eyes. He breathed into Messy's eyes. The boy straightened his neck back out so he could study Messiah's face, then he bent back down and before studying him again said, "Hawk is my name. Hawk's my name, and you should've known."

Dalton

DALTON DID WHAT HE COULD to keep his mind on his brother while he flitted away the waning days of summer, feeling spiritual, somehow, about the shortening days and the new tinniness in the rustling leaves. He kept house in the same way he had in the Army, dusting countertops with toilet paper, squeegeeing dried-on spots of coffee, rinsing out the garbage pail until it was clean. His ex-coworkers, still his housemates, offered him beers and warmness on their paydays but were cold and mechanical any other day, coming home from the job stinking and sore and ornery, snapping off the lights while he read, just as soon as all were in their beds. The trailer felt like it had shrunk in size with the heat of the day, and their arrival every night crowded Dalton's mind with unfamiliar language and stale antagonism, something like the opposite of camaraderie.

Each night came with dreams of Messiah and home, warped and incomplete childhood memories, a bird's-eye view of him and his brother, shirtless in their yard, waving sticks at each other like swords. Then came the vibrating, concussive memories of his mother in her bed, flashing before him, waking him as if he'd just been in a car crash. She is pallid, she is peaceful, she is sick, she is sick, she is tired, she is dead. The snores of Loera and Martinez

reminding him he was alive and alone. It was as if the men's snoring crawled through one ear and filtered through the quiet screaming of his brain, coming out the other end of his consciousness like sifted shards of sharp, dusted glass. His body jumped intermittently in bed and Dalton found himself shouting and grunting, helpless against his own inner workings. "Ya basta, ya basta," Loera would say. "Deja esto," he'd urge, shaking him. "Vuelve aquí. Aquí, estás aquí."

Weeks into this regimen of worry he kept catching himself in regrets, invading the tepid, tideless days again and again, and starting earlier than usual. There was nothing to stop him from flagellating himself with his failures, all preventable, his betrayals and moral entropy coming to smother him, spreading out like fly ash in the clear running water of time.

And that was simply how it was, and how he figured life was going to be: drummed out in little panics, the circle of trailers around him like rings on a cut-down tree, empty of souls save for the aural accompaniment of buzzing bugs. Dalton prepped to live, however he could, with no one else with him who might've cared whether he lived or died. And still no one came. Not even to arrest him. Time went by slowly, with Dalton all the while keeping his little brother stuck in his mind.

Kids were getting sick in the towns that dotted the riverbank downstream from the coal plant. Regional news.

It was growing uncomfortable in the trailer he shared with the other men. Once a week Loera would pull a small .38 revolver out of a footlocker at the end of his cot, unload it, dismantle it, and clean each piece with oil and a worn-down toothbrush. It was as if Dalton had never left the barracks. Gun cleaning and beer drinking. The idiot din of the television.

The bunny-eared TV was set up on the kitchenette counter that faced all their cots. The men tuned in to the news each night,

watching footage of picketers gathering at the processing plant. Interviews with lawyers and congressmen. Huddled around the TV, the roommates tried to make themselves out—pointing to a crowd of workers who were strolling across the footage, covering their faces and hiding from the cameras as they left work for the day—and argued about who was who and whether they'd be identified in any substantial way. They had taken to speaking almost entirely in Spanish now. But Dalton couldn't shake the feeling that some of this intense interest hinged on his presence there, as though he helped develop their theories of the case somehow.

Loera finished cleaning his pistol and laid out the rounds in a neat row on the cluttered coffee table. "Vasquez," he said. "You talk to the news?"

Dalton shook his head and raised his eyebrows, surprising himself at how happy he was to be asked. "I was already gone before any of this happened," he said. "Ausente trabajo," he clarified, deploying whatever Spanish he had. Loera and Martinez laughed at him. "Roll call!" they yelped. "Vásquez aquí!"

Martinez twirled his finger next to his temple and gestured at Dalton with his eyebrows. "Ausente aquí," he said. Loera pointed the revolver at the anchorwoman on the screen and clicked it through its cycle. He pulled the trigger five times, running it smooth all the way through before flicking open the cylinder, loading the rounds inside, and placing the gun down hard on the coffee table. The men smiled at Dalton and spoke to one another in a fast Spanish that made it hard for him to catch anything. He closed his eyes and tried to fall asleep, the blue flicking light of the television flashing through his eyelids.

Dalton told himself that the stretched-out panic and suspicion that had permeated their quarters for the past few weeks of his unemployment wasn't his fault alone. He figured all their jobs were on the line now. They were finding traces of coal processing runoff as far down as northern Virginia. An interstate issue.

After a week or so of thick air in the trailer, the talk hushing and quieting whenever he was around, Dalton knew he'd have to find a way to make enough money to leave. He also knew that he'd missed whatever opportunity there might have been to nab something easy with low competition. Everyone in the trailer park was planning a move. There was talk of plant closures and layoffs. Everyone, now, was looking for quick, easy work, scheming to protect their job or to get a new one. Dalton was the longest out of work, if only by a little, but he wasn't sure he was the most desperate. He could feel the tension rising.

Before, when he told himself he was just hiding out for a little while, he'd felt like he could just walk away anytime. Like he was deciding to stay put out of some stubbornness or idiosyncratic penitence. But it wasn't that simple. He prayed for deliverance of some kind or another, but it was TV and the static hum of bugs each day. It was warming well water, advertisements and the news, instant coffee and daytime dreams.

And then he heard screaming outside. He clicked off the TV and looked at the grey, convexed image of himself, the charged screen pulling loose hairs and dust onto itself in the yellow haze of hot noon.

Dalton walked out to see a man in a dirty undershirt banging on the door to the superintendent's trailer. Clark. Wyatt's right-hand man. He was drunk, Dalton thought, and was working himself up into a sweat, hollering at the door, kicking it and spitting on the bug screen. He stumbled backward down the rickety front steps and walked around the yard of the trailer, picking up trash and throwing it at the door.

"You change the locks? You change the locks on me? You fuckin' bitch!" Clark screamed. "All my shit's in there! I ain't got any of my shit!"

Dalton stood still where he was, not wanting to get involved, gauging whether Clark had even noticed him. The area of open

grass within the circle of homes felt shrunken now, locked in like a colosseum. His would-be opponent, however, was fighting with the walls.

Other than the huffing, the crash of hurling lawn chairs and beer cans, there was utter silence. Even the bugs quieted in the surrounding trees. Clark turned toward Dalton.

"What the fuck are you looking at?" He paused, smiled his dirty mouth, and spit. "Oh, you gotta be shittin' me. It's him, the fuckin' white Spaniard."

Sweat poured into Clark's eyes, doubling his scowl into a neanderthal grimace. "You fuckin' little— What the fuck are you lookin' at? Boy, go on!" Then he turned and stomped away.

Dalton heard a car start up and began making his way back to his trailer. Now the car roared into the grassy circle and barrelled toward him. Old Pontiac, missing windows. Dalton ran, leapt up the steps, crashed through the screen door. Then he turned and watched as Clark whipped the car away from the trailer at the last moment. He honked and shouted and swore, burning circles in the grass, screaming with his head out the window. Shouting about killing the superintendent. About how all his shit's locked up.

There'd been talk of a temp agency near the Walmart on the way to town. It was a pain to get to without a car, and carpooling there from the trailer park usually happened only on weekends when the employment office was closed. Still, a lot of the men were getting ready to go and see what sort of work was on offer there, and Dalton resigned himself to do the same even if it meant walking all the way. He was running out of money.

He awoke with the other men in his trailer, their morning preparations unfolding in silence as Dalton tried not to get caught watching them, jealous, somehow, that he was no longer part of the crew. He hitched a ride with them up to the highway and got out

with only a nod. The early light was sporadic and cool through the trees that lined the highway, and few cars were on the road.

There was a line out the door, each person asked to take a ticket to speak to an agent at the counter. Once Dalton made it inside he watched the president on the TV saying something about American jobs, and as he went on a man shouted, "Hey, turn it up!" An argument erupted around Dalton while he jockeyed for a ticket.

"What? Turn up what? You want to hear him tell some more fuckin' *lies*?" another man said. A third told him to shut his mouth. Shouting began.

Dalton pushed through the now mixed-up queues that were folding in on themselves and collapsing. Most of the men had perked up and were crowding the TV. At the front of the room he saw a shoulder-mounted camera scanning the tops of the men's heads as they shifted around. Dalton seized the opportunity to propel himself toward the ticket machine while the others were distracted by the fracas.

A young woman was among them. Clean-cut. She stood in front of the camera, elbowing out room for herself near the ticket machine. "Make sure you get this," she was saying. "Am I in frame? I'm in frame? Just roll." She gestured to some of the men who half-turned around as numbers were shouted from behind the counter. Those men were in the shot now too, and opened their mouths in protest but couldn't manage to say much.

The reporter was done up and dressed in clothes that jumped out against the beige-upholstered backdrop of her shot. She looked like an alien among the sweat-stained T-shirts and beer guts that surrounded her. She'd chosen to be there, had prepared for the moment. Everyone else was in frame by mistake, drawn and kept there by desperation. She was cool and easy among the hot and deteriorating.

She locked eyes with Dalton and he moved closer. She had black hair pulled up behind her head and straight bangs that ran

just above her eyebrows. Her nose was pierced in the middle with a little gold ring. When she smiled at him with white teeth and brown eyes Dalton felt a sinking awareness of his dirtiness, his grown-out Walmart haircut, his off-brand Walmart work clothes.

"Can I talk to you?" she asked him. "Here, see if you can come next to me, here."

Dalton nodded and stood by her, trying not to breathe in her direction. He licked and felt the fuzz on his teeth, squeezed his armpits closed, and grabbed for a ticket with T. rex arms. He noted the number, forty-four, and pushed the ticket and his hands in his pockets, flexing his chest and trying to stand up straight.

"What's your name?" she asked.

"Dalton," he said. "I don't have to give a last name, do I?"

"Not if you don't want. Were you a worker at Freedom Coal?"

"Not in the mines, no, but I was subcontracted for processing work."

"Great!" she said, as though Christmas had been cancelled but was back on. Then she settled into the moment.

Dalton rubbed his nose for errant boogers and blinked and sniffed and smiled, trying to get ready as she had. The cameraman pointed at them and the red light went on.

"We're here at the Kanawha County Public Works Assistance Office in a strip mall near Charleston, West Virginia, where dozens of workers have crowded inside to look for new employment following the layoffs, the downsizing, and the hiring freezes by the big three coal companies in the region. In the wake of recent allegations of illegal dumping and another failed collective bargaining push at Freedom Industries, workers from across this part of the state have been furloughed, collectively dismissed, or terminated with short notice."

The reporter said all this as though she'd said it a hundred times before; it rolled out of her mouth like a dinnertime prayer.

"Dalton, a worker recently terminated from his job with Freedom, is here looking for work. Is that right?"

He said yes it was, and the interview flowed on as the men behind them berated the president on the TV. He had to lean in to hear her questions, and he looked down at her tan arms and clean nails while she gesticulated, punctuating her questions and concerns. He returned his hands to his pockets. She asked whether he'd noticed any labour action at his last worksite. Dalton said he wouldn't know. This seemed to disappoint her, and she looked at him as though he might have been lying or playing coy.

At this pause he arched his neck to look at the hubbub behind him. The subtitles on the TV were coming through incorrectly. They cycled through Spanish, then a language Dalton didn't recognize, then technical symbols and numbers, then back to English, but he couldn't read them and speak with her at the same time. She tugged on his arm and asked him if he thought the governor had put pressure on Freedom WV Industries to fire him, or workers like him. "Well," he said, "I'm not too sure the governor knew I was working there." He returned to the TV.

The cameraman motioned to her to move on, waving his hand as if he was shooing Dalton away. "Wait, hang on, cut!" the woman said. She turned to Dalton. "I think you need to talk to me."

"I mean, I *am* talking to you," he said, unsure of himself. "But I just don't got anything else to say about it. I'm sorry. I mean, I didn't hardly talk to anyone when I worked over there."

"How long did you work there?"

"Just about a year. Maybe a little more."

The men behind them were bellowing at each other now, ignoring the camera.

"Do you know what happened at Freedom? Have you heard the news? What they were doing to the Elk River?" she asked.

"Yes ma'am, I think I do know. I was one of the people they had take the silica and chemical wash and all that down to the water."

"Are you rolling?" she asked her cameraman. He nodded and spun his finger around next to the camera to keep them going. "So,

Dalton, what was the under-the-table work like? What did they have you doing, exactly?" Her eyes were wide as if she'd just sat down on a roller coaster.

"I don't want to say all that on camera." He was looking at her directly now. She was in her thirties. She was taller than him and had a southern accent, sort of, but with a lilt unlike the local one. Hers was more like Dalton's. From somewhere less unreal.

"Okay! Cut it," she said to the cameraman, who broke away and trained his focus on the men still shouting at the television.

"What's your name?" Dalton asked.

"Laura. Can we please get you to talk about this on camera? I mean, it's all part of it, all of this—"

A man shouted at the TV screen. "I mean they killed Jack Kennedy! Yes sir, they did! Why can't they kill this sonofabitch?"

Shoving began. As the cameraman watched the scene unfold Laura tugged at him by the cord of her microphone, trying to pull him back toward Dalton. The microphone came unplugged.

"That's my president you're talking about!"

"Fool, you're in an unemployment line! What's he done for you?"

"Fuck that goddamn piece of shit, that no-good, cocksucking—"

The men fought over the sacred nature of the presidency, spitting pointedly on the floor and hurling slurs and epithets at one another. The cameraman had cut Laura loose for good and was filming everything.

The employment attendant was shouting out "Next!"

"Someone turn this up! God*damn*."

"Next! Number thirty-six!"

Dalton walked outside, breathed in a heavy lungful of mountain fog, and watched the sun move behind a gun-coloured cloud. Long enough, he thought, to have let thirty-six turn closer to forty-four, but when he looked through the glass the number above the attendant remained the same. The reporter and the cameraman were still inside, arguing with each other now.

Dalton asked for a cigarette from a spindly guy who'd pulled up smoking in his Firebird. The man gave it to him without a word. Dalton took deep drags as he watched the cars pulling in and out of the lots around him. Taco Bell across the way, a gas station to the right of that, Walmart behind. The Dollar Tree workers must have been switching shifts. He watched a couple get out of their tissue-strewn cars and pull their uniform polo shirts on over their outfits. The red number sign in the office said thirty-seven.

Dalton watched as a couple of other workers walked to their own cars. Cups in the seat. Cigarettes lit with the windows up. The glass fogged. NRA bumper sticker. Confederate flag air freshener. Bag taped to the missing window. The bag-windowed car pulled out of the strip mall parking lot, crossed the street on a yellow, and drove up the narrow ramp to the Walmart parking lot. He wanted there to be logic in all this. He wanted there to be some kind of system or sign, but he felt unsure whether there was a point to any of it at all. The whole busy corner just off the exit to the highway seemed to catch people like a tide pool catches fish, not knowing what or why they were being pulled in all these directions, the meaning of it becoming more opaque in the humid afternoon.

Inside, the men who'd been arguing were red-faced now, their arms outstretched toward one another, calming one another down. Laura was off to the side, yelling into her phone, her head bent, digging through her purse, her black hair concealing her face. The cameraman had sat down, resting his big camera on the floor. The ticket number hadn't advanced. Dalton turned back to the parking lot, observing the intermittent traffic.

A tapping on the glass behind him: Laura, waving at him to come back inside. Dalton waved a lazy wave and turned around, figuring he'd cross the street to the NRA-stickered car. They were the right kind of people to ask for a ride to the ABC store, and possibly back to the trailer park. Maybe if he brought home a few cans of Bud or some whiskey he could cheer up his housemates, then

maybe they'd let him in on how and where they were going to go work next.

He started off across the street. Looking back on the little strip mall, he saw that Laura was outside now, cellphone to her ear, scanning the road. She saw him and waved, watching him watching her wave, then she shrugged in disappointment as he kept on moving away. Like he wouldn't have just left her there. Like she expected something else of him, something better.

Messiah

THE SHARP ROCKS of the water's edge stabbed the soles of his feet and woke him from his waking dream as they walked back to where their clothes were. But their clothes weren't there, which seemed his punishment for letting Hawk get so close. He'd gotten so close.

The sun had gone down fast, replaced by a dense, fast-moving cover of clouds. "Where do you think they are?" Hawk yelled out to Messiah.

"We put them over there!" Messiah pointed, using his other hand to cover himself, embarrassed even in the distance. "Maybe a little further down!"

"You look up there and look quick!" Hawk called. "I can't see *anything*, god*dammit!*"

Messiah felt ashamed, as though the missing clothes were somehow his fault. He scrambled around in the darkness alone. Hawk shouted that he thought they might have been on the wrong side of the creek, but Messiah couldn't say. He thought Hawk would know.

Messiah's body was wet and cold but his cheeks felt hot, like he was sick. He heard rumbling now, the trees seeming to echo Hawk's shouts and cusses. Then came lightning. Then rain. A lot of rain. The rain splashed around them in the darkness, shocks of lightning

very close. In the afterlight of each strike Messiah saw shadows of his friend.

"Truck's gone!" Hawk said. "The motherfuckin' truck is gone!"

"What do you mean? Are we on the right side?"

"Oh, shut the hell up you goddamn ninny, this is your fault!" Hawk stomped around in his nakedness, looking as though he was conducting a ceremony. Rolls of sheet lightning flashed closer.

"Do we know how to get home?"

"No," Hawk said. "Not in the dark I don't."

"Then what are we going to do?"

"What do you think we're going to do? Huh? You fat pervert, what do *you* think?"

There was silence, and Messiah sat down in the mud. The rain had parted his hair and was streaming down his ears.

"You goddamn retard," Hawk continued. "I knew this would happen. You goddamn— Goddamn you!"

After a while Messiah said, "Well, I think we ought to follow this here creek. I saw smoke coming from a chimney up on top of that closest mountain."

"Shut the fuck up."

"I'll bet anything that this creek comes from up there. Worst that could happen is we'll find a bridge and someone will pick us up."

"No, you damned fool. We're going to go that way just so people *don't* pick us up. It's a good idea but you got the reason all wrong. I don't want to get picked up by some pervert out on the road. Maybe *you* do. You fucked-up sonofabitch." Hawk paused. "Okay, let's go. Might as well."

They started walking toward the water. Hawk shouted, "I sure hope you're happy! Goddamn you!" and slid into the creek. Messiah clambered in after him; the rocks against the shore hurt his feet.

"I don't know if I can walk on these rocks," he said. "We oughtn't be in the water when there's lightning."

"They get rounder once you go in a little deeper. Don't be a little pussy. Here, hold on to my shoulders and kind of lift yourself off the rocks a little bit, it'll help. Like that. Go on, bounce a little and float. Lightning ain't gonna strike you. You're like a rubber glove." He was back to being mean.

Messiah held on to the back of Hawk's naked shoulders as they waded uphill against the current and tiptoed on the smooth rocks. The lightning flashes imprinted negatives of the bank in their vision. The strikes were regular enough that they could follow along for a minute or two without running into felled trees or jutting rocks. Messiah's hands felt rough like apricot pits against Hawk's smooth shoulders. Yet he felt comfortable holding him, less worried about being close. It was right that they were going this way, he felt, deeper into the woods and higher up, closer to the clash of lighting, the rumble of something out of this world. He couldn't bear to get picked up on the road. The police would get called. Better to just tell the truth, or part of the truth, to whoever waited at the bottom of that smoke plume. About the rest he could never say anything to anyone.

"We'll just tell them we're molested when we get there," Hawk said. The lightning above was like staring into a flashbulb. It hurt Messiah's eyes and left the green ghost of the back of Hawk's head floating in front of him.

They walked and floated onward against the current. Some parts of the creek were deep enough to swim and some parts so shallow they enveloped only their shins. In one such shallow patch Messiah felt his genitals tuck up inside him. He had goose pimples that felt like they were jumping right off his skin, his blond arm hair standing on end. A blue lightning bolt forked down in stop-motion, in frame-by-frame jagged motion, crawling a thousand miles a minute toward the earth. It struck a tree a hundred yards away.

"Je-sus Christ!" Hawk shouted. "We ought to get out of this here creek for a while."

“I don’t think so, Hawk. I’m cold.”

“I don’t want to get fried up in here if lightning hits. Damn, that sounded like a durn gunshot.”

“Just go.” Messiah tightened his grip on Hawk’s shoulders and pushed him gently forward.

The rain eventually let up to a mere drizzle, but the cloud cover was so consistent that their whole world turned into an indiscernible greyscape of muddied, dripping figures. Following the smoke stream rising up from the top of the mountain, the boys reoriented themselves with each lightning flash, fighting against the instinct to flinch.

Alongside the creek they came to a break in the woods that led into a clearing. The opening was well-worn. Up ahead the creek looked like it widened into a pond formed by a bend in the down-flowing water.

“This’s gotta be it,” Hawk said, and Messiah could smell the smoke. They followed it down to a sturdy, night-blackened outline of a house beyond the clearing and another short treeline. It was almost dark now, but they saw a lit window set against a jutting wall of mountain. The house, large and half-stone, loomed over the slant of pasture through which they walked; Messiah realized it must be a tobacco field, the sticky nicotine leaves pulling at the hairs of his thighs and shins. The window like a candle in the dark. After a slow approach made slower by their cautious navigation around tools and sticks and briars, they came to a thinly wired fence.

“Well, go on! See if she’s electric,” Hawk instructed.

“No. Let’s go around.”

“Listen, I ain’t walking no more. We see the house. Go on and test the fence.” Hawk pushed Messiah into it, the wire catching him at the knee and sending him tumbling over. He got up and started pulling the black sticky leaves off him as if they were leeches.

“So I guess it’s dead?” Hawk laughed playfully.

Messiah turned and started walking off without him, fighting the urge to cry.

They found a coop and sheltered under its short-cropped awning, listening to the chickens humming and purring in their rickety old hut, their feet smearing the wet chicken shit and mixing it with mud between their toes.

"Look here, I've *got* parents," Hawk said. "Say we walked up onto that porch and they sucked us both in and strung us up like *Chainsaw Massacre*, then what?"

"I don't know," Messiah said. "I guess then we'd both be there together like we are now. Ought to go together."

They started creeping toward the house, hesitated and returned, then started again. Hawk pushed Messiah forward.

"What if nobody's home?"

"*Git* the hell on *up* there," Hawk hissed at him.

"What am I going to say? You go!"

"Say you're molested and need help."

He repeated "molested" back at Hawk and received a confident head nod. Messiah felt his eyes on his naked back as he advanced, but there was no tension now, only a sense of defeat. He took little steps up the slight slope leading to the porch, curling his toes into the wet grass, slipping as he went and covering his genitals with his hands.

When he got to the porch Messiah turned back and saw Hawk, a slinky, angular shadow, waving at him from behind the coop, making a pushing motion with his hand. "Go *on*! Go *on*!"

He turned and opened the creaking screen door, lifting the brass knocker with one hand and covering himself with the other, feeling even more exposed, spotlit now under the orange of the porch light.

Messiah knocked and waited and listened, the screen door scratching against its own joints and making a rusty moan out into

the night, creaking a little back and forth, matching his breathing. He pushed his ear up against the door and—

A flash of light. A void of time and sound. A snap.

He felt the wind sucked out of him and thought he'd been struck by lightning. But he felt himself, touched his soft belly and felt no charred skin, no bone or blood.

It was just the bug light zapping a mosquito or moth, illuminating the porch with a flash. Messiah went back down the porch toward Hawk.

"Hey! What? There weren't nobody there?"

"No. I listened. Nobody."

"You sure?"

Hawk reached out his warm palm and touched Messiah's shoulder to turn him around. The door opened, and out of the dark of the house came an old woman, long white hair seeming to pull her head toward the ground. She shuffled forward in moccasins, not bending her knees, her white legs hardly disturbing her thin nightgown as she approached.

She held a shotgun in her arms. And up it came.

There was a new, loud flash of lightning.

Messiah was struck and knocked back, sliding almost two yards in the slime of wet grass and the runoff of chicken droppings and rainwater. The rain picked up; buckets of water were being dumped from the sky now, less like individual droplets than the world itself getting thrown into an ocean. Above the ensuing thunder that clapped and rolled out over the mountains came a sharp laugh in a pitch purposeful, cursing, and menacing. Messiah rolled in the grass, oily and dark and painted with blood, screaming gasping heaves of anguish that got sucked up and drowned out by the rain and the thunder and the laughter.

The old woman stood there with the light from the open doorway streaming out around her and bent herself angrily toward them as though facing down a biting wind. She pointed her gun at Hawk.

Hawk dropped to his knees and chanted loudly that he was a Christian and that they weren't on drugs and that someone snuck up like a snake on them and came down to the swimming hole just to take their clothes and run off with the truck. *We was molested,* he said. Then, as though lightning came up from the earth and burst out toward them, another shot went off from the porch.

Messiah tried to lift himself up in the grass, warm now with his own blood. He watched as Hawk covered his face with his arms and stumbled back, pissing straight out into the wind from his nakedness—but he did not fall.

The old woman approached, her nightgown becoming translucent and sticky and ethereal as an onslaught of rain soaked her through. She came upon Hawk and cuffed him by his nape and proclaimed, "Lord! I have them! You have delivered them, Lord. The slick, peeled eggs of Jesus!" And she laughed high and loud, like a hundred women laughing out of one woman's mouth.

Messiah got himself up on an elbow, watching as Hawk, trying to cover himself with his hands, shrank at the old woman's fingernails hooked into the raw space between his collarbone and shoulder, shaking him now—half-lifting, half-pushing him toward Messiah by the neck like a puppy.

"Take him!" she said, breathing heavily and spitting up tobacco onto the front of her dress. "Look at him! Look at your brother! Take him inside!" Before losing consciousness Messiah gazed into Hawk's crying eyes and felt his muddy hands grab him. Messiah's arms slipped through Hawk's grip as Hawk dragged him through the muck, up the porch, and into the house, the rough and splintered floor of the porch tearing against his naked behind.

Clyde

CLYDE DROVE PAST a line of unfamiliar pickup trucks and SUVs spanning the whole spur road that scribbled up the backside of Buffalo Mountain. Specialty DON'T TREAD ON ME licence plates featuring a coiled snake. Hickok wasn't bluffing, he thought. He drove cautiously, careful not to throw gravel up from his tires, and looked inside the vehicles for anything that could tell him more about their sudden appearance. He wondered if he might be able to claim any of this crowd as being a result of his missionary work over the past few days. He suspected he hadn't been so successful on his own accord.

The night outside the Pulliam hunting lodge was wrapped around his head like a tightening noose. The men at Hickok's muster had walked Clyde back through the woods at rifle point, cursing and mocking him all the way. Then, when they got to his truck and flooded campfire, they shot a few rounds over his head and told him he'd better take off. *The next one's coming right at your back*. Lightning raked and exploded silently in the clouds behind them.

If these trucks belonged to the militiamen, Clyde thought, he was a dead man.

Clyde parked by his trailer and went in. All was as it had been except that it smelled like roadkill in there. Flies covered the door to Tyler's room. He went to the door and shooed them away; put his hand on the knob but didn't turn it. He moved to the bathroom to wash his face, to brush his teeth, but he could hardly breathe. He knew what was in the other room.

Clyde's shaving kit still sat neatly by the sink. He splashed water on his face and in his eyes. The air in the trailer was hot and stale. He opened a chest in the den that Tyler had kept chock full of liquor and drugs and cigarettes. It was almost bare.

He threw what was left of Tyler's little treasures—tiny liquor bottles, dusty-bagged pills, bottles of promethazine, half-empty Actavis codeine—in a broken-zippered duffle bag that held all the other alms he'd gathered on his trip. Then he rinsed the dust off the zinc communion plate that Tyler had used to pass out the alms and tucked it under his other arm.

Leaving the trailer door open, he headed through the woods toward the clearing where Grace was already delivering her sermon. Hearing her voice through the leaves, echoing off the juts of rockface and trees, gave him a foreboding feeling. He couldn't make out what she was saying, but her tone was menacing and sharp. She was in a mood.

"The only way a combatant for God will lay down his arms is if he's confronted by an enemy superior. The only way Christ can lose is if you lose your faith on this battlefield!" she was shouting as Clyde approached. "This here battlefield!" She was throwing her arms up and then hurling them toward the ground, pointing at the earth beneath her feet.

He started to think about how he'd go about setting up all the little bags and joints and tiny liquor bottles he had with him. He wanted to do this right. Looking over the orchard, though, Clyde saw what looked like a hundred people. He didn't have nearly enough of anything worthwhile for that many, but maybe it wasn't

about that anymore. Maybe today was finally all about the Gospel.

The forty or so chairs were all taken by elderly people. Children, some potbellied, some pale and thin, were strewn about the grass at Grace's feet. The tarpaulin revival tent hadn't been erected, Tyler and himself having been absent from that particular ritual.

When Grace felt especially spry and filled with old-time religion, she often forwent the tent and preached under God's sun, on God's green earth, to God's people, as she put it. She was preaching so now. Like a grey-haired sweet summer child with a new lease on life. Uncanny how she could move like a teenager when she wanted to. The scene resembled something like a political rally from a hundred years before, like something out of a history textbook.

She paused to catch her breath. Clyde figured only he knew how nervous she was about losing her congregants—how big crowds drove her wild with excitement, gave her energy to last her through the week, and how a poor turnout would plummet her into a depression. She caught sight of Clyde and smiled right at him as though she'd been expecting him all along. She reached out her arms before her like a child welcoming her daddy home and began to walk through the people toward him in a performance so overblown that it made Clyde feel like a prop. He saw in her eyes a glint of relief, the only betrayal of real emotion among all the flailing and proselytizing.

"I am offering you the way, the only way to salvation. Yes! Clyde is here, my deacon, friends." She was frantic now, pulling Clyde into the crowd. "My deacon," she said again for good measure. She gently pulled the tray from his hands and presented it to all those immediately around her. Dozens of arms thrust forward like a lunging brood of vipers to grab at the little baggies of one or two pills.

"Take these little bits of heaven into your life and embrace salvation now! Embrace it, my lovers, my friends, here, on this mountainside, embrace the Lord, embrace one another, and embrace the Great Awakening."

This was Clyde's cue to keep moving around, handing out alms as she continued. She'd taught him that these gifts were not to be perceived as an exchange for participation but rather were complementary to the sermon, a pathway forward and an offering of fellowship. "Listen close," he would say to the worshippers, urging them to think of Grace's sermon as they took their little prize for attendance.

As well as he could while being so encumbered, Clyde piled upon the communion tray the Mount Airy woman's OxyContin plus all the errant drugs, cans of snuff, and little liquor bottles. He walked through the rows of people, offering alms to all but the children, who were sucking on juice and wiping chips off their shirts as they stared at him.

Clyde had split most of the tiny pills in half, in quarters if he could. Times were tough and alms hard to come by. He ignored the eyes of the disappointed worshippers, walking clumsily and passing out the microscopic white bits of chalk to each person before him. A thin woman broke down in tears and held out her tongue as though Clyde was to place the communion there for her. He did so.

When Clyde got toward the back of the crowd he noticed some familiar faces from the militia muster grouped in the rear behind dark sunglasses, watching it all with crossed arms. No Hickok, though. Many had guns at their waist, and a few held long guns at the ready.

To Clyde's relief they waved him away when he approached; not only did he have very little to offer them but was also afraid they'd lift him up again and this time carry him off and throw him from the mountaintop. He nodded, a gesture of familiar camaraderie, but it wasn't returned. They stared ahead through their shades.

"The battlefield, my people, my blood. You can fight through to peace. You can fight through with prayer. Lord, let them fight through me! Let them see what it is to be taken up into the arms of the Lord. Now, in the cool light of day, without shame and without need for shelter, I am being pulled up to you. You all! You little ones"—she

gestured toward the children—"Do you see yourself in heaven?" The children nodded, mouths open, clenching their juice boxes.

"You are safe now, children. You are with those who love you, who understand you. You can be quiet. You are allowed to be peaceful. Indeed, you, little boy, you, little girl, the meek shall inherit the earth. And what an earth! We all know God, and know and know and know. But what if we were to become Him? To join Him?"

Amen! said some in the crowd. They were fiddling with their bags. Clyde, having finished his rounds, came back with a sleeve of tiny paper cups and an old ceramic shoulder jug filled with new corn whiskey he'd pulled from Grace's shed. He gave a little to all around him. The teenagers were thrilled. Grace was still rattling on about God's army.

"Those in the back, are those weapons of Christ?" she asked. The armed men stood silent.

"Look, friends, it starts in heaven. What is this light if not the fatherly smile of God speaking to us in the only beautiful language he has, the language that lets us see, the language that lets us move through his kingdom, the light. The people walking in darkness still, this is all their inheritance. This is all they have yet to see." She began spinning with her arms open, her mouth open, looking up at the blue sky. The cicadas and chorus of summer bugs buzzed through the air.

"So many still living down there," she went on, gesturing down at the lowlands, "they live still in a land of deep, spiritual darkness. But here, up here, a light has dawned. It is love. It is war if it must be, but it is love. It is the terrible feeling of knowing we have already crossed through into the sublime unseeable, the unnavigable, the horror, but always wanting more. We are a people together, a city on a mountaintop that cannot be flooded. You are the flesh; I am the cloudbreak, friends, I am the beam of glory breaking through the grey. I am the blood, illuminated. Let all see that pure spirit in which we now radiate.

"Now eat of this love, eat of this love, experience it. I said I cannot speak in God's language, but I can open up your ears and eyes. I can hear God's language and you, you can speak it!"

Some now stood in the sunlight, swaying and babbling incoherently. "We are atop the raging waves of the brutal earth. We are closer to heaven than most will ever be. Do not deny it now, look up, drink up! Yes, Clyde, let them drink. Oh, Clyde, won't you let them drink?

"That is what the world wants of you; whatever you may be fighting against now, speaking against now, they want you to drown yourself in that nasty blackness forever. But we *will not go!* Will we go?"

No! sounded the congregation.

"For we can be here, together, you beautiful patriots, you beautiful soldiers and maidens of the Lord, here, in the triumphant gaze of God, listening in the language of the Lord. What, now? Awake! Awake, damn you! And drinketh down of this, this transubstantiated miracle of blood. Eat now at his decadent body and taste, undeserving as you are, just a bit of our Saviour's grace and patience. Just for—just for a moment."

Grace shot her hands up into the air and stood frozen in the glaring sunlight. Patriots, she'd said. Clyde didn't have to wonder where she got that. It was directed squarely at the half-dozen men with guns.

A woman dressed in sweatpants and an American flag shirt began shaking and talking nonsense. She seemed to be fighting the urge to cluck like a chicken, pausing every once and again to enunciate her spastic movement. Others around her yelled *Praise Jesus! Praise Jesus!*

Clyde knew this would make Grace very happy, and he was happy for her. But he couldn't quite make out just what the point of the sermon was. He eyed the stoic newcomers in the back to see what they thought of it, to see if they were at all moved. They remained still and quiet throughout.

"We are up on the mountain, friends, far from the lake and fire of brimstone, and you will not be cast, not from this mountain, not from me, not if I can bear it, not if I can bear it. Praise Jesus!"

"Praise Jesus!" the congregation rejoined.

"Praise God!" Grace shouted, shaking now too, throwing her head back and stumbling around like a sick animal. Many joined in the epileptic reverie, rolling around like lunatics convulsing on the ground, smearing mud across their good clothes, pulling up clumps of grass from the ground, seizing and smiling. Grace continued praising the Lord, electrifying herself with her own conjured energy, pulling the sides of her body up and letting them drop as her arms reached toward the sky, flopping like a fish out of water. The children joined in, laughing and playing, making angels in the long grass.

"Praise him!"

The last parishioner licked the last of the dust from the pewter plate from his finger, gazed back at Grace, and began to cry as she stood, out of breath, and looking now, to Clyde, very old.

"Slay the third part of yourself. Slay not your vision, not your language, not the language of now, not the language of light and God, but slay your pride, which guides you now more than your eyes. Feel the Lord. Trust in Grace!" she said. "Trust, trust, trust!"

Trust! Trust! Trust!

Clyde cleaned up the refuse from the sermon. After all the ecstasy and revelling—as people walked through the forest toward their vehicles, some touching trees as they went, a few discarding their clothes and pulling on one another, kissing in beds of thousand-year-old layers of leaves, others punching one another in the shoulder, high and confident—after all that, the only things remaining were trash and a setting sun.

The new congregants, including the militiamen, had dispersed with the rest, moving peacefully down the road back to their trucks and cars. Clyde was still rattled by the sight of them. He thought

for sure Grace would know. He couldn't help wondering if she'd had a hand in orchestrating their presence. Maybe she had encouraged it, welcomed it. Hickok had called Grace his friend. He didn't like that.

After all the chairs were put away and the garbage bags hauled off behind the barn with the wheelbarrow, Clyde went straight on to his trailer. He resisted the urge to go up to Grace's house. He didn't know how to square his long absence with the little he had to show for it. And he didn't want to admit what a fool he'd made of himself at the muster.

The trailer door was closed again. Someone had been there. Clyde bit down and breathed out to prepare himself for a pair of revellers. It wouldn't be the first time two teenagers had gone in there to fuck around after service.

"All right now, go on and get outta here," he said as he flung open the door, but it was Grace inside.

"I told you to get alms, Clyde. I told you to put up the posters and get the alms and come back. This could have been yours!" She gestured widely with her hands. "But look, always by the threshold, son, sin crouches." She walked into Tyler's room, and Clyde followed.

A mass of white sheets wrapped around a human figure, splotched with brown, lay on the fold-out couch that used to be Tyler's bed. Candles had been lit ceremonially as if they were about to perform a wake. It smelled like spoiled milk, like an abattoir. He couldn't believe she'd left this for him. Flies buzzed all around.

He met her eyes after a few breaths, each of them huffing as though they'd just returned from a jog. He saw that juice from the mummified figure had pooled in a dip of the sheet. Tyler's body had been there since he'd left.

"I need to shave, Grace." He held back a retch.

"You call me Shepherd, you," she said. "Today of all days, you call me Shepherd, goddammit, you, *Clyde*. Save your two-faced

grumblings and shavings for Peter at the gate, damn you! You disappeared. I have had no groceries, no liquor, no wine, no help with *this*!" She gestured toward the body.

"And what is all this about you fighting and drinking with our new friends. What is all this I hear about you fighting with Pastor Hickok and acting like a damned fool? No! I don't want to hear it! I don't want to hear it!

"I've been sitting around this stinking mess all week. I expected you back much sooner, Clyde. I had plans for us, for you. No, no, no, no, no. No excuses. No excuses at a time like this. We are on the *precipice*! We are hanging on to mortality by a *thread*! But there is work to be done, and work to be done and work and work, and no! Not one word from you."

She was sweating in the still strip of sun that cut across her face. There was a long silence. Clyde made sure to close his mouth and to stand up straight, looking her in the eye.

"You're going to have to clean up this mess you've made," she said. "And you're going to bury it. You're going to bury it tonight."

"Yes ma'am," Clyde said. "I'll bury it tonight."

As Grace walked past Clyde he smelled her body odour, a mix of lilac and burning sweat like onions. She pulled her shotgun from behind the door and stepped out, letting the screen door shut between them. He looked at her, standing there in the freckled light of the rustling trees. Her grey-white hair stuck to her neck.

"That wasn't enough alms, Clyde."

"Grace," he said, "how did you get Tyler in here? Who helped you move it?"

She crunched up her face and shrugged her shoulders like a cartoon.

"*Who* in the hell do you think? We're gonna have some friends join us around here at the compound. This whole place, this whole ministry is about to grow to its rightful power. Courtesy of your friend Hickok. No thanks to you, Clyde. Now, your money's in

your underwear drawer," she said. "Ain't no underwear in there. Nasty man. You will be judged, Clyde! You *will* be judged. Now clean out this godforsaken trailer."

That night Clyde took the wheelbarrow and shovel from the side of Grace's house and wheeled them down to his trailer. There was no moon. He hauled the sopping body up over his shoulder and walked out the screen door with a cigarette in his mouth; the door closed on him, knocking the cherry off; it went down his shirt and he stumbled trying to snuff it out, dropping the body onto the wheelbarrow from the top of the trailer stairs. It sounded like a drum echoing through the still night.

Clyde lay the shovel over Tyler's body and then proceeded through the woods. The small trees that never had a chance stood in his way, still green and wiry; as he passed through the brush they snapped back from the wheelbarrow, hitting him in the face. He stopped about a hundred yards in and found a soft spot in the earth, free from any protruding rocks or stumps. He started digging.

He heard animals in the trees and thought back to the men firing their rifles over his head. Hickok had gotten to Grace before Clyde could even clean himself up. And she still let him be the errand boy, passing out little pills and bullshit. Flyering around and sweeping up after her party like a teenager. He held the shovel in his hands and fantasized about hitting Hickok in the head with it. *You'll get your chance,* he said to himself.

He could smell Tyler from where his body sat in the wheelbarrow, leaned up against a big yellow poplar. The shape of the sheet-wrapped mound was collapsing on itself as though it were melting. How was he to know this was his job? Grace had given him his job, just as she'd given him a hundred others before. And did he not always do what she asked? There was probably record attendance at the sermon. And she was still so ornery. He wanted a way out. Needed to finish this insane business once and for all.

Load his clothes and shaving kit into his truck and drive down that road for the last time. He was caught up in something big, something stinking like the body a few yards from him, bloated and grotesque. It was batshit crazy before, but here he was, digging graves. The men with guns. He couldn't believe she'd gotten them to move the body into his trailer.

The grave was easy digging, and after an hour it was about six feet long and four feet deep. He stood in it and ran his hand from his nipple to the edge of the grave. Deep enough. Now the noises in the trees started an unnatural-sounding stop and stutter. The steps of someone moving closer. The night was so dark. Clyde pulled a Maglite out of his pocket and reached his other hand toward the sheathed knife that dangled from his jeans. An animal?

Peering out over the grave, Clyde kept his eyes on the line of the ground, thinking if there was a break in the wall of foliage it would happen there first, and might give him some time to react. He did not want a black bear or even a coyote to jump in the grave with him. He thought the smell of Tyler's body might be what was bringing it toward him, especially a coyote. Silencc.

Then a gentle rustling of leaves and pine branches, slow and careful. Clyde clicked on the weak yellow glow of the Maglite and beamed it into the sound. A white line shone like the edge of the sun behind thick grey clouds and reflected back at him from behind a tree, ruffled in its movement, and disappeared. Not a coyote. Silence again.

He climbed out of the grave, took hold of the wheelbarrow's rough handles, and walked it closer to the edge. Then he tipped it toward the hole and the body slid off, an outer sheet catching a rusted edge of the wheelbarrow, spinning the body and turning it clockwise.

Tyler lay there naked and perpendicular to the hole in the ground. Despite the moonless sky his body seemed to emanate a certain light, a contrast to the dark earth and foliage around it. Clyde climbed in, trying not to breathe, lifted the stiff body above his head, and turned it. Holding Tyler's buttocks, Clyde set the head down into the hole

then shimmied up out of it, Tyler's legs dragging along the front of his jeans.

He filled the hole with the fresh earth and kicked whatever leaves he could over the site, vowing aloud not to return but knowing, for prudence, he would have to.

The next morning, just after daybreak, a sheriff tapped on the screen door of Clyde's trailer, which he'd left open to get the stink out of it.

Clyde was put under arrest. A neighbour had noticed something suspicious, the report said. Something about a roommate of his not returning, then his hauling a large white mass out to the woods with a shovel and returning with an empty wheelbarrow.

Dalton

MONTHS WENT BY. Dalton was doing some work on the weekends now to pay rent—odd jobs he'd pick up with some other guys from the park. Send-it-home work. It seemed to Dalton that half their pay was spent by the end of the month, so in the height of summer the men would try to make it back by painting houses for little old ladies, doing demo work and half-assed renos for new couples moving into Charleston.

They'd cram in a truck and go into town and sit around the parking lot of the local hardware store, waiting for someone to pick them up. Some would bring tools. Some had real skills. Hanging drywall, framing, plumbing. Dalton always tried to tag along and get what he could.

Sometimes the work would come, sometimes it wouldn't. On the worst, hottest days, the glare would send the ready-to-work men scurrying to find shade as the hours pulled the sun across the blacktop until it was noon, and by then it was too late to start a job anyway. Time was out of their hands.

Most of the men would start drinking then, divvying up a bottle of tequila or whiskey or corn liquor right there in the parking lot. Drinking like it was the end of the world. No one around cared

when the day drifted into these collapses of time. Usually they were disappointing only those very far away: a wife in Guadalajara, a cousin waiting to meet up in Texas. Dalton had just himself to disappoint.

They'd gotten a job this weekend, though, and it paid enough to cover the rent but not enough to get him anywhere new. His weekdays had been spent at the local library, modest as it was, crammed between a hairdresser and a vape shop near the exit for the highway. Power lines hanging overhead.

The crew he'd been working with dropped him off at the top of the gravel road that led down to the little holler of the trailer park. The rest of the men were headed over to the Southern XXX-posure strip club. Dalton couldn't afford it.

The sun was setting behind the trees to the right of him and there was dust in the air as he walked down the winding road toward his trailer. Bugs flew onto him in a blood-obsessed cloud. He swatted them away and scratched at his sunburned arms, trying to squeeze out the toxins from the most recent bites, like popping a pimple that wasn't yet there.

He saw an unusual truck parked on the torn-up grass in the trailers' inner circle. A brand-new Toyota. He'd been waiting for this. Someone to drag him back to the world, to hold him to account; someone to help him do what he needed to do. He felt like he'd swallowed a rock and that it was rolling all through the inside of him as he approached.

That woman was down there, what was her name? He could see her, the reporter, standing still in trim black pants, a baggy white dress shirt hanging loosely underneath a black blazer, her shiny black hair in the sun. No cameraman.

"You moving in with us?" He tried a laugh.

"They still let you live here?"

"Who's they? They don't give a shit who lives here. Just gotta pay the super."

"My name is Laura."

"I know." He straightened his shirt and hiked up his pants. Dalton was sweaty and smelled awful from sitting in the sun half the day. He walked around her, approaching in a semicircle. He settled into the shade of the trailer. She was so clean.

There were two dirty lawn chairs set out front. He picked one up and started brushing it off, realized the dirt was long since burned into it, and set it down. "I guess you don't want to sit in one of these."

"It's all right," she said, "as long as you'll talk with me a minute."

She exuded a sort of coolness he'd never seen in a place so hot and wet. She wasn't sweating. It was as if she was so used to air conditioning that she allowed herself to somehow enjoy the dog-breath heat of the West Virginia forest.

"I'd like to make you a coffee or whatever," Dalton said, dropping his bag. "But I don't think we have anything other than water or beer." It wasn't his beer to give.

"That's okay. Do you want to talk out here?"

"You don't wanna go in there."

Dalton dug through his bag for a cigarette but couldn't find one. Just loose tobacco and gum wrappers. Other trash.

As Laura sat down she pulled out a notepad. "I lost you at the temp agency," she said. "I had to do a lot of digging, but I found you. I think I got you nailed down."

"Listen," Dalton said. "It's been what, six months? I'm good now. What do you want to talk about?"

He wiped his hands on his pants and tried to sit back and act relaxed. He felt like her coming down here was a bad sign. If she could get to him then anyone could. Was this who he wanted to find him?

"I'm doing a journalism degree at WVU. I'm really into documentary filmmaking. I want to do a sort of exposé on the pollutants in the Elk River and where they come from."

"Well, I don't know anything about it, and I couldn't say even if I did."

"Did you sign anything? Like an NDA?"

He could feel the red rush of panic crawling up his chest. Dalton put his head between his hands and leaned over in the rickety plastic chair. Then he heard a car driving down the gravel road toward them and shot straight back up to look at her.

"Let's just go in."

"Okay," she said calmly, and smoothed out her shirt. He had to halfway pull her up the steps and shut the door before Clark's shitty old Firebird came barrelling into the roundabout.

They sat down on one of the cots topped with an unmade pallet of sleeping pad and wool blanket. He was humiliated. Laura seemed to take it all in. Like she was living in a movie. She didn't belong there. She was an actor on a set.

"Off the record, and for my sake, too, off the record. I know about Freedom WV Coal," she began. "And I know about the chemicals and layoffs. I know—from stakeouts we did, I mean we've got it on film—that you dug causeways that poured fly ash and 4-MM into the river. I know you were let go at Freedom and I don't know why." She paused. "Were you stealing from them?"

"You're wrong."

"I'm not wrong," she said. "I followed up. The man on the phone said something about fraud."

"You're wrong about me stealing. I couldn't even talk to most people I worked with, and—I just did what I was told. I wasn't laid off—I wasn't even on the payroll. I don't think. I don't even know the shit you're talking about. I just did whatever—do this, do that. Dug some shit. Dumped some shit. I don't work there anymore."

She sighed. "I know you've faked your name. I know that your name is Dalton Fuquay. It only took a few calls to tie everything

up. I'm surprised you're still here. The guy at Freedom told me he thought you were someone else. Vasquez? Come on."

"All right then," he said. "Go on and tell me what you think you know." He looked away from her.

"Dalton Fuquay. Discharged from the Army about two years ago. I know that your mother has passed away since. I know, what else, your brother was in state custody in North Carolina. It was in the paper, I mean—come on. Did you know about that? Her door was open."

Dalton felt like he could kill her, sweating in the stinking trailer. Old beer cans buzzing with flies in the garbage. Musty towels hanging on the edges of the other two cots. His hands tightened around the edge of his own, squeezing the blanket underneath. He shut his eyes as hard as he could and found himself holding his breath, blinking out as he looked into the wall across from them. He felt her shift her weight to face him. She crossed her legs. He heard Clark across the way slamming on the superintendent's door again and cussing. His car still running.

"All right," Dalton said after several long moments. He breathed finally and saw black spots swirling around his vision. "Do you have a number where I can call him?"

"Your brother?"

"Yes, my brother!" he shouted at her.

"I'm sorry," she said, and waited.

"I think they might still be looking for you. You didn't, I mean—You weren't there when she died?"

He saw her pull her car keys out of her blazer pocket. He softened himself. He put his head back in his hands and let his shoulders collapse.

"No," he said. "No, it wasn't like that. I was there, but. She was just very ill and it got to where I couldn't take care of her anymore. I left." Dalton felt the heat shooting up out of his face and head into his cold hands. It was as though a dam had broken in his brain.

Everything he didn't want to think about was all he could see. His mother's bald head. Jim Hickok's hands raised above the pulpit. His brother's blond hair falling to the floor at a Discount Cutz, Messy's eyes staring at Dalton from the barbershop mirror, his head floating there, suspended, blood from Romerin's nose mixed with tears dripping into his mouth, salt and iron, his own face caked in fly ash, the water sooty in the dirty bathroom as he washed it. His eyes burning for a year or more, the moment was becoming wobbly and cloistered with his breathing.

"I just left," he said.

He looked up at her. Her eyes were flicking around the room, lapping up details. He followed them and dreaded noticing it all alongside her. He wondered if she could see what he was seeing. The blooming brown stain in the corrugated drop ceiling. The dusty, broken blinds. The triangulated series of cots around the old TV. He wondered if this was all as unreal to her as it was to him. Newly unreal. She readjusted her blazer and pulled it tight over her chest. Her forehead wrinkled in thought under her bangs.

"I need something from you," she said, coming back to him. She scooched closer. He could smell her, newly clean and laundered. It made him feel ashamed. A clean world; an orderly, clean world. And now there was something new in her voice, like she was approaching a sick dog, maybe, trying to calm it down. "And I think I can tell you where your brother is. If you want, I mean. If you need help finding him, I can help. I just need you to do something for me." She seemed nervous saying it.

He'd never felt so helpless in his life. He was sweating, falling apart and loose, but he could just as easily have been naked and frozen, pinned where he sat by ice. Pure discomfort. He knew she could see now what was happening to him. That was the only real clear thing in the world.

"I'm not just a journalist, exactly. I mean I am. I'm getting the degree," she said. "But I work for an environmental non-profit, too.

It's like a summer job. Lawyers, you know, professors. I have a lot of help. I thought I was just making a documentary about the coal runoff here in West Virginia. I don't know—maybe for school, maybe for work. I was trying to do a little of both at once, but I started sharing some of the footage and, it's—it's out of my hands. There's gonna be investigations. Lots of people are getting sick. There's a class action lawsuit in the works. The EPA is emailing us. I mean it's all on the news. I know you were working in waste processing at Freedom. I don't know— I just want to talk to you about it a little. On camera."

"I know that," he said. "Yeah, I seen it on the news." He sniffed up all the snot he could and wiped the rest away with his forearm. None of this had to do with him and Messiah. He wanted to run.

He needed to get her out of here. She could go to the capitol building protests and bother someone else. He almost wanted to go outside and let Clark kill him instead of staying there with her.

"I heard all about it," he said. "I can tell you whatever, but I don't want to do it here. I haven't worked at Freedom for a year. I don't know what you want to know, really. I'm sorry."

There was a new turn in the commotion outside. A big clap on the side of a trailer. A car door slam. Clark must have gotten back in his Firebird. He was revving it now and honking. Dalton heard him scream something about Mexicans and white Americans.

"Not here," he said again, relieved almost to be rescued by the bullshit outside.

"Seen it on the news," Laura said back to herself. She said it like she didn't believe him, maybe, or like he was just ignorant. "All right, but I don't want to know what's already out there. And if you can really attest to exactly what's been happening down here. I mean, don't you want to leave? Don't you want to go home? There are people who can help you. I think we can at least get you out of this trailer. I mean, I think so. I can't promise yet, but— It just seems like you— I don't know. Don't you want to get out of here?"

"I just don't got a lot of money," Dalton said, trying to pay attention but keeping his eyes on the door.

"If you're not married to staying here maybe you can come with me. I live off campus in Morgantown. I mean we can put some things in motion. I just need someone to talk on camera about all this, to answer some questions I have about Freedom Coal."

Clark must have been throwing things at the super's trailer again. Laura winced at the sound of crashing trash. "Well, I'll ask to see if someone can help you with your discharge status," she said.

Dalton turned from her, not wanting her to see his face at the mention of his discharge. *Jesus Christ,* he thought. "I don't want help with that," he told her. He stood up and walked over to the kitchenette sink so that he could run some cold water on his head.

"Were you asked to leave the Army?"

"Not really. I got a failure to adapt. Three years active duty but, no. Just sort of let go." He ran the water in the sink until it was cool, then cupped his hands, filled them, and splashed his face and neck.

"Don't Ask, Don't Tell?"

Dalton filled his hands with water again, raising them up gently to his eyes. He blinked them in the cold. "I ain't gay," he said, and lifted his shirt to towel off his face. He saw her staring at his pasty stomach. He dropped his shirt.

"I don't care," she said, and straightened herself again. "I'm gay."

"Well, that's good for you," Dalton said. She was bullshitting. She was like a business-school Barbie doll, he thought. She wasn't like him at all. And he wasn't, anyway. He resented this attempt to make things equal between them.

He walked over to get a beer from the mini fridge on the counter. The large fridge hardly worked. They mostly kept dry food in there in old grocery bags. Bread and cereal, sometimes apples. Just to keep the food away from the bugs. The small fridge was for the important things, like beer and medicine. Loera kept body lotion in there, too.

He pulled out a beer and waved it at her and she shook her head gently. He'd have to explain all this to Loera and Martinez when they got home. The woman, the missing beer. Nothing was his. He closed the fridge door, pulled off the cap, and drank from it as he walked back toward her. There was a long silence as he gulped. "I ain't gay," he said again.

"Okay. Okay, but what about the rest?"

"The rest of what?"

"What if we could help. How can we help you— I mean, what do you need in order to talk with us. What do you need?"

"I need to use the latrine." He hated himself for using Army slang. Like that would impress her. "Excuse me." He walked into the bathroom, leaving her on the cot.

He didn't want to piss with her out there. The door to the bathroom didn't shut all the way. He sat down.

He wanted to think a little while. He wanted to tell her something like *I'll call you back and let you know,* like he maybe had other options. Someone had come to pull him back into the real world and he was acting as though he didn't want to go. Someone had come to remind him of what he'd lost, thrown away. There were pubic hairs all over the floor in the bathroom. Someone had trimmed in there and not swept up.

He had a snap feeling: If he let her leave that would be the last he'd ever see of her. Did she really know where Messiah was? He thought he might not have a chance like this again. He looked down at his skinny legs bouncing in his spastic, nervous way. Wet with sweat, pale white against the brown of his arms. He was miserable.

"GET THE FUCK OUT. COME ON, COME ON, GET THE FUCK OUT OF THERE!"

Glass smashed against the side of the trailer. Bottles flying at the vinyl siding. Laura let out a cut-short scream. Dalton was tripping over his unzipped pants as he came running, nearly falling,

out of the bathroom. Clark was rapping on the door with something heavy. Laura was already crouching behind the counter in the kitchenette. “Get out, you fake-ass little cocksucker!” Clark was slurring. “Who the fuck, who is fuckin’ in there with you? Come on out you little motherfucker!”

Messiah

MESSIAH WOKE TO A BANDAGED MIDRIFF and an old towel taped tightly around him. The sheets he lay on were soaked through and smelled awful. Sweat and the yellow weepings from his bandage. Urine, maybe.

The room spun around him as he tried to sit up. He hurt. He wished he could vomit. Wished he could go back to sleep. When he could steady his eyes, propping himself up on one elbow, he worked to get a hold on his surroundings. A white room, crosses adorning all three walls before him, a window behind him with blue sunlight pouring in.

There were footsteps outside the room. He grew dizzy again and lay back down, panting like a dog on a hot day. Someone walked in. He could smell flowers on them, flowers and something sweet like figs. He winced his eyes shut.

A hand rested on his clammy forehead and pushed back his hair. A dry, calm voice, a woman's voice, a familiar voice, was telling him to go back to sleep. She was calling him by his name. He groaned and hiccupped and kicked his legs to pull the sheet off himself, but the hand stayed on his head and steadied it, pushing it down

into the pillows. She was singing to him now, some kind of lullaby, like he was a baby. He loosened his jaw and started breathing out of his mouth and tried to calm himself. She told him to dream now like angels dream, to think about all the angels sleeping in heaven. She said "Come here" and moved the hand to the back of his head and lifted it up. He felt a spoon come to his lips and he let it inside. A sweet burn. Molasses and something else, chalky pills broken up into syrup. He kicked and thrashed again, feeling hot now, but was cooed and calmed, the woman's tissue-paper hands gliding across his forehead and through his hair, petting him until he collapsed back into blackness.

"Messiah, Messiah. That's you," she continued to say as she stroked his head. She told him to call her Nana. "Remember me, honey? Remember your old Nana?" She sang to him and kissed him and pet him, reminding him of his name over and over again, "Such a beautiful boy, such a beautiful, beautiful child of God," she said. "In whom I am so, so well pleased. Bless you, son. Bless you, Messiah. Rejoice," she said, "rejoice," and she let her voice crack down into a whisper. She petted him and cooed to him as he dreamed. And he did know her. And he was not afraid.

But no, now he was back at the State Children's Home, the Boys' Home. Somewhere in the dark sequence Messiah had grabbed his mama's lipstick, her makeup mirror, a cigarette lighter. He'd taken it from her room, upstairs in the old house. He was putting on the lipstick. He smelled it and rubbed it on his pursed lips. Then the sleeping children around him were awake. They'd come to watch. Then he was getting a spanking.

But that was okay. He knew it was okay. Dalton was going to be here, there, sitting next to him on the blue-lit bunk bed of the Home at any moment. Messiah had settled his mind on this. It was like watching a movie, where all the rest of the world kind of drifts away.

His mother was taking her long hair down. His mama didn't know he was watching. Messiah was at the kitchen table now. Grilled cheese. He dreamed of her in all ways. She took pills to relax. Her shoes on the hardwood floors. She relaxed. She sighed. A bottle of wine. The room was getting smaller and his feelings white hot.

He was being spanked again. The spanker sat him up and pushed Messiah off her lap. She left him in the room with his pants still around his knees. The other boys stood watching, quiet. And he looked down at himself and sobbed. His shirt was hoisted up too. His belly was soft and white like a baby's but he had sparse pubic hair coming up between his legs. He couldn't understand it and he didn't fight it. He knew that this didn't happen to other boys his age. He wanted to know why it was happening to him. He wanted to ask his brother.

No. Another dream. He was at the sawmill with Clyde. They were picking out wood. They flipped it and looked down the long edge, making sure it was straight. Clyde loved Messiah. Clyde told Messiah, "That brother of yours is gonna kill your mama."

Messiah could smell Clyde. The wood, the tobacco, the truck, the exhaust somehow rerouted through the air vents, the queasy feeling of driving through the mountains, the fresh air from the always-down window, the smell of dog and Old Spice.

They were building Dalton a bookcase, a surprise and congratulations of sorts because he was gearing up to go to college.

Messiah watched Clyde have a talk with the millworker in a dark storage area. The man had walked them through a maze of stacked wood: pine cut long, cherry unplaned; all organized by type. The man showed Clyde the boards he suggested for a bookcase. "You don't want to plane this yourself, you know—"

Somewhere there his mama was brushing her hair. He could smell it. Pantene and cigarette smoke and hairspray.

The man picked up a remarkably straight board and got Messiah to sniff it. "Smells good, don't it?" the man said. His mother's hair

again. Messiah agreed, and when he looked up Clyde was shaking his head and waving his hands back and forth near his waist as if to say no to that piece in particular. Messiah was there now. He stayed right there. But his brother would still not come. Wouldn't materialize.

The warehouse smelled like hamsters and sounded like a hundred air conditioners on all at once. They continued on to the corner of the warehouse where the wood was stacked in haphazard piles of different lengths and widths; some boards leaned on an angle and some boards were laid flat with heavy bricks or a piece of equipment on either end.

"I think this ought to do the trick, Clyde," the shadow of the other man said. "You get the walnut here, and I'll give you a deal. Tell you what. If you help me lift it over to the other side of the floor I'll run each piece twice through the planer. No cost, no sir. I can do that for you."

Messiah watched as Clyde again shook his head and eyed the warped discards.

"How about this? This is nice cherry," Clyde said.

"You said this here's for your boy?" the man was saying, his voice echoing around Messiah's head.

"Yessir," Clyde said, "but not this boy. This one here is a late bloomer. Don't need a bookshelf yet for you, do we, son? But we're going to fix that soon enough." Clyde waited there, his image evaporating into the dark of the surrounding warehouse. He said, "Ain't we, Messy? Ain't we gonna fix it?"

Clyde said it again and again: "Ain't we, Messy? Ain't we, Messy? Ain't we gonna fix it, Messy? Ain't we gonna fix that?"

Messiah came to only intermittently at first, catching markers not of time passing but what felt like his world shrinking. It was all this room, this smell of himself suffocating him. It was all the cracking of dried scabs and rough tape on his body, his buttocks raw and

stinging in the sweat like diaper rash. It was amazing that he hadn't had to go to the bathroom, he thought, but blushed at the realization that he'd been lying in his own bathroom, for how long he couldn't say.

He'd been lying on the floor on a pallet composed of three or four quilts, all nearly slimy with all that was coming from him. There was an old-timey bedpan in the corner and a plastic pitcher of something brown with condensation on the outside of it. Recently delivered. Fruit and herbs were floating in the pitcher, an unused glass just beside. He reached for it, and spilling only a little, managed to bring the jug up to his mouth and drink. As he pulled his mouth away he spilled some tea on his chest; it ran down over the dozen little birdshot pockmarks in his body.

He lay there looking around him for a long time. He found himself fixating on the idea of his brother. Dalton in his uniform, Dalton with his black hair over his eyes, smiling. Dalton arguing with their mother. Dalton holding their mother after she'd shouted so much at him that she'd nearly collapsed. He wondered when his brother would come in and take him home. His mama would take him home. These were his first thoughts.

Then the Perkins's house, then the creek and the hike up the mountain. The storm and the appalling lightning and rain, the freezing mud and the gunshot and the choking pain. He removed the bandage from his chest and stomach, the tape leaving big inch-wide welts across where it had been stuck to him. He saw what looked only like chicken pox scabs. Clean and white like when you're in the bathtub too long, he thought. The holes a little deeper and redder than chicken pox. His body ached to move.

He was nervous about the image he had in his brain of him and Hawk naked just come up out of the creek, their hands ridged like peach pits, all of Hawk wet and wrinkled like his bandaged skin, all of Hawk soaked through down to the very nooks of him. His hands on Hawk's shoulders. The two of them face to face.

He tasted bitter in his mouth and around his dry lips, the dust of something chalky wiped into his gums that both sickened and relaxed him as he explored his fuzzy moustache with his tongue. He was afraid and sweating and helpless. His mind wandered to the possibility that someone had seen them together. Someone had taken Hawk's daddy's truck, that was sure—someone had hurt him and then fixed him, but he had seen no nurse and no hospital. He waited for his Nana to come back in, but before the door opened he was back with the sleeping angels. He didn't even feel the washcloth come to clean him, Hawk's hands underneath him rolling him over and onto a new pile of quilts.

After another angel-laden sleep Messiah awoke again to pain and was still alone. He wanted to get out of this room.

His body told him that it wasn't yet time to move, but he struggled against the pain and got to his feet. He felt his breath torn away from him and fell to his knees. His searching hands pulled down on the dark wooden crosses nailed to the wall beside the makeshift bed. He pulled down the ornaments, sending them crashing around the room, thrashing in his attempt to stand. He prayed for someone to come find him. His brother. He fell to the floor.

Messiah struggled back to his feet and shuffled, leaning on furniture and against walls and then the doorway out into a hallway of that place. More crosses on the wall. He touched them as he steadied himself, walking toward what sounded like a woman praying.

The rhythm of the prayer was powerful and gaining momentum, a thrumming hum of incantations so streamlined he felt it was calling to him, murmuring against him or toward him, he did not know. The silence, this quiet eternity of pain, had finally broken. Another storm outside. Lightning crashing again. The world was sharp like cold water had been thrown over everything. Messiah tried to yell for someone to come and get him, to come carry him, but he couldn't choke out a word.

He felt it before he heard it, that same old rumble come to drag him into more trouble. Thunder rumbled through the house like the delayed echo of the gunshot. Flashes of light came bursting through the open windows and the wind excited and animated the house with creaks and whistling, the crazed jangle of wind chimes in a maelstrom.

The lightning was blinding. It froze the scene before him like the flash from an old camera, searing it in his mind. Each strike set a negative image in his eyes, illuminating the room in blue-white relief—ratty deer heads, stacks of Bibles, worn pelts on the floor, a nail in the wall surrounded by the discoloration of a discarded picture frame. A cross, a cross, a cross on the wall. Crosses everywhere. Messiah blinked, adjusting to the candlelight as he found the end of the hallway. He followed the voice of the old woman snaking, shouting, hissing from another room, her incantation pulling Messiah into it, toward her. The flash of the lightning guided him. Unused words, unreal words. Magnetic language came coughing out from under the woman's breath, strangely cheerful. Her great moans and gasps blended with the thunder rattling the uneven floor beneath him. He reached toward the figure there in the dark and collapsed.

Messiah rested in the doorway, watching the woman sway and chant to herself, surrounded by candles. She was staring out through the glass, shouting her laughing, loud-whispered language at her reflection in the window, blackened by the stormy night outside. She was lit by flames. When the lightning flashed her reflection disappeared. She walked toward him.

"Come here, Messiah," she said. She continued speaking soft words he'd never heard before—calming words, natural words, familiar words. As she drew close she paused, blew the candle out, and was on him, holding him and petting him in the darkness. The intermittent flashes of lightning erupted behind the window.

"Shhhh, hush now. Shhhh, shhhh, shhhh," she said. "I know it is hard, Messiah. Your brother gone and your mama gone. Yes, Lord," she said. "Yes, Lord."

She drew in a big breath and held it, squeezing Messiah's head to her chest.

Days passed in a merry-go-round of recurring headaches and shadows dabbing at his skin. Brown piss leaking into a mangled biscuit pan beneath him, the ammonia reek startling. The old woman was a dark blur in the haze of half-opened, sticky eyelids. She sometimes answered his moans. Sometimes they were met with silence.

In the musty afternoons of his awakening, Messiah heard her thumping, her hobbling around the house, stamping down hard on the floor to punctuate or interrupt her mutterings.

The mumbling, muffled sounds of obedience from Hawk made Messiah embarrassed. He couldn't stand to hear even the kindest words from the woman without feeling sorry for Hawk, even when she announced that she was running a bath for him. The bathroom was next to Messiah's room, and he heard her saying "Drink this, will you?" and "Now, that ain't so bad, is it, sweetheart?" and "Now thank the Lord. Now thank the *Lord*, I said," and Hawk would.

Wherever Hawk stayed was further off down the hall. Messiah couldn't hear him coming or going or exactly what happened to him at night—just that he yelped, he cried, and he moaned until he eventually quieted, his little sobs absorbed into the walls. The room, the whole world shrank around Messiah as he tossed and thrashed in and out of sleep.

Each morning Messiah was given a drink that tasted like a rain-filled ashtray. He knew he tasted medicine—the bitter, chalky pang of crushed pills floating in a sweet mix of water and sugar—something that reminded him of gas stations. The woman brought in a bedside lamp that hummed and buzzed next to his head. Once

he'd drunk that foggy brown mixture from a tin cup she would read to him from Genesis, or from Psalms. He prayed and asked Graham to tell him which part of the Bible he was in. All so familiar and all so strange.

Messiah awoke feeling lucid for the first time after being shot. The world, unlike his past few days, was clear as dripping dew. It was still and see-through and calm.

Hawk walked into Messiah's room, tripping on the broken, knock-off antiques and yard furniture that had been dragged there, all this clutter, spray-painted or half spray-painted, on newspapers that acted as the carpet. It occurred to Messiah that he was lying in a junk room on a daybed lounger with a ratty old mattress on top. He wondered where Hawk had slept. He asked.

"I haven't," Hawk said quietly, and then smiled as if he was hiding something. "Not really."

Hawk dipped a cream-coloured hand towel into a mixing bowl half-filled with water, most of which he'd spilled while navigating around the lawn junk and furniture topped with piled-up Christian prayer tracts and dust. Messiah looked at Hawk's wrists. They'd been cut up or dug into circumferentially. The thin red scabs that circled them screamed out at Messiah in their pain. He looked for worry in Hawk's face. He found none.

"Well, what does she say?" Messiah asked.

"What do you mean what does she say? Here—" And Hawk's red hands slowly peeled back the cut-up towel tied around Messiah's white chest. He set the bowl down and began to clean Messiah's wounds.

"Did you call the cops?"

"No," Hawk said. "Didn't think to." He smiled then, coy and unconvincing. It was a different smile from the one he'd had on when he looked at Messiah on the bank of the creek. "I thought we could stay here."

Messiah relaxed, exhausted by his effort to pull something

genuine out of Hawk. He let Hawk debride the pus-filled holes in his chest. The water was hot and cleansing. It hurt so bad but the water cooled as it trickled down Messiah's belly, wetting the underwear he was wearing that was far too small for him.

"I think we ought to stay," Hawk said. "I don't want to go back. I think she's got money. I mean I've spent the past two days doing chores for her. She keeps giving me, I don't know, twenty dollars. Doesn't matter what I do. Chopping wood, doing dishes. It ain't so bad."

"Who else is here?"

"Ain't nobody else. Well, I don't know. She's got people working on her land. There's lots of land. She's got people with little houses and camps working all day. She does a sermon for them on Sundays. She's like a kind of preacher. She prays a lot. All day almost. Can you stand up?"

Hawk bent over and slid his hand underneath Messiah's back and pulled on him without much success. All that was in the room was their eyes and shared air.

"Get the hell off me, don't *touch* me," Messiah said.

Messiah tore his wrists from Hawk's grip. But he was standing now. And now he stepped back, slipping away from Hawk's ineffectual grabs until Hawk gave up and started rummaging through the room. Messiah was left leaning against a wall. He watched Hawk move some of the junk around like it would help. Hawk made a big show of it, lifting furniture and old boxes and rearranging them loudly and dramatically, mimicking an adult fight.

"All right," Messiah said. "All right, I can move around. Let's go see. Let's go see her."

"We can fish, she's got a stocked pond," said Hawk. He was moving slowly, watching Messiah. "We can hunt. Beyond that treeline there's an orchard where she's been sending me to go pick apples before they drop. I went real early yesterday and saw a whole ton of

deer. She's got guns, too. Lots of them. And plenty of rounds: thirty-ought-six, twenty-two, whatever."

Messiah felt like he'd been asleep for longer than he'd been alive. "How long we been here?"

"Oh, I don't know, man," Hawk said.

They walked further through the messy house. Papers everywhere, as if a hurricane had torn through a museum. In the grey, clouded noon light, every detail struck Messiah as stark and purposeful and amazing. Beneath all the pamphlets and Bibles stood beautiful, decadent furniture. It all stood out to him like a black-and-white photograph.

"Look here," Hawk said too loudly in Messiah's ear, both of them huffing, one from pain and the other from excitement. "Look, she's got pews from a church. She's got cases of whiskey and all sorts of shit like that. She said she'd get me whatever food I'd like, whatever clothes I'd like."

"So how are we going to get outta here? Where's the road?"

"Later. Now come with me and I'll show you the rest of the place."

The two boys walked out of the house and started across the property, Messiah cricking his neck to get a better look at the house over his shoulder. It was the grey of untreated wood after many storms, yet not without magnificence. The shutters were real, and some swung off their latches, half-open. The glass had a sheen like oil on water.

Messiah noted the leafless brown vines, the skeleton of a Virginia creeper that wrapped the porch like stiff latticework. There were dogs running around, racing from the far side of the house then right at them, their crazed, smiling tongues flapping like banners, their breath joining the enveloping vapour with each quick pant and gallop.

"We're going down to the apple orchard I told you about," Hawk said. "They're almost in season. We can eat them right off the tree."

The lot they were on looked like it had been manicured by movie-set professionals. The grass grew plush, the surrounding trees grew thick. The forest was trimmed back just enough to make the clearing look like a stage. The sky weighed heavy with chirps and ringing, loud enough that Messiah wondered if his ears had been blown out from his getting shot. Ringing all around him. Hawk's voice was barely treading water in the wave of sound. Messiah felt an energy rise up within him from the wet grass between his toes, from the humid air, the overlapping cacophony of birdsong. He was in church. The sound was like how stained glass boxed him into a spiritual world; all was steeped in history, and all was above history, and all was natural and real in a mythic way, beyond questioning.

The boys kept walking. Messiah was fading. They moved further away from the house and down to a pond in a flatter area of the clearing. There was steam rising, somehow thicker than the fog that had settled above and around them; the atmosphere was a cloud, hazy and unreal. They came to a windowless shack that seemed built from spare barn parts. A thin man opened its door and peeked out, showing the boys a toothless smile.

"Who is that?" Messiah asked.

"It's her people," Hawk said. "It's people she got working for her. They're fine. Nice and all—they go to the church service like I said. They work for her, too. We ought to work for her, Messiah. She thinks we might."

Messiah watched as the man retreated into the shack. He heard the man say something unclear, something in a reverent tone. He heard children laughing.

"They got whole families living up here?"

"Not *they*," Hawk said. "*She*. She's got all kinds of things goin' on up here."

The boys traipsed along, Messiah leaning harder on Hawk's shoulders through the sparse woods where knotty sticks broke

beneath their feet. Messiah's towel bandage began slipping off, but the wet air felt good on his shallow wounds—shallower now, he felt, and sealed up with scabs.

Hawk was navigating, Messiah taking every step in an uneasy relationship with the soft ground, trusting his friend. It still hurt for him to breathe.

"Hey, Hawk, I don't wanna go. I think I need to stop. I don't want to go wherever we're going, I—" He caught his breath. "Okay. Okay, but don't—" He breathed hard in and out a few times. Hawk's shoulders relaxed.

An animal sprinted past them too fast for Messiah to see what it was. It dove into a culvert lined with rhododendron bushes. The jack pine in the thick of the culvert began shaking; there was a yelp and then silence. One of the dogs, maybe. Messiah's grip grew tighter on Hawk's shoulders and they continued. As the forest became thicker with trees and the trail grew harder underneath Messiah's feet the fog became thick as cream and swirling around the black trees. Hawk parted the bush line and the boys stepped into the orchard.

It was another small clearing, this one with tall grass, a square of which had been trampled down. The trees weren't quite in a row but were zigzagged, a diamond pattern thatched like a basket's weave. Hawk led Messiah through the first row and into the second, then the third, and Messiah couldn't decipher where he was. He was surrounded by trees and the sound of rustling leaves. It was as though no other place existed on earth. Hawk stopped walking and Messiah dropped his arms from Hawk's shoulders.

Hawk turned around and stared right into Messiah's eyes. No smile there. It was a look of encouragement and insistence. Hawk stepped off to the side. Behind him was a figure coming closer.

Messiah stood up straight, the pain lessening now in his chest. His breath deepened as if he'd come up from underwater. A hush came over the orchard. The world seemed to still. Messiah heard

the squish of small feet right in front of him and felt knobby, ice-cold hands reach up and under his bandage, popping off the tape and caressing his dry, shallow wounds.

Messiah shuddered and fell backward, scrounging at the ground behind him with the slippery butts of his palms. But something about the woman's eyes calmed him down. He looked at Hawk, who didn't seem surprised at all. Hawk nodded his head.

Messiah's Nana was wide-eyed. She was in a trance. Her white dress was soaked through with dew, and Messiah wondered whether she'd been in this orchard all night and all morning.

"Welcome home, son," she said. "Welcome home, Messiah. Welcome to heaven."

She fell to her knees and began to pray before him.

Part III

Messiah

IN HIS TIME ON THE MOUNTAIN, Messiah's blond hair had grown past his shoulders and sat now in braids on either side of his head. Willie Nelson style, he called it. He'd become a good driver over the past months, not without a few close calls with police, although none ultimately minded the speeding truck. It had state-issued plates that simply said FARM USE, acting as a sort of signal to the sheriffs and state patrolmen that this truck was just headed down the road, driven by bona fide country boys on local business. When Hawk drove he'd fly by them with a wave from the top of the steering wheel, a devil-may-care attitude that shook Messiah to exhaustion and so unnerved him that he took to driving most times. On nights like these Hawk would wind himself up, beating on Messiah's shoulders after a job, saying "Go faster, go faster, Messy! I can't believe it! Drive, drive!" He complimented Messiah's driving again and again, seeing how the encouragement worked on his friend. Hawk even called his ability to downshift the truck and act natural after a job "icy cool," which made Messiah feel truly remarkable. And in this way he learned to drive.

They followed the directions, a little further each week than the last, going out in widening circles radiating from Buffalo Mountain.

Messiah knew this because the adrenaline-sick trips home felt longer and longer. And even with his braids flying in the wind of the open windows and even with Hawk's encouragement, the longer drives took a toll. The regret had more time to pile up. As the excitement wore off and the reality of the splashing kerosene, of the burning pews, caught up to them, they grew quiet and retreated into themselves. Sometimes Hawk would hear his favourite song come on the radio and crank it up till the speakers rattled. And even then Messiah would find himself crawling inward to the familiar comforts of memory, fighting against it all to think about his brother, his mother, Graham, about all that loss set against the dry-eyed afterimage of flames. All that flashing against the panes of stained glass as the churches burned. All that they'd done for Grace and for God.

It got so that he'd start in early on this introversion and focused memory. Those first few giddy trips with Grace sitting between them on the bench seat, explaining the everlastingness of their destructive work—all that had grown into a cold routine. And like any driver on his way to work Messiah was elsewhere, even as Hawk asked him endless questions, went over the plan again and again, shouted directions, smoked cigarettes with verve. Messiah went inside himself.

Right now he was in the last moments of his mother saying goodbye when he left her. And there he'd be, the Blue Ridge fog parting before them like grey curtains cut by their beam light. The jerry cans of kerosene sloshing in the truck bed behind them. He struggled to remember her face as it had been. He saw a bald mannequin now, waving as though pulled by some string when he boarded the bus in the hot church parking lot, never really to return. Not really.

"All right we're gonna hit this motherfucker quiet," Hawk said. "Just like last time. You just waltz in. Someone was supposed to leave the door open for us. You just waltz in and drag out whatever alms you can find. Anything in a box with the warning label on it.

That's what they say. Don't worry about what it is, just worry about the label. If it's restricted, we want it."

They pulled into a quiet strip-mall parking lot in Galax. The black letterboard sign outside the methadone clinic said GUEST TREATMENT AVAILABLE! The lights inside were on. They circled the building and parked out back. A car sat in the lot with its lights off, but the windows were fogged up. Messiah said, "You think we ought to see who's in there?" Hawk ignored him.

"All right. I'll scoot over and keep it running." Hawk pulled out a little glass pipe, dropped a few shards of meth into it, and lit up. "I'll stay on the lookout."

Messiah got out and went to the back to grab the black backpack they always took on jobs like this. He pulled his hood over his head and pulled on some mechanic's gloves. Nothing moved in the little back lot. As he walked to the door he kept his eyes on the parked car. A beige Taurus with a dent in the side. *Can't be cops if it looks like that,* he thought.

Sure enough, the clinic's back door was open. Grace had worked another miracle. Still, Messiah knew he was on camera and considered the possibility of a silent alarm. The place looked just as it ought to look. Like so many he'd been in to get alms. The beige doctor's tables with the paper pulled up over them. Clean as a whistle.

Messiah found the little mini fridge hidden behind a set of faux cabinets. It had a combination lock on it. He pulled the backpack off his shoulder, unzipped it, and drew out a small pair of bolt cutters. He snipped the lock, took nine litres of methadone solution from the fridge, and put them in his bag. He listened hard for a buzzing.

He flung open every other cabinet and drawer in the office, careful not to touch his head or expose his hair. Nothing else worth grabbing.

The only other doors in the clinic's little office went to bathrooms. This was it, he thought. He zipped up the bag tight and

walked toward the back. The street lamp behind the strip mall had timed out. The truck was still running. As Messiah got closer, though, he saw that Hawk wasn't inside.

He threw the backpack in the bed and stamped over to the Taurus where Hawk was tapping on the window with the barrel of a 9mm he'd gotten from one of the revival's regular militia members. "Hellooooo," Hawk said into the window.

"Helllloooooo, hellooooooo."

"Let's go, Hawk. Jesus Christ."

They could make out a rustling in the car. A woman in the driver's seat wiped one line of fog from the windows and peered out. Silence for a moment. "Let's go, Hawk. Please."

"What did you see?" Hawk shouted now at the driver.

"She wasn't gonna see shit, Hawk."

"Hellloooooo!" Hawk yelled. He tapped and tapped the barrel of the gun against the window and started to laugh to himself.

"I'll get in the truck," Messiah said.

Messiah half-walked, half-ran back to the truck, about fifteen yards away. The door of the clinic still hung open. Lights were on now, and Messiah hadn't turned them on. They might be on a timer or not, or part of the alarm system, but he knew they had to leave.

"Okay, bitch," Hawk shouted at the Taurus. "Okay, then! Don't answer me. Are you— Are you on your phone?"

Hawk smashed the glass of the Taurus and the woman screamed. Messiah put the truck in gear.

"Why wouldn't you just talk to me?" Hawk asked again and again. "Why wouldn't you just say hello?"

Messiah drove toward them, put the truck in park, and revved the engine.

Hawk had reached in and unlocked the driver's door from the inside. When he pulled it open the woman fell out, already curled up, screaming and crying.

Hawk looked back at Messiah, who beckoned him to the truck. “Let it go!” he yelled.

“What the fuck!” Hawk shouted. “Goddammit. What the fuck! She’s going to call the police on us!”

Messiah got out of the truck and strode over to Hawk. He shrugged Messiah off him and pointed his gun at the woman on the ground.

“Don’t look at her,” Messiah said. “Let’s just go.”

Hawk pulled the trigger. He shot the asphalt next to the crying woman, the sound ringing out and back from the surrounding hills. Her companion was curled up in the passenger seat and turned away from them. Messiah grabbed Hawk’s arm and pulled the barrel away from the women. “They’re just waiting to work,” he said. “To clean or something! Look man, she’s scared. Let’s go. Let’s go. Let’s go.”

Hawk turned away from the Taurus and walked toward the truck. Messiah looked at the woman in the passenger seat. She’d pulled out her phone and was shaking, waving it in front of her face and chest, crossing herself with the blue light. Messiah stepped over the woman on the ground and leaned into the car, reached in and gently took the phone from the woman, and pulled himself back out. He picked up the other phone from the ground and pocketed both, then walked around the front of the truck and got behind the wheel and closed the door. Before Hawk closed his own door he stuck his arm through the crack and fired two, three shots into the black of the hills. The women screamed.

Dalton

HE WAS HEARING the same spiel on every local news station in West Virginia. The fallout from Freedom WV Industries' pollution was flowing southbound from county to county in the western part of the state, coal country, poisoning tributaries. Warnings, orders, advisories: they followed him on the airwaves as he drove.

The focus of the stories changed as he made his way through Virginia and into North Carolina. He flipped across stations to hear more about the various poisonings downstream from the coal plant. But as he continued south the news was all about fires. Arson at churches, robberies followed by fires at pharmacies and community outreach centres. The guilt he was running from, a fist squeezing tighter and tighter in his gut, was blending now with these new stories. The feeling that he alone was responsible for so much sadness built to such a pressure that his heart was about to burst with it. He kept listening. He was imagining himself lighting the fires, burning everything down. He listened maniacally as if it were more news about himself, as if at any minute he'd hear his name.

He'd tried to logic the sense away, yet it was still with him, a combination of hope and dread. Knowing he'd been mixed up with

the poisoned water north of him; fearing the sight of a burning building as he drove south. He wanted things to slow down.

His jaw ached and his chest and hips and stomach were still raw from where Clark had dragged him through the gravel outside his door. He hadn't been ready to commit to Laura's idea; hadn't known what he wanted to do as he sat there with her in the trailer. Now, though, he thought that maybe how it all happened had given him some leeway, the right kind of excuse to act out again, to set him on the road to North Carolina.

He'd zipped up his pants as Clark was still shouting, sending rocks and bottles at the trailer. When he'd heard Laura scream it had made him feel cowardly for even being there. He thought that if he could put himself in Clark's way Laura could leave. Maybe Clark would kill him, he remembered thinking. It might solve half his problems.

Dalton had walked past Laura to Loera's footlocker and pulled out the snub-nosed .38 revolver that Loera cleaned while the roommates watched TV together. It wasn't loaded. There was another crash at the door and Clark yelled, "Get out here, Vasquez! I ain't gonna ask again."

Dalton stuck the pistol in the waistband at the back of his pants and walked to the door and opened it. Clark was standing with his nose pressed to the screen, breathing whiskey and garlic into Dalton's eyes. Clark ripped open the screen door and grabbed Dalton by the back of the neck and threw him down the stairs. Dalton was face-down for half a second before Clark was on him, grabbing his arms and dragging him across the ground, the rocks tearing up the soft skin of his stomach, pushing their way down into his pants. His shoe had come off and his arm felt like it had been pulled out of its socket. Then Clark saw the pistol. He pulled it out of Dalton's pants and between breaths and swallowed burps said, "Ain't nobody

going to miss you, you piece of shit, you goddamn sonofabitch."

Having felt the gun leave his waist and having heard the click of the hammer, Dalton forgot that he'd brought it out unloaded. He'd covered his head with his hands and lain there, nose in the red mud, as Clark clicked through the cycle of the empty cylinder again and again. He pissed himself there. Clark had just laughed in amazement, thrown the pistol at Dalton's head, and walked away huffing.

Dalton got up, shook the rocks out of his wet pants, looked at the trailer's black threshold and shuddered. He couldn't even cry.

The screen door was half off its hinges when he walked back in. Laura watched him silently, with unblinking eyes. Sweat, maybe, streaking her face. He took off all but his underwear in the kitchenette then started the shower and rinsed off the mud and blood with cold water and Irish Spring. When he came back into the room she was still sitting there.

"Do you want to come with me?" Laura asked him.

He did. He took all he had and then some. He took Loera's gun and ammunition. He took Martinez's good boots and pocket knife. He took the communal toothpaste and the remaining cans of beer. He left no note saying goodbye or otherwise. He packed in silence and was silent all the way to Morgantown. She pulled into a hotel parking lot there and put a room on her credit card. They went up to the room together. As soon as Dalton lay down on the bed he fell asleep and slept until noon the next day.

Any thought about his predicament was purgatorial. Laced with guilt and secrecy. Laura appeared at intervals to tell Dalton about what he'd need to say and who he'd need to talk to. She arranged for him to sit down for a recorded interview but agreed it would be better to wait until the road burn on his face had healed. He got his head shaved at a barbershop in the Walmart and she bought him some new clothes. White Hanes T-shirts and Lee jeans and

socks and underwear. She got him a pay-as-you-go phone like something out of the nineties: it beeped and had soft buttons and played 8-bit songs when it rang. She gave him a little money and the keys to her truck, which she left in the hotel parking lot, telling him it was there for emergencies or in case she needed him to come in for an interview on short notice. Her daddy had another car she could borrow, she said.

He'd signed the papers and, he reassured himself now, had indeed intended on following through with his deposition when it came. He promised her he'd do whatever he could. Laura had told her non-profit she had a week more of work to do. Well, he thought, he had his own week of work to do, finding his brother.

He'd bring Messiah back to that hotel room and cut some kind of deal. He would make it right. He'd sworn to himself the morning his mother died that he would turn it around.

When he'd left the hotel he turned his phone off, not wanting to hear from Laura yet. The temptation to turn it on, to see if the deal was off, if the truck had been reported stolen: it amounted to enough existential worry to keep the phone turned off till he had a plan. He'd be honest with her, he thought. He'd tell her once he found his brother. Make it right.

After a night of driving Dalton found himself idling on Old 52 in front of his mother's house, surrounded by police tape that was now weathered and sun-faded, torn in places and lying on the ground like a ribbon-cutting ceremony come and gone.

Dalton waved cars past as they drove up behind him. He stared at the house for a good long while.

It was Friday, and he thought about his mother's last weekend. When the house stood dilapidating before him. Empty. He thought about his calling her from the phone booth, saying he'd come home. Her going to church alone. What it must have been like. Had she expected him to step through its doors with her? Her approach in

the lamplight outside their house that night. She held him. He saw her open mouth in bed. He waved another car past.

He did a U-turn and headed up to the church, the last place anyone had seen her alive other than himself. He knew Pastor Hickok would be there on a Friday afternoon. It was noon now. All the retirees getting set up for service. The church ladies. The AA meeting chairs getting pulled in a circle after their community cookbook committees. Hickok sitting up in his office, just making sure it all went his way.

Hickok would know where Messiah was staying. But the cost would be a conversation Dalton had been avoiding throughout his life. The cost would be acknowledging Jim Hickok. Looking him in the eye.

He pulled into the church parking lot, full and beaming with heat, just as some meeting or other must have been ending. Maybe a morning worship for seniors. The cars looked clean and tidy, parked just as they ought to be parked, only one or two spaces available at the back. People filed out the wide front doors in their khakis and yellow polo shirts, their dresses, their sport jackets.

As he got out of the car Dalton watched the congregants walking around under the canopy of trees on the manicured lawn, shaking hands. He climbed the steps, manoeuvring through the spilling crowd like a fish upstream, then walked through the front doors. He made his way gently through the crowded narthex and into the church proper. Some of the ladies lingered about, holding their hymnal books and notes, nodding to one another. None looked too long at him, unshaven and unclean as he felt after a long drive. They might have thought he was a repairman or the janitor. He could smell himself. The stink of cigarettes, the stale gas station coffee in his week-old moustache.

He was bathed in purple light now, the sunlight pouring through a stained-glass image of a sheep with purple backdrop, a cross dangling from its neck and a gold halo circling its head. The Lamb.

He walked past the organ player packing away her music sheets and pulling the insulated cloth over her instrument. Up the stairs and to the door at the back of the church through which he'd seen Pastor Hickok walk so many times to deliver a sermon. When Dalton was just a boy and before he knew about the pastor and his mother. Before she'd confirmed for him all the inextricability that kept them trapped there. The reason they couldn't just get out and go somewhere else to start fresh. He pushed through the door.

It wasn't Pastor Hickok. A man, maybe a little older than he, sat behind his desk looking at his cellphone. Wide shoulders and a fresh haircut.

"How can I help you?" the young man said with a self-assured sigh, the tone of a person pleased with their position, pleased to be needed but feigning business. His eyes still on his phone.

"I need to see Pastor Hickok," Dalton said.

The man looked up and stared. "Haven't seen you in a while, Dalton." It was the youth pastor, Graham, sitting there.

Dalton had finished Sunday school just as Graham started volunteering in the youth ministry. It was shortly thereafter that Dalton stopped attending church altogether. Once his Nana had left their house there wasn't anyone around who could make him go, and so he didn't. He'd hated hearing Messy and his mama talk about Graham. He was hating him while he looked at him, blaming Graham for this miasma of unattributable faults.

"Back from the Army!" Graham said. "People have been wondering what happened to you."

He was smiling now, looking Dalton up and down. He rested his chin between his thumb and forefinger, leaning an elbow on his desk.

"No," Dalton said. "Yes. I mean, I'm not here for church. I was looking for Jim Hickok. I need to ask him some questions."

"He's retired," Graham said, his smile wider now, as though someone had just informed him he'd won a prize. "I thought you might have known, buddy. No one called you and told you the news?

Not interested in your hometown anymore? No curiosity about our church here? Or what? Your brother?"

Dalton held himself still and breathed through his nose. He couldn't swallow.

"No, I'm not interested in your church." Dalton hesitated. "I need—I need to find my brother, Graham. Do you know where he is?"

Graham's expression changed to something dour, but he was playing at it. Mocking and serious. He got up and circled around the desk to meet Dalton where he stood.

"I'm looking for a family called Perkins," Dalton continued. "The last I heard Messy was living with them. A foster family. I just want to know where he is."

"I know the family. I've been to see them already." Graham was shaking his head now. He turned grim. His mouth frowned in an imitation of a concerned old man. "That's where he's supposed to be, anyway, but I think he's moved on. I went up there not too long ago to see how he was doing, you know. But he's run off."

"Run off?"

"He's not there. He ran off with one of their own children. The Perkins family. They're upset! I mean, you know I want to make sure Messy's okay. But no one can find him. Not either of them."

Graham paused for effect, then shook his head again. "Yeah, buddy. Very sad. Damn shame. They couldn't tell me anything about where he'd gone. And no one knew where you were hiding either. A ton of people called here looking for you, too. The theory was Messiah had run off to wherever you'd disappeared to. Like maybe you two met up. They told me he was looking for you. Calling you."

Dalton felt sick to his stomach. He gathered himself. "All right, then. Well, I guess I'm gonna go up there and find out where he is, then. I'll take care of it."

"You telling that to me or to yourself?" Graham said. It was an obvious opportunity for preaching, for delivering some kind of wisdom. It only pissed Dalton off that Graham had managed to get there.

"Well, like I said, I've tried asking the family he was with," Graham continued. "And I don't think they know where he went."

Dalton stared down at the floor, working to control his face, then looked back up at the pastor. Graham had big veins running down his neck into his collar. Dalton felt small just looking at the robed man as he stood before him, tall and long and athletic.

"I asked around after your mama passed away. And Dalton, I am *so* sorry for your loss. Of course, you're welcome to look. I mean I want to find Messy too. I can tell you where they live."

"I'd like that very much."

"They're up near Fancy Gap," Graham said. "You know, just north of Mount Airy. Take the Squirrel Spur up the mountain and you'll see the red mailbox with Perkins written on it in white paint. East side of the road. You'll see it before you hit the parkway."

Dalton reached for Graham's office door, then looked back at him sitting in his chair again, looking pleased with himself.

"Well, can I get Pastor Hickok's number?"

"No," Graham said flatly. "He told me that if you came around here sniffing after him, well he told me to tell you not to bother. He's disappointed in you for all this. His words, buddy, not mine."

Dalton turned and stepped into the hallway.

Graham raised his voice like he was yelling down a tunnel, despite not having lost sight of Dalton. "Tell Messy that I say hello! If you find him. Tell him I'd like to see him sometime if he can make it down here. He's always welcome. Always was my favourite kid. Send your grandma my regards too."

Dalton shook his head and slammed down the stairs.

"God bless you, Dalton."

Dalton paused and looked back. Graham was at the top of the stairs, hanging over the railing. "And thank you for your service."

Grace

Dear Pastor Grace,

It comes to my attention that we are sharing a member or more of each our flocks. I write to you also about the return of a wayward lamb whose presence is not welcome, and to congratulate you on your ministry. I am not jealous but honored, and know that your Revival has done its work indeed, and helped me find my place here in the Word. Our friend, true to your word, had done his work well, I take it.

It pains me to have exposed the sins of your daughter, but I feel it is redemptive in the grand narrative that God has written out for us. Pastor Hickok has retired slightly early, and through whatever prayer and divine will was mixed in with my labor and luck, I am leading Sacred Hollow and its good people. I have all but condemned the relationship between Hickok and Ms. Jane in my sermon, but I feel that it was necessary for the public good and toward good order in the congregation. It is all out in the public now, and Jim has moved on to greener pastures. I hold no ill will toward him but wish you each all the best in your endeavors.

I understand the wrath you speak of and trust we are safe from it. No more exchange between us should transpire. If the Lord wills the coalescence of our covenants and congregations then it shall be so, but to my mind I think it is best to keep them distinct.

If you are able, I would like to request any more photos or correspondence between Jane and—I should say—Mr. Hickok that you have in your possession, just to secure my accusation against him. I worry he may appeal and try to come home to roost, so to speak. His wife remains unconvinced of his dalliances and sinful travails, as you put it, and I feel as though my position is still not secure. I have worked hard in the name of Jesus Christ since I was a small child, and this is my calling. I know you feel the weight of The Word as I do, and will spend no more time convincing you, as your work has been a great help to us here in Sacred Hollow. We are set to purge a butcher from our ranks, as you say. Indeed, we may be set to purge quite a few. I thank you for all your notes and messages. Our church has begun an evangelical broadcast on the internet, and interest in a more decisive, pugilistic Word is spreading across the nation like wildfire.

Of interest to you, I think, and preemptively in exchange for any more evidence of Hickok's transgressions, I will tell you that Ms. Jane's son Dalton paid us a visit just this Friday. I do not suspect anyone but myself took notice of him. He claimed to be looking for Messiah. I told him that I do not know where that boy is. That little Messy's adventures remain a mystery, and something I am urging everyone to forget. Let us tie off this loose end together.

I have told the sheriff about Dalton's return, and that he was armed and frantic, which he was. The sheriff explained to me that Dalton is twice wanted for stolen military property, and, he suspects, the murder of his own mother. If you have any means of keeping him far from here, please exercise them. Please continue to keep us safe. Please burn this letter.

Any further correspondence, if at all needed, let it come tucked away in a promotional Bible, packaged, and addressed to me. I am confident that our respective sheriffs want the best for both our ministries but let us not be careless.

— Pastor Graham White

Grace folded the letter and did as Graham had asked. She took a match from the drawer under the kitchen counter, struck it, and watched the letter burn in the porcelain sink.

Gunshots outside. Grace walked to her window overlooking the side of the mountain. Four men in fatigues combed back and forth across a little clearing, arranging new gallon jugs to shoot. These were men from Hickok's militia. Perhaps one man Clyde had brought before he *disappeared*, as she had informed everyone. Grace could see Hawk's backward-ballcapped head bobbing along to instructions, along with Messiah's, golden in the fading sunlight, statue still. The two boys raised rifles and fired at the jugs. Masculine applause.

Jim Hickok was knocking at the door to Grace's house. She checked her appearance in the mirror and ran her fingers through her hair. She paused, sighed, then wrapped it up in a bun and went to the door.

"Come on in, then," she said to Hickok. "Leave them out here, will you?"

Hickok told the men waiting behind him to join the others down the berm and get them to police up their cartridges and cigarette butts. "Go on, then," he said when they hesitated. He walked into the house.

They went into Grace's living room. Outside its windows the clouds were flat and uniform, striated in cascading lines across the horizon. The sun indirect and tame.

"I'm told your prodigal son has returned, Jim."

"He's not my son, Grace. And he isn't quite prodigal, no. The prodigal one is already here, I'm told. But yes, I heard Dalton came by the church."

"We don't need to debate Scripture, Jim. And he may not be welcome back in the prodigal fashion, but he is your problem if he's anyone's. He isn't mine."

"It's our problem, Grace. One of many. I don't want him coming up here. The sheriff's already holding one man on my word, and I can't ask him to hold another. And I can't risk him in the same jail as Clyde. The whole thing will fall apart, I'm afraid."

"Well, we'll just have to deal with him, Jim. I mean, you'll have to do that. I gave you all that I have. It's your show now. Just about all of it is yours except the revival itself and the Word, and that is all I intend to apply myself to."

"You don't want to see your grandson at all, Grace?"

"I think I've invested quite enough in that boy. And no, I don't want his brother to see him, neither. No. Not yet. There's a good many people up here looking to Messiah to break out and become what I've moulded him to be. I want that to stand."

"All right, then," Hickok said. "I need to know when we'll be ready to build. About half the people around here are scared and need a new church. We said we're going to give it to them. I want to build up soon. Deeds are in place, contracts in the works. I just don't know how it's going to shake out yet with the media. I need for you to slow down with the *alms*, as you call them. I don't have any problem with a little wine, but if we're going to take this—if we're going to build what we say we'll build—then I want it to be clean, Grace. The crazymaking times are gonna have to be behind us."

"They will be," she said. "I just know I'm shaking hands with the devil, Jim, but—"

"We'll slow it down, then?" He was encouraging her. "I want this to be a new kind of community. Something pure and American. Something beyond the reach of corruption and nastiness. I want a new world, Grace."

"I do too, Jim," she said, "I'll slow it down."

"Okay then. I'll see if I can find Dalton and I will see if I can talk to him. If he was the prodigal son, I think he'd have to come to me."

"Well you better open them arms, Pastor Hickok," Grace said.

Messiah

"WE GONNA GO to Croft's Creek Primitive?" Hawk said.

"Why you lay it out like that? Like I don't know what the fuck you're talking about?" said Messiah.

"What do you mean?"

"We're gonna hit another church. Why you want to name it?"

"I didn't name it. Just what it's called."

"I suppose we ought to," Messiah said. "List ain't getting any shorter otherwise."

"Why you think she got us doing this shit? Ain't hurtin' nobody I guess."

"I don't know. I know she's mad at the non-believers," said Messiah.

"What exactly do you mean by that?"

"I mean just what I said. I mean I don't think she's too happy with how people 'round here been treated. Our congregation. Her flock, you know."

"And you think the best way to fix that is to set fire to little churches all over? Half of them look like they ain't been used in years."

"I don't think that's just her idea, Hawk, and I don't worry about the best way. They got a big plan for the revival up there. I do what

those militia boys tell me to do, and I get what we're supposed to get because my Nana told us so. I don't know what else to do. She's got me doing this, and I don't got anyone else."

"Well, I do." Hawk blew smoke out the window in a stream of punctuation, then popped a pill and swallowed it dry.

They were sitting in the truck in a dark parking lot in front of a strip-mall pharmacy, one of the Mountain Community Pharmacies and Clinics. Hawk had just pried open its door, walked in, and taken its morphine and oxycodone. His bag was full of the stuff.

Since they'd started attending Grace's revival the two had been "training," as it was called, with a group of men from "the militia," as it was known. This had amounted mostly to walking down the side of Buffalo Mountain and shooting guns at jugs set into the red clay berms that sloped upward from the winding roads.

The men had given them maps and taught them how to read them, telling the boys exactly where they were supposed to go. The instructions were explicit.

"Hey, can I ask you something?" Hawk said.

"We'll go in a minute."

"No, not that. Okay. Do you remember?"

"Remember what?"

"You remember my mama's house?"

"Not really." Messiah motioned for Hawk to pass him a lighter.

"You remember the day we went swimming? I know you do, man, just say yes so I can tell you something. You remember?"

"Yes. I remember that day. You still gotta go in, though."

"Well, I was thinking. What if we hadn't done that. Would we still be there?"

"Probably be in school," Messiah said. "You wanna go back?"

"Naw. Shit. No, I don't. No, no. I don't think so. I just wonder. That's all. I don't know if I miss it or not. You got Grace's house. Nice floors in there. Good bed and white sheets. She makes it so I

gotta take care of myself out there in the trailer. You still just a kid. Acting like you're living in your mama's house."

"We gotta go to the church," Messiah said quietly. "I think I'm in trouble."

"Hell yeah we're in trouble. *You're* in trouble. And I ain't going to no goddamn church."

"We just gotta get it done. Let's get out of here and get on with it."

"I just don't want to do it, that's all. I just want to go home and smoke, man. You know?"

"It ain't an option, Hawk. We gotta do what she says."

"Does she cuddle you, Messy? Does she kiss you? Does she tuck you in at night? What got you so religious other than your nasty old grandma? You know how stupid this is? Why can't we just do it another night?"

"I don't want to do it all, I don't think," Messiah said, "same as you. But what else am I supposed to do? What else is there for us? I mean now, I mean after all this."

Messiah was looking for the words to make his position real. He was looking for a way to explain.

Messiah set a couple canisters on the ground in front of the church. Then he picked up the tungsten hammer and tapped on the running stained-glass window next to the white front doors, and with the quietest crunch it fell apart. The glass sounded like ice cubes hitting the ground. He reached in, found the bolt, and turned it.

He opened one of the doors and stepped inside. It was like a mausoleum. Still and organized. When he went back out to get the gas cans he looked over at the truck, darkened now. He checked his pockets to make sure he had the keys.

He lifted up the canisters and climbed the front steps of the small wooden church. Once inside he began trailing a line of fuel

behind him as he walked between the rows of pews, throwing the emptied jerry can down the aisle toward the door.

Now he gathered up the sheet music from the organ, spread it across the stage, and doused it in kerosene from the other can. He put about a quart of kerosene inside the organ itself, then coated the wooden cross at the backdrop of the stage, then filled the stage instruments, amplifiers, and musical equipment with the rest.

Holding both canisters upturned in his hands, he let them knock against his thighs as he walked out of the little building, the old wooden stairs creaking beneath him as he descended. He set the canisters in the bed of the truck and moved around a spare tire, a tarp, and a soggy long-gun case till he found the wet box of fire-starter logs. He returned to the steps of the church, lit the plastic of the log, and let it get going. Then he set it down gently on the trail of gas.

It went up with a whoosh. He watched the flames follow the fuel across each row of pews, most lighting up right away, the fire travelling like an usher collecting the offertory from one row to the next. The burgundy carpet caught fire and started billowing lines of thick black plastic smoke. Messiah stepped back onto the front steps and closed the heavy white doors at the front of the church. The light cascaded through all but one pane of stained glass. It was beautiful in its projection. A magic lantern. Coloured shapes danced up and around the grass, followed him down the sidewalk. Like sitting in front of a Christmas tree. Messiah stopped to admire it. He looked up at the warmth radiating out through the glass and into the stark black night. The Lamb of God and Jesus and Peter beside a rock adorned with a cross, Mary and the Lamb, more glass renderings of Jesus, Jesus weeping, a cross and a ribbon, an open Bible, a rose, a rendering of the Ten Commandments. Panes of gold, purple, deep green, blood red, all illuminated, all shining out into the moonless night from the fire inside.

Back in the truck, Hawk had thrown up on himself. The brown smoke billowed into the atmosphere and blended into night.

The truck seemed to drive itself back to Grace's compound on the crest of Buffalo Mountain. The zigzagging, ascending rocky road was practically a river of mud, the last breath of a shore-busted hurricane exhausting its clouds with one final deluge on the unsuspecting mountains.

"Wake up, Hawk. I need your help driving. I can't hardly see."

"Just drive, Messy. I ain't feeling so good."

"You gotta stop sneaking these pills," Messiah said in a mock maternal tone, glancing at Hawk's ballcap over his face, his skinny chest rising and falling too slow. It didn't match Messiah's feeling at all. The truck slipped and caught itself in unanticipated thrusts in the mud, sending its rear into a fishtailing whip as Messiah tried to get enough traction to keep climbing.

"If this rain don't stop I think we're gonna have to pull off over here and wait it out," Messiah said. Hawk seemed to choke a little on his own spit. He gasped a weak, disinterested gasp and settled back into his nap.

Messiah veered into a turnoff where cars had dug a two-ditch path down to a group of trailers and campers that jumped out at them through the brush as the truck's headlights set upon them. Messiah killed the engine but kept the lights on. A door to one of the smaller camper trailers swung open and a teenage girl ran out into the headlights.

"It's him!" she shouted back at the doorway. "It's Pastor Grace's Messiah!" She was already soaked through. The too-big undershirt translucent, clinging to her body, showing a swollen potbelly above her grey sweatpants as they grew heavy with water. She hiked them up high like a man might thumb his suspenders after a meal. She didn't seem to mind the rain.

"Get up, Hawk," Messiah said. "I don't want to talk right now. Can you talk to her for me?"

The girl was standing just outside Messiah's window now, fogging it with her breath. She tapped on the glass and smiled.

"Let me come up there with you," she said, and Messiah caught the transition from her smile to her look of worry as she glanced at the open trailer door swinging in the wind. "Messiah," she said, looking back at him. She was acting ecstatic. "Messiah! Please!"

And Hawk hadn't moved.

Buffalo Mountain seemed to have swallowed itself. Where there was once a small pocket of gospel searchers who'd come up from the surrounding lowlands to till Grace's fields and get paid a fair wage, now there were jungles erected in every little turnbuckle of the dirt road up the mountain. Men, half drunk, patrolled with guns, spitting tobacco into the dry earth, overhunting the forest, burning wet trees at night.

The trees had worn themselves out, sharpening and becoming needle-like in the new wind tunnel of Grace's recently paved road. They toothpicked its sides and accentuated each maelstrom and weather malady that blew through that mountain dip. The deterioration surrounded Grace's house. It was a burden to get oil for heat, the delivery drivers ceasing to fill their orders on account of the difficulty they had trespassing through the mountain, what with the threat of marauders on junk ATVs and the constant blare of battery-run stereos playing Johnny Rebel and Hank III next to generators that hummed along, powering Christmas lights and hot plates deep in the kudzu night.

There were cross burnings and rituals, cat skinnings and unofficial marriages lighting up the mountainside, strange and quotidian miracles occurring on any given night of the week. Corn liquor made from silage stolen from surrounding farms was cooked up and drunk,

green and unready, harsh and unbearable. Teens and twentysomethings were armed with pocket knives and pistols, those tender years hardened by the relentless sunlight of the summer mornings that burned their eyes red and their necks to leather.

Nightly fires in barrels and sporadic forest fires from lightning or cigarette ash pockmarked the cleared plains of the side of the mountain where people poured white lightning into watermelons and the women drank and the men drank and their sons drank, and they had almost no daughters. Big rivets from mud tires filled with rainwater sat stagnant in the foggy mornings and stank with gas and ash from the barrel fires. Dark-red minivans sat tireless on bricks and on old tires and on pallets taken from Lowe's and the local hardware store. The pallets rotted in the wet morning dew, having avoided getting burned and cooked over by the older-than-their-time ladies who sat around the fire snuffing ground tobacco and twice-cut cocaine in the Saturday and Monday afternoons of the summer sun and the winter wind. They became saturated and soft, and the rusted vehicles sank into them, and all sank into the red mud.

Messiah watched all this and let it become him. The idea of it mirrored not at all what he was hearing on starched-shirt Sunday afternoons. Grace's revival was monied now, and some people from far off the mountain would come and put huge bills in the collection. Messiah just about never saw them outside the service. Television cameras for a live web feed. The khaki pants and the big white smiles, that's not who was there—out there sleeping along the gravel road up the mountain, out there breathing and living in the woods, the real heaven—when he and Hawk would return home from a run. These were big-monied smiles now. Starched Ralph Lauren collars in pastel; ghosts in the Sunday afternoons that dissipated during the week and re-emanated from Grace's words on those new holy days, those holier than holy. Those days mostly absent of the lonely,

unclean workers whom Grace loved so, that salt of the earth. These were kings of the lowland crawling up to heaven for a visit, and Messiah felt separated from it all.

Nighttime turned alien and got coloured in grey, the world truly touched by God only in the early-morning weeping noise of air-sucking generators left on all night and the smell of burned plastic that mixed with the fog and hung in the atmosphere, that smoke mixing with sun, beautiful and deep in the air, the dirty air of a once-clean place clearing only for Sunday, for Sermon. The souls the only salve of the land.

But where was the redemption? And when would it come? Hawk slept. Messiah watched Hawk sleep.

Dalton

HE WAS DRIVING as straight as he could toward the Blue Ridge Parkway, the twisting road curling like black twirls of smoke before him. He switched to the FM band and the radio came alive. He scanned for the news, found it, and listened. More fires, more sickness. No starlight, no moon.

He recognized some of the burned-down places: pharmacies in King, a Baptist church in Pilot Mountain, another in Beulah, a Methodist church in Sandy Ridge, a Primitive Baptist congregation in Ararat. The station played a clip from a press briefing in which local sheriffs, Virginia's Bureau of Criminal Investigation, the North Carolina State Bureau of Investigation, and many of the towns' mayors and preachers gathered in Mount Airy to discuss the fires:

"We, as of yet, can't seem to find a motive suitable to explain this pattern of arson and vandalism," a spokesperson said.

"We have yet to identify the number of attackers, although we suspect that this is not the work of a lone wolf. This level of destruction is unprecedented in our region. Many of the victims of this string of arsons are local businesses that are Christian-owned and -operated, and the rest are themselves Christian places of worship. Our coalition, with assistance from the FBI, is compiling a list of online radicals in

the area with anti-Christian sentiment. We're checking message boards, forums, and political websites for statements of responsibility. We are looking into radicalized groups in western North Carolina and Virginia, and, with the encouragement of our determined citizens, will begin increased patrols, traffic stops, and random vehicle checks. At this time we have been offered assistance by local militias and veterans' groups who are themselves coordinating to keep our community safe. These men are organized under the Second Amendment and are dedicated to keeping our country safe. If we do not see a cessation in this sort of terroristic violence, well I can just come out and say that we are looking into deputizing some of these groups to man certain checkpoints and provide community patrols. We will not tolerate the terrorism of our local places of worship. This committee urges anyone with information to come forward."

The recording ended, followed by a pause before the announcer turned to another story. Dalton searched the radio again, keeping his eyes on the dim sides of the angular road, looking out for deer or other animals, feeling himself to be in a wild, wild place. He scrolled through the recordings of impassioned worship and shitty preaching that often came on after suppertime, listening for a second to each one, hoping it might concern recent events. He stopped at a man's voice halfway through a segment:

"*. . . don't see how there's any doubt about it! The sheer number of illegal aliens in this state is at an all-time high. Certainly, no American—born here, living here, working to contribute to our economy, paying taxes, raising a family, attending these church services—certainly, certainly it isn't him who's setting fire to our churches. I would be on the lookout for unfamiliars. Listen, here's our reason for the roadside checks. If you weren't born and raised here, we're gonna be looking for you. I'm not going to have an invasion with criminals driving around our towns, burning things up and hurting people. Mark my words, after the checkpoints are set up these crimes will stop. Whatever coward, or group of cowards, is trying to*

scare the great people of North Carolina, the Piedmont, and the mountain region has come to the wrong place."

The narrative complete, the blame squarely placed, Dalton felt satisfied with the radio, for now. He reached over to click it off.

He had worried visions of police pursuits, of gunfights and speeding through guardrails, all in the grainy style of cop shows on television, but nothing of the sort manifested. It was a calm, cool drive as he worked his way onto the Blue Ridge Parkway and flew through the rush of bugs zipping into the windshield. He turned his headlights on and off, on and off to watch the world disappear and reappear. He drove and didn't think.

He found the Perkins's mailbox by moonlight and turned the car off the highway onto a little cemented pullover just beyond a bend in the road. He leaned the seat back and put his hat over his face. He listened to the night noises. Only one or two cars drove past in the night, one honking crazily and swerving all over the road as they zoomed past the truck, shaking it with the wind of their wake. Their tires screeched down the mountain road and out of earshot.

Dalton lay awake, then, till morning. When it came, he took a new toothbrush out of its package and a bottle of water from the rear of the truck and brushed his teeth on the roadside, spitting into a pile of dead leaves by a faded Mountain Dew can, some other trash piled up by the wind and inconstant traffic.

He rinsed his hands with water from the bottle and splashed his face. He smelled his armpits and the lack of offence made him happy, satisfied to smell a little like smoke and sweat and worry. He straightened his shirt and checked the zipper on his fly and walked up the narrow driveway to the Perkins's home.

It was a little post-war house tucked away behind three cars parked perpendicular to the gravel driveway, rusted out. Toys were scattered across the driveway in various states of disrepair, having

been run over, it seemed, maybe a thousand times by slow, bald tires. He walked up to the door and heard kids screaming and crying inside along with a woman's voice shouting "Shut up! Shut the hell up!" He tried the doorbell, but it was unconnected, then knocked on the screen door's plastic pane. Dalton took in a few deep, muggy breaths, the summer heat already beginning to set in, mixing with the fog of the mountain to make a steam bath out of the damp little enclave where they were all tucked away.

He waited a moment and then knocked again, the children still yelling but the woman having quieted. He heard a rustling behind the door, then it swung open.

She stood before him in sweatpants, a muumuu draping over her big shoulders below a greying, frazzled helmet of hair. Even with her tinted brown glasses and in the low ambient light of morning, she squinted at him and almost bared her teeth in focus and concentration. "Who're you?"

"My name is Dalton Fuquay, ma'am," Dalton said, clearing his throat and straightening his posture. He put his hands behind his back in parade rest. "I been told that you were taking care of my little brother, Messiah Fuquay?"

"Police already came about that. Runaway. I already paid 'em back that month's cheque."

"I'm not the police."

"I know you ain't the police. I'll call the police though if you don't get on out of here. I know about you. Where were you at? Why was he a foster at all if you looking for him? I paid them back, I told them he left, and I don't want nothin' else to do with it, thank you very much."

She started to close the door.

"No, ma'am, please—"

A child started a fresh cry inside. She kicked at something behind the door.

"Go on, git— Git, I say, damn you. It's the cats."

"Ma'am, I'm just wondering if you know maybe where he went off to."

"Not he," she said. "They. I don't know what you know about your younger brother, young man, but he's got something wrong with him. He took my son and my husband's favourite truck, and they run off. I don't know where they run to. If you want to ask the police, you can ask them. I already answered all their questions." She started to close the door again.

Dalton opened the screen door and stepped toward the door frame, ready to put his foot in the way. He caught his tone and softened it. "Ma'am—I just really need your help."

"I'll help you," she said, raising her voice. "Oh, son, I'll help you." And she stepped out onto the porch.

"Let me tell you something, and I'll be straight with you. That boy costed me a thousand dollars a month. And he ain't even mine. I'll tell you what, if I could find him the world would know it, because I'd whip him senseless. Gone and taken my boy from me. Don't you think I'm concerned about my own child? Well, I'll tell you. When I find him, either of them for that matter, either your little brother or my good-for-nothing son, I'm gonna whip them till they go blind. I don't care if it's tomorrow or a hundred years from now.

"So just tell them that when you find them, the little motherfuckers and bastards. It would save me a lot of grief if I could just get ahold of them and put them in the ground so the state would get out of my hair. They come sniffing around here like I did something wrong. And I wanna know now, son, how you come to find out where I was? I washed clean my hands of this business. I haven't complained, or filed suit, or nothing at all, and you come up here like I got some kind of something to *hide* from you?"

Dalton backed away from her. She heaved as though she were recovering from a fight that hadn't happened. A cat pawed at the

door and a toddler with nothing on but a striped shirt stood behind the bug screen, pulling at the cat's legs. "No ma'am," he said. "I'm just trying to find him too. I'll give him a whipping for you when I do." He turned to walk away.

"Let me tell you something, son. I got a little secret for you," she sneered. "I used to run a business here, and all this has got it so I got no kids to take care of. And you don't forget, boy, I got one of my own children missing. Didn't occur to you to ask about him. Well, if you find him you let me know." She was almost whispering in baby talk.

"I got another little secret to tell you." She was smiling maniacally now. "A little secret. I know one thing for certain. And I can't get enough away from this rats' nest to prove it." She laughed. "They can't have gone far. A girlfriend of mine told me they seen Hawk at the gas station even a week ago. With someone who sounded like your brother but with his hair grown out like a woman. Said Hawk looked skinny and grown. Said the other boy had on clothes that didn't fit him. But I don't know." She was laughing at herself. As though all of this was a funny old family memory. "You can't believe anything you hear. Do you believe it? Ha!" She giggled like an overexcited schoolgirl, hiding her mouth behind her hand in a vaudeville gesture. Dalton walked down the steps away from her. "You find them, and you come directly to me!" she shouted down after him. "Boy! You, boy!"

Dalton was halfway down the drive, walking backward and bowing and waving gently, trying not to trip on the toys.

She screamed now between two hands, leaning into her shouts, "Put it in the paper, you little sonofabitch! He did this because his daddy is a sonofabitch too!"

He turned onto the narrow mountain road, got in the truck, and pulled away, looking behind as much as ahead as he rolled through the Blue Ridge.

Dalton pulled off to get gas. Wherever he was, it was little more than a school and a stoplight and two competing gas stations across from each other. Down the road there was a diner attached to a one-storey motel that backed onto a steep rock cliff with the Blue Ridge Parkway running over top of it. The southernmost gas station displayed their gas for sale at one cent cheaper than its northern competition. What the northernmost station had, though, was a long row of flags flapping in the mountain wind and affixed to its awning with twisted wire: DON'T TREAD ON ME with the coiled snake, the stars and bars of the Confederacy, a white III% against a Washington blue backdrop, and something that looked like hatched white symbols on a black flag resembling a deconstructed swastika—all that and many, many bright signs beckoning drivers to pull into its Old Tyme Mountain Country Store and Gift Shop and Garage.

Recent construction had covered up half the building's own sign, so instead of GARAGE it just said RAGE.

Dalton listened to the pump click until the tank was full. He went inside and walked through the store, up and down through the aisles filled with cookbooks—*100 Possum-Cookin' Family Classics* and *Trailer Trash Cuisine for One*—and bumper stickers—DON'T BLAME ME, I'M WITH JOHN BIRCH and THE SOUTH WILL RISE AGAIN!

He touched the greasy cast-iron pans that were MADE IN THE USA! and flipped through a few tracts stacked up on one another. There were Jesus comics that you could find in the bathrooms of the Bible belt, some explaining how Thanksgiving was a victory celebration for the Christians of America. One with Jesus absorbing a wall of bullets to save the troops in Iraq. He stood there awhile, studying these things. He looked through some gift T-shirts featuring caricatures of Obama eating a plateful of dollar bills, or the shadow of a praying soldier that read BRING THEM HOME! ARMY VETERAN OIF/OEF, or the rebel flag carried by a cowboy bleeding from a bandaged wound on his head. One simply read THIS LAND IS OUR LAND. He felt he was truly losing his mind.

"Can I help you?" a man said from behind the counter.

"Yessir," Dalton said. "I need to pay for my gas and, um, well, I guess I'm curious about your flags."

"What flag you want?"

"I'm just curious. What's going on with the flags?"

"You gonna buy a flag or ain't you?"

Dalton set down the tracts and walked from the country store part of the building to the gas station part of the building. He scooped some hot nuts from a kettle near the out-of-order ATM, pulled a Coke from the fridge, then went on to the counter and met the man there. He asked for a pack of Camel Lights and some matches and told him he was on pump number one.

"I know which pump yous on." The man sighed a flamboyantly exasperated sigh. He flipped up his trucker hat and scratched his head. Then he turned and looked at the wall of cigarettes and dip, reached his hand up under his shirt and scratched his belly, then turned back to Dalton. "What cigarettes you want again?"

"Camels," Dalton said. "What do all these flags mean? Who buys these?"

The man stopped ringing him through and stared Dalton down. "Are you stupid?"

"No."

"Listen, I don't give a shit what each of 'em means. I know that if you sell 'em people around here'll buy 'em. I got patches of each by the register. Look right there." He gestured toward a pile of Velcro patches. "You got any more asinine questions?"

"No sir."

"Just the boiled peanuts, the Coke, the cigarettes, and the gas, then?" The man smiled sardonically at Dalton.

"Yessir, and a map, please." He paid and walked out.

He'd gotten the truck started up and was looking back at the RAGE sign when he saw a corkboard on the front of the building that he must have missed on his way in, tattered by time, some of

the papers stuck to it completely bleached by the weather, but some fresh and new. Dalton remembered what the Perkins woman had said. Messy and the other boy had been seen around here.

He got out of his truck and let it idle. He walked back to the front of the store and saw the station attendant looking at him. Dalton looked right back, trying not to break eye contact as he reapproached. When he got to the corkboard he flipped through some of the pieces of paper and flyers, business cards and tear-off *Call Me* sheets, until something caught his eye. One piece of weathered white paper was stapled right atop the thick layer of flyers.

It was a photo of his grandmother, distorted and grainy, having been photocopied and photocopied again and again, with her hands lifted above her head. There was a drawing of the sun above her, its rudimentary rays darting down around her. Beneath the photo it said:

> REVIVAL – GRACE'S CHURCH OF THE REDEEMER – EVERY SUNDAY – EAST SIDE OF BUFFALO MOUNTAIN – COME ONE COME ALL – ALL WELCOME – PATRIOTS WELCOME – MOTHERS WELCOME – OLD TIME GOSPEL – PAYING JOBS WEEKLY – REFRESHMENTS PROVIDED – SHINE AND MUSCADINE WINE – GOOD PAY WEEKLY FOR VOLUNTEERS – EVERY SUNDAY – NOON

It had directions to get to the revival tent, but it didn't have a date.

She was there though, hands up toward the Lord, he thought, the camera praising her. *Come Join Pastor Grace's Revival on the Mountain!* it said, an addendum scratched in poor handwriting.

He tore the flyer off the board and folded it and stuck it in his pocket.

He saw another, recently pinned, fresh and new, adorned with some of the same flags and symbols he'd seen around the gas station, this time hand-drawn. It was the call to muster that intrigued

him. "In Accordance with the 2nd Amendment," it read. This one detailed the time and location, too:

> PULLIAM HUNTING RESORT. SATURDAYS, 6 PM. PATRIOTS, CHRISTIANS, VETERANS, POLICE OFFICERS, ACTIVE-DUTY WELCOME. WEAR NO INSIGNIA. RECEPTION WITH WEAPONS TRAINING TO FOLLOW. INFORMATION AND ORGANIZING. BYO AMMUNITION. WEAPONS UNLOADED UPON ARRIVAL. REGISTRATION REQUIRED. DONATION ENCOURAGED. PROTECT YOUR NATION!

He tore this one off the board as well and folded it and stuck it in his pocket.

When he looked up the station attendant was an inch from the window, staring at Dalton with his nose just about pressed against the glass. Dalton nodded and turned around and walked back to the idling Toyota, opened the door, took one more look at the man. He'd come out through the door of the gas station and was squinting at the truck and mouthing something to himself. Dalton drove off slowly.

He pulled into the little motel next to the diner and parked as best he could behind a dumpster, wanting to avoid anyone looking for the truck from the highway.

He told the motel clerk the story about his lost wallet and phone and his emergency trip home, and how he ran out of steam on I-77 and how he'd been driving for days. "I just pulled off the parkway to find some place to stay, and well, I'm happy to see y'all here."

"You gonna pay tomorrow?"

"I'm going to stay maybe for a few days. I'm going to call my bank and get a new card sent to me here, if that's okay. I'll call my company commander tonight." He stood up straight for effect.

"What's the name?"

"Vasquez," Dalton said. "Corporal Vasquez."

"You don't look like yous in the Army," the woman told him.

“Well, I’m on leave.” Dalton felt he was going to be sick from lying such an obvious lie.

“All right, well, do you got any proof?”

“Not my ID. I lost my wallet. But—I’ve got my uniform,” he said cheerily.

He started rifling through his bag. He pulled out his beret and showed her. She was unimpressed. She gave him the key anyway and said that when the card came it would be three hundred dollars for the week, flat rate for veterans.

“Thank you for your service,” she said, and sighed as the door closed.

His room was at the opposite end from where he’d parked his truck, which he thought was ideal. Dalton turned the key in the cheap knob and the door creaked open with a push. He looked over the blue-lit room in the summertime dusk, his shadow darkening the rough beige carpet and the maroon bedspread. He dropped his bags on the floor and put his .38 on the TV stand, walked to the bathroom, and pissed. He tore off his jeans and shirt and ran the water until it was as hot as it would get and stepped in and breathed.

The motel provided a bar of soap and a single-use razor. He lathered up his face and head and shaved all of it blind in the mirrorless shower. The Walmart haircut hadn’t been close enough, he thought, and he wanted to look sharp and disciplined in case he had to use the lost military ID story again. He wanted to leave all he’d grown behind, and to be new.

He stepped back from the water and rubbed himself with the soap until it was a thick foam. Using the suds as a sort of lubricant, he tried to masturbate but it was no use. There was too much burden. His shoulders too tight. He stepped forward again and the hot water burned his freshly shaven head. He thought of his mother’s baldness, her retching echoing throughout their house. His leaving was something like that, his abandoning and abandonment, his abandon.

When he got out of the shower he saw the lines he'd shaven into his scalp, uneven like a poorly mowed lawn, red and bleeding in places. He patted it dry with a rough towel. He washed his shirt and underwear and socks in the sink and laid them out over the flat screen TV to dry. He put the cellphone Laura had given him on the nightstand and plugged it in to charge, though he'd drained no battery.

His Nana, he thought. He couldn't believe it. He unfolded the revival flyer and smoothed it out on the bed next to him. He looked at the Xeroxed, grainy daguerreotype of her face. It looked so empty and white. So flat. She'd been preaching, living just over the state line from them. Here, in Virginia. And for how long? "Say hello to your grandmother," Graham had said.

He unfolded the flyer for the militia muster. He studied it. Dalton remembered a few of the signs and symbols from some of the various bad-boy contraband he'd seen in the Army. Pamphlets, magazines, YouTube videos of white supremacist shit that guys in the barracks would show him. This flyer was in a near-identical style to the one for his Nana's preaching, but was more recent. *Patriots*, they both said.

Dalton lit and then took a pull from his cigarette. He sat naked on the stiff bed of the motel room, listening to the cars cut up and down the Blue Ridge.

Grace

"THE FIRE IS NOW READY. The furnace is now hot, and it is not something for us to walk into, no. We are the embers. We are the forge for sin. And we will repent! We are the work of Satan but still the good of God. Friends, while the devil moves us and moulds us, God has yet to withdraw his hand from our working shoulder!"

Grace was walking through the crowd of about fifty people in their church clothes, touching all their starchy shoulders as though they'd gathered only to keep her aloft.

"There is, in the souls of you wicked people, nothing much left but the carnal torments with which to whip yourselves. Yes, you—you are all in the possession of Satan and his myriad devices. Yes, already. And where is your escape? And where is it? Our flume? Our exodus from the crucible? Open your damned hearts, open the flume. Open your damned wicked souls. See God in the air. See God everywhere.

"Oh, you are in the flames already. Don't deny it. But as sure as you look upon me today, you are saved. We are already martyred, friends. It is no security, you feel, to be saved. Shame! It is no security that you do not yet see death. Shame!

"Admit it to yourself!" Grace shouted. "Conscript yourself to the destiny laid out before you. Hell hounds, wielders of not the

sword of angels but the close, sharp pocket knives of knaves and sinners: these are your supposed kin, your supposed countrymen. Let us begin anew. Let us become the future, here: true souls consecrating the firmament with blood and faith. Beginnings do not beckon ends, my wanderers, they disrupt them. Ends imply only misunderstandings of sequence. We are new, and deference to our calling is nothing but the blind immolation of circumstance. You—are—not—condemned! You are free!

"God doesn't come in to spoil your sleep. He doesn't come to wake you in the morning—breathless, sweating, vulgar, shaking, ugly, damned, futureless. God lifts you from your sleep into the one true life. Accept that. Accept death and find truth.

"Look into the burning hot core of you. You are only saved in death. You are awake now. See yourself: you are awake! God loves mostly what lies within the palisaded perimeter of this place, here, this sacred, worshipful place. Why else would you come? Why else would you ascend to be near to heaven? We march. We beat the drum! Join me now and help me expedite these lost souls"—Grace flung her arms toward the mountain's shoals—"help me sort these souls on their way to heaven or to hell. I am not afraid to say it! It is the end now. It is the beginning. Let those who profess it come to believe it. We will expedite these poor souls. We, here, the redeemed, have been put on earth to populate heaven. Say it! Say it now. Say that you will expedite!"

We will! they said.

"Say you will!"

We will! they said.

"Amen!"

Amen! they said.

People stood and touched their faces. They reached their hands to the sky. Some began to speak in tongues. Grace, in an unbleached cotton slip, shook her arms violently, shaking her hands out at the crowd like so many lightning flashes, punctuating her words.

"Save some room for the saved, now. Save some room for the saved. We're only fighting devils. Save some room for the saved! Oh, the arrogance of Americans. The ignorance. All this temporary madness, incendiary gladness! We either hasten the end, yes, we either hasten our salvation, or we hasten others to their very real, very assured damnation. It is the beginning and the end. Know it! Wake up and see God!

"But let me show you a new path up the rocky mountainside. That crooked path to heaven, away from the lowlands, away from the catfish and scum, away from the ugly hum of television towers and weak-willed fake power. God wants you near. He wants you here, on the mountaintop. He *calls* you near. And what seems unmeasurable, what seems contingent, what seems unknowable is all here for you. It is all already set in motion. The world is writ! Motion, action, deed: static in the eye of time. In a world ever expanding lies worlds ever shrinking. The beginning and the end.

"And there are consequences to your sin, but they are already written. Take your sins as ammunition in the fight for God. Expel, expel! Expedite! I will bear witness to the soundness of this for you. Who and what you are is a distraction from the who and what you shall be. And you shall be redeemed.

"You are now in the immaculate garden. You are now coming home. Come out now into the safety of God's new day. Abandon the terror. You have sinned, yes, you have sinned. And the wages of sin is death. So let that death be worthy of God's grace. You have sinned, indeed. But no more. We cease to fear death. We embrace eternal life. We cease to fear death. Do you hear me? Say it. We only see truth! Say it! Truth!"

Truth! Truth! Truth! they said.

Amen! they said.

Messiah

THE MILITIAMEN HAD TOLD Messiah and Hawk that things had quieted down and that it was safe to go out and make an example of another church, a ritual they were calling a Crusade now. "Safe for another Crusade," they said.

The boys were driving along winding roads outside of Hillsville, backroads where the kudzu was strangling trees, choking tall, powerful plants and telephone poles and power lines, swarming the ridgeline. The trees on either side of the road reached up over the blacktop, blocking out the moonlight. As their headlights pierced the darkness before them the crickets and cicadas hummed in their roaring truck engine's wake. Without warning Messiah cut the lights and gunned the gas a little.

"Stop that! Stop that shit, goddamn," Hawk said. They both laughed, and the weight of their task seemed lightened. Hawk lit a cigarette and held it primly out the cracked window, relaxing now that they'd left the fright of all-encompassing darkness behind them. Messiah turned on the radio. Flipped from Christian conservative talk to honky-tonk country, to the news, to a station that seemed to air only ads for local barbecue spots and pharmaceuticals. He left it there.

"Where are we going? I thought we was gonna do another church," Hawk said.

"We are. We're gonna hit one more in Fancy Gap. We just gotta go to this trailer park like they said, get the alms they got there, and then if we got any nighttime left we can hit the church."

"I don't wanna hit that one, Messy."

"You don't never want to do anything at all. But it ain't up to you." Messiah's voice cracked under the pressure of sounding so determined.

"I think that's the church we used to go to. Back when we went to church," Hawk said.

"How come you don't go there no more?"

"I dunno . . ." Hawk trailed off. "I mean, I'm at Grace's church. I'm my own man, Messy. Got my own church. But I'm thinking I don't care. I'm thinking it's bad luck."

They hit a series of spurs in the road and Messiah slowed down and focused. The night air resounded with the buzz of cicadas mixed with the truck engine's thunder.

"You're always back there," Messiah said. "You gotta be here. Me and you."

"Well, how about this. How come we don't ever get caught?"

"I don't know," Messiah said. The thought had occurred to him too. "Grace doesn't want us in jail and, I don't know. The fact that nothing's ever come of it makes me think it's supposed to be this way. We're cleansing, remember, she said that. Expediting."

"I don't even know what that means."

"That big guy with the moustache that's been coming to Grace's sermons. He's a cop, ain't he?"

"I dunno," Hawk said again.

"Well maybe ask him. I got a feeling that's why we ain't in jail. I worry we gonna run out of churches and Grace is gonna make us burn down her own tent."

Hawk laughed at this. "I think we're about done, Messy. I think all this is about ready to come to a close."

"What do you mean?"

"You said we running out of churches? Well, I think we might actually be just about out of churches Grace is interested in. You know why we do this?"

"I know without knowing." Messiah surprised himself at his parroting of his grandmother.

"Well. That's good for you, Messy, but I know why we do it, and it's for money. There's money in this somehow. She's getting paid. She said to me that she ain't no better than a travel agent in all this. Just moving things around. Something about speeding things up. Something like if she helps in speeding things along, well, there's people with money who want to speed it all along."

"Speed what along?"

"The whole thing. They want to kill the system. Some of them guys in the militia, you know, they asked me to muster with them. They said you can't wear no patches and you gotta keep your gun unloaded. And I said I don't even have a gun that they didn't give me. But that isn't what it's all about, Messy. It was serious shit, I think. They was talking to me about what all Grace's preaching is actually about. I mean what is really going on. It's to speed things. To speed it up. End of the world, you know. We gotta get there. We gotta, you know, just like you said. We gotta be here. Me and you and what we gotta do."

They drove along. "You know where it was?" Hawk asked.

"Where what was?"

"The militia muster. The meeting."

A car sped toward them on the wrong side of the yellow line and Messiah had to jerk the truck out of the way.

"I said you know where it was?"

"Don't care," Messiah said, and looked back, half-expecting the car that chickened them to be crashed and in flames. It rounded

the sharp mountain corner, its brake lights bathing the trees in red.

"All right, this is it." Messiah cut the engine, letting the truck drift silently the last hundred yards or so before they reached a dirt road turnoff.

"You been here before?" Hawk whispered.

"Yeah, I bought some alms from them once. Same guys you about to go *muster* with. Whatever, you know, same guys. Three Percenters, whatever."

"What does that mean?"

"I don't know. Shut up and let's go. They ain't there tonight. That muster," Messiah sneered, "is happening at one of them resorts. All the men supposed to be there. Just a kid and a woman in this trailer tonight. Their whole stash just laid out. That's the word."

"That's the word?" Hawk repeated. "Then what the hell is *this* for?"

He gestured to the military rifle that sat between them, an M4, stolen; marked FT. BRAGG, N.C. It was loaded with a twenty-five-round magazine, the initials DF painted in Wite-Out on its side in creepy lettering.

Messiah said he didn't know, but that he'd been told to bring it and use it just once, even if it was to put a hole in an empty window. "That's just what they gave us. I *knew* you were scared to shoot it the other day. Look, you're scared of it right now!"

"Shut up!" Hawk hissed. "Be quiet anyway. I ain't scared of shit."

The two of them closed the truck doors gently and walked through the woods on either side of the dirt road toward a little trailer in the brush, hidden from the road but white in the moonlight as though it had been coated in radiated paint. They tiptoed across what counted as a lawn, moving from one discarded vehicle on flat tires to the next on blocks. Messiah's sneakers were soaked through with dew.

"Okay," he whispered. "We knock. If it's a man we just check in and ask to buy. We keep this gun out of sight. Just set it to the side of

the door frame." He passed the rifle to Hawk awkwardly in the cramped space. "If it's a woman we bust in and scare her. Oughta be easy."

"We're good," Hawk said. But they could see each other shaking, like always.

The screen door had been pulled off its hinges, punched through and discarded, leaning against a slimy wood railing that lined the steps.

Messiah knocked on the door.

"Hello?" a woman from inside said. At that Messiah ran his shoulder into the door and fell inside. Hawk poured in after him shouting. A child started crying. Bundles of drugs were lined up on almost every surface, even stacked in the sink on top of the dirty dishes. They were practically all there was in the place.

The woman inside stood up quickly, fumbling with a handgun that fell to the floor. In her confusion she dropped a cigarette down her tank top, screaming then and slamming her free hand against her chest to beat the cherry out. She looked down her chin to see if she'd burned herself and then looked up at them. "Who the fuck are you?" she said in a slurred voice. Hawk kicked the gun away from her toward the crying toddler on the floor.

"Just—just don't hurt the baby," she said, soberly now. The child wailed.

Messiah flapped open a duffle bag and started pushing the tightly wrapped bundles inside. It smelled awful in the trailer, like burning plastic and hairspray, and he wondered how the woman could smoke in there without the whole place exploding. Everything was giving him a headache.

"Would you turn around please?" Hawk said to the woman.

He'd walked up behind her and lifted the back of her shirt with the muzzle of his rifle.

"Okay," said Messiah. "Let's go."

He scanned the trailer for more packages but none were apparent in the mess. "Let's go," he said again. He walked toward the

door and peeked out. The outside was quiet. "Let's go, goddammit!" Messiah's voice cracked. He picked up the woman's gun from next to the red-faced child, screaming now and beating his little fists into the carpet.

"Let's go, man, come *on*." To his relief Hawk stepped back from the woman and toward the door.

Now Messiah ran down the stairs; once he got to the treeline he knelt and looked back but didn't see Hawk. He put the gun in his duffle, zipped it up tight, slung the handles around his shoulder, and started jogging toward the truck.

When Messiah got to the road he heard a car engine in the distance, so he slipped into the draw-off ditch and ran, bent over, all the way to the truck. He didn't see Hawk there waiting for him. He threw the bag in the truck bed, got into the driver's seat, put the key in the ignition, and waited.

It was two, three minutes. Messiah heard a loud, deep gunshot and knew it was the assault rifle. Birds flew up from the clearing beyond the treeline down the road. Another shot went off, closer now, the same gun. The engine in the distance was coming this way, and it seemed as though it came faster now. Chances were pretty good they could hear the shots.

A minute passed, and then Hawk came stumbling into the rearview mirror. Messiah started the truck and waved for him to come on, to hurry.

As they pulled onto the road a big diesel pickup turned the corner in front of them and flashed its high beams. Messiah drove slowly, trying to be as calm as he could be. He waved two fingers above his steering wheel all but directly into the truck's blazing floodlights. The big truck barrelled past without slowing and turned onto the dirt turnoff that led to the trailer. Once they were on the main road Messiah gunned the gas to the floor, slowing only to turn at every junction, getting as far off a predictable path as possible. But after many such genius moves of misdirection they still wound

up on the Blue Ridge Parkway, not far from Grace's house, almost right outside Fancy Gap.

Hawk was still breathing heavily. He was running his hands back through his hair and tugging his face taut, his eyes wide and unblinking. Messiah slowed down as they passed the Perkins's house. Hawk was staring out the passenger window looking down the driveway to the dim little house, the dust and dirt and fold-out chair where his mama always sat sipping sun tea.

The truck they'd taken the day they left hadn't been returned, but all else seemed just as it had been. Overgrown lawn. The moonlight illuminated an empty and faded plastic sandbox just beyond the mailbox, still there with a crack in it, suitable only for breeding mosquitoes. Toys spread all over the yard, and trash.

"Why are you slowing down?" Hawk said.

"I don't know, don't you want to see?"

"Messiah! Get— Drive, man. Go on! Why would you take me here? No— I can't look at this. You gotta fucking drive. Please!"

Hawk was still staring out through the windshield and into nothing as they pulled into the mountain church down the road in Fancy Gap. "I been thinkin' about it," he said. "We can— We can just go. We got money on us right now; we got all these drugs. I mean I think we should. We can go, Messy."

"Where you wanna go?" Sweat soaked Messiah's shirt around his collar. His body ached. He already knew what Hawk was going to say.

"We don't have to do this one. We didn't have to do any of 'em. We didn't have to do none of this."

"No one has to do anything. Get out here and walk home if you want. You know how to get home. Get on home, then. Always calling me a baby. Look at you. I can't make you do anything, but I'm gonna do this one for my Nana."

"I told her I don't wanna do this one. I said, well, I asked her what this preacher of this here church ever done to her. She said it

ain't what he done to her but what he done to humanity. What does she mean? What does she ever mean? I just don't understand it, Messy. I feel like I'm losing my goddamn mind."

"You ain't scared, Hawk," Messiah said. "We were just in a trailer and that woman had a gun pointed at us. You just shaken. *I'm* scared. I'm scared to burn like Grace said my mama burned. I'm scared to burn like she said my brother burned. I'm scared of that. She said God made us in His image, and she said that in doing so he made us vain. You think you can cut it on your own, you just cut and run, then. But you can get taken up to heaven just about whenever. And I thought about it a long time. I thought about it since I was little. I can't reason no other way I came to be in this life if she wasn't meant to guide me. She's all I got left, man. I don't got a brain to think about it any other way."

"You do have a brain, Messy. Listen to you talk now. All talk. When I met you, you was just a retard and now you're like a gospel preacher yourself. You got all the words you need to do just what Grace does. You got whatever Grace got. You can cut it out with me. I am saying we can do it on our own. We don't have to go back, you know. You changed and, I mean, I don't want to worry about it but I do."

Hawk heaved his breaths in and out. "Now I told her I didn't want to hit this one and I ain't hitting it for her. I'll hit it with you, and I mean *with* you. You're my friend, Messy. You're my man.

"I don't know why you can't see that," Hawk continued. "You should've known you had a real friend here." He paused to look at Messiah. "A real friend, man. And that is actually all you got. You know that. You know and I know your brother ain't coming for you. You just sitting around waiting. I don't know. Trying to go to jail or get killed while you wait. But I'm trying to tell you: you're my brother now, Messy. We went past that house just now and I knew it. I know that yard of that house, every square inch of it. Man, I can't go back there. I'd rather take a chance, you know? Let's just skip this one."

Messiah felt Hawk lean in close but kept his eyes on the church, taking in whatever it was Hawk was saying while trying not to look at him. He cut the ignition on the truck. "All right, we'll do it together then. We'll talk on the drive back. Maybe we save some alms for ourselves. Maybe you're right, but you ain't my brother, Hawk."

They stared at each other, the bugs screaming outside. "You're something else," he added.

"Okay," Hawk said. "Okay then, let's go."

They got out of the truck and situated themselves. Hawk took his time. He tightened his belt, looked at his face in the side mirror, scratched at something on his little beard. Then he pulled the long rifle out of the truck bed and slung it across his shoulder. Meanwhile Messiah pulled the two cans of gas and kerosene from the back. Now the two of them walked up to the church in the symphony of bugs and summer wind through the surrounding trees.

"They don't lock this door," Hawk said.

"How you know?"

"When we went to church—well, before all them other kids and fosters and babysitting kids—when we went to church, this is where we'd go. I just know there ain't no lock on the door. It ain't the first time I snuck in here. I ran away a few times, Messy."

Messiah tried the knob of the little white door, and sure enough he was right. "This thing'll go up like a tinderbox," he said.

They walked through the pews like usual, but Messiah thought he'd save a bit of gas to make sure they could light the fire from the stairs of the church. He worried that if they set the little lectern on fire they might not be able to get out quick enough. He'd seen a dozen of these churches light up and he knew now how fast the fire moved. When Grace first showed them how to do it she'd said it moved with the speed of prayer.

Messiah remembered that first night, that first church after he'd healed. After Grace had rubbed his legs and stomach with

corn liquor to draw the pain and stiffness out. He'd had a cold shower. He'd felt awake to everything.

Hawk had fumbled with his work and Grace had shouted at him to hit the Bibles. "They burn long," she'd said. "They are the only true thing in this house of sin." That was in a Baptist church in Cana. "Pour that kerosene on the pews, there, Hawk," she'd said.

Messiah remembered wondering the same thing Hawk had tonight. Why this place? Why this at all?

They walked down the steps and out into the moonlight. Wind was carrying all the noises across them, staying just a little while in their ears. Everything moved. Messiah's sweat felt cold on his back and the kerosene smell made him light-headed.

"This is my last one, Messiah. So help me God. This is my last one." Hawk knelt down to fish through the box of fire starters and lighter fluid. "I ain't doing none of this no more. That was too much mess for me to clean up."

"What was too much mess?"

Hawk was struggling with his lighter. "You got any matches? That kerosene is gonna dry up."

"What was too much to clean up?" Messiah asked again.

Hawk returned his attention to the box of ignitions, looking into the bowels of the church through the open door. "God*damm*it."

"Hawk, what are you talkin' about?" Messiah was desperate now.

"That woman, I dunno, man." He shook the lighter and paused, then kept flicking it. "It was once she figured you'd left. When I went out she jumped out at me on the steps of the house. She grabbed at me and pulled my hood off and said, whatever, she said *Oh my God* and I knew she knew me. Not me like now but from when I was a boy. We were too close to home, man. I said I didn't want to do any of this shit."

"What did you say to her?" Messiah's heart sank. Something like the crushing enormity of the dark sky descended on him and

he felt he would break under the weight. "What did you say, Hawk?"

"I didn't say shit." Hawk tried the lighter again. "I hit her with a round."

"You what?"

"I hit her with a round. Shit, you said I was supposed to let one off. I hit her with a round."

"You killed her?"

"I don't know, Messy. Do you have any goddamn matches?"

"You killed her? In front of her baby?"

"Not— No. I don't know, man. But I'll tell you one thing: we can't go back. Everybody is gonna know it was us. I don't think I killed her but, shit, I guess I wish I did. We can't go back." Hawk stood up and turned to Messiah.

"What was the other shot?"

"What do you mean?"

"What was the other shot? I heard two shots from that big gun, Hawk."

"I'm gonna go out to the truck and get a pill or two," Hawk said. He dropped the lighter and clapped his hands clean, wiping them on the back of his pants and shooting a smile at Messiah. "Gonna just go get another lighter from the truck or something. This shit ain't gonna work."

Messiah didn't react.

"I'd just as soon get the hell out of here," Hawk said.

"Stay right there." Messiah's voice was unsteady. He didn't move so much as he saw himself move. He drew the 9mm and pointed it at Hawk.

"What do you want me to say, Messy? You want me to tell you somethin' you don't know? Hold on, now."

Messiah flexed the gun out at Hawk, who stayed where he was.

"All right, all right, you want to know? I did just as you said. I did just as Grace said we're supposed to do. I expedited another soul

out of this world of sin. I *expedited*, Messy. I did what you woulda done. I let the round go and I sent a soul to heaven and it ain't for me to judge. I did what she said. Now put that thing down and let's just go."

Messiah stared down his arm at Hawk, the gun feeling heavy in his hands and trembling. He squeezed the trigger to a click.

"Jesus Christ are you gonna shoot me? Did you know that wasn't chambered? Messy what did I say? I want to go. Messy I want to leave." Hawk was crying now.

Messiah pulled back the slide and chambered a round. As soon as he lifted the gun Hawk fumbled with the sling of the rifle and tried to get it up in one arm and pointed at Messiah. Messiah pulled the trigger again and shot Hawk in the leg.

"Oh God," Hawk said as he fell. "Oh God I— Messy. Oh my God."

Then he screamed some unintelligible screams, heaving and pulling at his jeans. Messiah heard sirens in the distance across the rolling hills of the mountains, carried by the wind. He tucked the 9mm in the back of his pants and picked up the can of gas and poured it alongside Hawk as he screamed. Hawk threw the fire starter at Messiah, then pulled at the sling for the rifle that was wedged beneath him. Messiah let him struggle. "Hawk," he said, "you ain't my brother." He said it again and again.

Messiah set down the can of kerosene just beyond Hawk's arms on the cracked white paint of the church stairs. He shot the can. There wasn't an immediate explosion but there was a sizzle, the flames crawling all along the steps, the melting plastic dripping and running down the wood. The flames pulled themselves toward Hawk's struggling body as he inched away from it. Hawk pulled at the rifle sling and pulled at the banister and pulled at his pants and pulled at the steps as the fire chased him with the speed of prayer.

Dalton

THE FLYER SAID to wear no insignia and to unload weapons upon arrival. Group affiliation and rank forbidden. He packed up in the afternoon and looked around the motel room for anything else he thought he might want to bring. He knew where the spot was, just south of an overlook called Lover's Leap that had been so popular in his high school years. A place to drive up to and make out. The legend of Lover's Leap was a blended story about ill-fated lovers who'd leapt to their death, flinging themselves off the cliff and down the mountain to the gap below to avoid persecution and to die in love and together.

Dalton had gone up there, too, but not with a young woman. He and Tyler drove there often in the year or so before the nightmare that tore them apart. Tyler liked to shoot off his daddy's gun there, firing it into the gully at the bottom, aiming for things that'd been thrown off the edge: washing machines, bags of trash, refrigerators. They drank Southern Comfort together and talked. Dalton remembered tasting Tyler's cigarette lips on the mouth of the bottle. They'd shoot that gun right down the slope of the mountain into the blur of green.

Dalton thought that if that was all it had come to, if it had ended there, then that would be quite all right. A time when there was nothing concrete to look forward to but nothing yet to truly regret. The two boys talking about Tyler's daddy, Dalton's lack of one. Telling Tyler he had a hard time living with Clyde. Telling Tyler he was scared his mama was going to die. The taste of the tip of the bottle. Their shoulders touching. The crack of the gunshot echoing off the ridge. The black swoops of bats cast in the orange sunset. The story could have ended there, sure. As happy and as all right as he'd maybe ever be.

Tyler had said that if they shot off too high or too far into the distance the bullet could fall almost straight toward the ground below. If it went far enough it could drop right down into someone's bedroom. "Wouldn't want that, would you, Dalt?" No, no he wouldn't. He didn't. The memories of that part of Virginia felt warm all the same. Warm and orange and green and up high.

He saw that some men had parked their trucks right on the side of the road near the catty-cornered crossover circled on the map. Some big men, some small, some old, some young, some bearded, some bald-faced. All wearing ballcaps and most wearing Oakley sunglasses. They put on their militia regalia just outside their big trucks—'98 Ford F-150s, brand-new Dodge Rams with dually wheels—most of these lifted up on their suspensions and clean, with oiled, deep-tread mud tires. Other vehicles were rusted out and hanging low on blown-out suspensions with Gadsden flag licence plates and Rebel flag stickers. Some of the men had donned flak jackets and ammo pouches. All were armed. Every man wore black tactical gear or camouflage of different origins, from different conflicts. Desert camo from Operation Enduring Freedom, digital camo from a deployment to Afghanistan. He watched them remove their patches and Velcro insignias, setting them in their

glove compartments or on their dashboards, shoving them into their pockets.

Truck doors slammed. The men walked in little groups, twos and threes, some solo, through the fields and toward where the muster was marked on the flyer map. Dalton held the ratty piece of paper off to his side like an admittance ticket. Crinkled paper rattling; his hand shaking.

He hadn't thought to wear any old army clothes, following the men in just a white T-shirt and jeans. He was happy he'd parked the truck far away. He hung a ways back from the others but tried to stay close enough to hear what they were saying. They fell into formation once they reached the clearing, a mechanical sort of synchronized swimming that Dalton was accustomed to navigating: the sidling up next to another man next to another, standing with their feet shoulder-width apart and looking forward. The men around him harboured a nervous excitement that was palpable. Maybe it was the breathing set against the silence of the clearing. Dalton wondered who they were waiting for, some kind of company commander perhaps. His .38 was in his jeans pocket, unloaded. He felt naked and vulnerable. Some of the others had two or three guns on them—on a chest holster, at their waist, a magazineless long rifle slung across their back.

Three men were walking toward them now down the hill from the hunting resort. Dalton squinted in disbelief.

The man in the centre rested his hands gently on the shoulders of his compatriots as though to steady himself while they descended. It was like a royal procession.

As the three came closer there was no doubt about it. It was Hickok, the pastor of his mother's church. The silent partner in all things Fuquay as far back as Dalton could remember. And Jim Hickok was even more than that. He knew it all already but had sworn to never think of the man as what he was, what he ought to be

to Dalton. What he ought to have been to his mother. What he should have been, anyway.

Hickok was flanked on one side by an overweight man in a bolo tie and a ring on almost every finger, a big magnum nestled in an ornate holster; on the other was an athletic young man with a baby face and a fishing hook on the brim of his ballcap: the guy from the ABC store who'd seen Dalton before he left town for the last time. What was his name? *I know you; you was in the Army*.

Dalton bent his knees then reshifted his weight to stand behind the big man in front of him. The two escorts fell in line with the rest of the assembled militia as they arrived on flat ground. Hickok situated himself in the centre, facing the ad hoc formation. Dalton was two rows back from the front, furious with himself now for not having brought his hat or even sunglasses. Pastor Hickok stood with the sun haloing him as it set behind the ridge.

"All right, men. Thank you for joining us today. I'm gonna say a few quick words and then I'll let you get on with your training." Hickok paused, gathering his thoughts and preparing to speak. He furrowed his brow, held his head high, and clapped a loud clap to get their attention. "Okay, well. I am saddened to say that one of our regulars at muster couldn't make it. Seems like we got a tragedy on our hands here. A man has lost his wife and child to the crime that is enveloping us all like so many flames. As a man of God, I am feeling a divine stirring around and underneath me, something telling me that hell is about to break open and we will have to fight. Something evil is facing us, and I think that's the real reason you're here. You know that, don't you?"

"Yes sir!" the men shouted. Dalton looked down at the love handles of the man in front of him, spilling over a cinched combat belt that cut into his flesh. When the man responded the love handles ballooned on either side of the belt and shrank again when the man caught his breath. The man's flak jacket hardly fit him.

"Men, well, there ain't no easy way to put this. I know many of you and I know you're doing what you can in your professional capacity: church men, business leaders, policemen, reservists, and on and on, but there's something that these institutional positions just simply can't do, a service of an even higher calling that we are meant to perform. Something that it takes numbers to do. Something that takes more than power to do, something that takes honour and bravery to do. We gotta come together and protect this corner of God's earth. You understand?"

Again the men shouted "Yes sir!" in unison.

"This is just the first step to that. Something's gonna give soon and we're gonna formalize our efforts, one way or the other. We're gonna do just what I'm talking about—we're going to heed the call. You men, you'll be on the front lines of the war for America *in* America." He looked down. "And it hurts me to say this." He paused then looked back up, holding his hand over his heart. "We've gone from arson and simple burglary to murder. And someone is going to pay. I believe in time a great many will pay.

"Can you believe what is happening in this godforsaken country? Are you going to let it happen? You think this sort of terrorism is coming from your brothers and cousins? Do you think it's coming *from* the churches? No. There's something deeper going on here, and it's a war on God. It's top-down. It's a war on Jesus. It's a war on white America," he said, red in the face.

Dalton's knees nearly buckled. He pulled himself tall and kept his head down, his eyes trained on the man's love handles before him, praying that Hickok wouldn't notice him. He stared at the man's hips, the pistols resting on either side of his belt, floating up and down with the man's breath. He felt like he could run if he had to.

"So y'all think about that today, and if I can help you sort something out a little more permanent, a little more serious, well, we'll see if we can get some money for that. There's going to be a strategy

meeting after our squad-movement exercises in the woods. And so I want you to know that you're not alone. If you have something to contribute, if you can take the quiet war to the street, I would like to meet with you. You have your country behind you; more people than you could ever know are waiting for a change. Every moment, every day. You've got your country behind you, and we won't let them take our God away. We won't let them take our country away. Will we, men?"

"No sir!" they shouted.

"All right, then," he said. "Carry on."

The men fell out. The man with the rings started shouting orders about weapons drills and safety checks. Dalton turned immediately away from the crowd, who broke out of ranks and went to get a little of Pastor Hickok's attention. He began to walk away.

"Get that young man for me, will you? Get him to come over here," he heard Hickok say. Dalton felt two hands on his shoulders turning him around and walking him gently toward Hickok. He looked up briefly and saw the pastor standing there smiling, his arms flung wide open as though he was expecting an embrace.

As Dalton approached he kept his eyes on the ground like a prisoner on his way to the firing line. The sun had turned orange, and the shadows of the men splayed out all around him like so many spider legs across the pasture grass.

"What are you doing here, Dalton?"

The walk up to the resort was soundtracked by husky whispers behind them. The men accompanying him and Hickok had loaded their magazines into their rifles.

Once inside, Hickok dismissed the others. The two were alone, surrounded by tall walls and rustic joists and ancient wood beams that extended across the length of the empty dining hall. Animal heads hung from the walls.

"Son, I'll ask again. What are you doing here?"

Dalton couldn't answer because he didn't know. He was one step behind his own logic. Beacons and signals lying just beyond his absolute cognition had lured him here, like a sailor drawn to a mirage. This wasn't his idea.

"Do you remember?" Hickok said. "I mean, I told you after that incident at school. I just wish you'd try to do something. I mean just do anything else. I told your mother too—"

Dalton glared at him.

"I told you that for the good of your mama you ought to look forward and try to stay out of trouble. I just don't think this is your world, son. You were supposed to be off somewhere else, doing something else. Anything. The Army. College. Anything, Dalton. What happened?"

"I didn't think it was your world, either." Dalton looked into Hickok's eyes, looking for meanness, caginess. He assessed the man, older and wirier than he remembered; his barrel of a diaphragm had been whittled down to a hard log that held him upright.

Hickok looked as though he was suppressing a laugh, like there was some kind of joke here that Dalton was unaware of. But this man was always performing, always at the pulpit. "What the hell happened to your head, son? It looks like you took a weed whacker to it." He paused to assess Dalton, it seemed, and Dalton straightened himself and tried not to blink. He waited for the lesson to come.

"My world is something different now," Hickok told him. "And this—this is just expedient for the time being. I have been organizing these little war games and get-togethers for a while now. I have other plans, too, for my retirement. All my preaching and all my work. All my shepherding of a nice little country church, and the country slipping away from me the whole time. I thought I had to *do* something. Did you ever want to just do something, Dalton? To know that if you put your back into something you could make it right? I want my country to be totally, perfectly right. I have the time to do something now."

Hickok paused for a long few minutes, breathing through his nose. He was looking at Dalton as if he was saying something but his mouth didn't move. It was as if he was waiting for Dalton to get to the punchline of a joke, as if a whole other conversation was happening in the exchange of silence.

Hickok started up again. "But I'm concerned about *you.* You know, I thought you were going to come back and see me. I felt that you were. I guess I missed you at church the other day. Heard you stopped by.

"Do you know the law is looking for you? They want to know if you were in Jane's house when she died. I haven't heard much lately but when they first came asking, I mean, I didn't know what to tell them. And now, well." He paused. "I'm sorry about your mama, boy."

To this Dalton had no response to give. He closed his eyes and saw his mother, or, closer to the truth, felt the trace outline of her inside him. The feeling of having swallowed gallons of oil from a drum that came up in him whenever he was faced with the memory.

"I loved her, Dalton," Hickok said to the silence. "She was—you know. I know you think it was your fault, maybe, but it was God's design. Or I hope it was."

"You don't know shit-all about what I think, shit-all about nothing."

"Well, I'll tell you one thing, son, and it's that you might do well to speak with the sheriff about this." Hickok stared at Dalton with practised benevolence. "Because they suspect you had something to do with it. They know you were there. It isn't a secret, son. People saw you."

"That's bullshit." Dalton was sniffing now and wiping his nose.

Hickok grew stern and condescending. "And now you're coming around again with a gun stuck in your pants and you think you're gonna blame her dying on somebody else. You'd think you might have learned by now. What are you gonna do, Dalton? Are you going to do the right thing this time? You going to make it right? Or

are you going to fuck up again and run away? All you done your whole life."

Dalton stood and stormed toward the door.

Hickok raised his voice. "Don't go through that door, boy! You go through that door and I can't help you!"

Dalton stopped.

"The sheriff's got your number, son, and it's you and your brother and Grace, all the way down. She's got your brother up there, Dalton. Grace's got him up there doing God knows what. Buffalo Mountain. All this news, these fires, this cold-blooded murder. It's Grace, son. It's your grandmother. And it's Messiah, too."

Dalton couldn't believe what he was hearing. He put his head in his hands and pushed his palms into his eyes. His ears were ringing. He moved his hand to his neck. He felt like it was going to burst.

"I'm just looking for Messy. I'm going up there to get him tomorrow. I'm going to go up to my Nana's and I'm going to get him." Dalton was trying to sound determined.

"Well, son, you shouldn't go up there tomorrow. I am telling you this: you will regret that choice. You should lie low awhile. You could stay here at the resort. I can help you clear your name."

Hickok was softening his tone. "We can sort you out. I can start to do right by you, Dalton, but you need to do the right thing. You are free to leave, but you cannot go up to the revival tomorrow. You need to promise me that, for your own good."

Dalton strode to the door, pushed it open, and walked out, unpursued.

He woke up the next morning in the motel room off the Blue Ridge Parkway, swimming in the cyclone of his own vision.

He'd stumbled out of the resort in a near-delirium, and by some miracle had gotten to the truck and driven it back to the motel. He'd lain on the bed with his clothes and shoes on, panicking, unmoving,

eyes open in the sweltering unreality of the room, its puttering fan blades slicing the air above him. He crashed from exhaustion.

But he was going to the revival. The flyer was smoothed out neatly on the bedside table next to the complimentary Bible. He would make it right.

Dalton hadn't turned on the baseboard air conditioning unit and the air in the room was stale. His clothes were wet and sticky. He felt like he wasn't alone. He looked around the room to make sure the pastor wasn't in there with him.

He got in the shower and let it run cold over his hot, rashy head where razor burn was breaking out all over and turning to pimples. He ran the bar of soap over the hot spots and let the cold water drip into his eyes. Then he turned off the faucet, sat on the bathroom's vinyl floor, and listened to the tap drip.

He tried to remember what Hickok had said. To imagine Messiah with a lighter in his hand. A barbecue lighter, a match. Little Messiah with his fair hair. Dalton wanted to reach out and grab his brother's hair. He wanted to pull him close.

He walked himself dry around the room, arranging pillows and shoving his crinkled clothes that he'd washed and dried back into his duffle bag. He smoked naked and ashed onto the carpet.

He dressed and turned on the cellphone. It buzzed and buzzed with messages that he couldn't concentrate on enough to figure out how to check. It settled down. He turned on the TV. Some of the pixels had been watercoloured and rainbowed by his drying clothes; one corner of the image bled out onto itself. He flipped to the local news.

A commercial played for a painkiller. The phone chirped out "Für Elise" in an 8-bit tone. It went through the whole famous movement. Dalton looked over his shoulder at it, lying there on the bedside table, but he didn't move. The news showed the remnants of a church burned down the night before. A church in Fancy Gap, a few miles away from where he sat according to the map displayed on the screen, repurposed from the weather report to show the

triangulation of arson that plagued the region. The anchor had big blond hair and seemed unmoved by what she was reporting.

The phone rang again. Beethoven again in Nintendo sounds. He reached back and picked it up and looked at it. Laura again, the only number programmed. He let it ring, then checked the messages.

"Dalton. I am going to say some things to you and then I'm going to hang up." There was a long pause.

"I told you I'd look for your brother," Laura's voice said. *"I made some calls and asked around. Dalton—"* She started to break down, heaving into her words: *"I don't know what's going on. I don't even know you. I don't know why I'm calling!"* She was half-laughing into the phone. The message ended. He listened to the next one in the queue.

"I called about your brother," she said, more calmly now. Sighing away the ludicrous necessity of the message. *"I'm telling you this not because I think you can help me at all anymore, but because it's what I know.*

"I don't even know how to say to you, to tell you— Dalton, I am so sad right now. I've called a hundred times and then it rang today and— I just can't believe you'd do this to us."

There was the sound of her crying through the phone. It made Dalton's eyes hurt to hear it, almost.

"I will tell you what I know. I know you went off the map after you got discharged. Of course I know all about Freedom Coal. But when I made calls down there looking for you—you were flagged. There's a warrant out for you, Dalton. I don't want to know where you are. This isn't what I asked for. I'm sorry to do this, but I need to cut contact with you. I want you to leave the Toyota parked wherever it is and never touch it again. I will wait for you to call me back, but I won't hold my breath."

Dalton left the motel Sunday morning without talking to the woman behind the desk. He left the TV clicked to the news and left it playing loud.

The truck hummed down the rolling lanes of the Blue Ridge Parkway. He knew reasonably well where Buffalo Mountain was, but it was easy to get lost once you got off the parkway and got tangled in the spurs and dirt roads that snaked through every hill and holler.

There were only a few turns he'd have to take to get to the revival, and it wouldn't be hard to reach it if he followed the map closely. He laid the flyer with its rudimentary map on the seat next to him and raced through the blurring green tunnels of forest. The kudzu, the rhododendron, the pine, the sparkling shale blasted out to make room for the road: it all jumbled together beyond his concentration as it zoomed by.

He pulled onto the road up to Buffalo Mountain and took the truck into low gear. It was a steep climb. As soon as he got on the winding spur he saw tents and clotheslines alongside the red dirt berms and natural drains. He saw a thin woman pull herself out of a camper trailer like a baby being born, her hair wet and in her eyes, a cigarette in her mouth.

There were shacks, too. Lean-tos against big trees and felled logs, junk flowing out of them as though their insides had exploded, throwing white garbage all across the grass. Burned circles from movable, impermanent fires seemed to radiate out from the centre of every little would-be home. People shuffled around and paid no attention to the truck roving up the mountain. The revival was set to start in less than an hour. Were they going?

As he got closer to the pinnacle he approached sawhorses that looked as if they'd once operated as formal checkpoints but had long since been abandoned, manned only by an aura of danger. The apex of the road widened into a makeshift traffic circle that led off into half a dozen drives, only one of which was gravelled. Dalton knew to follow it.

He parked the truck a little further along. He kicked his seat back, and pulled his hat down to watch the people crawl in, and so they did.

They clearly didn't belong to the squalor he'd seen on his approach. Nice new trucks and SUVs like those parked near the militia muster, covered now in a light dusting of red mud, slowed to a halt in the circle. Nice-looking families got out and adjusted one another's clothes. Some big men, too. He had the distinct feeling that they'd all got up that morning ready to attend an opera, some kind of production way beyond a backwoods revival preacher. His Nana. He wanted to hit himself and come to himself. The parts of what he was seeing weren't matching together in his brain to form anything he could understand. The nice families shuffled down the gravel drive to a clearing that sloped down the other side of the mountain.

A man rustled in the trees opposite the gravel drive. He wore a camouflage jacket and Oakley sunglasses and had a long gun like something he'd have shot in the Army. The man looked bunched up; he might have ballistic armour on underneath his jacket. He shouted to someone Dalton couldn't see.

By a quarter to twelve fewer cars were driving up, but in their wake came walking collections of people, some of whom Dalton might have seen climbing out of their little cabins and RVs on the way up the mountain. The quality of their clothes, and their relative discomfort walking in them, seemed the only discernible difference between them and the churchgoers of the low country. But there was more to it than that, surely. Sunday best, to be sure. Sure, and unusual.

Dalton got out of the truck and tossed the keys onto the front seat. He'd left all his things at the motel room but knew he wouldn't go back. Whatever happened here, he would not go back. He walked behind what looked like the last family headed toward a clearing in the woods dotted with well-pruned crabapple trees. He could smell their body spray and un-ironed clothes with their spray-on starch. Tobacco smoke wafting in the air behind them.

In the centre of the trees stood a woman in a nightgown, gently bowing to the oncoming people. His grandmother. Like a vision of her, older now and turned all to white from head to toe. Next to her was a tall, broad young man with braided, almost-white hair. He held out a brass-looking plate to the families when they walked toward him. They each picked through its offerings then chose one, fiddled with it, smiled. Then the young man gestured and grinned big, ushering them toward a big circular amalgam of chairs among the trees.

It was Messiah. A stretched tall, gaunt spectre of his brother. As children chased one another around their laughter rang echoes behind Dalton's eyes.

People dipped cups into a big old household propane tank cut in half, set up on sawhorses to make a punch bowl. The woman in the centre of the chairs waved at each little girl and boy and their parents, at each man who sauntered up. Dalton stopped and stood about a hundred yards away. He looked open-mouthed at the white-haired young man standing profile in the sun, illuminated like a stained-glass cut-out. Dalton squinted into the glory illuminating him, shining between the clouds.

A soft wind rustled through the trees. Dalton heard the gentle wail of sirens to the east, maybe at the bottom of the mountain. He heard helicopter blades in the distance. He stood at the edge of the gravel driveway and could not bring himself to move forward, to approach this new world.

Together

THE FIGURE WAS LEAN and baldheaded and had a bent to him as though he were carrying a heavy rucksack, but Grace knew just who this was. The prodigal son. She'd been expecting him. And now here he was, exaggerated and gangly, walking slowly toward them as one might approach a wounded but dangerous animal. Now it was her time to be the father, to open up wide her arms and to give it all away. Hickok hadn't kept Dalton at bay. She smiled and prepared herself to be martyred.

She swung at Messiah's shins with her cane, telling him to go inside, go inside. "They aren't coming for you, son," she said.

But Messiah was staring at the figure in the sun. "My brother," he said. "Dalton!" he yelled out.

The sound of the sirens was audible to all now. The most respectably dressed congregants woke from their shuffling and turned, walking briskly past the man on the drive to their cars behind him. The most devout, those wearied, harried, permanent fixtures of the mountain, ran from place to place, gesturing at one another before ducking back into the woods to their hollers, their trailers, their little jungles.

A crackle of radio squawk from the congregation. A man with a long rifle jogged up to Grace. “Shepherd, Shepherd, I don’t know what happened. We had men down the back side of the mountain. I don’t know. Hickok is telling us to stand down. What do we do, Shepherd? What do you want me to do?” He was wiggling out of his jacket, huffing and puffing, revealing armour strapped atop a black T-shirt, his gut hanging out under the ballistic plate.

“It’s fate,” she said. “It’s the beginning and the end.”

She laid down her cane and slipped her feet out of her shoes. She pulled her nightgown over her head. She let it drop to the ground and stood there naked in the cauterizing light of the Lord. Her arms were open and waving to the hovering helicopter now visible to all. She smiled an open-mouthed smile and drank it in.

“The trumpet will sound!” she shouted. “And the dead will be raised again! And we are imperishable! We *will* be changed! We *will* be changed!”

The helicopter whirred around Grace’s house, buzzing the tops of the trees, bending them down. Dust and sound everywhere. The worshippers fleeing in all directions. A loudspeaker announced itself as ATF and ordered all to raise their hands and sit on the ground. Some of the remaining congregants did.

The man on the drive walked toward Grace and Messiah and did not raise his hands.

“Messiah!” he screamed above the cyclone of the blades. “Messiah!”

“Yes, Lord, shout it! Make him shout it!” Grace called out. “Rejoice with me, Lord! I have found my sheep which was lost! Come here, Dalton. Come here to your Nana, boy. Come here to your Messiah!” Her hair blew about her in a wild tornado.

Messiah stepped toward his brother. Behind Dalton were the sounds of sirens and shouting and another loudspeaker muffled by trees. Dust came up around him and flew into his eyes. He kept

walking toward the two white-haired figures. A phalanx of officers formed into a black mass behind him.

The two brothers were just feet from each other now. From the treeline, from the entrance of the gravel drive, came the clamour of boots and slamming doors and chambering rifles. Men shouted Dalton's name and ordered him to get on the ground.

"You left me," Messiah said. "You left us, Dalton."

The brothers reached out their hands toward each other.

Shots rang out, echoing across the mountainside.

EPILOGUE

A NEW LIGHT dawned upon them. The birds sang sweetly and flew from church to church, perching in clapboard cathedrals, the light lifting the wings of those beautiful things, angels springing up and singing. The ash and char of the world transubstantiating back to green, and all that evil was undone; all the evil of the world gone and undone, that new light coming like a break in time, an epoch meant to last forever. All contained. And the birds arrived on Grace's Mountain, diving and gliding. A swirling hurricane of song on the crest of the world. A hundred thousand magnolia warblers in the wobbly sunwake of the unreal new day. And the sun's rays shone through them, opaque as the Ghost, those tiny-winged angels, all come to see the miracle now, the oneness, alighting on trees, and to sing it.

And there they were, the miracle. A family in the eye of the hurricane of angels, with a glory breaking through the muscular clouds suspended above the mountain, choired by mourning doves in the everlasting new cool morning, that quiet crucible of song and light, and the family joined them in song and rejoiced. They prayed and sang and stayed without pain forever in the new light, the fresh rejuvenation of the flesh and the earth, that crucial moment, that miracle of spiritual birth. God has come again to the Blue Ridges.

The wind pulsed through the mountains like the tide, plunging over each ridge like an ocean wave, the shiver of each gust shot through directly with a spell of lightning current and sermonic power rattling through the rhododendron, lifting the skirts of the dew-burdened branches, flooding in and shaking out time itself—the rain, the tears of the earth evaporated and swept away by a groundswell of returned breath, the mountain's mouth exhaling, rattling the windows of each old house and the plank of each old barn and lean-to, rattling the plastic of each abandoned Winnebago and the polyurethane siding of each trailer until all was still and peaceful. New life breathed into this everlasting moment, this perfect place and time.

And the scene was nearly set.

The wind raised the hairs on the mother's scalp and nape, and there she was in the garden, in the white-hot sunlight, overexposed. And the child's white hair, the hair of a little boy munching on Easter lily leaves like they were God's green gum, and all was well. And he was pulled up from the baby bed of kudzu by his brother, dark and handsome, smiling down on his little Messiah and lifting him by his armpits into the air. The hair raised too on the bare arms of the old woman caught unawares by the unexpected rightness of it all. And she was straightened out now, and a smile came to her face, and her eyes closed in peace, and she turned to the sun and let the pink light shine through her and enter and cleanse her mind, and the wind and the light, the new light was sending a shiver through her body, and she smiled, electrified and sated, sharing in the abundance of song and illumination, and the elimination, finally, of evil from the earth. And life is ignited again in this sprinkling newness, this spring in the hills.

The cobwebs of the past and all the potential were swept away now with this reckoning of air and suspended time, and all was clear and well again but still somehow not their own. The world was new. The world now was heaven, where nothing was untrue,

where nothing was faded, where the light gleamed glorious, where the trouble of the earth ceased and where the joy was everlasting, where all was still but reflective and rippling around them as though they were submersed in the sublime, that sunwake shine of time.

And God, like an auctioneer or line dance caller, shouted from over yonder, overwhelmingly large from the sky. He shouted to the family, all dancers on the pine board floor of the earth now, he shouted to these dancers "Promenade," and shouted to them to cling close to their partner, and the old mother and the daughter held hands and swung and spun each other, never losing sight of each other's eyes, and the children danced. Jane wept ruby tears onto her full cheeks, so youthful and alive, and the tears wetted her blouse, there in the sun of the mountain, and then evaporated, glistening and shining up toward the sun, gracing her cheeks upward and they were dry again, and she wept again, tears for the safety and health of her boys and her life so full, and she wept forever and smiled, and her chest fell and rose, fell and rose, even and strong.

And it was always beautiful spring, and it was always summer, the days forever getting longer and more vibrant, then fresh and new, then crisp, then warm; and such is heaven, there in the miracle birdsong. And the flowers were coming always into bloom and the air was sweet and cool. And the leaves were colourful. And the fruit ripened and became plentiful, and they ate from it always and were rejuvenated and alive, and nothing was wrong.

And the mornings were always sweet and tucked-in and half-dreamed, and the stars, if ever there were a night, were always immaculately bright, save the momentary dip in the light that served only to spur on the most awe-striking sunrises and fire-ceremony sunsets, these fires set to diminish, to relinquish their eyes to these magnificent glimpses at the infinite stars that shone of course all at once and forever and ever.

And the grass grew tall among them and blew in the wind, the gentle and intimate breath of God, blowing brisk on their sun-warmed bodies in the pleasant lamplight of His own making, here, in the miracle of their wakefulness and the strength of their conscious sleep, and all was filled with psychedelic dreams somehow more true than the timeless, malleable rock of the earth that would forever remain unchanged and giving.

Yes, dancing. God shouted now for their arms to interlace with their partner's, to make their shoulders inseparable as they strutted, as the fiddle from heaven swayed and played, soundtracking those cascading days, as the high lonesome tones cut to the very gut of them, the very gem of them, their history pouring out their eyes, each of them birthed again and again between the slightest crack in the flesh of clouds, that illuminated minuteness of space between the flesh of them and the flesh of all things, this dance, this play, this cycle, this woefully perfect day collapsing into stasis, then beginning again just to end, the beginning and the end, as the sun all but conjoined them further and further into themselves, and Jane wept.

God yelled out now for them to twirl, and now they twirled, and the world spun in accordance to hasten their spinning, and the heavens grew dizzy, and God laughed a big echoing thunder down on them that came only as a swell in birdsong and in crickets, cicadas, and bees, the rustling of leaves. And Dalton and Messiah were just babies now, smiling in their suspenders, waddling between their mother and grandmother who spun each other, dancing and loving, drunk on the collapsing crescendo of the Lord's fiddle and heaving, laughing, waiting for the song to come to a close, happy and out of breath, and knowing their power, as with each twirled step an earthquake shook and a whirlwind blew from the mountaintop, stretching out and shaking all the world. And with each shared glance that maelstrom spun around them, that glorious terror of everything else being held at bay here, inside the refuge of the eye, here in the never-ending sun, here where all was contained,

here where the sure message of untold newness and potential, of revival, reached all those who dared to hear it. Yes, dancing. Shout to them, dear God, and call out their moves, because you are the conductor and creator of something. Something beautiful. And it is always, always and forever, just like this, just like this.

And now the dance was done but was never done, and the evils of the world had rejoiced in their own defeat and the sun was a cauldron of overflowing magma fate, burning and shining on Grace, Jane, Dalton, and Messiah, and the twists of the mountain road were wet and flooding into lakes with Jane's tears, true tears of true love and true relief at this unimaginable bliss, this existing now within stars, now below the stars, existing now just for the wonderment of stars; and the family rejoiced.

And the sound of the ancient rock hummed beneath them, falling asleep to dream it all again, the two boys now grown and shaking hands and writing cheques and smiling and remembering to all they meet their sweet mama, their Nana; the boys stood tall in the face of accidents of fate and they bettered their peers and made something of themselves, made a life out of love, and Jane was very, very proud. And when she awoke, if that's what she did, they were babies again and again and were stretching themselves awake and smiling in the golden morning light. And it was all an accident, she felt, that there would ever have been even the semblance of doubt that the world would surely burst into such colour and into such crisis of beautiful song and buzz. This was real and true and suffering was unimaginable. Even the doubt itself was joyous and assuaged by the ever-present morning and the ever-alluring dusk, the vibrant sky and the consoling touch of her mother's hand running through her thick hair, braiding it and smiling, and *We will all know it in the morning,* she thought, *all the answers would come in the morning*. And so, they did.

And now the dance was done and now it was morning and now it was night again. All but the cardinals and bluebirds having

retreated to the never-ending clouds beyond the trees, the cardinals were joined by a symphony of silent lightning bugs, Christmas lights in the beautiful forest around their garden, around their frozen slice of time. And Jane fell asleep on a wool blanket overtop grass overtop earth as soft as down and as still as death and she rested and was safe in her family's care. And her boys held her as she died, and they wept. And Grace held her as she died, and Grace wept. And the morning again, and the mourning doves' blessing.

And Jane was born again, and the cycle forever and ever was born again, now in that new light of in-between forevers; her babies, her boys, her love, her mama, God and the plenty of it all, and the fear of wasting it softened by the assurance of forever, of forever and ever, and ever and ever, and ever and ever, *Amen.*

Acknowledgments

This book is the culmination of countless miracles, the first and that which took longest to perform was done by my mother, Elizabeth, from whom I was taught how to love and to learn and to tell stories, and from whom I was taught how to truly live through time and to remember the world as it was in order to remake it as art. Thank you for the gift of my life, Mama, and thank you for loving me and my brother as you did. I hope it is clear to you now as you reminisce with angels that this story is an exorcism of all the terrible outcomes from which your love and perseverance saved us. We will be together in heaven, and we will be laughing and crying, holding each other, looking at the million moments of our life in eternal awe.

An ongoing miracle wakes with me each morning and loves me (a miracle in and of itself) and holds all the pieces of our world together with the iron twine of her soul. I love you, Kaitlin.

I have dedicated this book, of course, to my brother, Jacob. Jake, you are nowhere in these pages, my brilliant, sweet, serious man. You are too good. But you are in all the writing of them. You are everywhere around me, and I could never lose you. I can see you now.

Thank you, Michael, for raising me, for loving me, and for being the best man I will ever know. Thank you for loving my mama; for preventing our lives from unravelling; for caring so deeply.

I thank all my family. I write for the love and grace of my grandmothers, Peggy and Yvonne, and for the family these strong women have given me. Thank you, beautiful Tamsin. Thank you to my cousins, aunts, and uncles, that huge extended family, each of whom will be surprised to find that I have a brain in my head at all. Thank you to my stepfamily and their families: Karen, Ceara, Matt. Thank you for being so kind and loving. Thank you for being so generous and intelligent, Karen.

Thank you to my father, for loving me, for believing in me, and for steering me out of hell. Thank you for rescuing me, quite literally bloodied and bruised, from the pitfalls of my youth.

There is perhaps no greater spiritual debt I owe to anyone in my writerly life beyond my dear friend and brother Cody Caetano. You have put a chunk of your very big soul into this novel and for that I can never repay you. The energy of your drumming heart moves so much of the literature in this country that it is difficult to quantify. I look forward to growing into elder artists together. You move steady and you see clear. Your belief in me is all I need to keep writing.

The complete world of this text only exists in one other person's mind. Lara Hinchberger has read and edited, re-read and re-edited, cut and added, suggested and surgically serrated, moved and motivated every shred of this book as it stands and has done so a dozen times. Thank you, Lara. Your commitment to language, character, and story is unmatched. I am convinced that I am the luckiest artist in the world to work with an editor of your calibre, but even luckier to be your friend. I am so honoured to work with you. It has been one of the great privileges of my life.

Thank you to Karen Alliston for the magnificent copy editing and understanding.

This novel began as a series of poems and vignettes in 2017 in a writing class at the University of Toronto. I have unending gratitude for those early readers, teachers, and friends who guided me through the first part of my ideas. I am especially grateful for the guidance and encouragement I received from Professors Nick Mount, Bob McGill, David Chariandy, Al Moritz, Andrew DuBois and Adam Hammond. Your labour is invaluable, and I cannot thank you enough.

Thank you to the entire team at Penguin Canada and everything each of you do for Canadian arts and letters. Thank you to all the booksellers and literary workers of the world. To all the bookstores in Toronto. To the libraries and library workers. Heroes!

Fancy Gap and so much of my writing life would not be possible without Pasha Malla, the first and only real writer to take a chance on me when I desperately needed a friend and mentor. You are one of the most gracious and patient artists I have ever known. Thank you for your years of work editing, trimming, troubleshooting, reading, shaping, and championing this book before it could even be called a book.

Thank you to those early readers and editors of my very rough drafts, Sydney Gautreau and Julia Henderson. I am so grateful for your guidance.

Thank you to the first readers of the *real* manuscript, Danyse Golick and Chris Sandison, for your invaluable suggestions, generosity of mind and spirit, and for being such wonderful understanders of the human condition. I need everyone to know how talented each of you is at the art of feeling and meaning-making.

Thank you to Dimitri Karakostas for all your art. Thank you for your boundless energy and productive capacity, for your sense of humour, for your deep understanding of the psychosphere of the novel, for your belief in art as the last and only human institution worth anything in the world. I will teach a class on your collected works when you die.

Thank you to my incredible friends. If you are reading this, that means you. God bless the Canadian writers and artists who I have come to love so completely. Yes, you!

Thank you to my brothers, Trev, Dave, and Geoff, for our eternities of friendship and love.

Thank you to my army buddies, Jimmy and Jay. We didn't let ourselves get lost. I am so proud to be your friend.

Endless gratitude to my creative partner, Neil Rimmer, for all our projects together. My wonderful man.

Thank you to my family in and around Toronto: Amy, Mike, Kate, Mariel, Ruby, Carson, Claire, Kathleen, Delaney and Bethany. All the people who have taken care of me. Danielle and Meaghan. My comrades: Abby, Walter, Sam, Jess and Cassandra. Adam and Vaughan. Thank you all for keeping me relatively safe and relatively sane. Thank you for being such a wonderful friend, Professor Rose, I owe you such a debt of gratitude.

It is a miracle that I have so many friends and teachers and artists in my life that I so love and so admire. God bless you all. God bless the turbulent world.

God bless my dog, Cowboy. I love him.

And on go the miracles. Thank you, reader.